# WINDS

*of*

# GLORY

## A NOVEL

# GARY BYE

**Winds of Glory: A Novel**
Published by Granite Point Publishing
Pomeroy, WA



ISBN: 979-8-9867002-3-6 (hardback)
ISBN: 979-8-9867002-4-3 (paperback)
ISBN: 979-8-9867002-5-0 (ebook)
FICTION / Literary

This is a work of fiction. Names, characters, businesses, places, events, locales, and incidents are either the products of the author's imagination or used in a fictitious manner. Any resemblance to actual persons, living or dead, or actual events is purely coincidental.

Cover photograph by Resa Cox .

Cover and interior design by Victoria Wolf, wolfdesignandmarketing.com. Publishing management by Kirsten "Kiki" Ringer, KLR Literary Management. Copyrights owned by Gary Bye.

QUANTITY PURCHASES: Schools, companies, professional groups, clubs, and other organizations may qualify for special terms when ordering quantities of this title. For information, email garywbye@gmail.com.

This book is dedicated to those people living
in small towns and rural communities who
understand why their worlds are special.

To reach a port we must sail, sometimes with the wind,
and sometimes against it. But we must not
drift or lie at anchor…

—Oliver Wendell Holmes, Sr.

# CHAPTER 1

# WIND

A SILVER PADLOCK HUNG waist-high on the chain blocking the road.

"What now?" Ronnie Jepson asked. She glanced over at Brock Gallagher, who was surveying the site in front of them.

"Now we walk." He turned the car around, found a pullout nearby, and eased the Lexus off the highway.

Ronnie studied Brock's face to see if there was any hint of his intentions. His jaw was set, his eyes focused. But his features revealed nothing. *Still handsome*, she thought. She'd fallen for him nearly twenty years before when they were in high school. Now, ironically, despite life's twists and turns, they were together again.

"We're going through the fence," he said. "Gotta get closer to check this out." They walked to the barrier and Brock put one foot on a lower wire, raised the upper one, and motioned her through. "Keep your bottom down."

"Keep your eyes open and off my bottom, Mister." She stretched her leg through the wire. "They have guards, you know."

"And if they catch us, they'll line us up against one of those things and shoot us." His smile betrayed his amusement at her worry.

"*No trespassing. Violators will be prosecuted.* I read the sign."

"Just bat your pretty eyes at the poor watchman. He'll usher you away while he takes aim at me."

They slipped through the barbed wire, watching for any vehicle that might be approaching. There was no sign of movement, and the only sound was the steady whirring of giant blades spinning above them. They skirted around the base of the machine, away from the road, and slowly knelt on the soft ground. Brock took Ronnie's hand and gently pulled her down.

They lay on their backs staring up, the sun brilliant in the spring sky after a winter of darkness. Scattered clouds drifted eastward across the heavens from the flatlands. "Like angel hair," she said softly. The movement accentuated the dizzying sensation they felt, as if they were untethered from the earth. The cool soil beneath them seemed the only thing keeping them anchored, otherwise they might drift into the endless cool blue. Above them, the slowly spinning blades marked time and a swooshing sound routinely interrupted the silence like a giant bird's wings brushing their cheeks.

"Is it beautiful or monstrous?" Ronnie whispered, looking up at the 500-foot giant, sleek and glistening in the sun.

"Both," Brock said. He squeezed her hand as he spoke. "Too big to fit into my brain."

They'd come to see for themselves what the wind tower project would look like if completed. It was only days after the latest visit by

Anthony Marcellus, an arm twister seeking signatures on a lease agreement for the Gallagher farm acres. A wind company, with international backing, had identified the area along Cold Creek as a prime location to establish a wind farm. Brock's mother, Irene, was one of the first to receive a letter, then a visit from the company.

Brock knew it was because the Gallagher farm edged up close to the top of Piney Ridge and was always buffeted by the wind. Irene, weakened by her cancer, was troubled by this intrusion into her world. She wasn't receptive to the idea of giving up what she loved the most, life on the farm, to a bunch of strangers in business suits. Community meetings followed. A split developed between those who welcomed the company's proposal and those who resisted.

So, Brock and Ronnie took the three-hour drive to this existing wind farm to see for themselves. Since Brock's separation from his wife, Celia, and the death of Ronnie's husband, Cort, the couple were regularly spending time together. They found solace in one another and, after an evening snowed-in together on the farm a few months earlier, the passion they flirted with as teenagers was rekindled.

Ronnie propped herself up on an elbow and looked down at Brock. She was serious now. "The bank says they're throwing some pretty big numbers around." She knew Brock's mom was struggling with the idea of leasing their ground for development. "They say it could really help the economy for people in Glory Grove."

Brock stared up at her. She looked contemplative, waiting for his reply. But he didn't speak, distracted momentarily by the warmth in her face. Without makeup and dressed in blue jeans and a flannel shirt, she was the picture of health. Her auburn hair glistened in the sun. Her cheeks were pink from the cool air. Lying next to him beneath this giant turbine, she quickened his heart as she had always done. For a moment he forgot why they'd made the trip. He purposely refocused his thoughts.

"It's going to be a hard decision. Seeing this is going to make it harder." He motioned with his arm toward the hundreds of giant machines stretching before them across the horizon … like an army of otherworld invaders. "I can't even imagine these things blocking the view on Piney Ridge."

"I know," she sighed, and thought of the special moments they'd had together on the ridge and the beauty of the remote area. "But people are tempted by the promise of money, and a chance to move out from under their financial problems. You and your mom have to consider the long-term implications of it. At the bank, we see how tough things are for farmers and ranchers. Remember how I struggled to make your budget balance."

"Oh, I remember." A mischievous grin formed on his lips.

She put her hands on his face and squeezed his cheeks. "You'll figure it out. But I may have to shoot you first." With a laugh, she curled up next to him and buried her face in his chest.

CHAPTER 2

# EARLIER

**MONTHS BEFORE THEIR TRIP** to the wind farm, Brock arrived back at his boyhood home just as the sun was setting. A light dusting of snow still covered the ground. As he stepped from his car, Sassy, the family's border collie pup, rushed to greet him.

"Hello, girl, did you miss me? "He reached down to cup her head in his hands and rub her ears. "Sure, you did, I've been gone almost all day. At least you didn't forget me."

Her tail wagging accelerated with each stroke of Brock's hands. It created a loud thumping sound on the floorboards of the old farmhouse's front porch. As he wrestled with the pup's wiggling, he heard his mother's voice.

"Back so soon? That was a short trip to Seattle," Irene said as she stuck her head out the front door to see what Sassy was excited about. She was surprised to see her son, but her face lit up with a smile.

When Brock left early that morning, he intended to visit his former athletic director at Brighton High School. He'd coached there for seven years. Despite his intentions to stay away from football for a time, he'd ended up taking on the head coaching job in the tiny farm town. The result had been a storybook run for the team, albeit with a disappointing ending. He'd given up that job at Brighton to tend to his ailing mom in Glory Grove, and now he wanted to explore his options of perhaps returning as the head football coach in the large Seattle school.

But more importantly, while in Seattle, he planned to resolve issues with his wife, Celia. She had written to him weeks earlier to ask for a separation. Their marriage had come apart when Brock went home to the Grove to be with his mother. While he was away, Celia, an employee at a Seattle art gallery, found companionship with a well-known New York sculptor. She had come under the influence of his celebrity in a drug-fueled world.

At a low point, she entered a rehabilitation facility, but soon abandoned the therapy. Brock struggled with the realization their marriage was coming to an end. Their bond, once aided by mutual respect and cooperation, was fractured by their differences in lifestyle and values. But Brock hated losing—in the games he coached and in his life. Losing his marriage felt like … failure.

As he traveled west to Seattle, Brock battled snowy roads and the turmoil in his mind. He wrestled with his love of farm life and his fondness for the boys he coached for one season at Glory Grove. He'd taken over a desperate football program and led them on a championship run for a state crown. While he drove, he reflected on the affection he felt for his high school girlfriend, Ronnie. An attraction that had begun years ago was returning. At the peak of his emotional conflict, his car went into a dangerous slide, crippled by a flat tire.

Parked by the side of the road in a snowstorm, he struggled with the physical task of making the repair. It was there he reached his breaking point. In his moments of indecision and despair, the image of an elk appeared—real or imagined he wasn't sure—calling him back to his rural roots. He found a moment of clarity and a decision was made. He turned his car around and headed east … back to his hometown. It was where he belonged.

Brock's mother tried to reassure him. "Well, whatever you decided, I'm sure it's for the best. Sometimes, what's meant for you won't get by you."

Brock nodded at his mother's oft-used saying as they walked into the kitchen. "I thought a lot while I was driving and decided I had more reasons to stay in the Grove than to move back to Seattle. Funny though, how a flat tire up on a mountain pass kind of steered me back here."

"It's the first time I've ever been grateful for a flat tire," Irene said. She poured him a cup of coffee from the stove. "What now?"

Brock smiled as he slid into a chair at the kitchen table. His mother was still struggling with cancer, and he didn't need to burden her with details of his life's crises. "I'll just keep moving forward. 'There's always something to do on the farm.' I can remember Dad saying that even when I was little. But now …" He paused, lifting his cup as if saluting her, "We need to get ready for Christmas. I'll go find you a tree."

"And not just any tree." Her eyes widened. "It has to be a special one from up on the ridge. I like the ones the FFA kids sell in town, but I'd love to have one again from our own farm. It'll bring back so many memories. Your father and I always went up on the ridge to bring home our own Christmas tree."

"Okay, then. That's my number one priority. Maybe I can get Ronnie to go with me."

"I don't think you'll have to ask twice. I'm sure she is a little lonely now that Cort has passed, but you wouldn't know it to look at her. She really keeps it together, even with all she's been going through. Some of the bachelor farmers around here can't wait to swoop in. Got their horns up."

Brock almost choked on the coffee he was trying to swallow, struggling not to spit it across the room. "Holy cow, Mom, don't you think it might be a bit early for talk like that?"

"Not in a little farm town like this. Pretty women don't come along very often."

"I suppose." He regained his composure and took another sip from his cup. "Maybe I should stay away for a while and let her get her life back in order. But she seems happy when we're together, thinking of old times, and now especially because we both lost something in our lives and are trying to move ahead." He wrapped his hands around the coffee cup warming his fingers. "With the football season over, we might finally have time to sort it out."

"I wouldn't wait too long. Just saying."

"I'm still married, you know."

Irene bit her lip. "I know. Just tell me to mind my own business."

"Sure, but you know, I'll always take your advice." Brock looked over and stared into his mom's blue eyes. "You've never steered me wrong. At least not yet anyway." He grinned like he was a teenager again, trying to please his mother, working for an extension on a midnight curfew.

"Getting kind of sticky sweet with this conversation don't you think?" She bobbed her head and laughed. "Let's talk about the farm."

"I agree. The cows will start calving soon." He pushed back in his chair and let out a deep sigh. "Nice to be back."

Brock didn't wait long to drop in on Ronnie at her house. She'd find out soon enough he was already back in town, so he wanted to get in front of the rumor mill. He told her of his mid-trip decision to return.

When she heard his story, he could hear the relief in her voice. "I'm happy to hear it, I thought maybe we'd lost you for good," she said, "but what made you turn around?"

"A flat tire."

Ronnie rolled her eyes "A flat tire? That's it?"

"No, that and thinking of the football team … and the farm … and a young widow." He gave her a sideways glance.

"Those are good enough reasons," Ronnie said. She leaned over to straighten the collar on Brock's shirt. "But is this widow so far down on the list?" She was teasing with a grain of truth in her statement.

"Okay, maybe my reasons weren't exactly in that order." He laughed. "Anyway, I stopped by to invite you to join me on a Christmas tree hunt. I'll ask Tim and Peggy to come too." Tim and Peggy Palmer were two of their oldest friends, who were working on getting their marriage back together after a long separation brought on by her alcohol addiction. Tim had played high school football with Brock and the previous fall helped Brock coach the Grizzly football team.

"Is this a date?" Ronnie asked.

Brock shook his head. "Just an old friend get-together. Or maybe a double date. Call it what you want. Can you come?"

"Sure. I could use another tree. And if I know Tim, he hasn't even thought about it yet, unless Peggy has done it for him. They seem to be getting along pretty well. Everybody is holding their breath hoping they can make it work."

Brock remembered how much happier Tim was when he was with Peggy. "Let's hope for all our sakes they can work things out. We'll see how well they can get along on a Christmas tree hunt. And by the way, with all this tree cutting, we're going to work up an appetite, so I'll bring the ax if you bring some food."

Later that day, Brock had a visit with Tim and his old friend agreed he and Peggy could join in the tree hunt. "Hell, yes," Tim said. "Peg has been buggin' me for weeks to get a tree, but damned they're expensive. If I can get one off the ridge, it'll solve that problem."

"Sounds like she's trying to turn you into a proper family man again," Brock said, as he pictured Tim's home as it looked before Peggy came back to live with him. Beer cans, hunting magazines, and clothes scattered throughout the living room. "You and that big son of yours have to clean up your act a little?"

"Yep, and it's a hassle, living with a woman again." Tim's face turned into an exaggerated clown frown. "She's watching Hallmark Christmas movies now when Luke and I should be watching football. We might have to get another television before things get serious."

"Well, just be glad she's willing to put up with you. You could use some refinement." Brock stared out the living room window as if looking for someone. "Trust me, since I'm single again, I miss having a wife."

Tim nodded. "That sucks about you and Celia. She just couldn't fit in here, could she?"

"No, and I never fit into her crowd either. Honestly, we were never a very good match. But we had some good years. I'm grateful for that. Just wish it could have ended on a happier note." He looked up at Tim. "She has some demons to deal with, with the drugs and all."

There was an awkward pause in the conversation. Tim rocked back in his chair. "That hits close to home. It's a struggle for Peggy, too. She's been sober for almost six months now but says she thinks about drinking every day. I've cleaned out our house of every bottle, so she's not tempted. But now I'm cranky as hell." He smiled. "I miss my nightly brew."

"Hang in there, Tim, you're doing the right thing. She's worth it. And it won't hurt you to back off a bit. But if you really need a drink, I'll pack a couple twelve-ouncers in my saddle bag when we head to Piney Ridge. Then we can slip away from the girls for a few minutes and have a toast to the trees we bring back." Brock laughed when he could see Tim nodding his head, happy with the thought.

Brock changed the subject. "By the way, Uncle Richard says one of our cows didn't come in with the herd when he started feeding hay. When we take the horses up for the trees, we'll see if we can find the old girl."

A few days later, Tim arrived with his horse trailer. He'd brought along two extra saddle horses for the women. They climbed aboard their mounts and rode as a foursome up the ridge behind the house. "Good luck. Have fun," Irene hollered from the back door.

Sassy raced out in front of them and nearly wore herself out examining one curiosity after another, taking in the sights and smells of a clear crisp Saturday morning. With the temperature in the teens, the riders were all bundled up, waiting for the sun to warm them.

As they rode, conversation bubbled up between the women about the latest happenings in town, while the men talked about the Grizzlies. The high school basketball team had been practicing for a couple of weeks and had games scheduled in the coming days. The town was shifting its attention to the possibilities of making a championship run like they had done in football.

"How do you think the basketball team will do now with some of the new players on the team?" Tim asked as he pulled his gelding up next to Dolly, the old mare Brock was riding.

"Well, we know they have some good athletes … same kids we coached in football. So, it just depends on how Coach McHue handles them and how well they can work together," Brock said. "We'll see how that plays out. We'll be getting reports from the boys real soon."

# CHAPTER 3

# RESCUE

IT WAS A FORTY-MINUTE RIDE up a steep ridge to the area where they'd find the young fir trees. As they rode, they scanned the surroundings for the missing cow. If she'd fallen ill, they might find her carcass, or a skeleton licked clean by coyotes. Brock was riding along the edge of a steep ravine, a narrow gulley formed by centuries of natural erosion. Granite outcroppings edged out from the banks. Scattered along the depression were lines of packed soil showing where cows had trailed in and out of the area.

As they approached a timbered section of the ridge, Brock noticed one of the areas in the ravine void of vegetation. There was no grass on the bottom or banks. He spurred Dolly forward around the bend and tugged on her reins to bring her to a stop.

"Tim, get over here," he shouted. "I've found her."

Tim wheeled his horse around and galloped to Brock's side. "Look at that." He whistled as if dramatizing the scene he was staring at. A black baldy cow stood at the bottom of the channel, staring blankly at the giant tree which had fallen, blocking her exit from the area. Her ribs were protruding, evidence she'd been there for some time. A trickle of water from melting snow had left a few pools in scattered depressions, enough to keep her hydrated. But she'd licked clean every scrap of vegetation she could reach.

"What now, Brock?" Tim asked. "I have my pistol in the saddle bag. Do we put her down? Or do you think she can make it back to the barn?"

Ronnie and Peggy had joined them, sitting silently on their horses.

Brock stared down at the cow, not wanting to give in to defeat. A dead cow was a sure sign of failure. "Let's give her a chance. But there's just one way out. We're going to have to move that tree."

Tim slipped off his horse. "Figured you'd say that. Wish we'd brought a chainsaw, but you got that ax you brought for the Christmas trees. Let's start hacking."

The men tethered their horses to a nearby tree and watched the women go on ahead with Sassy to scout for Christmas trees. They began working, taking turns chopping on the timber. Throughout the morning, they peeled away splinters from the narrow end of the log. As Brock began the final cuts, he turned to Tim. "Ride up the ridge a ways and see if you can find a pole long enough to use as a lever. Then maybe we can wedge this old thing around and give her an escape route."

When Tim returned, dragging a ten-foot pole behind his horse, they dropped it into the channel, positioned it under the log, and began reefing. "Good thing you're still packing the weight from the nightly brews you were talking about. Any lighter, and we wouldn't have any leverage at all."

"Makes up for your skinny-assed little quarterback frame," Tim shot back, laughing, as he gave another strong push.

With successive heave-ho's they managed, inches at a time, to scoot the downed tree away from the gulley wall. "Okay," Brock said. "Let's see if she has enough strength to head down the hill."

They skirted around the cow, but she didn't move. She was so accustomed to the blockage that she couldn't see the opening. So, both men got behind her and locked hands. With her weakened condition she didn't fight. Gradually, they guided her to the narrow slot they'd created.

"Now girl, it's up to you," Brock said. "Make yourself free." He patted her rump. "Okay Tim, on the count of three. One, two, three …"

With a synchronized shove, they forced her past the end of the log, and she stumbled through the opening, stood for a moment to get her bearings, then began to slowly walk her way out of the prison that had been her home for too many days.

Tim flopped down onto the dirt bank and despite the winter temperatures, sweat poured from his forehead. "She'd better not die now," he said, as he spit some of his chew onto the ground. "After all that effort, I'd be pretty pissed at old bossy."

Brock sighed and eased himself down on the tree trunk still laying in the gully. "Well, we've done our good deed for the day," he said. "But we still have a couple of Christmas trees to find." He slowly turned and stared up at the saddle bag on his horse, then turned to Tim. "Should we crack those beers?"

"Yep, just don't tell Peg," Tim said.

"Wouldn't think of it." Brock rummaged through his saddle bag and tossed a can to Tim. They flipped the tabs and with the thirst they'd built up working with the tree, they inhaled the beer.

"That's good timing," Brock said as his eyes scanned the ridge. They'd finished just as the women were coming down the slope. Like a couple of seventeen-year-old schoolboys, they quickly stashed the empties and innocently stood waiting for the women.

Peggy spoke first. "You men just hanging out waiting for our arrival?" She swung her mop full of hair side to side and laughed. "If you're done here, we'd better go collect some Christmas trees, because it's going to get dark soon. And spending a night on the ridge in December won't be the same as it was when we were teenagers in the summer."

Ronnie ducked her head and Brock thought he could see her blushing, remembering such a night. "Okay, girls, lead on," he said, smiling.

The couples returned from Piney Ridge as the sun was setting. They all turned their collars against the wind. None of them had dressed for the evening cold, assuming they'd be home well before dark. But they'd fashioned their own windbreak, as they each had a fir tree strapped to the back of their saddle.

When they neared the barn, they could make out a figure in the fading sunlight. Tim let out a small whoop. "Will you look at that, Brock. The old girl made it back." The wayward cow stood motionless by the corral gate ready to join the herd.

"Today you win," Brock mumbled. His breath was visible in the chill as he dismounted and opened the corral gate. "Go on, bossy," he said. "You deserve a meal for hanging on as long as you did. Sorry it took us so long." He patted her hip as she staggered through the gate.

Tim turned to the women. "Have you noticed with Brock, it's all about winning?"

Brock stared up at the trio. "Hey, I'll take every win I can get. It's been a long day and I'm beat. But I've learned a couple of things through all this." He swung the gate shut and latched it closed. "First, it's good to have friends like you. And second, the best thing about cows is they don't talk too much like some people I know."

They dismounted and unpacked their Christmas trees.

CHAPTER 4

# HOOPS

**IN THE FALL OF THE YEAR**, Brock coached the Glory Grove High School football team to an appearance in the state championship. Despite a disappointing loss, the community was flush with pride in their success. It was reason for celebration, but the loss denied Brock the state championship he so desired.

Now, with the end of football season, there was an empty feeling among the many sports fans in the Grove. They'd been caught up in the championship quest and the team's unexpected rise to prominence. It had ended suddenly and left them wanting more. But like all small towns that focused on high school sports, they quickly turned their attention to the same group of boys playing on the hardwood.

Before Brock took the reins of the football program, the failed seven-year tenure of Conrad Newton as the Grizzly football coach had the people paying more attention to basketball. But, as with football, there were no trophies in the trophy case for their basketball teams.

Coach Buster McHue had been a fixture on the bench for over twenty years. His ever-expanding bald spot and growing midriff was often the point of conversation amongst the crowd. The conjecture was, his hair loss came from the constant head rubbing he exhibited as a game would spin out of control, shots failed to drop, and his boys failed to defend. The team seldom put up more wins than losses, running a slowdown offense with a scripted screen game with pick-and-roll options. After decades of being the Grizzly basketball coach, Buster had little to show for it aside from his aging appearance.

With the recent success of the football team, Grove citizens, including the men in the coffee groups who met early each morning in their favorite eating establishments, were talking about basketball, hoping for some success with their winter sport. It would fill their conversations for three months. The men were especially curious how the newcomers, Jimmy Ivory and Luke Palmer, who had ignited the offense for the gridiron team, might bolster their chances for knocking off some of the town's more disliked rivals in basketball.

"Old Buster inherited some real players," Don Baker said one morning at the Cozy Corner Drive-In, as the morning coffee crowd gathered around their favorite table, sipping on the fresh brew. Don, who had been an assistant for Brock Gallagher's football team, always arrived at the drive-in early—he had his own set of keys—to brew a pot before the owner arrived. "It'll be fun to see what he can do with those boys. It's going to take a few days before they get over trying to knock their opponent to the ground."

The men, who had all faithfully followed the football team, agreed there could be hope for a good season.

"Maybe Huey will be rewarded for all the years he's put in walking up and down in front of the bench," Homer Johnson, one of the old-timers, said. "Couldn't ask for a nicer man, but he's still coaching like it's the fifties. And he's going to struggle to get along with the Knighton kid and his old lady. Even when they win, it's hard to cheer for that kid and his loudmouth mom. Someone should put a sock in her mouth."

"Come on, Homer … tell us what you really think," another man cracked. "We're sure going to have fun talking basketball this year. A lot of games for you to analyze. And Homer, we'll put you in charge of Goldie Knighton." He set his cup down and let off a trumpet-like laugh.

Goldie Knighton always sat in the top row of the bleachers in Glory Grove High School's gymnasium for basketball games. But it was a small gym and Goldie had a big voice. Most of the folks in the 500 seats could hear her when she yelled, including Coach McHue. And she let her opinions be known. Usually, her angry words were directed at the men in striped shirts, but occasionally they were aimed at the coaches or the players on the court. Her son, Cole, only received constant praise from his mother. "Good job, Cole," she would sing out. "You got this. Make me proud."

Goldie usually sat alone in the bleachers. Other fans avoided sitting near her, not wanting to be associated with her harangues. And in a similar fashion, she'd also spent most of her adult life alone after her husband, Clarence, a long-haul trucker, left on a trip to the Midwest and never returned. He wasn't dead, she knew that, but as her resentment of him grew, she wouldn't have mourned even if she learned he'd met his end in some horrific accident. However, she gave him credit for the one thing in her life that was good. That was her son. She'd raised him by herself since he was seven and guarded over him like a mother hen, inserting herself into every facet of his life.

To the boy's credit, he loved his mother and tried his best to please her, even when she made his life uncomfortable. He stayed away from the other boys in school who teased him about his mom. And he worked hard enough in the classroom to get by and not draw attention to whatever he was doing. He didn't distinguish himself from the other kids until the fourth grade, when he picked up a basketball and found he had a knack for handling the smooth round sphere better than others his age.

The two local men who directed a youth basketball program recognized his potential early on. "That kid is going to be something special," one said to the other. But they were somewhat reluctant to make him part of their team because of the interference they knew would come from his mother. "It's a win/lose kind of situation," they'd said, shaking their heads at the promise of having a winning team with Cole on it, but with the annoyance and irritation of dealing with Goldie as an in-your-face parent.

When Cole reached high school age, it was Coach McHue who had to deal with the situation. He had experienced too many years of failed seasons to care much about the downsides of having Cole Knighton on his team. He needed to win games. He'd heard the whispers as he walked through stores in town or sat in church or went to local gatherings. He'd been the Grizzlies coach for a long time and had no hardware to show for it. There had been petitions to have him fired but since no one stepped up to seek the job, he'd languished in the position … waiting and hoping for a time when the talent was there for him to make a run at the trophy that always seemed out of his reach.

Now, it was like he'd scratched off a winning lottery ticket and discovered a big prize. A quick young athlete named Jimmy Ivory had moved from the inner city to Glory Grove with Brock Gallagher when Brock returned in the summer. And not long after that, a muscular sixteen-year-old named Luke Palmer was shipped home from Denver to live with his dad while his mother, Peggy, was serving a jail sentence. McHue had watched the new boys reinvigorate the Grizzly football program and help take the team to the state championship. When he learned they would turn out for basketball, he quietly celebrated.

"If I can get those new boys and Justin Jepson, who is already being recruited by college football coaches, to mesh with Cole Knighton, we may finally have the team I've always dreamed of," he confided to his wife, Eunice.

"But Cole doesn't even have friends of his own," Eunice said. "He's always angry and stays to himself." She taught in the elementary school and had watched him grow up. "It might be a challenge to get them to work together, Buster. You'd better not get your hopes up."

"They don't have to love each other, just make more baskets than the other team." He slumped down in his recliner.

Eunice sighed. "Sounds simple enough. But you know everyone will be watching. Especially Goldie."

Buster growled. "Gawd a'mighty, why can't it just be simple for a change? I'm too old to be a babysitter or a psychiatrist."

"Hey, that's why the school pays you such a big salary for being a basketball coach, isn't it?" She laughed and handed him his nightly shot of Jack Daniels. "Maybe it'll all come together, you know, like a jigsaw puzzle. Just assemble the border and slip all the other big pieces into place. Can't be that hard, can it?"

At school, the boys were all still energized from the success the football team had experienced in their magical season. The week after the football championships, thirty-five boys showed up for basketball tryouts. Cuts were quickly made, and at the end of the first week, Coach

McHue called the team together and announced his plan. "Jimmy, you'll play the point. Jepson and Palmer, you play the forward positions, and Knighton, you'll be on the wing. Baker, for now, you'll play the other wing unless someone else can take it from you. In fact, any of these positions are up for grabs, so don't get too comfortable. Keep looking over your shoulder."

"Sure, Coach. But there's nobody over my shoulder." It was Cole Knighton. As a sophomore, he would claim the role of a slick shooting guard. He moved with the grace of a whitetail deer. Even as a freshman playing on the varsity, he could knock down twenty points with a silky-smooth jump shot. At five foot eleven and with a wiry frame, he'd chosen not to play football in the fall to save himself for the hardwood. And he'd arranged with Principal Lester Colquit to have access to the gym, through the custodian, so he could practice on his own. But he'd grown to resent all the attention the football players had garnered in the fall and kept to himself when they came together for basketball.

At the team's first practice, Coach McHue could see he would continue to have problems with Goldie. As the team was warming up, running laps around the court, following his orders to stay outside of the out-of-bound lines, she slipped into the gym and sat in her usual spot in the bleachers. Luke Palmer was the first to notice. "Who's the chunky red-headed lady?" he asked Justin Jepson as they jogged together, nodding toward Goldie.

"That's Knighton's mom," Justin said, under his breath. "She follows him wherever he goes."

"Kinda sucks for him, doesn't it?"

"He's used to it, kind of responds to her commands."

Luke caught his breath as he rounded the corner of the court, making sure not to step on the playing surface. "Well, what does old

Buster think of her being here? In Denver, no parents were allowed at practice."

"Well, no one wants to get into it with Goldie. Especially Coach McHue. He just tries to get along with everybody."

"Okay. But I'm sure glad my parents don't show up at practice. They'll get worked up just watching games. You remember my dad at that one football game … cost us a win."

"Yep, but he learned his lesson. Changed his ways after that. But I'm not sure Goldie will ever learn. You'd better get used to her sitting up there. She was there all last season when Cole was a freshman. He worked his way onto the varsity. She'd even yell at us if she thought we weren't passing him the ball enough."

Just then, the whistle blew, and the coach brought the team to a stop. He stood in the jump circle at center court. "Lay-ins," he bellowed. "Both ends of the court. Let's go."

After two weeks of practice, the season started. In the first non-league game, the only trouble the team experienced was when Luke, a fullback and linebacker on the football team, was tagged with personal fouls for his over-aggressive play and had to sit on the bench. He watched as the team struggled to keep pace without his muscle inside.

Brock and Ronnie were at the game, sitting together at the end of the bleachers, trying to be inconspicuous, quietly watching the action. Townspeople in the bleachers, including the church ladies, were whispering about the two, making judgments about whether it was too early for the young widow to be with a married man, or if a married man, separated from his wife, should be so comfortable with a recently widowed woman. Thankfully for the couple, the game was entertaining enough to keep prying eyes mostly on the players.

Meanwhile, Tim Palmer and Peggy, who extended her stay in Glory Grove for another few weeks, were happy to see their son on the basketball court. The couple sat in the front row, center court, close to one another and focused on Luke. This was also the first chance many in the crowd had to see the muscled boy without a helmet and pads. They couldn't help but be impressed by the size and muscular frame of the junior who'd moved in from Colorado.

"I could do without the eagle tattoo on his arm," one woman said, wagging her finger in his direction. But the other mothers were thrilled knowing if the game became too rough, Luke would be on their son's side. He was even more intimidating to the opponent when they felt his strength muscling them away from the basket.

Peggy reminded Tim to keep his opinions of the referees to himself. She knew Luke could be tagged with early fouls due to his physical play. "Let's let Luke enjoy the game without worrying about your outbursts," she said, with a sharp elbow into his ribs. She had remained sober since coming to Glory Grove and didn't need any drama in their lives as a temptation to calm her nerves with alcohol.

But a few minutes into the game, it was Peggy who became increasingly annoyed by the constant yelling from Goldie Knighton sitting behind them. "I'd like to stuff this bag of popcorn down her throat," she whispered to Tim as she crumpled the bag in her hands.

Tim pulled his cap, with the county road department logo, down harder on his head and swayed back and forth in his seat. "Peggy, I'm trying to remain calm. Don't get me riled up. But damn it's hard. Between her screaming and the one-sided referees, my blood is starting to boil."

Peggy patted his arm. "Let's go out at halftime and join the smokers in the parking lot. Twenty-degree weather ought to cool us down." She snorted a laugh and swung her tousled hair back and forth reacting to her own suggestion.

As the second half unfolded, Cole Knighton felt rewarded for his decision not to play football. The hours he spent in the gym by himself, putting up shot after shot, perfecting the motion, had him ready for the early season. He quickly became the star of the show. He'd set a personal goal for himself. He wanted twenty points in the scorebook in each game and set out to hit his mark. But, even when his shooting touch left him, he didn't slow down his attempts. The lack of self-awareness quickly turned his teammates and their parents against him.

"You might try passing the ball once in a while," Luke muttered as the team huddled during a time-out.

"Up yours, bigshot," was the response he got in return.

Luke stepped toward the mop-haired sophomore with a clenched fist, but Justin Jepson, the team captain and always the cool-headed leader, slid between them and held Luke back. "Not tonight, Luke," Justin scolded. Coach Buster didn't say a word. The game resumed and Knighton kept shooting.

In the end, he put up the game-winning shot at the buzzer and the crowd erupted in cheers.

CHAPTER 5

# DRIVER

**MOST NIGHTS AFTER BASKETBALL PRACTICE,** Jimmy Ivory rode home with Brock's Uncle Richard. Since moving to the farm with Brock after the death of his own mother, Jimmy had grown fond of the bachelor farmer, a man with a head full of silly jokes and a mind full of wise advice. Jimmy missed his mom and his friends in Seattle, but he found a welcoming environment on the farm and with his teammates on the football team.

It was now Richard who was assuming the duty of ferrying the young man around to his school events and basketball practice. "You need to take some driver's education at the school so you can get your license," Richard said as they drove home one night. "I'm going to get tired of chauffeuring you around," he reached over and shoved his young friend's shoulder, laughing.

"I bet you'd miss my company," Jimmy said, a wide grin on his face. "Who else you got to talk to besides the cows."

"Smart ass." Richard drummed his fingers on the steering wheel. He loved the give and take which had become their customary routine on these drives. He hadn't wanted his nephew to leave the farm so was thrilled when Brock returned with plans to stay. He'd become comfortable working with him. The farm was in better shape with another man involved in the work and helping make decisions. And he didn't want to deal alone with Irene and her failing health. Right now she was doing well, but still recovering from her surgery. And above all, Richard knew if Brock returned to Seattle, Jimmy would go with him. It would leave a big hole in his life like a missing partner in a team roping rodeo event.

"So how was practice?"

"A lot warmer inside the gym, that's for sure. I didn't play much at Brighton, since I was so small, but over here the coach is letting me play. I'm jacked about that." Jimmy was slapping his leg in time to the music on the radio. "But there's a couple of new guys playing I don't know very well. This one guy's giving me a hard time about my size. Keeps trying to push me around. I can ignore him but he's going to get on my nerves if he keeps it up," Jimmy said, staring out the window at the Christmas lights on the farmhouse they were passing.

"Do you put up lights for Christmas?" Jimmy asked, changing the subject.

"Naw, don't see much sense in that. I don't have a wife nagging me about decorating, or kids to entertain. Nope, just peace and quiet at my house."

"My mom used to put up a little tree, in Seattle. Wasn't much, but she loved Christmas. She had music playing all the time. I'm missing her more with Christmas coming up." His eyes blinked a couple of times, remembering. "But Irene says we'll get a tree. Maybe we should get one for you too. Just some scraggly old Charlie Brown tree." He bit his lip, trying hard not to laugh.

Richard punched Jimmy again. "Hey, me and a Charlie Brown tree. Bah humbug." He made a Scrooge face at the boy.

# CHAPTER 6

# TEACHER

**THE DAY SCHOOL LET OUT** for Christmas vacation, Brock got a call from Lester Colquit, the principal at Glory Grove High School. "Brock, I heard you were still in town. I'm glad you're going to stay around for a while."

Brock tried to keep from laughing. When he'd first met the principal the previous summer, the man had done everything possible to keep him away from the school and the football team. But through a season of coaching Lester Jr. in football, Colquit had become one of his biggest supporters. He could tell from the high-pitched nasal timber of his voice that the principal was about to ask for something.

"Brock," Colquit started to speak, then shifted his voice to a more authoritative tone. "We have a teaching job open at the school. Our young history teacher gave up trying to control the classroom and handed in his resignation. The board says the job is yours if you want it."

"Thanks, Lester, I do miss the classroom and the kids." Brock said.

"I probably should get off the list of the unemployed. I think I could step into that role. Can you give me some details?"

"Sure. As you know, we're a small school, so you wouldn't have over twenty kids in each class. You'd teach three history classes each day, plus one class in government and another in junior high social studies." He paused for a second or two before dropping one other requirement. "And there is one other thing. Each teacher here is expected to take on at least one extracurricular activity. Of course, it'd be football in the fall, but this winter and spring, we'd have to slip you into wherever you're needed."

"That's fine, as long as I don't have to coach volleyball or basketball. That's way too easy a place to make enemies."

"Duly noted," Colquit said. "But actually … the board wants you to step in and help Coach McHue with the basketball team." There was an uncomfortable silence for a moment and then the principal continued. "People have watched enough games to think these boys have a shot at being a contender for a league title. I guess that doesn't come along very often here in Glory Grove, so they would like you to give Buster a hand."

Brock took a deep breath. "Lester, I'm no basketball coach. I wasn't even a good player in high school. I'm not sure I'd be any help."

"The board thinks Buster needs help getting those boys headed in the right direction. They all saw what you did for Grizzly football and think you could help make it happen in the gym."

Brock knew he could be spreading himself thin. Coaching basketball wasn't in his plans. And playing second fiddle to Buster McHue wasn't something that fit his character. Besides, basketball meant a lot of late nights and weekend travel. And he had commitments at home. His mother's health was deteriorating. And he'd become the guardian for Jimmy Ivory, who had grown up in a rough part of Seattle and was still adjusting to life in a small town.

Still, he'd been without a paycheck since June, aside from his football coaching. And his wife Celia's short stay in a rehab program in Seattle, plus her spending on travel and partying, had depleted the couple's savings. There were also the extra expenses he and Jimmy had added to the farm operation just by being there.

"I do need a paycheck," Brock finally admitted to Colquit. "If you hire me, I can promise I'll earn every penny. But I don't want to get on the bad side of Coach McHue. He's a nice man and I know he's trying his best."

"I'm sure you will do your best, too," Colquit said. "I'll make sure of that." He laughed his high-pitched snicker. "I saw what you did with the football program in three months. I'll expect you to do the same for our history classes. And as far as basketball goes, we'll let you work it out with Coach McHue. I'll run this by the school board so we can make it official, but let me be the first to welcome you to the faculty."

# CHAPTER 7

# CHRISTMAS

**BROCK DRAGGED THE CHRISTMAS TREE** into the farmhouse and propped it up in the corner of the living room. It stood in the same spot where it had been every year that he could remember. Irene watched from a corner chair with a smile that reflected the gratitude she felt for her son's efforts. "This is better than any present you could buy me," she said, gazing up at the tree. "I can't wait to see it with all the ornaments."

"That's good, because I'm not sure you're getting anything from me," he said as he wrestled with the tree, persuading it to settle into its stand. "You know what a great shopper I am."

"That's okay, not much you could get an old lady like me." She rocked back in her chair. "I probably don't have many Christmases left in me anyway," she said.

"Mom, you never know. But that's why this one needs to be special,"

Brock said. "And we need to make it a good one for Jimmy, too. This will be his first one without his mother."

"What do you have in mind?"

"I don't know. Just to try and make him feel like this is his home and we are his family."

"It does feel like he belongs here. It's only been since June, but memories build quickly on a farm. Especially with football, and harvest, and now the cows. He's already experienced a lot. I've grown very fond of him. And if you've noticed, so has your Uncle Richard. When those two are together, they jabber like a couple of magpies."

"That's because Jimmy still laughs at all his dumb jokes. Anyway, let's put our heads together and see what we can come up with for gifts for him."

When Richard and Jimmy returned from a quick shopping trip to town for cattle supplies, Jimmy stepped into the living room and let out a whistle. "That's the best tree I've ever seen."

"And it's from the Gallagher farm," Irene said. Her face was beaming like a happy child.

"Thanks to Tim and me," Brock countered. "We spent all day searching for this perfect tree … and chopping a lost cow out of a prison. But since you like it, I guess it was worth it."

"Can I help decorate?" Jimmy asked, looking over at Irene.

Irene laughed. "Of course, I can't wait to see it all dressed up."

"Yes, sir." Brock joined in. "You can be the head decorator; let me get the ornaments." He disappeared for a few minutes into the attic and came back lugging two giant boxes of Christmas lights and ornaments.

"Where do I start?" Jimmy asked.

"Wherever you like," Brock said. "Just dress it up until it looks like Christmas. There is no time to waste; that chubby little man in the red suit could be coming down that chimney any minute now."

So, they spent the next hour hanging lights and balls from the tree limbs. Jimmy asked about many of the ornaments that piqued his interest—the ones with writing or photos on them.

"We could never have a tree this big in our apartment," Jimmy said, "but mom would put up decorations I brought home from school and the ones she'd bought for me. I think some of them might be in the boxes you hauled here from Seattle."

"Then go get them," Irene said in a faux scolding manner. "Let's see what you have. This is about your Christmas, too."

Brock thought it might be best if he left them alone for a while, so he excused himself. "I need to go check on the animals," he said.

Jimmy spun around and headed to his room, returning a short time later with a ragged cardboard box of Christmas decorations. He carefully pulled them, one at a time, from the box, studied each one, now a memory from his childhood, and then found an empty spot on the tree to attach them. As she watched, Irene could see the emotion on the teenager's face ... not tears, only melancholy.

"Now the tree is even more beautiful," Irene said, as she gave a big sigh. "Thanks, Jimmy, for bringing part of your home to ours."

Jimmy didn't say a word, just sat down beside her, rubbed his eyes, and stared up at the tree. Finally, in a serious teenage voice, he said, "It's real nice, Irene ... it's real nice."

She reached over and patted his arm. "You don't have to say anything, Jimmy. Let's just sit here and enjoy it for a while. I think we're almost ready for the big day."

Christmas morning was cold, and there were a few inches of fresh snow on the ground. Brock stirred the embers and added logs to the fireplace. Richard and Jimmy went out together to feed the livestock, while Brock stayed inside to help his mom with breakfast. Jimmy carried a steak bone as a treat for Sassy, who bounded out of the doghouse they'd filled with a giant quilt.

"Merry Christmas, Sassy," Jimmy said as he pulled her up to his chest and let the little dog lick his face. Jimmy kept begging Irene and Brock to let the dog in the house, but they assured him a farm dog was fine outside with enough blankets and shelter from the wind.

When they returned, Irene and Brock set out a full breakfast of scrambled eggs, hashbrowns, and sausage from the pig they'd bought at the county fair. The house was filled with the aroma of farm food and the noise of a crackling fire. "A big breakfast on Christmas morning … can't beat it," Richard said. He stretched his legs under the table and waited for the others to join him.

After they finished eating, Irene, although weakened from her illness, pestered the men to move to the living room for the opening of presents. "Okay, Irene," Richard said, "but you know we're not little kids anymore, well, unless you think Jimmy fits that category." He winked at the teenager.

Jimmy hopped up and extended his hand. "Come on, old man."

They gathered around the tree and Jimmy went into action, handing his presents to the adults. He'd found a Glory Grove Grizzly cap for Brock, red with white trim and a double G on the front. "Thought maybe next fall you could show a little more flash and style on the sidelines when you're calling plays," Jimmy said.

Brock adjusted the band and slipped it over his unruly shock of hair. "Perfect," he said. "Now I'm ready for football."

For Richard, Jimmy purchased a joke book full of *dad jokes*. He knew it was the perfect gift for the man who made him choke back laughter as he pretended not to understand his lame jokes. "You need some new material, I think," Jimmy said. He knew Richard would memorize the entire book, ready to spring each one on any unsuspecting listener who wandered into his path. "You'll probably have the whole book memorized by next week," Jimmy said.

"And I'll tell every one to you, starting on page one," Richard said as he thumbed through the pages, laughing at the new material he was reading.

Jimmy was nervous about the present he'd made by hand for Irene. In the farm shop, he and Richard had designed a stained wooden plaque with a metal plate attached to it. On the plate, Jimmy had used the welder to carefully lay a bead in the shape of a cross upon a hill. They chipped away the slag and buffed it on the wire wheel until it sparkled. He held his breath as Irene carefully unwrapped the package.

She pulled the paper from the box, and gently lifted the plaque away from the wrappings. She held it up in front of her eyes. "Oh, Jimmy," she murmured. "Did you make this? It's beautiful."

"Do you like it?" He held his breath.

"It's one of the nicest gifts I've ever received," she said. She looked into his eyes. "Thank you so much."

"Okay," Brock said. "Guess we can't hold a candle to that. But we do have a few things for you, Jimmy."

Brock wiggled a small box out from under the tree and handed it to the teenager. "I think you might be able to put these to good use," he said.

Jimmy didn't expect much. His Christmases had always been a bit of a disappointment when he was growing up with his mom, simply because they were poor. He knew that. His mom tried to make the season happy for him. And her love made up for the lack of things that some of the other boys in the neighborhood received for Christmas. But there was always a sense of melancholy that came with the season. Now, here, surrounded by the Gallagher family, he suddenly felt a sense of anticipation for the gifts that lay before him.

He opened the package from Brock … an expensive pair of athletic gloves used by receivers on a football team.

"No excuses now for dropping a pass," Brock teased. "But you'll have to wait a few months before you can try them out. Ol' Buster wouldn't appreciate you wearing them during a basketball game."

Jimmy slipped them on and worked his fingers back and forth in the soft leather. "Man, if I can touch it, I can catch it," he boasted.

"We'll see about that," Brock said. He let his mind wander to the many passes Jimmy reeled in during the Grizzly football season. If the gloves made him better, the Grizzly team would have an even bigger weapon.

"Okay," Irene said, putting the brakes on the football talk. "I'm a little nervous about the present from me. It's old and small, but I hope you like it." She slid the little box over to Jimmy, who was sitting beside her.

Jimmy rattled it by his ear and held it up to his eyes. "Hmm. Don't have a clue. Guess I'll have to open it."

He quickly stripped off the paper and lifted the lid from the tiny box. His fingers grasped a weathered pocketknife. He held it up in front of his eyes, turned it over, and rubbed his fingers along the sides. He wondered about the significance of the knife.

"It's not new, Jimmy. But it's special to me and I want you to have it. It belonged to my husband, Max. It was his favorite. I asked Brock and he said he'd also like you to have it. Max always said, 'Every man needs a pocketknife if he's going to work on a farm.' You've become a big part of our farm so I thought it was the best present I could give you. I hope it's all right."

Jimmy sat staring at the knife.

Irene began to worry that he didn't like her gift, but she gave him time to speak.

Jimmy cleared his throat and whispered, "It's too much, Irene. I don't know if I should have this. Are you sure your husband would want me to have it?"

"He would be tickled pink. It's not doing any good sitting on my dresser. And I won't be around forever, so it was time to find a good home for it. Just think of me when you use it." She smiled, tears in her eyes. Brock and Richard were also fighting off their emotions, remembering their dad and brother, knowing if he were looking down, he'd be smiling at the scene taking place.

"What about me?" Richard suddenly burst out laughing. "Don't I get to be a part of this?" He pulled a giant box from behind his chair. "I think Jimmy needs something a little bigger than gloves and a jackknife," he said, grinning. He launched the box toward the boy. "Go ahead. Open it."

Jimmy was dizzy. What could Richard give him, more valuable than the expensive gloves or more meaningful than Max's knife? He pulled the string off the giant package.

"Might want to use that knife in your pocket to get the box open," Richard said.

"Okay, but I'm a rookie at pocketknives," Jimmy confessed, nervous about using the tool in front of the men. He'd never owned one before.

"Just don't go bleeding all over Irene's carpet," Richard said.

Jimmy extended the folding blade and ran it across the seam of the box. Inside he found a second box. "Okay, I get it," Jimmy said, squinting over at Richard. "How many boxes?"

"Oh, a few," Richard said, laughing.

By the time Jimmy found his way to the final box, there were seven others in diminishing dimensions, scattered at his feet. The final container was no bigger than a matchbox. "What'd you get me, a pack of chewing gum?" Jimmy asked, staring over at Richard.

"You'll see. If you want, I can trade it for that."

Jimmy slit open the crease in the final cardboard container. He silently pulled out a set of keys and dangled them within inches of his eyes. He swallowed hard and looked around the room at the family.

"Okay, I'm not sure what this is."

"Keys to the old pickup," Richard said, sitting up straight in his chair, beaming, loving the idea of surprising the boy. "Thought it was about time I stopped chauffeuring you around. Of course, you have to get a license first, but when you do, you'll have your own set of wheels."

Jimmy raised his arms in the air, just the way he did every time he scored a touchdown for the Grizzlies. He stood up and paced in a circle around the room, stopping to slap hands with Brock, Richard, and Irene.

"Merry Christmas, Merry Christmas, Merry Christmas," he said with each gesture. When he finished, he plopped down on the floor, lay back gently against a chair, and stared up at the tree. "Thank you, family."

"You're welcome, Jimmy," Irene said.

# CHAPTER 8

# TRAINING

**IN THE LULL BETWEEN** Christmas and New Year's, Richard proposed something to Jimmy. It was another lesson about working on a farm. Since the Gallagher farm pushed up against Piney Ridge at the foothills of the Blue Mountains, raising livestock meant sharing a border with wildlife—deer, elk, bear, coyotes, and many smaller species of animals. Since the reintroduction of wolves into the area, ranchers were on guard. In rare instances, they suffered depredation from the alpha predators. It resulted in expensive losses of valuable animals and heartbreak and anger among those who found evidence of a savage killing.

For their part, the Gallaghers hadn't experienced any losses to the wolves. But they knew it was a possibility. The more common loss came from the ever-present coyotes who shared their home with the cattle. Given the opportunity, they would kill and devour a vulnerable newborn calf. Most of the time this happened during a hard winter, when their traditional food source of field mice and game birds was hard to find.

Richard kept an old rifle in the cattle barn for ready access in case of an attack on one of their animals. The pump-action .270 Winchester was passed down from his father, and Richard used it on deer hunts in his younger years. The old rifle felt good in his hands and reminded him of his father. It hung in a convenient location in the barn's feed room, with ammunition nearby. It was used infrequently, mostly to ward off a brazen coyote who'd come too close to the cattle, or a transient neighborhood dog who took pleasure in stirring the herd.

One day as Richard and Jimmy were moving cows from one lot to another, Richard called the young man to his side. "Jimmy, I think it's time you learned how to fire a gun."

The novice cowman cocked his head in disbelief then shook it side to side. "Thanks, but I don't think I'm a gun guy." His response was almost like an apology. "I promised myself I wouldn't ever get into the gun thing," he said. "You know, the last time I was with my friends in Seattle, I saw a brother get shot. I was standing right next to him, so the cops hauled some of us off to jail. I'm not going to start packin' and take that chance again." Jimmy's gaze was to a far-off place, remembering the close call he experienced the night before the championship football game in Seattle.

Richard waved Jimmy over. "That's not what I'm talking about. This isn't about a teenager acting big and tough by waving a pistol around or guarding your drug turf. This is about protecting our livestock. I'll teach you how to carry and fire a rifle … and how to do it responsibly. You're man enough now to learn the right way, even if you never have to use it. But I want you to be prepared."

Richard lifted the gun off the hooks that held it to the wall. He pulled off the towel draped over it to keep the sparrows from roosting on it. "First thing, Jimmy, is to check and make sure it's unloaded. Never leave a gun with shells in it."

That was the beginning of the lesson. Richard went through every detail of the proper handling and care of a firearm. As a boy, he and his brother Max had been trained by their father. The training was strict and formal. They were told how serious the carrying of a weapon was. The final lesson had left an indelible impression on Richard. The words were seared into his brain.

"Never, ever, point a gun at another human being unless you are prepared to pull the trigger," his father scolded. "This is not a toy. It's a tool to be used for good." Richard's final advice to Jimmy was like an echo from Richard's past.

When the lesson concluded, Richard said, "Let's drive up the ridge a ways, so we don't spook the herd, and fire off a few rounds." Jimmy nodded as he was handed the gun. "What's the first thing you do?" Richard asked.

The teenager stood speechless, staring at the weapon in his hands.

Richard sighed. "Short-term memory?" he laughed. "Come on, kid, check to make sure it's not loaded, okay?"

"Right, right," Jimmy mumbled.

"Now, when you get in the pickup, make sure the muzzle is pointed down to the floor and away from your body."

Jimmy was tense. He was new at this. He'd never carried a gun. Now with all the safety talk, he was almost afraid to touch it.

Richard noticed. "Relax, Jimmy, it won't bite. Just remember the things I've taught you."

"Okay, boss, but you've got me as nervous as I was on my first day of varsity football."

Richard threw his head back and laughed as if responding to a joke. "Well, you're still here, so I guess you survived it. I suppose you can survive this too. Now let's go."

When they arrived, Richard parked in the same spot his father had taken him for his first live fire training—a gentle slope with a gully separating them from scattered trees on the opposite hill. "This is a good spot," he said. He took the rifle out of Jimmy's hands and showed him how to insert the five-round clip.

"Now, when you're ready to shoot, always brace yourself, either by finding something to lean against or getting on the ground, kneeling or sitting." He reached into his pocket and handed Jimmy some foam ear protectors to muffle the noise. "Stand back behind me and I'll fire off a round so you can see what it sounds like. Then you can have a turn."

Jimmy's heart picked up a beat. He wiped the nervous sweat from his hands and pushed the earplugs in tight.

"Okay, stand back," Richard said. "I'm aiming at that old stump across the way. I'd guess it's about one hundred yards off."

Jimmy backed away and watched as the middle-aged gunman flopped down on the ground into a kneeling position and took aim.

"Open your mouth a little," Richard said. "That'll reduce the blast in your ears. This old girl can be plenty loud. Here goes." He steadied himself for several seconds before he slowly squeezed the trigger. The resulting concussion made Jimmy jump. The violent blast reverberated and echoed down the canyon, rolling on for several seconds. Across the gully, chunks of wood flew from the rotting stump.

"Nice shot," Jimmy whispered. He breathed in the smell of gunpowder. A chill went through him. He couldn't wait to take his turn.

## CHAPTER 9

# INTERVIEW

THE DAYS FOLLOWING CHRISTMAS were a time to relax. The men fed the cattle and prepared for calving season … stocking up on the supplies necessary for tending to baby calves. For Jimmy, basketball was on hold for a few days until the games resumed. Irene was resting up from the Christmas excitement, and Brock focused on lesson planning for when the school bells rang again.

It was one of those quiet mornings. Irene was washing dishes in the sink when the phone rang in the farmhouse kitchen. She quickly dried her hands with a dish towel and picked up the receiver. It was Ronnie calling for Brock.

"How are you doing, young lady?" Irene asked as she motioned to Brock to take the call.

"I'm good, but a little confused," Ronnie answered. "I need some good advice from your handsome son."

"Well, handsome may be correct, but I'm not so sure how good his advice might be." She laughed and handed the phone over to Brock. "It's Ronnie."

"Mom is a tough one to impress," Brock said. "What's going on?"

"Something pretty big has come up. I got a call from the bank's main office in Spokane. They want me to come up for an interview. Seems one of the branches in the city has a manager's position open. They think I might be a good fit. It would mean a pay increase."

Brock closed his eyes and drew in a large breath. 'Wow, that came out of nowhere. Bet that was a surprise. I know you're good at your job, but how did they hear about you?"

"I don't know. Seems the big boss heard the story about Cort's passing. Maybe they just feel sorry for me. And there was something about Justin and football. I think the boss saw him play in the championship game."

Brock's eyes widened. He had been around coaching long enough to have suspicions about sudden offers being made to parents when their son or daughter had exceptional talent. And Justin's skills were exceptional.

"Are you going?"

"Well, I am curious. I may see what they have to say."

"Sure, can't blame you for that. When will you go? Do you want me to keep you company?"

"Could you? I'd really appreciate it. We could go up and back in a day."

Brock chuckled, thinking of the subtle inference of any extended stay. "I think I can make time for an old friend. Besides, it's almost New Years. So, this can be our end-of-the-year get-away."

Two days later they were on the road in Brock's car. It was still December, so the wheatfields alongside the highway weren't yet waking from their winter slumber. Small ponds in the low spots of the fields were fringed with ice. In a couple of months, those places would have mallard ducks paddling in the receding puddles.

"Spring can't get here soon enough," Ronnie said, excited to be on the road and away from the Grove for a few hours. "I love it when it warms up and the flowers start blooming." She bubbled with small talk and laughter. The prolonged nightmare of her husband's accident and death and the necessary adjustment to a new life were beginning to drift into the rearview mirror.

Brock didn't match her spirit. The job offer to Ronnie worried him. He'd begun to treasure the time he was spending with her and dreaded the loneliness that would come if she left. He didn't want her to leave but couldn't blame her for considering the promotion. It would make her life easier. Still, there was the gnawing suspicion about the timing of the offer. He'd done some calling around and could make a connection between the bank president, whose son was a star receiver on his private high school's 4A football team, and that team's need for a quarterback to replace a graduating senior.

Brock carefully hinted as much to Ronnie. "You don't think this offer might be because of your son, do you?"

Instantly, Ronnie's buoyant attitude shifted. She stared over at him. "Why couldn't it be about me ... don't you think I'm capable of running a bank?" Her eyes flashed.

Brock swallowed hard then accelerated to pass a slower car. He backed off quickly from his speeding ... and from his question. "Of course you're capable. I've seen your work. You'd make a great bank manager. We both know you could do it. It just seems to be kind of sudden. But," he paused and looked over at her, "now that I'm back in the Grove I'd hate to see you go."

She leaned over closer to him. "I know. But I've never lived anywhere away from the Grove. And a change does sound kind of exciting. Things are tight financially for me right now. Cort left us with some debts we didn't expect. And Justin is looking at colleges for when he graduates. I don't know how we can afford that." She dropped her head and stared down at her hands.

Brock set the cruise control on the car, leaned back a bit in his seat and didn't speak. Neither he nor Ronnie attempted any more conversation for several miles.

When they arrived at the bank headquarters, they stepped up to the waiting secretary. Brock suddenly became aware of Ronnie's appearance as if she were in a spotlight … a red-carpet moment. She was at her best, dressed in conservative business attire—gray slacks, an off-white satin blouse, and a navy blue jacket. Gold earrings glittered through amber curls. Her heels made her reach almost to Brock's chin. And even though without makeup she was beautiful, she'd put on enough to look dignified in the formal business surroundings.

"I'm Veronica Jepson," Ronnie said. "I have an appointment for an interview with Roland Donigan."

"Oh, yes. The president is expecting you. I hope you had a nice drive. Mr. Donigan will be with you in a minute. Can I get you something to drink while you wait, for you and your husband?" She looked over at Brock.

Brock winked at Ronnie and then turned to the secretary. "I'm just a friend. But thank you for the offer. I would like some coffee. If you don't mind, I'll wait out here while Ronnie does the interview."

"Of course. Sorry, I should never make assumptions." She blushed ever so slightly. *But you're both wearing wedding rings,* she thought. "Would you like cream and sugar?"

Ronnie said no to the offer of coffee but couldn't help but smile, with a bit of a schoolgirl giggle, at the awkwardness of the comment. It came at the perfect moment to ease her nervousness. She was now ready to impress the boss.

Roland Donigan stood up as Ronnie entered the room. He'd never met her before and was immediately taken in by her appearance. He knew about her son, Justin, from witnessing the state championship football game played three weeks earlier. When he'd been told the backstory concerning Justin's father's death and then discovered Ronnie was an employee in one of their small satellite banks in Glory Grove, he immediately considered putting a plan in place to bring her to a branch bank close to the main office. It could benefit everyone involved. However, he'd wanted to ensure she had the personality and skillset to take on a top position in one of their banks.

"Good morning, Mrs. Jepson, it's a pleasure to meet you," Donigan said, a gleaming white smile on his face. "I hope you had a nice Christmas." He motioned to a chair and waited for her to be seated before settling back behind the mahogany desk.

He looked to Ronnie like he was in his mid-forties and was a man who took pride in his appearance. The open collared shirt he wore revealed the tan he'd acquired on a recent vacation to a Mexican resort. And she could smell the fragrance of his cologne. A few silver hairs colored the sideburns of his dark brown hair. She also noticed he wore an expensive watch but no wedding ring.

He opened a folder centered on his desk, scanned it quickly, and then got right to the point. "Veronica—may I call you that?—I've gone over your employment records, and it shows you've been with us at the bank for over fifteen years. Ten of those were as the assistant manager in Glory Grove."

"That's correct, and you can call me Ronnie, that's what everyone calls me," she said, nodding politely.

"Okay, Ronnie it is. John, the manager of the branch in Glory Grove, says you're extremely talented, both in dealing with people and working with budgets and accounts. Says you would be more than ready to take the next step in your professional career. I know John and trust his judgment."

"You're aware I don't have a college degree?"

"That's not an issue. Your experience with the bank has given you all the education you need."

"Well, John is a good boss. He trained me well and I enjoy the work. What do you have in mind?"

Donigan hesitated, studying her face, slightly distracted by the dark green color of her eyes and the soft texture of her skin. "Well, I was thinking perhaps with your current situation—and I'm very sorry about the loss of your husband—you might be interested in a position we have coming available here in Spokane."

"I see," Ronnie said. She sat up straighter in her chair. Her thoughts were spinning. Although she was halfway expecting the offer, she was filled with gratitude for being considered for such a move. Her life in Glory Grove had been dictated by the single awful night of her high school prom. Since then, she had adjusted to that reality and accepted it. Now life might be offering her more.

"That would be a big step," Ronnie said, her voice soft but confident. "My son will be a senior next year. It'd be tough for him to have to move and leave his friends."

"Ronnie, I've heard about your son. His name's Justin, isn't it?" Donigan asked. He rolled a gold pen in his hand and then set it back into its marble-based holder.

"Yes, that's his name."

Donigan continued. "I have a son about the same age. He's an athlete just like your boy. I know it'd be hard for Justin to leave Glory Grove. But I'm sure he's now thinking about college. It's incredibly expensive these days. From what I hear, Justin has the athletic ability to earn a college scholarship. But, realistically, he needs the exposure of playing for a bigger school. He'd have that chance here. More television. More print press. And more college scouts." Donigan thumped a finger on his desk with each "more" he uttered.

He lowered his voice, sounding like a sympathetic friend or parent. "I think a move might be the best thing that could happen for you and your son. Let's give it some time. We don't need a decision today. We won't be naming a new manager for a few months. Let it play over in your head. But I think it would be a great move for you and Justin. And of course, there would be a significant pay increase that goes along with the promotion."

Donigan looked at his watch, then casually stood, indicating the interview was over. He stepped around the desk and extended his hand to help Ronnie up from her chair. He guided her towards the door with a hand on her back. "It's been nice meeting you, Ronnie. I wish we had more time to talk, but I have another meeting I have to get to. I know it was a long trip for you to make for a short visit, but I wanted to see for myself if everything they said about you was true. I'm happy to say you seem like the perfect person for our manager's position. I hope we can make it happen."

Ronnie turned toward him and brushed a lock of hair from her face. "I appreciate your time, Mr. Donigan." She hesitated for a moment and took a measured breath. "I'm sure we'll talk more in the future. I'll have to give this some thought. And I'd need to know more about which bank I might be going to and what the salary would be. I'm not going to make a snap decision, but I really want to thank you for your time."

"Of course," he said. "It's been my pleasure."

She smiled up at him, and again, he was put a bit off balance by her natural beauty and her Irish green eyes. "Have a very Happy New Year," he said. He extended his hand, shook hers gently, and ushered her to the lobby where Brock was waiting.

# CHAPTER 10

# ENERGY

WHEN THE RURAL POSTMAN DELIVERED the mail to the Gallagher farm the day after New Year's, there was an official-looking document among some of the late-arriving Christmas letters. It was a seemingly tiny blip on the Gallagher family radar … an unexpected letter from a company no one around Glory Grove had ever heard of before. Its name was Wind Driven and its sudden appearance in the county had people talking. The company wanted to visit local landowners in the area to discuss the possibility of acquiring leases on their land to create a wind farm. Farmers along Piney Ridge were the first to be contacted.

"What's this mean?" Irene asked as she handed Brock the opened letter. "I don't think we have any interest in giving up our land," she said flatly.

"I don't know, Mom. Let's see what you're looking at." He quickly scanned the simple letter requesting a meeting at their home. "It's probably nothing, but we'd better give it a listen, so we know what's going on."

The following Monday morning, the phone rang, and Irene answered. She agreed to a visit by the company's representative. She made sure to mention someone would be there with her, and then set a time when the man could visit.

On Wednesday morning of the visit, the farmstead was shrouded in fog, looking like a country home on the English coastline. It was the kind of day that always dropped Irene's usual happy mood down a notch or two. Brock was starting his teaching assignment that day and Jimmy was also heading back to school. Richard agreed to sit in on the meeting. None of the family expected anything to come from the proposal. "Sounds like more of a snake oil pitch that comes around every so often," Richard grumbled when he read the letter.

At ten o'clock, a dark green SUV slowly approached the farmhouse, as if the driver was taking a survey as he drove, then coasted up to the yard fence. A man inside the auto shut off the engine and pulled out papers from a briefcase. He sat still for several minutes, purposely reading a document, then raised his head, gathered his papers, and opened the car door. Sassy instantly rushed to his side, tail wagging, ready to accept a simple pat on the head, or even better, a happy rubdown from a stranger. The man pulled his papers closer to his chest and shied away, not out of fear, but an attempt to keep dog hair off his tan khakis. "Get back," he scolded.

Irene pulled back the curtains and peered out the living room window. She had been anticipating his arrival. Anthony Marcellus had been polite on the phone when he made the appointment as a representative of a global energy company. He had three other visits scheduled for the day with some of the Gallagher neighbors. Richard, who'd promised to hurry through his chores so he could be there, hadn't arrived yet.

When the man knocked on the front door, Irene opened it and welcomed him. "Mr. Marcellus?" She smiled at him. Even if she wasn't excited about the business of putting wind turbines on their farm, she would always greet a stranger with politeness. "I hope you didn't have any trouble finding your way here."

"Not at all," Marcellus said. He shifted his papers to his left hand and offered his right for a handshake. "Please call me Tony."

He was careful not to squeeze her hand too tightly, noting how frail she looked. In his mind, he was pleased to see her appearance, knowing older women could often be a little easier to charm. Many times, they didn't want to be bothered with all the facts and figures, but just needed a few moments of friendly conversation.

"Let's sit in the kitchen," Irene said."It's easier to talk there and my brother-in-law should be here soon."

Marcellus followed her into the kitchen and sat down at the table covered with a checkered patterned tablecloth. He was happy to find her alone for their first introduction. "You have a nice little farm here," he said. "Have you lived here very long?"

"Just since I married Max, nearly fifty years ago," she said. "I fell in love with the place as a new bride and I still love it here. It's my little bit of heaven."

"You're so lucky to have had that. But farm life isn't easy, is it?" he said, sounding as if he felt sorry for her.

"Oh, it has its ups and downs. But we've been able to work through the hard times. So much depends on the weather and grain and cattle prices. We've always been able to balance our budget but a few times it was just by the skin of our teeth." She raised her head and looked across the room at the picture of her husband that hung on the wall. Her blue eyes closed slightly as she remembered the times when there wasn't an extra penny to be had.

"Well, maybe what I can offer today will make things a little easier for you." He shuffled his papers, searching for the brochure which introduced his company. Irene noticed how soft and white his hands were, and how his pants and jacket had not a single wrinkle.

As Marcellus searched for the brochure, they heard Richard's pickup rumble up the driveway and stop beside the hog shed. Minutes later, he burst through the back door of the house after pulling off his mud-covered overshoes. Marcellus started to get up from his chair, but Richard motioned him to stay seated. In his sock feet he plopped down into a chair beside them.

"Hi, I'm Irene's brother-in-law, Richard," he said. "I'd shake your hand, but I've been working with the pigs."

Marcellus unconsciously looked down at his fingers. "Thanks, I appreciate that," he said.

Irene suddenly patted the table. "Oh, I'm not a very good hostess, am I? Mr. Marcellus, would you like some coffee? I know Richard will. He's been up with the cows since the sun came up." She gingerly pushed herself up from the chair and walked to the kitchen counter. She pulled three cups from the cupboard, making sure to pick out Richard's favorite, the one that said "Knock Knock" on it, and poured coffee for the three of them as the men made small talk about the weather.

When the coffee was served, the sales pitch began. Marcellus began laying out the reason for his visit. Wind Driven was part of an international conglomerate, Global Energy Systems, holding market shares of wind, solar, and petroleum energy products. They were expanding their wind energy portfolio and found the eastern part of the state had potential to meet the minimum wind requirement to establish a large grid of towers; the state government was eager to push green energy. The company was ready to do meteorological testing and to begin the process of gathering enough acres by leasing farmland to plan a wind farm. The Gallagher farm, on the edge of Piney Ridge, was in the center of the large piece of property the company was hoping to lease.

"This could give a big lift for your county's economy. It would create jobs for the people who live here," Marcellus said. He sat back in his chair and smiled, his lips closed. "Some of those young people who leave home looking for work could be employed right here."

Richard listened intently, then quickly came to the question that was foremost on his mind. "What's in it for us?"

Marcellus seemed pleased with the question and was ready with an answer. "Richard, I think financially you'll find it a wonderful opportunity that most people can't pass up." He focused on Richard's face, sensing he was more interested in the project than Irene. "The company would pay you five dollars per acre per year while testing takes place, which could take up to two years. Then, if towers were placed on your farm, you would receive royalties from each tower on your property on an annual basis. If the wind is right, each tower can generate energy producing between $15,000 and $20,000 for you each year. From our original survey of the county, it looks like your farm might have ten or more towers."

Richard absorbed the statement. He did the math quickly in his head. He blinked two or three times and let the idea sink in. His hand shook, not enough for anyone to see, but Richard felt it.

# CHAPTER 11

# LEAGUE

**THE PRIOR AUTUMN,** the Glory Grove Grizzlies scrambled to put together a nine-game football schedule when the program was reinstated after a one-year hiatus. For some games, the team traveled further than usual, and for others, they played games against teams from bigger schools. They initially struggled to find success before gaining traction and winning the games necessary to make the state playoffs.

But the basketball schedule was, as it always was, fixed—with six early season non-league games with schools outside their league, then a dozen league contests with schools of their own size. In the current season, after those early games were completed, the town was buzzing about the results. They'd notched six wins and most of the games had not been close in nature. Cole Knighton, the sophomore guard, was making a name for himself among the opposing teams and coaches, even if not endearing himself to his teammates and their parents.

After the Christmas break, the league season began with a home game against Pine City, a traditional opponent. "Should be an easy win," Buster McHue confided to Brock in the teachers' lounge a few days before the contest. "Especially if Knighton is on his game."

Brock had just begun his tenure as the replacement for the history teacher who'd resigned at the end of the semester. He was also now officially an assistant basketball coach under McHue. The whistle around his neck felt familiar; but the gym sneakers on his feet did not. "Yep, I've been watching. He's a good one, for sure. I hope he can blend in with the other players. Most of them played football for me and became close, like family. They just need some time to warm up to Cole."

"I haven't seen any problems," Buster said, ignoring the rancor boiling up among the players. "Those others are just lucky to have Cole as a teammate."

"I suppose you're right. But when crunch time comes, they'd better all be on the same page."

"We'll be fine, Brock. I've been at this game a long time. For boys' basketball, it's more about who can make baskets than it is about getting along. It's not like football."

Brock fought back his urge to counter McHue's conclusions. *I'm an assistant,* he told himself. "Okay. But I've spent a lot of time with these kids, so if you need any help to figure them out, I'm right here. "

"Thanks Brock. I appreciate the offer, but I think I can handle it. So far, it's worked out pretty well. We're 6–0. Haven't been there for a long time. Feels pretty good."

"Well, we can hope for the best against Pine City. The football team handled them pretty easily. But I heard they have a big kid named Milo Ruttinger, who didn't play football. Word is he's pretty good. If Luke can handle him. I'm sure we'll have a good night."

When the home fans gathered for the game, the boys tried to fight off their nervousness. The crowd in the stands for the preseason games had been big, but this one for their first league contest was larger and more boisterous than the Grove had seen in years. It seemed to the fans as if something good was about to happen.

The ritual of game night was a staple in Glory Grove, as it is at any level of the sport. And like every venue, it had its own unique ceremony. The varsity boys huddled in the doorway of their locker room, like thoroughbreds milling about ready to file into the starting gate, peering out as the girls finished their game. When the horn sounded to mark the end of the contest, the girls trotted into their dressing area, deliberately avoiding eye contact with the boys, trying not to distract them from their mission.

The pep band instructor had prepared his students for this moment. When Justin Jepson jogged onto the floor with his teammates following, the band struck up the school fight song. The large trumpet section blasted the ears of the spectators across the way. It echoed off the brick walls surrounding the court. Each boy had a ball in his hands and when they reached center court, they were greeted by the larger-than-life Grizzly Bear mascot—he'd been recruited from the wrestling team— who with outstretched arms leaped high into the air in a frenzy of exuberance to chest bump the team captain.

Justin Jepson had been chosen captain by his team before the season began and had the privilege of going up against the bear. He knew the boy in the suit, and they had a side bet as to who would be the first during the season to fall to the floor from the collision. So far, both had kept their feet under them. The only objection to this demonstration of animal/human conflict came from Luke Palmer, who coveted the privilege of going up against the bear.

"Can you believe this?" Luke shouted at Jimmy, as they broke into lines to begin their warm-ups.

"These small towns must like their basketball," Jimmy swiveled his head toward the stands. "It's different than Seattle, but this little gym makes me feel like a fish in a bowl. I think I stick out a little." He grinned up at his big friend.

"Yep, Ivory, you'd better not screw up, 'cause everybody's gonna see you." He playfully shoved his Black friend into one of his teammates. Jimmy was the only person of color in the gym.

"I won't stick out as much as a giant with tattoos," Jimmy shot back, glancing at the eagle on Luke's arm. Luke's body barely squeezed into the basketball jersey.

As the team went through their warm-ups, cheerleaders practiced their yells and old men lined up for popcorn at the concession stand.

Both teams were pumped by all the noise and attention. When the opening tip dropped into the hands of a Mustang player, Luke swatted at it like a mixed martial arts fighter and nearly knocked the boy into the bleachers. The referee's whistle stopped the game before it had barely begun.

"Calm down," Buster McHue hollered from the bench, but Luke had come out of the locker room ready for action; by the end of the first quarter, he'd rung up two more fouls. McHue parked him on the bench for the entire second quarter.

Luke wasn't the only Grizzly struggling to find a rhythm. If Justin got his hands on the ball, which he rarely did, he couldn't find the target, and watched his shots bounce off the back iron. Jimmy was running the offense as the point guard, but once his pass hit Cole Knighton's hands, he knew it wasn't coming back. Cole was rushing his shots, determined to reach his twenty-point goal.

Cole's mother Goldie was in the stands, center court, back row. Her back was against the wall and red hair hung to her shoulders, clashing with the red Grizzly shirt she was wearing. Her loud, piercing voice rose above all the others as she screamed encouragement to her son. "Come on, Cole, you got this, keep shooting!" she screamed. "Make me proud!" Other parents could only shake their heads.

"Maybe she should cheer for some of the others," Peggy whispered in Tim's ear. "She thinks her son is a one-man team." Tim could only stare silently at what he was watching. His hands were rolling the program into a twisted pencil shape.

At the half, Buster took his team to the locker room trailing by a half dozen points. He didn't chide the team for their performance; he only assured them it would turn around in the second half. "We'll get Luke back in the game, drop into a zone to keep him out of foul trouble, and try to stop Ruttinger. Then we'll be okay," he muttered. "Just calm down and play ball." He scanned the stat sheet his student assistant had handed him. "Cole, we need more points from you … if you're open, keep shooting." More than one of Cole's teammates rolled their eyes.

When the second half started, Luke quickly got his fourth foul. When a loose ball rolled between him and Ruttinger, they both dove for it. The collision sent Luke sprawling. The referee's whistle blew, and he signaled to the scorer's table. "Foul, number 15," he said.

Luke jumped up, red in the face. "What?" He stared into the official's eyes, flirting with a technical foul, sure in his mind it was a fair play.

"I gotta call 'em like I seem 'em, young man," the referee said. "We're not playing football here."

"I wish we were," Luke grumbled to himself, then looked at his dad, shook his head, and headed back to the bench.

"It's okay, son," Tim said, mouthing the words so Luke could see and gave him a sympathetic thumbs up.

In the stands, Luke's girlfriend, Ashley Summers, laid down the clarinet she was holding. *This is going to put him in a very bad mood*, she thought.

Luke returned in the fourth quarter and made sure not to foul, but too often it allowed the pudgy giant, Ruttinger, to work his way into the lane and score. As the clock ticked down in the final quarter, Cole, now desperate to add to his box score and save the day for his team, continued to hoist shot after shot, even when harassed by the opposing guards. He wanted to keep his star status intact. When the buzzer sounded to end the game, the Grizzly players stared up at the clock as to remember the ten-point deficit that would be recorded in the official scorebook and the *Glory Grove Gazette*.

"Same results as last year," Homer Johnson, the grizzled Grove fan, mumbled as he lifted himself off the bleacher seat. He threw his canvas coat over his shoulders and headed for the exit. "All this talent and old Buster can't win a league game."

Inside the locker room, the players and Brock looked around and waited for the head coach's words of wisdom. But none came. McHue was still standing by the scorer's table, dealing with a very angry Goldie Knighton. No one in the locker room spoke. Instead, the players sat, looking at one another, trying to find someone to blame for their misery.


Luke showered quickly and swung open the locker room door that emptied out into the school parking lot. He fumed. First, because he couldn't control his physicality and spent most of the game on the bench. And secondly, because he couldn't stand the actions of Cole Knighton. He turned to head home and in the glow of the streetlight he saw Ashley waiting for him. His mood lightened a bit.

"We don't have to talk about it," she said, knowing Luke well enough that he would anyway.

"Yep, that was a shit show, wasn't it?"

"I think the refs had it out for you."

"Wasn't their fault. I think I'm still trying to play football."

"Well, you were pretty good at it," she smiled, bobbing her head, bouncing the curly blond hair hanging from under her winter stocking cap.

Luke blew a long breath and watched the vapor rise in the night. "Damn, it's hard being mad when you're so perky."

"I figured you needed some cheering up. It's only one game." She laced her arm around his elbow.

"But it's a tough way to start the league season," he grumbled.

"Maybe we need a better coach."

"Oh, Buster's fine. But I wish he'd stifle that little show-off."

"You're talking about Cole, aren't you?"

"Of course. Who else? Sometimes I'd like to strangle that little weasel."

"He's a good shooter. And kind of cute." She cringed after she said it, thinking of Luke's reaction that might come.

"Not cute when he's playing his selfish one-man game. He needed to play football to see what it takes to be a teammate."

"Then you might have strangled him for real," she kidded, trying to lighten the moment.

"No." He stared over at her. "You know I'm not a violent person … well, except when it's within the rules."

"I know. You're just a big teddy bear … at least with me." She put her hand in his big paw, and they walked through the cold night, away from the school.

# CHAPTER 12

# SAVED

**BY THE EIGHTH GAME OF THE SEASON,** Tim and Peggy were fixtures sitting courtside. "Damned near as much fun as watchin' him play football," Tim confided to Peggy on their way to another Grizzly game.

"It would be even better if he would spend more time on the floor and less time on the bench with his fouls," Peggy said. She had watched his games in Denver and recognized his tendency to get in foul trouble. But both she and Tim reveled in the joy of watching him play with the starting five. Still, the loss to Pine City had everyone scratching their heads.

Men at the Cozy Corner Drive-In tried to put a finger on it. "They need to be more disciplined," Homer Johnson said. "Move the ball around a little. Maybe let Justin Jepson take a shot once in a while."

"Come on, Homer," one of the others said. "You think that big ol' redhead, Goldie Knighton, is going to cheer if her boy doesn't take every shot? "

"Buster needs to get a handle on her. I swear she's got his underwear so knotted up he can't think straight, let alone coach a team. But I hate to see all this talent going to waste."

"One thing's for sure, Palmer isn't doing us any good sitting on the bench for half a game. Good gawd, Buster needs to tranquilize that kid before he takes the floor. He's like a giant bull in one of them China shops."

It was that kind of talk that had Peggy Palmer fuming … at the people saying those things about her son and especially at Goldie Knighton, whose yapping from the back row grated on her nerves like a tooth in need of a root canal. So, in the next league game, against the Bristol Bay Bobcats, Peggy was on edge before the game even began.

"Palmer," Goldie yelled, early in the first quarter, "get your big behind in there and set a screen, what do you think you're out there for?"

Peggy could feel her heart race. She saw stars dancing in front of her eyes from a sudden rage. She jumped to her feet and wrestled her arm away from Tim, who was trying to hold her back. She stomped up the bleacher steps and made her way across the bench to where Goldie was sitting.

Peggy was a thick, well-proportioned woman, but not as big as Goldie Knighton. Still, her time in jail had taught her how to show her toughness. She wasn't afraid to stand up to bullies. With the anger she was feeling, she wasn't hesitant about giving Goldie a piece of her mind. "Why don't you keep your trap shut, lady?" she spewed. "Everyone here is sick of your big mouth. Those are just boys out there trying to win a game … as a team. Why not just cheer for the team for a change? It's not just about your spoiled brat little boy."

What came next would be talked about in the coffee shop gossip sessions for days. The men argued over who slapped who first, but all agreed they would have paid to see the fight go for a good ten rounds. As it was, only a couple of good punches were thrown before nearby spectators rushed in and separated the women. When they were pulled back from one another, Goldie was standing, flushed face, screaming, "Anytime, honey … anytime. Bring it on. Nobody shuts me up. Don't even try."

Peggy burst into tears and grabbed onto Tim, who'd chased her up the stairs, trailing behind because of his bad knee. "That's enough, Peg. We need to leave now," Tim said. The boys on the court had momentarily turned from their game to watch the commotion. Luke ducked his head, embarrassed by his mother's actions, while simultaneously impressed by her boldness in his defense. But he joined his mother's sour mood when Cole Knighton casually walked over to him and sneered, "There's a lesson for you, Palmer. Nobody messes with me or my mom."

When they got home, Tim tried his best to calm Peggy down. He had seen her frustration mount through the early part of the season as she watched Luke struggle with his foul problems while having to listen to Goldie screaming from the back row. But he hadn't expected the sudden ferocity of her actions. "You kind of lost it there," he said in a soft voice. "I can't say as I blame you, but you don't want to get yourself into a big pot of trouble like that."

"I couldn't help it." She threw her coat onto a dining room chair.

"It's just a game," Tim said.

"You wouldn't say that about football, would you?" She paced back and forth in front of the sofa.

"That's different."

"Sure. Helmets and the elements. I don't see much else."

Tim rubbed the back of his hand over his forehead as if he were trying to find just the right words. "Basketball is harder for parents. Their kids are exposed. Mom and Dad can see close up when their kid's feelings are hurt. And they spend three months rubbing shoulders with other parents they may not even like. Goldie is a good example of what that can lead to." Tim flopped down into a recliner.

Peggy looked over, still flush from the affair. "So, what was I supposed to do? Sit there and listen to that loudmouth piece of crap yell at my son?"

"Yep. I had to learn that lesson in football." He sat up in the chair. "Now it's your turn. We just have to try and not make it hard on our kid. Sometimes I think he's more mature than we are." He paused. "Come here, Peg."

She kicked off her shoes and slowly walked over to where he was sitting. She slid in beside him in the recliner. "We'll break this chair," she said as she closed her eyes.

"Don't care. You need a hug. Gotta calm you down before I go to work. My night shift begins in a few minutes."

Peggy laid her head on his shoulder. "Maybe I don't belong here in the Grove. Everyone is watching all the time. And now the whole town will be talking. You and Luke are probably better off without me."

"Don't say that. That's not true. We want you to stay. We'll work this out." He kissed her on the forehead and nuzzled his face in her hair. He rested there for a moment, then pushed his big frame out of the chair. "Wish I could stay but Luke will be home soon. I'm sure he'll have something to say about tonight. But he loves you. This thing tonight won't bother him for a minute. He probably just wished you'd have smacked her a little bit harder."

Tim slipped into the adjacent bedroom and grabbed his work clothes. "I'm changing, then I'll head out. Be back first thing in the morning. You'll be fine."

Peggy lay back in the chair and closed her eyes, knowing the one thing that could calm her down wasn't in this house. She wasn't fine … she was angry and depressed. So she waited until she heard Tim's car pull out of the driveway, then put on her coat and headed out into the night.

Ashley Summers was working late at the convenience store. She had drawn the short straw and had to be there to help the manager until closing time. She was weary, and agonized over missing the Grizzly's second league game. She hadn't heard the outcome yet when Peggy walked in the door. It was unusual to see her at the late hour, but Ashley assumed she was there for some staple the Palmers needed for the next day. "Hello, Mrs. Palmer," she said. Peggy's sad face hinted that the Grizzlies had lost again. Ashley wouldn't ask.

Peggy nodded but didn't stop.

Luke had told Ashley about his mom's history and her trouble with alcohol, so Ashley watched as Peggy strolled down the aisle studying the offerings and then stopped in the section displaying a long row of wine bottles. She saw Peggy's hands tremble as she reached up and pull down one of the nondescript cheaper brands and cradle it, along with the small sack of chips she was holding. She made her way back to the cash register where Ashley stood.

Peggy had seen her son with Ashley and knew they were friends, so she tried to act nonchalant about her purchases. She lowered her head slightly before speaking. "It's for Tim," she said, a tight smile on her lips. "I want to surprise him. He's had a long week. The county crew has been digging out from this latest snowstorm." She pulled some bills from her coat pocket and handed Ashley a twenty.

"Yes, ma'am. I'm sure Tim will be surprised. He deserves a break. That last storm dumped a lot of snow. But I'm kind of surprised with the wine; I thought Tim would be more of a beer guy." Ashley laid the bill on the cash register and started to make change, but remembered that because of her age she wasn't allowed to sell alcohol. She called the manager over but knew he'd make the transaction since Peggy wasn't underage or inebriated.

The sad-eyed manager, tired from a full day on the job, thanked Ashley for bringing him over. "We need to follow all the rules," he said. "Wouldn't want to lose our liquor license." When he finished counting out the change from the purchase, he nodded politely to Peggy and returned to his usual duties.

For a second, the two women stared awkwardly at one another. Ashley was only sixteen years old but sensed the deception from Peggy. She gently slid the bottle in a brown paper bag across the counter. *At least I wasn't the one who sold her the wine*, she thought.

Peggy raised her head and narrowed her gaze. "Let's keep this a secret," she said as she tucked the bottle into her oversized coat pocket.

Ashley knew Peggy couldn't be refused but was troubled by the transaction. She cared about Luke and was fond of his dad. She'd been the first person to meet Luke when he'd arrived on the bus from Denver, sent to Glory Grove to live with Tim. Within the first few months, he found himself liking the little farm town. Ashley secretly hoped she was a big part of the reason why.

When Peggy was released from jail and joined them in December, it was after a major turnaround in her life. She'd come clean of alcohol and now everyone in town was watching to see if the Palmer family could live out a happy ending. Her planned short visit to the Grove had been extended for several weeks. Ashley saw how thrilled Luke was to see his mom and dad together again.

Ashley didn't know all the details, *but this doesn't seem right,* she thought. As soon as Peggy exited the store, she grabbed the phone and called Luke.

"Hi, Ash, what's up?" Luke guessed she was calling to see how the game turned out. He wasn't surprised to hear from his friend since he knew she was working late. "A slow night behind the counter?"

"Yes, it is slow, but thought maybe you'd want to know your mom just left the store."

"Yep, she was already gone when I got home. We must be out of milk or eggs or something. She can't keep up with the way my dad and I eat." He laughed.

"Well, I know it's none of my business, but, umm … she bought a bottle of wine … said it was for your dad."

Luke erupted. "Like hell, he won't touch the stuff. Dammit to hell. When did she leave?"

"Just now. I didn't see where she was headed. Anything I can do?"

"No. My dad's doing the night shift and won't be home 'til morning. But mom can't drive so if she's on foot she can't be far. I'll go and try to find her. And I'll call Coach Brock. Maybe he'll know what to do."

"I'm sorry I sold her the wine."

"It's not your fault, Ash. But I've gotta stop her. We've been down this road before, and it always ends badly."

"Well, I'll be here for another half-hour if you need anything. I'm so sorry this is happening. I hope you can do something."

Luke reached Brock by phone and let him know about his mom, then hopped into the family's old pickup and began his search. The town was small and only had one main traffic area, so he headed up the main street. There was little traffic late at night, so he drove at a slow pace, peering down the side streets as he looked for signs of his mom. His search came up empty. The only movement was a single stray cat that scurried in front of his pickup.

*Where would she go?* Luke wondered. *Thank God she didn't take the pickup.* He'd watched how her life disintegrated in Denver when she was driving drunk. In the final episode, they put her in jail. The thought of her doing the same in this little town frightened him … both because of the harm it would do her and the embarrassment it would cause him and his dad. She might leave Glory Grove for good.

He turned toward the school. Again nothing.

Where would she go to be alone with a bottle? He knew she wouldn't return to the house, knowing he'd confront her. And there was no other place in town where she could be alone and free from others … *unless, the park?*

He made a quick U-turn and sped toward the park near the football field. The gazebo was well lit. She wasn't there, but off to the side, sitting in a rocker swing—the one made for two people who could pump and rock the swing back and forth—sat a lone solitary figure. It was his mom.

Luke guided the car into the gravel parking area next to the grass lawn and pulled his big frame out of the vehicle. His heart was filled with anger and sadness, and he needed to find a way to express both of those emotions to the woman he loved. He knew she was weak. And it was because of her troubled life that he had become the person he was … strong and angry to any outside observer, but sad and frightened in his own mind. He needed to tell her. She needed to know what she was doing to him and his chances for happiness.

He approached carefully, and she didn't hear him coming. Lost in her thoughts. When she finally heard his footsteps, crunching on what was left of the autumn leaves, she looked up but didn't move. "She told you, didn't she," Peggy said through clenched teeth.

Luke stood, looking down at her. "Ashley was just trying to help, Mom. She's a good friend and was looking out for me."

"Well, good for her, I guess. I remember now what drove me away from this little town." She turned her face away. "There are no secrets here."

Luke shuffled closer. "I love it here."

"Why?"

"Because people here care about each other."

"Maybe too much, sometimes." Peggy grasped the bottle in her hands.

"They care about me." He sat down across from her in the swing. "And they care about you, too."

"Maybe they shouldn't," Peggy said as she laid the bottle in her lap.

"You're going to throw all this away if you open that," Luke said, staring down at the wine.

"I don't think I can go on without it. It just hurts too much."

Luke stiffened. "And what do you think it does to us if you start again? Why can't you just be happy with what you have?"

Peggy closed her eyes. "I'm not a good mom, am I?"

"Not if you do this. And I need a mom. I need you. Can't you see that? My life is so good right now. I have you and Dad together. I have a girlfriend who cares enough about me that she called to help tonight. And this town has taken me in as one of their own. Why can't you see?"

"But it's hard, Luke." Tears were falling down her cheeks.

"You don't think my life has been hard … worrying about you? Watching you try to kill yourself with alcohol? Dang it, Mom, think about someone besides yourself."

Peggy began to cry harder, sobbing. "I'm so sorry." She handed the unopened bottle to her son. Her shoulders shook as she covered her face with her hands.

Luke moved across the swing, teetering for a second as all his weight shifted the swing upwards. He laughed as he sat down beside her and put his arm around her. "Got a little out of balance there for a second, didn't we."

She leaned into his chest, and they sat motionless for several minutes until they heard Brock Gallagher's black Lexus pull up alongside Luke's pickup. Brock stepped out slowly and moved silently toward them, not sure what he would find.

"You guys okay here?" he asked when he was within speaking distance.

Luke looked up, relieved to see Brock. "I think so," he said. "We had a talk." He handed the unopened bottle to his coach. "I'm going to take Mom home now."

"Guess you didn't need me then," Brock said, his hand on Luke's shoulder. He turned toward his old friend … a friend he didn't want to lose. "You have a good son, Peggy. But I'm always here for you guys. And I mean always. You don't have to do this alone … ever."

# CHAPTER 13

# CALVES

**CALVING SEASON WOULD BEGIN** in January for the herd of crossbred Angus cattle the Gallaghers kept on the farm. It was agreed all family members, except Irene, would take turns checking on them throughout the day and night to avoid any disaster. "We're going to need your help," Richard said as he drove Jimmy home from basketball practice one evening. "It will get dang cold that time of year. Temperatures can drop into the teens or even single digits. A calf born during those hours can chill and die within minutes."

"Why do cows have their babies when it's so cold?" Jimmy asked, as he stared out the pickup window at the willow trees dropping the last of their yellow leaves onto the highway.

Richard chuckled. It was a question he'd had to answer dozens of times for people who didn't understand their farming operation. Growing crops was their priority … their cattle was a secondary business.

"Well, cows can calve anytime during the year," Richard said, pleased by the young man's curiosity. "They calve nine months after the bull gets romantically involved. Same waiting period as humans."

The bachelor farmer smiled, knowing what was going through Jimmy's mind. "We turn the bulls out exactly nine months before we want the cows to start calving. If things click, the calves start arriving right after Christmas. It may be colder than the North Pole then, but it's the only time we can all give our full attention to the cattle. The rest of the year we're so busy farming we can't spent a lot of time with the cows, other than to make sure they have food and water. Maybe it doesn't make sense to a lot of people, but it makes sense to us."

Jimmy nodded, taking it all in … making a mental note.

Richard continued, concluding his lengthy complicated answer to Jimmy's simple question. "The other thing is, with January calves, they can fatten on their mother's milk all year and then be sold in the fall as feeder calves at six or seven hundred pounds. We don't have to put any feed into them."

"I don't know anything about cows," Jimmy said, shaking his head. It was becoming clear he was expected to become a part of the cattle business. Hauling hay and driving a truck in harvest were an adventure. Welding metal and showing pigs were fun things to do. But working with these 1200-pound beasts they'd brought down from the mountains gave him the same nervous sensation he got before every football game … a step or two away from panic.

"You'll catch on pretty quickly," Richard said. "We treat our little herd humanely, but you need to understand it is a product we produce to sell. It's part of our farm's income. The animals all eventually end up in a meat locker for human consumption. Humans need protein and beef is a great source. You can love 'em, but don't get too attached."

Jimmy tried to understand, but he wasn't sure why he would ever love a cow.

Richard further explained. "If a calf fails to survive the birthing process, it means a big loss to the farm's income." He didn't mention, however, how it also took an emotional toll on the family. And about the pain one would feel seeing a lifeless calf on the ground with a distraught mother cow standing helplessly over it. He knew Jimmy would only understand that feeling if he was able to witness it. But he hoped that day didn't come too soon.

The "cow checking" observations were broken into intervals. During the day, Irene could see most of the herd from the windows of the farmhouse and she could call for help. But with darkness settling in early in the evening, the men took over. Richard would make a check at sunset before heading home to his house, and Brock would take his turn, with a spotlight in hand, when he returned from school. He'd take another walk through the herd, this time with Jimmy at his side, before they went to bed.

Jimmy was given pointers on what to look for when a cow was close to calving … how they would separate themselves from the herd and become agitated, pacing about the pasture. "Then she will begin alternating between pacing and laying down and pushing," Richard said. "The first noticeable part of the actual delivery is when the cow pushes out a large water sack like a balloon, which hangs under her tail."

"Once that water sack appears, it will take about an hour before you see feet emerge. If you see two little feet and a nose appear as she labors, that's a good sign." Richard explained. "That's a normal birth. It's the exceptions to that when difficulties arise."

"What do I do if I see any of this happening?" Jimmy cleared his throat. "I won't know what to do."

"That's when you go and wake Brock up or give me a quick phone call. We don't expect you to do anything until you've notified us. Then you become a helper."

"Whew … thank God." Jimmy exhaled deeply.

That day arrived one Saturday morning. Richard and Jimmy had finished feeding the herd with the hay bales they'd stored from the summer before, and Richard had gone home for his lunch. Brock was at the school to do some prep work for his class. As Irene and Jimmy sat in the kitchen having their own lunch, Irene stirred from her chair. She could peek out the kitchen window and see the cows, which had spread out throughout the pasture where the bales had been dropped.

"I think we might have something going on," Irene said. "Come look."

Jimmy popped up from the table and stood next to Irene. "What?"

"See the cow by herself, over by the fence? I think she's pacing and swishing her tail back and forth. Go out and see what you think."

Jimmy threw on his coat and overshoes and scooted out the door. He opened the old aluminum gate and wound his way through the herd, with Sassy by his side, until he got close to the cow in question. "Number 392," he said to himself. He had begun to know each of the cows by their numbers and markings. "What's going on?" he said out loud, not really expecting an answer. "You thinkin' about having your baby?"

Sassy trotted over to his side, hearing his voice. The cow moved away with an agitated trot. The herd was accustomed to the little cow dog, but now this cow seemed less inclined to want her around. She had gone fifty yards when she dropped to the ground and rested. But just as quickly, she jumped up and moved away again.

*Okay, I think this is what Richard was talking about,* Jimmy thought. He scurried back to the house to tell Irene.

"I'll call Richard, but you and I are going out to watch," Irene said. "We have time before the calf comes." She loved watching the birth process. Next to the excitement of wheat harvest, calving season was her favorite, even if it meant sleep deprivation, numb feet, and freezing fingers.

They moved through the cow herd at a safe distance to avoid making the expectant mother more nervous. By the time they could get a good view, the water sack was fully visible.

"This is good," Irene said. "A nice sunny day and no wind. It should turn out well. Unfortunately, some of these deliveries happen in the middle of a cold, foggy night when you'd rather be tucked away in a nice warm bed. So, let's enjoy this."

They watched, while quietly chatting … about the cows and school and basketball and how Jimmy was adjusting to his new life. "I miss my mom," Jimmy admitted. His head drooped for a moment before he stood erect and continued his thoughts. "And I really miss football, but basketball is okay too, 'cept some of the guys on the team don't get along. In football, we were like family."

"Give it time. You'll either find a way to come together or the team won't have a lot of fun or win many games."

The cow stopped pacing and dropped to her side and began to push. After a series of strong contractions, two tiny feet appeared and minutes later a pink nose was visible. Then the cow lay still again, like an insomniac trying to rest but with eyes wide open.

"Do we need to help?" Jimmy asked.

"Not yet. It may take another thirty minutes or so before it's out. Sometimes you can do more harm than good by jumping in too fast."

As they stood watching, they could hear Richard's pickup rumbling up the driveway. He pulled off the road, slipped through the barbed wire fence, and strode across the pasture toward them.

"Does this old girl need an audience … to cheer her along?" Richard asked. He pushed his steamed glasses up on his nose, grinned, and grabbed Jimmy by the shoulders.

Irene jumped right in. "We just thought it'd be good for Jimmy to watch this process in the light of day with the sun shining," she said. "Then when he finds something in the middle of the night, he'll know what's happening."

"Good idea," Richard said. "Gotta turn this young fellow into a cowman."

As they talked, cow 392 gave another giant push, and the front shoulders of the black baldy calf slipped into the sunlight. The cow, energized by the change, jumped to her feet, the calf swinging free behind her, held by the hips. As the mama cow pivoted to find her calf, the baby swung perpendicular to the cow's body.

"Like a dog chasing her tail," Jimmy whispered.

Then, just as he spoke, the calf's hips slipped out of the cow and the baby—along with a small waterfall of fluid—cascaded to the ground.

"Is that normal?" Jimmy asked. He turned to Richard, his eyes wide in amazement.

"Not always like that, but not uncommon," Richard said. "Most of the time the cow waits for the calf to come all the way out before standing up, but either way, it doesn't hurt the calf. Unless the baby lands with its head down and suffocates from all the birth sack and fluid. Especially if it's cold and the sack freezes around the calf's head. It can happen. But this one is plenty healthy."

The cow spun around and began frantically licking the newborn.

With the stimulation of the mother's rough tongue, the little calf began struggling to its feet.

"That's amazing," Jimmy said. "It's already trying to get up." He rubbed his hands together, both to warm them and with the excitement of the moment. "Is it a boy or girl?"

"You mean bull or heifer," Richard said. "Gotta get the words right. Let's go look."

They eased over to the new calf, making sure the cow wouldn't be too protective and chase after them. With a wary eye on the mother, Richard cautiously lifted the calf's back leg and looked down. Two tiny testicles told the story.

"It's a bull, Jimmy. How about that? One done and a whole bunch left to go. The fun begins."


Jimmy was moved by the experience ... watching new life, slick and wet, struggling to its feet in a matter of minutes, moving with rubber legs to search for its mother's udder and a first taste of warm milk. When he and Richard stepped in to determine the sex of the new calf, he'd reached down and touched the newborn and felt its body quiver and shake beneath his fingers. He'd never experienced anything like it.

Jimmy was full of questions as he tipped his old cowboy hat back on his head and looked over at Richard. "How much does it weigh? Why does the cow lick it so much? How does it know where to find the milk?"

Richard answered each question, knowing the experience was better than anything the boy would learn in school. And every answer created another question.

As Jimmy watched Richard place a tag in the little bull's ear, give vaccinations, and treat its navel with iodine, it was, "Why does the mother try to eat the afterbirth? Why do you put iodine on its belly button? How often does it need to drink?"

"Good questions; you'll be a real cowman by the end of calving season if I give you all the answers," Richard said. They stood, leaning against the fence, watching the new pair drift away to join the herd. "But it won't always be this easy. Lots of things can go wrong. That's why we keep a close eye on the herd all the way through calving season. We won't have them all calved out for a couple of months. By the end, you might wish you'd never seen a cow."

"Well, we're off to a good start, don't you think? Gonna call that calf Firstus, since it's the first one I've seen born. What do you think of that?"

"Very clever." Richard shook his head. "Hope you can find better names for the rest of them. I suppose the next one will have to be Secondus. "

"Now that's just old man stupid," Jimmy said, as he took his floppy hat and swatted at Richard. They laughed as they retreated to the house to record the birth of the calf and drink the hot chocolate Irene had prepared.

After the first calf arrived, the family came up with a carefully drawn-out observation plan, where each of the family members would take a turn checking on the cows, both during the day and night. The plan included Jimmy, although he was given clarification. "If you see something suspicious, let one of the other men know, so if there are problems they can be there to help."

Within a week, several more calves arrived … all unaided by the men. Jimmy had been nervous the first time he had to do a check by himself. "I'm not sure I'm ready for this," he'd confided to Irene one morning at breakfast. Irene always liked to have breakfast ready for Jimmy and Brock in the morning, although she found herself getting weaker as the days passed. Sometimes she had to force herself to get out of bed in the morning, but she'd sit up on the edge of the mattress for a few minutes, convincing herself to stand up for at least one more day.

"You'll be fine, Jimmy. You were able to watch that first calf be born, so you have a pretty good idea what to look for. I'll be here if you need help." After the first few times alone with the cows, the teenager became a bit more comfortable with the routine.

One Thursday, Richard dropped Jimmy off at the house after basketball practice. "I'm going to hurry home so I can get some rest before my ten o'clock check," he said.

"Sure, boss. I'll put on some boots and make my rounds." As Richard drove off, the border collie bounded up to Jimmy's legs, eager to join him for their nightly stroll through the cows. He stroked her shiny coat for a few minutes, then hurried into the house to change into work clothes.

"I'm headed out," Jimmy hollered to Irene, who was busy in the kitchen. He grabbed a spotlight and started for the pasture. There was a nip to the January air, and he wasn't going to linger. But when he'd made his way into the middle of the herd, he noticed a cow moving away from the others, standing by the fence switching her tail, side to side.

Jimmy watched for a few minutes before making a decision. "Okay, something is happening," Jimmy said to Sassy. "I'm going to go call Richard back, 'cause I'm not ready to do this by myself."

Soon the lights from Richard's pickup could be seen heading up the driveway. He pulled up to the barn and hopped out. "What you got, Jimmy? Thanks for calling before I climbed into bed."

Jimmy hoped he hadn't bothered Richard with a false alarm. "One of the bald-faced cows is alone down by the fence. I'm not sure, but I think she's starting to calve."

"Let's go take a look." They walked, side by side, down the fence line until they found the cow. By this time, it was clear she was giving birth. When Richard shone his flashlight at the cow, two feet could be seen protruding under her tail. "Okay Jimmy, good call, she's calving, but what else do you see?"

"I don't know. Am I missing something?" He couldn't read Richard's face in the dark but knew from his voice he wasn't joking.

"Well, those feet should be pointed down, with a little nose between them. Look closely, those feet are pointed up. Those are hind feet. The calf is coming backwards. It's going to be a breach delivery."

"Can she have it that way?"

"Nope. Not usually. We'll have to get her in the barn and put some chains on those feet and pull it out."

"You're kidding. Chains? Will it live if we do that?" he asked, trying to picture what that might look like.

"It will if we do a good job. Two men can usually get a breach calf out quick enough to keep it alive."

With a little persuasion, the young cow was in the barn and secured with a head catch. She didn't struggle much, accustomed to the men and seemingly happy to have someone helping with her discomfort.

Richard procured the chains, light in weight, but strong enough to pull the calf from the cow. "Okay, Jimmy, slip on this plastic sleeve, then reach your hand in there and secure the chain around the ankle of the calf."

"In there?" Jimmy looked over at Richard, making sure he wasn't kidding.

"Yes. She won't mind too much. You have to get the chain secured around the ankle. Once you get that one on, we'll do the same with the other foot and then you and I are going to get that baby on the ground."

Jimmy gently inserted his hand into the cow's vagina. He was surprised by the warmth of what he was feeling. He found a foot but struggled to get the loop of the chain around the hoof and above the ankle. The fluid inside the cow made the chain and his hand slippery and somewhat unmanageable.

"Take your time, but don't take all night," Richard said, serious but still with humor. "You're not hurting her. Just get it done."

Once the chain was over the hoof, Richard pulled tight on it and waited for Jimmy to secure the second one. "Okay," Richard said. "Since it's breach, we need to pull straight back, to keep the umbilical cord intact as long as we can. That keeps the calf from getting deprived of oxygen." He paused for the last command. "When I say pull, we'll give it a strong tug." He looked over at his young friend. "Ready?"

"As I'll ever be," Jimmy whispered. "You just tell me what to do."

"If we can save this calf, you can name the little critter. Now when she pushes, we pull, then once the hips are out, we won't stop pulling until the head and shoulders are free."

"All right," Jimmy nodded.

As the cow strained with her contraction, the men began to pull, increasing the pressure on the cow's cervix. She moaned and fidgeted in the chute. The men's muscles trembled with the strain. Richard was breathing hard, his shoulders starting to ache. But Jimmy's time in the weight room made up for Richard's weakness. Still, their efforts yielded no results. "This is going to be a hard one, I'm afraid," Richard said, sounding much less confident than he was just moments before.

"What now?" Jimmy asked, looking over at his mentor, as he stood shoulder to shoulder with the man.

"Try harder," Richard said. "We'll get down on the floor and push with our feet to get more power." He sank to the floor and motioned for Jimmy to follow. "Okay, get your feet right up under the tail and we pull hard when she has another contraction. The cow humped up her back and pushed. "Now," Richard said. "Pull hard."

The calf's hind legs began to slip from the cow, but only by inches. They relaxed the tension, and then when the cow pushed again, the men pulled, straining with every bit of muscle they had. Again, more of the legs appeared, but then the movement stopped. The hips were stuck.

"Damn it," Richard muttered. He let out a groan. "I'll have to get the puller." He rolled onto his knees and lifted himself up to a standing position. "Be right back."

Jimmy scrambled to his feet, now alone in the barn, just him and the young anxious cow. He looked at her with the calf's hind legs extending from under her tail, bewildered by what had transpired. *I don't think this is working out the way it's supposed to*, he thought. "Hang on, bossy," he said softly to the cow. Her eyes seemed to be pleading with him for help. "We're trying our best."

Richard rounded the corner of the barn, carrying a six-foot pole with a chain attached. On the end was a curved bracket shaped like the rear end of the cow. "Lift her tail," Richard said. "We'll slip the leather strap over her back and the bar under, then attach the two pulling chains to the ratchet. We'll have to crank the calf out the rest of the way. There's still a chance we can get the little bugger out in time."

They got the mechanism in place and with Jimmy holding the pole straight back, Richard began moving the handle back and forth like he was pumping the lever on a car jack. Inch by inch the calf was more exposed to the night air and out of its mother's body. As the widest part of the hips broke free from the body of the cow, she bawled a loud expression of angst. Jimmy had never heard a sound like that before and hoped he wouldn't again soon.

"Okay, Jimmy, grab the handle and help me ratchet this baby out as quick as we can." Jimmy did as he was told and the footlong bar flew up and down at a furious pace, until the calf's chest, neck, and head followed the hips, and the calf fell to the floor in a bloody pile of fluid.

Richard threw the long device across the room. "Get the chains off and we'll drag the calf into the corner into that straw pile." As Jimmy fought to extract the chains from the calf's legs, he looked into the eyes of the newborn. They blinked and stared, unfocused and dimming. "I think it's alive," Jimmy said.

"Maybe, but that was a rough pull," Richard said. "It might not make it." He grabbed the hind hooves and dragged the oversized black bull calf into the corner. *Damn, it's big … too big for a young cow to deliver by herself,* he thought. He dropped to his knees and watched to see if the chest was moving, then took his fingers and pulled the mucus and phlegm from the mouth.

"Jimmy, go get a bucket of cold water … and hurry," Richard commanded. Jimmy sprinted out of the barn toward the faucet outside the corral. While he waited, Richard grabbed a long piece of straw and shoved it into the calf's nostril, trying to trigger a respiratory response. There wasn't one.

Jimmy jogged back with the water, trying not to spill, and handed it to Richard. The older man grabbed it and dumped all five gallons onto the calf's face, hoping the shock would bring it around. Still, the newborn didn't respond.

"Isn't there something else we can do?" Jimmy asked, pleading.

"I know it was alive a few seconds ago." But Jimmy saw the look on Richard's face and watched the man shake his head and drop his shoulders. Richard collapsed to the floor, resting his back against the barn wall, catching his breath, in silence for a time.

"It's gone, Jimmy. That pull was too much." He pulled in a big breath and let it out like he was surrendering. "I wish we could have saved it. It was a nice calf."

Jimmy's heart sank. He felt sympathy for the man he was watching. He could see the disappointment on his face, how the lines around his eyes seemed deeper and more pronounced than usual. Richard wouldn't cry, he knew that, and he would have been embarrassed if Richard saw the tears in his own eyes. *Cowmen don't cry*, he told himself. The calf had come so close to beginning a new life, and yet it ended before it began. The young mama cow was now looking over her shoulder, searching for the baby that would never find her udder.

Jimmy felt his lungs contracting as if they also wanted to stop breathing. He was falling into the dark place that seemed to meet him at every corner. He remembered how he'd found his own mother's lifeless body just months before. *Why is life so hard?* he thought.

# FRICTION

**WHEN BASKETBALL PRACTICE BEGAN** the week following Peggy's breakdown, Brock sensed the animosity between Luke and Cole. The actions of the two mothers were being reflected by the teenagers. Words were not spoken between the boys, but the tension between them was apparent in their on-court attitudes.

Even though the Grizzlies pulled out a victory over Bristol Bay to even their league record, the win was overshadowed by the behavior of the two mothers. Both were notified by Principal Colquit on Monday they would not be allowed entrance to the two games the following week.

Luke was still troubled by the emotional event with his mother in the park. He wasn't going to bring the subject up to his teammates, but when Cole mentioned under his breath how he was "glad Peggy wouldn't be in the gym to hassle my mother," Luke's anger rose. "Sure, and it'll be nice playing a game without hearing your mom yacking from the top row." Luke glared at his teammate. "Are you sure you can play ball without mommy cheering you on? You freakin' little tool."

Coach McHue and Brock had their backs to the players and didn't see when Knighton slammed a ball into Luke's face. Luke rubbed his nose, checking for blood, and instinctively took after the slender sophomore, but before he could reach him, Justin Jepson grabbed him by the shoulders and held him back.

McHue caught the movement out of the corner of his eye. "Hey, Jepson ... Palmer, knock off the horseplay. Save your energy for the games. We've got some big ones coming up this week."

Luke's eyes blazed. He stared at Knighton. "You can't run forever," he said.

Without Goldie in the stands, the crowd for the Grizzlies' next game seemed strangely subdued, even though each game was a necessary stepping stone toward a possible spot in the district playoffs. When the team traveled to Wallitas to play the Chiefs on Tuesday night, the Grove fans were overwhelmed by the noise and size of the home crowd. The Chiefs were a team made up mostly of Native Americans, accustomed to winning titles in basketball. Their fans filled the gym to capacity for every home game, were vociferous in their support of their boys, and were full of negativity toward the visiting players. Drumbeats from older warriors seated in the front row were incessant ... a purposeful distraction for the visitors.

The atmosphere should have raised the energy level of the Grizzly team, but instead it seemed to unnerve the players, especially Luke and Cole, who weren't speaking to one another. Before the tipoff, in the locker room, Brock reminded the team how hard the Chiefs had competed in football. "They are a tough bunch … used to winning. We were lucky to pull out a win in football, so you'd better be ready to bring your best game."

But Cole and Luke weren't thinking about the Chiefs. And despite attempts by Justin and Jimmy Ivory to calm their animosity toward each other, it immediately fed into their play on the court. If Luke posted up, ready to take the pass and drive to the basket, Cole would purposely ignore him and force a pass to another teammate or let loose with an ill-advised shot over an opponent who had him covered with a hand in his face.

"Feed Luke!" McHue yelled again and again, but Knighton ignored the coach.

The coach turned to Brock, sitting next to him on the bench. "What the heck? Got any advice?" he quizzed. "They're not listening to me."

"Oh, they've got some personal problems," Brock said. "But they're not going to settle it here tonight." He paused. "You might try benching Cole or Luke, let them think it over, but you'd be giving up a lot of offense if you do." Brock knew losing was right around the corner if things didn't change.

"Right now, I'd like to bench the whole bunch of them," McHue said, as he slammed his clipboard on the bench. And as the fourth quarter wound down with the Grizzlies trailing by over twenty points, McHue was good to his word. He parked the entire starting five on the bench, letting the reserves run out the clock. Cole and Luke stared out, sitting as far from one another as possible.

Brock could only watch as things unraveled. When the buzzer sounded to end the game, the Wallitas crowd celebrated their twenty-point victory among themselves and could be seen laughing as they watched the Grizzly boys leave the gym. The Grove fans hurried toward the exits, sour looks on their faces. Their hope for a championship season was dimming rapidly.

In the locker room, the players dressed quietly. No one spoke until Coach McHue burst through the door and waded into their silence. In a manner uncharacteristic to his nature, he raised his voice. "That was one of the worst exhibitions of basketball I think I've ever seen by a Grizzly team," he said. "I don't know what's going on here, but you all better pull your heads out or you can wave goodbye to this season. Because you'll never win another game unless you can figure it out."

Brock watched as the boys reacted to the harangue. Heads dropped. Eyes drooped. He remained silent. *I'm not in charge, but something has to happen.* He hated losing. The ship was sinking. It was just a question of how long before it reached the bottom.

The other boys on the team knew the game was lost because of the friction between two of their best players. They resented the selfishness shown by Luke and Cole. But how could they solve the fracture? Now it wasn't just Luke and Cole who were upset … it was the whole team.

# CHAPTER 15

# COURTSHIP

**THE BANKER, ROLAND DONIGAN,** was intrigued by his first encounter with Ronnie Jepson. He didn't need to be convinced she was a qualified replacement for the retiring branch manager. Her references had already assured him of that. But he had wanted to meet her in person to see what she was like. When she'd walked into the room for a short interview, his male instincts nearly trumped his business acumen. *There is something special about this woman*, he thought.

Donigan had been divorced from his wife for three years and lived alone, although after the divorce, he frequently found company with other women. He was a handsome man, a former athlete who kept himself in shape with a routine of running and weightlifting. He had become one of the town's most eligible bachelors. But he wasn't ready to pursue a meaningful relationship. He was busy with the bank, and he shared the responsibility for his two children with his former wife. Mostly, he gravitated toward their participation in competitive athletics.

His eighth-grade daughter was making her mark in basketball. And his son, a sophomore in high school, had been named second-team All-City League as a receiver for his large private Catholic school.

It was his son's participation on the football team that led to Donigan's first meeting with Ronnie. He'd watched her son's amazing performance in the state championship game and later learned of her husband's passing. *This makes perfect sense*, he thought. Hire Ronnie as a local branch manager and bring Justin to his son's team. They needed a quarterback.

As he sat scheming, a third factor entered his thinking. Even though the meeting with Ronnie had been short, he was enamored by her appearance and demeanor. He toyed with the idea of pursuing the auburn-haired woman with the green eyes. She aroused thoughts of serious dating again. He was intrigued by the situation. *It's almost too good to be true*, he thought. It was full of promise. He needed to see her again … the sooner the better.

When the phone rang in the Jepson home on a Wednesday evening, Ronnie expected the call to be from her son, Justin, advising her of his whereabouts. Since Ronnie's husband had passed away in an accident, Justin was attentive to his mom's every need; he worried about her being alone. But when Ronnie picked up the phone, it wasn't Justin.

"Mrs. Jepson, how are you tonight? It's Roland Donigan from the bank. I assume you made it home okay from our interview."

"Oh, hi. Yes, sir, we made it home fine." She turned down the volume on the television to focus on the call. "Clear roads all the way. I think spring may be just around the corner."

"We can hope so. I just wanted to check on you and see if you've given any more thought to moving up the ladder and taking on a manager's position?"

"Of course," Ronnie said. "It's been on my mind. But like I said when I left the interview, I need more information before I can make any decision."

"That's why I'm calling. I've talked with John at your branch and asked if he could spare you for a day. I'd like to spend a little more time and flesh out some details. I hate to ask, but can you come back up this week? Maybe we could go out for dinner and talk these things through."

Ronnie tightened her grip on the phone and lowered herself onto a chair. The offer of a new job had become serious. It presented a huge opportunity for her. But was she ready for a major shift in her life so soon after Cort had passed? Justin was in his junior year of high school. And her rekindled relationship with Brock might end just when they'd begun to spend more time together. But she couldn't ignore the offer.

She caught her breath. "I can probably make arrangements. But I want to go to my son's basketball game on Friday. If I came up tomorrow, would that work?" She stared at the ceiling as she listened to Donigan speak. The receiver in her hand was like a magnet and the man on the other end of the line seemed to be pulling her to him.

"Perfect. Let me reserve a room for you at the Fairmont. My schedule is full all day but if we meet for dinner at six, we can go over all the details of the job while we dine. They have wonderful food at their restaurant. Even if I can't convince you to take the position, I promise you a good meal."

Ronnie's head was spinning. It had been years since she had dined in a classy restaurant. In her life, she felt it was a treat to eat at The Steak House in Glory Grove. How could she say no to this? She gave in to the offer. "That would be wonderful. I'll take off from work early tomorrow so I can be there before six o'clock. You're very kind to treat me so well."

"Well, we value our good employees. There will be a room waiting for you when you get into town. I'll call on you at the hotel at six. Goodbye for now."

Ronnie hit the off button on her phone and laid it on the table. She put her head in her hands and breathed. "This is all happening too fast," she said, as she lifted her head and stroked Franny, the housecat, who had crawled up into her lap. "You should be glad you don't have to make decisions like this."

Franny looked up and swiveled her head towards her human. Ronnie rubbed the cat between the ears and watched her stretch her limbs in appreciation.


On Thursday, Ronnie checked into the Fairmont, Spokane's best hotel, and was surprised her room was on the top floor. With her small suitcase in hand, she took the elevator and stepped out cautiously, feeling like she didn't quite belong at this level. She spied the room numbers on a directional sign, turned left and walked down the plush carpeted hallway to her room. She slid the card into the keylock and swung open the door. "Oh my gosh," she said out loud to no one.

The room was expansive ... a king-size bed was stacked with pillows. Flowers sat positioned on the coffee table in front of the wide-screen television. She walked to the window, opened the curtains, and looked out. The downtown lights twinkled as darkness enveloped the city—a silver shine stretching to the horizon. She felt a bit out of place in this environment, but realized she needed to hurry to freshen up before Donigan called.

At exactly 6:00 p.m., there was a soft knocking on the door. "Here we go," Ronnie said to herself as she took one last look in the mirror. Luckily, she'd found a dress she liked online right after Christmas, and since it was on sale, she treated herself. It was an emerald green, velvet midi-wrap dress with ruffled sleeves. When the package arrived, she opened it and held the dress up in front of her. She ran her hand over the material. *This is gorgeous*, she thought. But she didn't know where she would ever wear it in Glory Grove. Now she smiled as she saw herself in the mirror. *Flattering without being too revealing—perfect for a dinner with the boss.*

She'd brought a gold necklace, with a matching green stone, from her jewelry box. All her jewels were the inexpensive costume variety. She could never afford the real thing, and on the rare occasion Cort gave her jewelry as a present, she always assumed it came with a small price tag. She added simple gold loop earrings to complete her outfit, which hung a few inches down her neck. She wanted to look as if she were in a friendly meeting, but with enough style to fit in at a four-star restaurant.

When she opened the door, Donigan stood before her smiling. It took him a moment to catch his breath. "Hello, Ronnie," he said. "You look lovely, if you don't mind me saying. Is the room to your liking?"

"Yes, yes. But a bit overwhelming. This room's as big as my whole house," she said, wondering if she should invite him in or wait to be invited out.

"I thought the flowers would be a nice touch," he said, as he brushed by her and walked over to the bouquet.

"They are lovely, but do you treat all your employees like this?" she asked, as she moved away from the door.

"I do if I'm trying to convince them to make a life-altering decision." He smiled over at her. "I know how hard this might be for you.

But I try not to take no for an answer. I'll do what it takes to win you over."

Ronnie was surprised by that statement and considered it a compliment. *No one has ever said that to me before,* she thought.

When they sat down to dine, and the waiter laid a menu in front of her, she almost had to keep herself from gasping. She scanned the fare … and the prices. *Oh my gosh,* she thought. *How do people afford this?* She tried hard not to show her uneasiness.

Before they ordered from the main menu, Donigan asked the waiter to bring a prawn cocktail for an appetizer and a gin and tonic for himself. Ronnie waved off his drink offer. She considered the choices on the menu but didn't follow suit when Donigan ordered the most expensive entrée on the list: prime rib from Wagyu beef, medium rare, with mushrooms, a tossed salad with heavy Italian dressing, and breaded broccoli. Ronnie wavered—her habit in a restaurant was to always consider price and calories—but found a moderately priced meal that still spoke of sophistication and extravagance.

"I'll have the pomegranate duck breast with a berry salad," she said, looking the waiter in the eye, trying to act and sound as casual as possible. Donigan ordered red wine with a French name Ronnie couldn't pronounce. She hesitated, tempted to tell him she didn't drink, but didn't want to be impolite. She hadn't allowed herself to drink wine since the regrettable experience she'd had after her high school prom. It had led to an unintended early pregnancy and a life with a man who had mistreated her and kept her isolated from friends and the community.

When their dinner arrived and Donigan poured her a small amount of wine in a delicate glass, she conceded. She'd be careful not to over-indulge. He was sophisticated and intelligent, unlike her late husband.

She trusted him. This was a business meeting to talk about a potential promotion with the bank.

Music by the pianist at the bar adjoining the restaurant drifted through the darkened room. His repertoire of classic love songs added to the ambiance of the establishment. As they waited for their meal, Donigan started to tell of his plan for her. Ronnie would be offered management of a branch, east of the downtown area, but close enough to be within a quick drive to the main office. Her salary would increase by fifty percent, and she'd receive a full insurance policy for both her and her son.

"That's not all," Donigan said, becoming more enthused by his offering. He swirled the wine in his glass as he spoke. "You'll have use of a company car and three weeks of paid vacation. But the best thing I can offer you is to personally arrange to pay the tuition for your son, Justin, at St. Peter's High School, where my son goes to school."

Now Donigan was flush with excitement as he spoke. "It's a school in the state's largest classification for sports. It has a first-class football program with a terrific coach. But Ronnie, they need a quarterback, and Justin could step right in." He slowed his words for full effect. "He would get lots of exposure in the media and, by playing for a big school, set himself up for a chance to move right up to a D-I college when he graduates. Think of how that would improve his life and yours. You don't want him to be saddled with student loans."

Ronnie felt the wine slow her thinking. She tried to focus. It all sounded too perfect. So many of her worries for her son would be alleviated and it would be a fresh start for her. The thought of Justin playing for a bigger school caught hold in her imagination. She'd watched some of the state championship games with the large schools, and seen the packed stands, dozens of cheerleaders, big bands, and fawning parents. She suddenly wanted that for Justin. He deserved it.

Donigan rested his case. "I know it is a lot to think about. And you can take your time, but the more you consider the potential, the harder it will be for you to say no." He leaned back in his chair and smiled like a courtroom lawyer who was sure he'd won the argument.

Ronnie was relieved when the waiter came with their meal. Donigan was charming, and even though he kept saying there was no pressure, she felt it beginning to mount. Her accountant's mind was spinning with the details. It was a lot to add up. *It's like I've been offered the golden ticket for a brighter future*, she thought.

They settled into small talk for the rest of the meal. He recounted his days working his way up through the bank until he reached the top. He admitted he'd had an easy path, born to influential parents and an education at an elite business school.

She countered with a very dissimilar story … of hard times, being raised by a single mother, and being a teenage mother herself. She wasn't embarrassed to tell the truth, although she did not reveal how her marriage had begun. Or how her husband's auto accident had happened only because of Cort's intoxication and anger. She was proud of the work she had done at the bank in Glory Grove and what a gentleman her son was becoming.

"Can I offer you more wine?" Donigan asked, as he filled his glass for the third time.

"No, thank you. This is the best meal I've ever had, and I'd hate to ruin it with too much wine. But thank you anyway." She was still a bit lightheaded from the first glass she'd had.

The longer the evening wore on, the more Donigan was drawn to the woman across the table from him. He'd grown up around mostly self-important, pretentious people, and always held them at arm's length, searching for their motives … what angle they were using to win a certain situation. Ronnie Jepson had not one bit of that. He sat silent for a time, just watching her and listening to her speak, softly and sincerely.

They finished dinner with flaming crème brûlée, something Ronnie had never tasted before. It seemed heavenly. When Donigan offered the last inches of the wine carafe to her, she agreed. She'd measured her consumption and knew a few drops would not hinder her thinking. Donigan paid the bill—Ronnie couldn't imagine the cost—left a large tip, and extended his hand to help her from her seat.

"This has been wonderful, Mr. Donigan. You are very generous" she said.

He shrugged off the compliment. "Don't worry, the bank is paying. And from now on it should be Rolly and Ronnie, don't you think?" He slid his hand down her arm.

Ronnie nodded and smiled a half-smile. *Sure, but should I be calling a future boss by his first name?*

"Let me walk you to your room." They maneuvered through the crowd beginning to assemble in the dance portion of the bar. "Hey, Ronnie, would you like to dance? Don't you think you owe me one?" His eyes were teasing while imploring her to agree.

"I love to dance," she said. The best parts of her marriage were the nights Cort would take her to a western bar in the next town over from Glory Grove and they'd dance to a live band. Now, she was reluctant to agree to dancing with a potential employer, but the little bit of wine she'd had wouldn't let her say no.

He walked her to the dance floor to join the other half dozen couples moving gracefully to the music. He took her in his arms, and they quickly found perfect synchronization. Ronnie remembered the rough strength of her late husband, and how he'd physically directed her every move. Donigan was a good leader but did it in a gentle but sure way. *This is like a dream*, she thought. She closed her eyes and floated in his arms, free and contented.

One dance led to another, and then another. Then several more. They laughed and chatted and casually held hands between dances. The food and the music and the dancing were the most pleasure she'd experienced in one evening in her adult life. Ronnie became aware of others on the dance floor watching them with admiration for the way they moved, assuming they were a married couple or two people falling in love. *Odd,* she thought—a job interview had turned into an evening on the town with this very handsome man.

Now it seemed like the moment was about more than a job. She was hesitant to let it end. But it was late, and she was expected back in Glory Grove the next day to help her mother with some housework before the Friday night game. She looked at her watch. Her eyes widened. "It's almost midnight," she said.

"And I can assure you, there is no chariot waiting for you that will turn into a pumpkin."

"I need to turn in. I've lost track of the time." She rocked back on her heels and grinned apologetically.

"And it's been great, hasn't it?"

"Yes, Roland, but it has to end, doesn't it?"

"I think that's not a question, but an order." He offered his arm. "Okay, I'll walk you to your room."

They took the elevator to the top floor, and he walked her down the hall, his hand gently touching her back. He didn't want to let her go. He had been with other women, but none like her. When they got to her door, she turned and reached out to shake his hand … to thank him for a memorable evening.

"Ronnie, this has been delightful … more than I expected. I know this was about business, but I think it could be more than that," he said, his voice a low whisper … the deep resonant sound he'd used with other women in intimate situations. "I don't know what you're thinking, but I suspect you might feel the same." He ran his hands up her arms and pulled himself into her body, embracing her tightly with a controlling grip. They'd danced closely all night, and he wanted to be even closer. He could feel the contours of her body. Other women had often succumbed to his charm. "May I come in?"

Her body stiffened. Her breathing paused. The flashback was instantaneous … to a night so many years ago when she'd been convinced to drink wine after the prom. She was there again, back in a car with Cort Jepson, who was moving violently, grasping at her clothes, and forcing himself on her. At sixteen, she couldn't break free. Now, she shook and felt nauseous, but was determined to stay strong.

"No. No. I can't. I won't." She put her hand on his chest, but he resisted.

"I'm not going to hurt you. I care for you. I want you … for more than the bank." He held her tight.

Ronnie kept her hand on his chest. "I'm sorry, Roland. Maybe I've sent the wrong signals. I've had a wonderful night. Don't ruin it … please." She stared straight into his face, her eyes unblinking.

He pulled his arms back like a hawk moving away from a prey willing to fight back. But, like a banker negotiating for the best outcome to a disagreement, he recovered without hesitation. "You're right, I'm coming on too strong. I've had too much to drink. I'm sorry. I hope you'll forgive me."

He stepped away, his shoulders squared, downcast but still in control like a chastened but defiant child. "Please, let's pretend this never happened. Maybe in the future. I still want to see you working for the bank and working with me. It'll be on your timeline. But I don't scare away easily."

"But I do." Ronnie let out her breath. "You scared me. I'm not used to this. My husband hasn't been gone long. I need time. Forgive me if I gave you the wrong impression."

"We're good, Ronnie. I understand. No harm done." He straightened his jacket and stood erect. "Please consider my offer … on a professional level of course." He reached out to shake her hand and she instinctively met his grasp and relaxed her posture.

"Thank you, Mr. Donigan. Good night." She turned and slipped inside her room, closed the door, and consciously flipped the deadbolt lock over its holder. She walked to the king-size bed, kicked off her shoes, and flopped down on her back, eyes open, trembling as she stared at the ceiling. She burst into tears.

# CHAPTER 16

# DADDY

**FORTUNATELY FOR THE GRIZZLY TEAM,** their next opponent, the West Hill Warriors, scheduled for Friday night, had only a single win for the season. They were undersized and young, and their coach was new to the program. McHue, after discussing the situation with Brock, decided to start his reserves. They performed admirably throughout the first quarter and kept the score close.

Most of the starters, duly chastened, took the floor in the second period and stretched the lead out to double digits by halftime. McHue kept Knighton on the bench while Luke played and then brought him in for Luke after a time-out. Grizzly fans were confused by the coaching moves, while McHue and Brock were relieved Goldie wasn't in the stands to scream her objections to their strategy.

When the game was over, the coaches were pleased with the win but still concerned. "Well, it got us a victory, but we can't keep this up," McHue said, rubbing his head. "We'll get killed by better teams."

"I know," Brock agreed. "Somehow we've got to bring these boys together."

A very different attitude took over the following day. The rift between Cole and Luke suddenly took a back seat to a new development. The news came from Cole Knighton himself. "My dad's coming to watch me play." The other players stared at him as if he'd announced he'd met Jesus on the street in front of the school.

It was the most excited anyone had ever seen Cole. Most of the Grizzly basketball team didn't even know Cole had a dad. Of course, they knew his mom, Goldie. She was always present in his life and would be back in the stands for the upcoming game. But there were only rumors about his dad. Some speculated he was dead … perhaps from a tragic accident in his truck. Others thought maybe he was spending time in jail. The few years he lived in the Grove, he'd earned a reputation—among those who could remember—as a bit of a drunk who had trouble keeping his driving privileges.

Brock and Buster noticed the extra spring in Cole's step and how much more talkative he was among the other boys during game prep. "Maybe it's a good thing … his daddy coming to watch a game," McHue said. "He's always had a chip on his shoulder, because of his mom. Now it seems he may be coming out of his shell. Hopefully, it'll sharpen his shooting. He's been in a bit of a slump."

"Maybe better for the basketball team. But I hope it's better for him too. He seems troubled," Brock said. "And when a kid gets to thinking too hard about something other than the game, it can throw them off. If he hasn't seen his dad for a decade or so, it's bound to be emotional. We'll have to wait and see."

Clarence Knighton had sent a note to Goldie, telling of his visit. She recognized the writing on the front of the envelope and her brain exploded. When she read the note, scribbled on a pad from some auto parts store, she wanted to tell him to drive his Kenworth eighteen-wheeler right off the nearest cliff. She never wanted to see his face again, least of all when Cole was playing ball. Those moments should be reserved for the parent who cared the most … the one who had raised him and protected him from the world. Not the scumbag daddy who never sent a dime to help her feed their boy. If he showed, and she had serious doubts he would, she vowed to stay as far away from him as possible.

The Saturday night game with Brookside was the fifth league game of the season. A sizable crowd gathered in the home gym, including a smattering of parents and fans from Brookside. It was still early in the league season, and despite their two losses, the Grizzlies had a chance to make a run. Brookside was never a serious contender for the league championship. The Grizzlies were still in the hunt if they could knock off the Bombers and string together some wins.

By the time the game started, many of the Grove fans had heard the rumor about the potential return of the missing Knighton father. As they watched the teams warming up, many eyes in the gym were focused on the entrance to see if the mystery man would make an appearance. Cole also had his eyes fixated on the door, hoping his father would step proudly through the entrance, if for nothing else, as evidence he did exist.

Brock watched the team warm up and could tell Cole's mind was wandering. As they ran warm-up drills, his shots were off; his passes often went awry, and he fumbled with balls thrown to him. Brock's intuition as a coach told him the boy was beyond distracted. *He's a mess,* he thought, *as tense as a schoolgirl on her first date*, and certainly not ready for his typical offensive performance.

"Buster, Cole's struggling with this," he told the coach.

"Oh, he'll be all right. Once the whistle blows, he'll shake off that 'daddy' thing," McHue said.

McHue was wrong. Brock knew it but was hesitant to speak up. He'd been a varsity coach for years and when he was in charge, he didn't accept interference from his assistants. There could only be one boss. Period. But in this situation, he was tempted to break protocol. He knew instinctively, Cole's mind was somewhere else, and the coach should be preparing for the situation. Jimmy could be told to help the others find ways to score, and Justin could be in Cole's ear, urging him to focus.

Brock's stomach churned, wanting to help, but as an assistant he had to stay within his lane. He kept scanning the gym entrance for Cole's father. But he questioned whether an appearance or an absence would most settle the boy's nerves.

When the game began, Brock's predictions proved true. Within the first few minutes, Cole had thrown the ball away a handful of times and missed all his shots. His mother's chirping from the stands didn't settle him down, in fact, it compounded the awkward situation, reminding her son he had a mother and no dad.

Still, the Grizzlies were within striking distance as the half ended. Luke had pulled back on his desire to flatten the opponent when battling for a rebound, and Jimmy, sensing Cole's struggles, more often found Justin open for mid-range jumpers. As the clock ticked down to end the half, the Grizzlies had possession of the ball, time enough for a last shot. Jimmy walked the ball down the floor, taking seconds off the clock so the opponent wouldn't have time to respond before the half.

With eight seconds showing on the clock, he began his drive toward the basket and felt the zone collapse on him. He triggered a quick pass to Cole on the wing and watched as the sophomore rose up from beyond the three-point line and calmly sent the ball airborne, the fingers on his shooting hand dropping down to finish in a gooseneck position.

"Squeeze the orange," Cole uttered to himself as the ball dropped through the net, without a ripple of the twine. "Make your daddy proud," he whispered.

The crowd applauded the play, stood to ease their posteriors, and began moving to the concession stand and the restrooms. Cole waved off the backslaps from his teammates and searched the crowd for the one person he wanted to see. He let his mind imagine his father, standing and cheering for the son he'd come to watch. He hoped he could recognize him from the few family pictures he'd seen. He saw his mom, alone, which he expected, but saw no one else who resembled the photos. He quickly dropped his gaze, disappointed by the man he didn't see. He stiffened his shoulders as he followed the other boys into the locker room.

Coach McHue, pleased by the last-second play, stood in front of the team, oblivious to the personal situation playing out with his star sophomore. "We just need to clean up the turnovers and we can run away with a win," he said, trying to sound confident. "Y'all know you're a better team than they are." He hesitated for a moment, then turned to Knighton, who was leaning back against a locker, staring up at the ceiling. "Nice shot there at the end, Cole. Keep it up."

"Got it, Coach. I'm feeling good. Can we go warm up a little?"

The other boys looked at one another. "Jeezus," Luke muttered to himself. Only Jimmy heard.

"Just do your thing," Jimmy whispered. "We can win this without him if we have to."

"Just wish he'd pull his head out of his butt. Tired of his whiney little act. He's not the only one with problems."

As they stood up, ready to return to the hardwood, Jimmy nodded, knowing he and Luke shared their own tough history. But earlier in the year, they'd found relief in the family of teammates they'd developed through football. Somehow it was missing with this team. And they both knew it was because of Cole Knighton.

"Can I have a word?" Brock asked Cole, as the team began to exit the locker room.

"Rather not, Coach," Cole said. "I just need to get back out there."

"Sure thing," Brock said. "I just wanted to let you know, Coach McHue and I have your back. Your teammates do too."

"Don't need their help," Cole said. He spun away, headed out of the door, and searched the stands for his dad.

Clarence Knighton did not appear. By the end of the third quarter, people stopped looking. Those that remembered the man had doubted all along that he'd show up. They hoped, maybe for the kid's sake, he'd come for a game and disappear again. The town was better off without him. And Goldie didn't need him in their lives. They joked she might become homicidal if he stayed around too long. So, no one in the stands was disappointed when he didn't appear.

Cole, on the other hand, was broken. He'd wanted a dad, even a disreputable one. He'd let it be known his dad would be here and now he was embarrassed again by his absence. He let his disappointment slowly turn to anger as he played, lofting shots from further and further away.

Driving through zone defenses that collapsed around him, knocking his shots down and sending him sprawling to the floor.

Coach McHue was frustrated. "What the hell is he doing?" he asked Brock, midway through the fourth quarter.

"He's mad at his dad," was all Brock could say.

"His dad's not even here," McHue said.

"Exactly."

McHue called for a time-out and sat the sophomore on the bench. "We need you to calm down, Cole," he said.

"To hell with this, I'm out," the sophomore snapped. He grabbed his warm-up jersey, put his head down, and sprinted for the locker room.

"I'll go with him," Brock said.

"Let him cool off alone," McHue said. "We still need to win this game."

Brock's stomach tightened. *I should go*, he thought. A storm was brewing, and he wanted to turn on the sirens, board up the windows, and calm the wind. Cole needed him. He stood and took a few paces toward the locker room.

"Stay here, Brock," McHue ordered. "These boys need you too."

"We'll get it done," Justin said as he stepped between the two men.

Brock sat as the boys trotted back onto the floor without Cole. Justin, Jimmy, and Luke looked at one another. They weren't wearing helmets, and they weren't on a grass field, but now that Cole was gone, they each felt the old connection they'd developed during football season. A family, working for a common goal. Their passes were sharp, they worked to free each other for open shots, and they rebounded with determination.

As the clock wound down, they had done enough to secure a victory. The crowd cheered, and the men from the coffee shop began talking among themselves about the drama they'd witnessed and their interpretations of what had happened. There would be enough to fuel their morning gossip sessions for several hours.

When the boys and their coaches returned to the security of the locker room, Cole had disappeared. Brock gritted his teeth, trying to convince himself everything could be worked out. But he felt the gravity of the situation pulling him down.

Across the room, Buster McHue couldn't repress his happiness over the win. The team was still in the hunt for a league championship. He'd deal with Cole at the next practice … maybe have him run a few extra laps as punishment for his poor behavior.

But his good humor didn't last long. Principal Colquit stuck his head in the door and called the coach over. "Goldie is outside waiting for you," he said. "Better go calm her down."

McHue closed his eyes, took a deep breath, rubbed the hairless spot on his head, and plodded toward the door.

"Close up for me, Brock," he said. "This could take a while."

As the game was winding down, Cole sat alone in the locker room. He ripped off his sneakers and stripped off his jersey and shorts. He moved with a fury he'd never felt before. In minutes he was in his jeans with a hoodie pulled tight around his head. He fought back the tears and tried to funnel his disappointment into a rage that might keep him from dropping to the floor and sobbing.

He'd let his hopes lift him during the week and now they'd been dashed into jagged pieces which would be hard to reassemble. He'd embarrassed himself and encouraged the scorn of his teammates and the anger of his coach. He threw his gym clothes into a duffle bag and slammed it into his locker. He yanked the dressing room door open to head out into the night.

But outside in the cold, darkness filled him, trapping him in its clutches. He tried to breathe but couldn't take in air. He felt paralyzed but instinctively turned back toward the locker room. *That is where I belong,* he thought. He'd had the gym to himself all fall while the other boys played football. It was like his own personal space.

He knew the way down the stairs into the weight room. It was where he often went, during the summer, after he'd put himself through hours of shooting, dribbling, and running in the summer heat of the gymnasium. He'd cool himself by laying on the weight bench, where he could dream about the games he'd play when basketball season started. He'd imagine the thrill of shooting … scoring the winning baskets to lift himself into hometown hero status. But tonight, he had other dreams. Dreams to punish others. Dreams to curse the teammates who wouldn't accept him. And a dream to let his father know how much he'd been hurt.

As the dream formed in his mind, a weight seemed to lift from his shoulders. If he acted, he wouldn't have to feel the stares of people in the stands, those who might pity him for his loss. And he wouldn't have to apologize to his teammates for playing so poorly. And he wouldn't have to deal with Coach McHue and Brock Gallagher, who alone seemed to be able to read his mind. *All those things will go away,* he thought.

He reached into the box of jump ropes stashed in the corner … cotton ropes used by the wrestling team for cardio workouts. He began knotting the ends together until he had one long rope stretching for fifteen feet. His hands were steady while he grabbed the end and, remembering the lessons he'd learned in Boy Scouts, he tied a knot. As he worked, he could hear the horn signaling the end of the ball game. Had the team won? He wasn't sure. Perhaps. He didn't know and truthfully didn't care. But the thumping of hundreds of feet showering down on him as the crowd left the building assured him the gym would soon be empty, and he could finish his task.

He lay on the bench for a long while, the rope lying on his chest. He stroked it with his hand and tried not to think of his mother, only about the man who had failed him again. Finally, he knew it was time. He silently climbed the concrete steps, the rope in his hand, and opened the door to the locker room. It was dark, only the smell of boy sweat and dirty towels lingered. He didn't need light; he knew the way. Stepping carefully around the shower stalls, he moved through the hallway until he could see the gym through the door. A single light shone down as it did day and night … *the eternal light*, he thought.

There were chairs parked at the gym's entrance for the ticket takers and he lifted one carefully, not making a sound, and carried it to a position under the basket. He looked up, thinking it was in the right spot. He stepped onto the chair, careful not to collapse it onto his legs, then steadied himself and, with one hand, tossed the noose end of the rope over the back of the orange hoop. *I never miss*, he thought, just as he said to himself each time he let the ball fly out of his hand, in practice or in a game.

But now what? How could he anchor the loose end? Tying to the chair wouldn't work. Maybe the ball rack? Again, not heavy enough. Finally, he remembered the half hitch he'd been taught in Scouts. It might take a few tries, but he thought it'd work. And after several attempts, he looped the end securely around the basket itself. The noose hung head high, a perfect height.

He stepped down and backed away from the basket, looking at what he'd accomplished. But he wasn't ready. He walked to the ball rack and carefully picked up a ball. It felt so good in his hands as he ran his fingers along the seam, one of eight dark lines circling the sphere. A basketball … the one thing that gave him comfort. He spun it, rubbed it against his face, swung his body around, took three steps toward the opposite basket while dribbling … he wouldn't be called for traveling … and let fly. The ball spun, a nice arc with perfect rotation. He watched as it kissed the twine on its way through the net.

"Still golden … I make my mama proud," he said, as tears appeared in his eyes.

Cole Knighton was done with basketball. He was done with life. He walked very slowly across the top of the key, past the free throw line, until he could grab the rope, step onto the chair, and slide the noose around his neck. The clock was counting down in his head. *Time to let fly for a perfect finish.*

After the game, Brock Gallagher hurried into the locker room, hoping to catch Cole. Perhaps he could calm him down … help him deal with the disappointment of a missing father. But Cole was gone. His absence increased Brock's anxiety. *I should have followed him.* The thoughts kept repeating like a stuck record.

Brock knew Coach McHue would be busy dealing with Goldie, so he stayed with the players in the locker room. The atmosphere was jovial. The team had pulled out the victory without their star sophomore, and it made everyone happy.

"We got it done, Coach," Luke hollered across the room. "And I didn't foul out."

"Hey, nice change," Brock shot back.

"And I even scored a few points," Jimmy said, as he sat in front of his locker. "But where did Knighton go?" He directed the question toward his big friend Luke, who was working his way toward the shower.

"Beats me. Little shit kind of left us high and dry walking out like that. Now he'll probably be upset that we won without him."

"This time, maybe. But we're going to need him for our next games," Jimmy said.

The boys weren't overly worried, but Brock was deeply concerned. He knew Cole Knighton was on a thin edge. The sooner someone talked to him the better. When McHue returned from his go 'round with Goldie, Brock quickly excused himself and headed back into the gym to have a word with her.

She was walking toward the exit … head down in deep thought. Dark strands of hair covered most of her face. Brock approached her slowly.

"Goldie."

She turned. "What?"

"I may be overstepping here, but I'm concerned about your boy. He was pretty upset about his father not showing up. He loves to play basketball and it's not like him to walk away from the game."

"I was happy that loser didn't show up."

"I understand. But Cole was looking forward to it. He was distracted during the game, and it showed by the way he played. I think someone needed to talk to him. But he'd already left the locker room when we got there."

"I'll check on him when I get home. He needs to understand he shouldn't count on his dad to ever be there for him. I'll try to get that through his head."

"Would it be okay if I came along to talk with him?"

"It's really none of your business. I can handle this myself. Don't try to get between me and my boy, okay? I know how to deal with him."

"I understand, but if he needs someone to talk to, please call. I'd like to help if I could."

Goldie's eyes flashed. "Thank you, Mr. Gallagher, but I don't need another man messing with my family. Now if you'll excuse me, I need to be going. And since you're always sitting on the bench with that dumb old head coach of yours, tell him to pull his head out and figure out how to win a few games. He's got the best player in the league, and he still loses games. Really pathetic." She turned and curled her shoulders inward before heading to the exit door.

Brock returned to the locker room. It was nearly empty. The boys were gone. Buster was studying the stat book in his office and the janitor was tidying up after the boys. "I'm getting a few things from my classroom and heading home," Brock said to the coach. "I hope we can work something out with Cole."

"He'll be fine. Just needs to cool down before the next game on Thursday. I'll make him apologize to the team and run a few laps, then we can forget about tonight."

*Not enough*, Brock thought, but didn't say it. "I hope you're right, Coach. But I told Goldie if Cole needs to talk, I'll be there for him."

"Good for you, Brock. I'm not very good with stuff like that. I'll let you handle that end of things."

Brock walked down the dark hall, his footsteps echoing off the bare walls. He slipped into his classroom, flipped on the lights, and slid in behind his desk. He studied the pile of papers waiting to be corrected from the history quiz he had sprung on the class. *I'll start in on these now*, he thought; maybe it would take his mind off the boy.

He liked to get tests returned quickly so students could measure their standing in the class. This was a simple, multiple choice, twenty-question test; it wouldn't take long. Then when he got back to the farm, he'd check the cows. Perhaps the anxiousness over Cole's meltdown would have faded by then.

He worked through the papers, pleased to note the basketball players in his class had all put up decent scores. The team didn't need any more distractions during the season. Even Luke, who struggled with his studies, was doing fine. As he finished the last of the nineteen papers, he leaned back in his chair and let out a deep breath. He could see his reflection in the exterior window and instinctively pulled his stomach in and forced himself into an erect posture.

He wasn't ready to be considered a frumpy old history teacher. He laughed at himself for his vanity. Who really cared what a jayvee basketball coach in a tiny little farm town looked like anyway? Maybe in Seattle … but not so much in Glory Grove. He'd made the choice. This was his life now.

He piled the papers neatly on his desk, gathered his coat and a few books for lesson planning in the morning, and shut the door to his classroom.

He usually used the back door to the school to reach his car, but something told him he should take one more walk by the gym, which connected to the main school building. The hall was dark and there wasn't a sound other than his footsteps. When he reached the door to the gymnasium he peered into the cavernous facility, where only hours before there had been the constant squeak of gym shoes, cheering, and the clapping of hands from Grizzly fans.

Now, it was silent. The gym was dark, save for a single overhead light. It reflected softly off the blackness of the gym floor The only shadows came from a single folding chair, oddly placed under the nearest basket. He saw a smallish figure slumped over in the chair like an old man who'd fallen asleep in his favorite recliner.

Brock froze. *Oh, dear God … no, no, no …* his mind convulsed. It wasn't an old man. It was a boy. And he had a rope around his neck. He'd found Cole Knighton.

# CHAPTER 17

# RECOVERY

**BROCK FORCED HIS LEGS TO MOVE** forward as he approached the boy. A knot formed in his stomach, thinking of what he might find. Cole lay slumped back in the chair, his face pale, eyes closed. His head was tilted at an awkward angle against the chair's metal backrest. The end of the rope lay in his limp hands. In the dim light from the single bulb in the gym ceiling, Brock studied the boy. *Please, don't be dead.* He dropped to one knee and watched the boy's chest. He didn't see any movement. *Dammit, Cole, what have you done?*

Brock grabbed his wrist to see if there was a pulse. When he did, Cole went rigid, inhaling with a start. The movement sent Brock back on his haunches, but he gathered himself as he stared down at the young sophomore. He wasn't sure what to say, to calm whatever emotions were going on inside Cole's mind. Finally, he said the only words he could muster.

"What's going on, Cole?"

"I couldn't do it."

"What were you trying to do?"

"Trying to die … but I couldn't get the rope tied right."

Brock responded quietly, hoping to calm the teenager. "Wanna talk about it?"

"Not much to say. I'm just all messed up."

Brock patted the young man's arm. "Let me sit with you for a while." He walked over to the gym entrance and lifted a second folding chair, carried it over, and set it down next to Cole. He reached down and gently removed the rope from around Cole's neck like he was removing a lasso from a frightened calf. He tossed it against the wall. Instinctively, he lowered himself down next to the boy and when he did, Cole collapsed against him and began to cry.

"What am I going to do?" His voice was restrained and tight. Not mad, but sorrowful. Brock tightened his arm around him and let him talk. "I tried to hang myself. I had it all figured out. But I couldn't do it. I really wanted to." Brock could see the tears running down his face. "But it was just so lonely and quiet here in the dark. And then I thought what if my dad came in late and found me? Maybe his truck broke down or something. He was supposed to be here tonight." He struggled to catch his breath between sobs. "I just wanted to see him. Just to have someone besides my mom cheering for me."

"Other people cheer for you too, you know. Maybe you just don't hear them." Brock turned to look directly at the boy. "I cheer for you."

There was a long pause. "But the other guys on the team don't like me. Luke, and those other football players. They don't cheer for me."

"They might if you gave them a chance. For sure they don't want to see you with a rope around your neck. Every one of those guys has his own set of problems. You'd understand that if you'd give them a chance."

"But I'm different than them."

"And no one really cares. Do you remember how different Luke was when he came to town … all dressed up like a gangster from the city? But he learned to fit in. And Jimmy. Don't you think being the only Black kid on the team makes him feel different?"

"Sure, but now everybody likes them."

"And why?" Brock stared into Cole's face.

"I don't know. 'Cause they were great football players?"

"And you, Cole Knighton, are a great basketball player. The only difference is they formed a real bond with the other football players. And you haven't quite done that with the basketball team. But you can. I know you can. And when you do, your differences won't matter, and the team will just get better and better."

"But I let them down tonight. I played awful." He shook his head slowly back and forth. "And walked out on them."

"They were fine. The game was close, but we won. But in the future, they are going to need you. They know that. They know you're the best player on the team. None of them would argue that."

Brock hesitated a moment to let his words sink in. "But before we talk about basketball, we first have to get you back on your feet. We can't ignore what you tried to do tonight. That's serious business that needs to be addressed. I don't know your dad. And maybe he'll never come to town. But if he does, he's not going to want to find out you ended your life because of him. And Cole, your mom's world would be turned upside down if you took your own life."

"She's part of the problem, you know."

"She loves you."

"Too much sometimes." He cringed at the thought of his mother.

"Maybe we can help her, too," Brock said.

"Good luck with that." A faint smile appeared on Cole's lips.

"I'll talk with her." Brock nodded his head and let out a bit of a laugh. They both knew talking with Goldie would take some courage. There was a moment of silence and then Brock asked, "Do you just want to sit here for a bit?"

"Can we go sit in the stands? I'd like to hold a basketball."

"I'd like that," Brock said. "Maybe you can show me how to improve my shot. I was a pretty poor shooter when I played here." He saw the boy's lips tighten in a sad smile with the thought of his coach and his pathetic jump shot. "But then I need to call your mom, so she doesn't worry. And I'm going to have to tell her that you're with me and that I'll bring you home in a little bit."

"Does she have to know?"

"She does, Cole, because we're going to have to get you into some counseling right away ... even tonight, because the sooner we get you some help, the sooner we'll get you back out here where you belong. Sadness is nothing to be ashamed of ... it can be worked out. I know you had a bad night tonight, but we need to get it behind you.

Brock stood up and headed for the ball rack. "You and I will find a way to make tomorrow a better day." He picked up a ball and softly directed a bounce pass toward the boy as if it were a lifeline.

Brock was met at the door of Cole Knighton's home by Goldie. She could tell by the look on her son's face that something was wrong. "What's going on?" she said. Her eyes flashed with anger and worry. She stood across the entrance, blocking the way for her son and his coach to enter the house.

"May I come in?" Brock asked. His voice was calm but insistent.

"Why?"

"We need to talk about what Cole did tonight."

"I know. He walked off the gym floor. Let's not make a big deal about it, okay?" she said, her voice rising as she spoke.

"It's more than that, Goldie."

Goldie's eyes swung over to her son. "You tell me, Cole. I need to hear whatever it is directly from you before I'll believe anything these coaches say."

Cole dropped his head and kicked at the worn welcome mat at the door. His lips quivered and he could barely mouth the words. "I tried to kill myself."

"No. No, you didn't. I don't believe it." Her arms crossed in front of her chest.

Brock edged around Cole and stood between him and his mother. "He did, Goldie. I found him with a noose around his neck. Your son is very depressed, and he needs some professional counseling. It really can't wait. As his coach, I know it's something he'll have to do. I'd like to come in and talk with you about it and then we'll make arrangements."

Goldie closed her eyes and let out a guttural sound from deep inside her chest, alternating between sobs and screams. She swung away from them and stumbled towards a hardback chair in the living room. She slowly sank to her knees, laying her head on the seat. She pounded the seat with her fist. "It's that damned father of yours, isn't it, Cole? He should never have sent that letter."

"But, Mom, I wanted to see him. Even if he's a worthless old truck driver, I wanted to see that I had a dad … like the other boys. And then I played awful. I let my team down. I just wanted to end it all." Cole walked over to her as if he was going to lift her up, but he didn't stop. He passed by her and crumpled onto the sofa.

"I think Coach is right. Maybe I need help. I don't know what else to do."


Brock spent the next two hours talking with Goldie and her son. It was midnight when he called the nearest hospital, thirty miles away, and explained the situation. They said they'd take the boy and would have a counselor available to work with him. An attempted suicide demanded that the person be seen immediately.

Finally, Goldie was convinced, and she and Cole loaded into Brock's black Lexus. They left Glory Grove and rode in silence. Brock had done what he could to calm Goldie and now she was deep into her thoughts … angry at her long-absent husband, while trying to deal with the hurt in her heart. But grudgingly, she was relieved someone had been there for Cole when he needed them.

Still, she was sad it wasn't her. Most of all, as the car made its way to the hospital, she couldn't stop imagining how she would feel if her only child had taken his life. From the back seat of the car, sitting behind Brock, she could see the profile of her son's face. Her entire reason for living centered around Cole. If he had ended his life, it would also have been the end of her. The thought of such emptiness made her convulse. She clenched her hands together in prayer until her fingers tingled. She also needed help.


Brock stayed long enough at the hospital with Cole and Goldie to get them checked in and to consult with the psychiatrist who was there to meet them. Later, he reserved a hotel room for Goldie near the facility, so she'd have a place to stay until Cole was released. He returned home in the middle of the night exhausted. When he turned into the driveway, he noticed a spotlight moving through the cow pasture. Brock waited in the car while Richard rambled over.

"Everything okay here?" Brock asked, when Richard got close enough to hear.

"Yes, but what in blazes are you doing out at this hour?"

"Had a problem with one of the players. Had to take him to the hospital."

"Something serious?"

"Pretty serious, but nothing physical."

"Cole?" Richard was slowly nodding his head before Brock even answered. "I saw the way he left the game."

"Yeah. He had a meltdown, bordering on suicide. He won't be playing again for a while."

"Figures," Richard said. "That boy is under a lot of pressure, with the team counting on him for points and his mama yelling at every game. It's no wonder he cracked. But it makes it hard on you and Buster, doesn't it?" Richard stared down at his nephew. From the interior lights, he could see the worry on his face. "God, Brock, it must be hard being a coach. Not all fun and games, is it? I'm glad it's you and not me."

"I do what I can."

Richard spun the spotlight in the air, the beam of light streaming into the heavens. "Gotta say, though, it's a good thing the kids have someone like you to look out for them." He tapped the top of the door frame with his gloved hand. "Now go get some sleep. The cows are in good shape here."

"Thanks, Uncle, but I might have trouble sleeping. Have to decide how to tell the team."

"Tell them everything but nothing. Just make sure the rest of them keep their heads on straight. Don't want anyone else to go off the deep end."

"That's what I'll try to do. They need to hear it from me before the rumors start. But it's a highwire act. I'll be stirring up their sympathy and dealing with their frustration with Cole at the same time. Most of all, I have to make sure they understand suicide isn't something daring or bold, or an easy way out of their problems. They've got to realize suicide isn't a solution to any problem … and it's permanent. If they ever get to that point, they have to reach out for help. There is always someone who will listen."

"Sounds like you've got your speech ready. Let's hope they have their ears open."

On Monday, Brock met with Principal Colquit and Coach McHue to fill them in on the details. He'd called McHue earlier to tell him of the incident and what had transpired afterwards. McHue was dumbfounded, and sorry he'd not taken the incident seriously enough. *What would I have done if this ended badly?* he thought. "I'll be forever grateful to you, Brock. And I'll start paying more attention to what you say. It's a wake-up call. Maybe I'm too old and not cut out for this job anymore."

"Buster, you are the right man for the job. Coaches all learn as they go. This is just another lesson."

The men all agreed the team should be informed and Brock should be the one to do the talking. The boys were called into the locker room during the lunch hour for a private meeting. As they straggled in, there was an air of curiosity. The coaches weren't smiling, and their body language told them this wasn't a time for frivolity.

"This must be something serious," Luke whispered to Jimmy as they found their usual spots on the locker room bench. "Do you suppose somebody died?"

"Hope not," Jimmy said. "I've had enough of dying." He turned away from Luke and stared at the coaches. But his mind went to his mother's recent passing and to Irene's failing health. *Please God, no more death for a while*, he mumbled, as he thought of her and how fragile she'd become.

Brock called the boys to attention. "Guys, thanks for showing up here. I have something to share with you and it's not pleasant to talk about. You're here because you are part of this basketball team. It's like a family, and as part of a family, you each have a role to play in keeping it together. So, here's the deal." He paused and took a deep breath. "After the game Saturday, Cole Knighton found himself in a bad place emotionally. He had a moment when he thought he could end his depression by taking his own life."

There were groans from a few of the boys … silence from the others. Brock purposefully stopped talking for a few seconds to let the news sink in. He hadn't used the word *suicide*, knowing the players would instinctively try to picture the scene. But he wasn't going to describe what he'd found. No one needed to know.

The boys sat still, some staring at Brock, others looking down at the floor. The silence lingered until it was broken by a timid voice coming from the back of the room. It wasn't one of the team captains or anyone on the starting five, but the freshman, Les Colquit. "Is he all right? He's a good player," Les said. "He shouldn't have done that."

"Yes, he is a good player, Les. And he's a good young man. He just felt alone and needed someone to listen to him when he was hurting. He didn't think he had anyone."

Luke sat with his head down and took a long slow breath. He wanted to speak up but instead clenched his teeth tighter together. *So what if the little jerk thought about killing himself? It wasn't my fault, and it's not my problem.* Cole had done nothing to act like a friend or try to be a good teammate.

Brock noticed Luke's reticence but continued. "This is serious business. Life is precious, especially for a teenager. You are a team of basketball players and every one of you has something to offer. Take care of each other. You are the next generation, growing up in the Grove. You will go out and do important things."

Brock's mind wandered for a moment about his own life's journey … about his moments of uncertainty and sadness. Then he continued with the message he hoped would be planted in each boy's brain. "There is a lesson here. Each one of you has a wonderful life in front of you. Don't waste it. For now, enjoy these high school years. Take the time to make them special. And this … being part of this team is special. But always remember, life is precious, and how you live it impacts all of those around you. God has given you this one life, do something with it."

Brock turned to Coach McHue, who was standing off to the side. "Coach, are you okay with what I'm saying?"

McHue just nodded his approval, not saying a word.

Brock turned back toward the boys. He needed to add a few closing remarks. And he needed to ask for the boys' help in keeping the whole incident from becoming fodder for gossip. He stared hard at them, demanding their attention.

"Guys, what is being said in this room, stays in this room. Do not go out and start telling secrets like a bunch of old gossipers. Keep this to yourself if you can. Right now, Cole is getting the counseling he needs. He will get better. He'll return to school soon. We don't know when or if he will be back on our team. But if he does come back, and we should all hope he does, show him some love. He may be troubled and embarrassed for what he has done. It will be up to you to help him get over that feeling."

# CHAPTER 18

# LAWYER

**THE AREA FARMERS WERE INVITED** to a meeting in the Joseph County courthouse with an attorney who wanted to represent them in their negotiations with the Wind Driven Corporation. If they were going to sign leases to allow wind towers on their property, they needed assurances that it was in their best interest, and that the leases were written with no loose ends or fine print that would come back to hurt them later. As Brock and Richard Gallagher climbed the wooden stairs leading to the second-story courtroom, each step, barely five inches in lift, emitted a slight creaking noise that echoed down the empty hallway below.

"I'd hate to be a criminal headed to my trial," Richard said. "These creaking stairs might make you think you were headed to the gallows."

"So, you're feeling guilty, are you?" Brock asked while keeping pace with his uncle. Although the family hadn't decided about the lease, Brock guessed his uncle was more inclined to sign a lease than he or his mother.

"Guilt-free as a bachelor in a nunnery," Richard grinned as he took the last step onto the landing of the second floor. He exhaled as he recovered from the exertion. "This will be an interesting meeting."

"Mixed emotions, for sure. Maybe we should have ushers to guide the pro-wind people to one side of the room and the anti-wind people to the other."

Richard paused for a second before stepping into the courtroom. "Where would you and I sit?"

"I'd probably sit right in the middle of the aisle," Brock said. "This is a tough one. It's a decision we'll have to make as a family. I wish this outfit had never shown up in the Grove. But I guess it's progress." He suspected the final decision could even divide their own family. Of course, his mother would have the final say, but she would lean on both Richard and him to help her decide.

Soon the room began filling with farmers, ranchers, and those local businessmen who would be impacted by the influx of construction crews who came to erect the towers. There were also curious onlookers who thought they might witness some conflict among neighbors, which they could gossip about.

Some preliminary introductions were made by the head of the committee that screened the lawyers specializing in dealing with wind companies. Then the attorney, Cameron Duncan, dressed in a dark gray business suit to match his thinning hair—his dress an obvious contrast to his audience—began to speak.

"It's a pleasure to be here," he said. "I've always had a deep respect for the people of Joseph County. You have some of the finest people on this side of the state. You all aren't known for having the best farm ground, but you are known for being some of the best farmers." His voice was calm and monotone, barely rising or falling in pitch.

"If he were a preacher, I'd be asleep in ten minutes," Richard whispered to Brock.

The attorney droned on. "I hope to get to know you as we begin negotiating leases with Wind Driven."

"Who says we're signing leases?" A voice deep and threatening came from the back row. It was Harold Olson, the Gallagher's neighbor, who lived just up the road from their farm. Harold's son, George, played tight end for Brock's football team. George was a big boy for his age—started on varsity as a freshman—and Brock found out early George got his size from his dad.

Harold called Brock early in the football season to see if he could come talk. When he showed up at the farm and walked up the sidewalk to the house, Brock looked out the window and smiled. He'd never met George's dad before but was impressed by his stature. He was a mountain of a man, thick and powerful looking with ruddy cheeks. *Viking blood,* Brock thought. If young George grew up to be his father's size, the Grizzly football team of the future had a weapon.

When he met Harold at the door and they began talking, he found the man to be polite, with nothing but positive things to say. He'd only come to show his support for the football team. "Coach, I hope I haven't kept you from your business. I just want to say in person how happy we are you've taken the football job. We were surprised to hear our son George is on the starting rotation, but we'll give him and you all the support we can."

Brock was impressed. "Would you like to come in and have some coffee?"

"No, sir. I've got to get back on the tractor." The conversation was over. He spun around and walked quickly back to his pickup. That was the last time Brock had seen Mr. Olson, except occasionally sitting in the stands during practice, or after the game with his son. Despite their very short formal visit, Brock had respect for the man.

So, when Olson boldly blurted out his question at the community meeting, Brock was shocked. This business had struck a nerve with his neighbor.

"Some of us don't want anything to do with your windmills," Olson said. His voice was etched with anger. "I've seen those wind farms, and they are a blight on the countryside. I know some people here might be impressed by the dollar numbers Wind Driven is throwing around, but there are others here who just wish them and their lawyer would go away. If you get your way and we all *sell out*, you're going to scatter those giant monstrosities through our farmland and ruin everything with blinking red lights and massive roads cutting through our fields. And we know there will be dead eagles lying on the ground. It's a proven fact. Some of us just want to farm the land we've inherited. So don't think we're all going to jump on board and sign anything."

There was a hush in the room. No one expected an outburst like that, especially from Harold. Folks knew he was bashful and would barely speak when meeting someone on the street. It was as if someone had yelled a profanity during a church service. Men rocked uncomfortably in their seats. And the farmers who welcomed the wind towers wished they could rebut Olson's outburst, but no one spoke, leaving the room uncomfortably silent.

Duncan's complexion paled with every word Olson spoke. But he regained his composure. "I appreciate your opinion, sir, but this isn't a forum for the pros and cons of wind energy. I'm here to help each of you understand what the company will do for you and what you will commit to if you sign a lease." He stepped forward just enough to show he hadn't been cowed by the outburst. He quickly returned to his monotone delivery, as if by slowing down he might throw cold water on the emotions that were building. "Let's look at the details in the handout we passed out."

When the lawyer finished his presentation, Brock and his uncle filed out of the room with the rest of the crowd. "Harold got a little fired up," Richard said. "Didn't expect that from him."

"I'm sure there are others who feel the same way," Brock said, as he made his way down the steps from the courtroom. "Sorry to see people having to take sides. But I understand both positions. And after looking at the maps of the proposed project, our farm is sitting right in the middle of the whole thing."

"So, what if we don't sign? Is that going to change anything?" Richard asked as he reached the landing.

"I don't know, but I think there is going to be a lot of pressure on us to jump on board. If we sign, it will make others think there is no stopping this thing."

"So … what do you think?" Richard glanced over at his nephew.

"I think I don't know. But I know my mother doesn't want anything to do with this business. She'd hate to see the ridge turned into a pin cushion for massive wind turbines." Brock paused to step outside the courthouse doors into the chilly evening.

He continued talking as they moved away from the crowd. "Mom has lived most of her life loving the farm and the wide-open freedom we have living next to Piney Ridge. She'll be heartbroken to see that come to an end. But she's also smart enough to know the income from those towers would ensure we can keep the farm for another generation."

"It would make life a little easier, that's for sure," Richard said. "Every time we felt the wind blow, it would mean more money in our pocket. That's a hard thing to resist."

Brock could see how dangling *free money* in front of the farmers was having an impact … even on his uncle. And why not sign up for free money? It was a huge temptation. But was there such a thing as *free money?* Certainly, there would be a price to be paid.

# CHAPTER 19

# DONIGAN

**COLE KNIGHTON WOULD BE MISSING** from the basketball team for an extended period, as per the advice of the psychiatrist at the hospital where he'd been treated. His mother took the professional's advice to heart and vowed to ease off on her histrionics at the ball games. She wouldn't attend the games anyway, with Cole sidelined.

Brock was on the bench with Coach McHue as the basketball team warmed up for their home game with Timbertown. He scanned the crowd to see who all was there. Tim and Peggy were back in their usual spots and his uncle sat high to his right across the gym. Richard tried to attend the home games unless the cows were calving. He paid close attention to the way Jimmy played so he could give his critique the next day … all in good humor, of course.

As Brock swung his gaze to see where Ronnie was sitting, he spotted her mid-court, across from the scorer's table. She was with a few of her friends from the bank and they were in casual conversation, waiting for the game to begin. As Brock studied them, he noticed a man climbing the stairs heading straight for the women. At first, he couldn't place him, but suddenly recognized him from the brief introduction they'd had at the Spokane bank a few weeks earlier … it was Roland Donigan.

Brock watched as Ronnie's face turned a shade of soft crimson when Donigan reached her. Was hers a welcoming look or one of shock? He wasn't sure. Those sitting around Ronnie noticed how the handsome man seemed pleased to be with her.

Ronnie's heart beat faster when she saw him. She'd put the memory of her night with Donigan out of her mind. He'd left a few calls on her answering machine at her home, but she didn't respond … trying to take time to sort out her emotions before giving an answer to his offers. She was tempted by the proposition he had made during their dinner in the city. But when she thought of the way he'd come at her later outside her hotel room, she found herself gripping tightly to whatever she was holding.

"I need time to wrestle with a decision like this," she'd told Donigan. But he now was sliding into the space made available by Ronnie's friends, who had scooted away to let him in.

"Hello, Ronnie," Donigan said. There was a velvety texture to his voice, like dark chocolate. He smiled at her, and she remembered how handsome he was—tan, a stylish two-day growth of beard, wearing a soft leather jacket with matching driving gloves. He stood out in the gymnasium, like a movie actor stopping for a burger at the local drive-in filled with men in overalls. "I thought I'd take the time to come watch Justin play basketball."

"That was a long drive for a basketball game," Ronnie said politely, steadying her voice, trying not to seem surprised by his presence in her little world. She sat still, trying to look comfortable, aware of the many eyes directed at them.

"And of course, I really wanted to see you and talk to you again." He leaned into her, speaking softly as if he were visiting with an old friend. "It seems my phone calls aren't going through. I hope you've given the bank's offer some serious consideration."

Ronnie sat up straighter. She felt as if walls were closing in on her. It was an emotion she'd lived with since her teenage years. Someone always pushing her into a corner. There was a pounding in her head. Was Donigan the devil, offering money, prestige, and celebrity for her son? Or was he simply a sophisticated, handsome man offering the things any grown woman would want? If he was the devil, it would be easy to fall under his spell. But a little voice inside her was saying, *no, no, no … leave me alone. I can't do this.*

Her eyes scanned the crowd. They were watching, like this was the newest carnival attraction. They were waiting to see if she'd grab the prize. She ignored Donigan for a moment and saw Brock standing with his team. He was staring at them, looking calm. But it seemed there was the slightest movement of his head … just an inch or two, side to side. "No," he seemed to say. But was it "No, don't do this" or "No, I don't care"? Or was the movement just her imagined desire for him to stand up and shout across the floor, "No, Ronnie! That isn't for you. I'm for you."

She turned back to Donigan. "I'm sorry, Roland. I don't think I'm ready to make a decision like that. And certainly not tonight. You'll have to give me more time. I'm still dealing with Cort's death. And I'm not going to disrupt Justin's life right now. This is a decision he'll help me make." She looked down at her handsome son, innocently running onto the court to begin the game. "If you need to move on and make a decision right away without me, I can understand."

Donigan slumped back in his seat, laughing. "All right. You are a stubborn woman, hard to convince. We'll give it more time. In the future perhaps. But I hope you won't mind if I sit here with you and watch Justin play. You know I've heard good things about him. And I really want to see him have more opportunities to show his skills on a bigger stage."

Across the floor, Brock watched the pair. In the past, he'd been aware of men flirting with his wife, Celia, both when they were dating in college and later in their marriage. It was an annoyance, but until she had run off with Jovan, the creepy little sculptor with his shaggy haircut and sophisticated charm, famous for his artistic talents and high-priced creations, he'd never felt threatened. Now, watching Donigan with Ronnie made him unexpectedly angry and jealous. The towel in his hands was being squeezed tight.

Still, at this moment, he was helping lead a basketball team. As the boys gathered around the coaches, Buster McHue spoke first. "Okay, fellas, you know the drill. Without Cole, we'll run the offense through Justin. He'll have the hot hand. Luke, you battle those boards. Don't let anything get inside you. If you do that, we can make short work of these guys."

Brock clapped his hands, straining to focus his attention on the team and away from his personal life. He joined in on the team cheer as they broke the huddle, and without thinking blurted out, "And play like your future depends on it." The boys cocked their heads and stared at Brock, bewildered by the seriousness of the command. McHue's reaction was silence and a furrowed brow, wondering what he'd missed.

As the coaches watched the game unfold, things were different from earlier contests. Without Cole, the ball movement was better; players were sharing the ball until someone found an open shot. If it didn't find the mark, Luke would chase down the rebound, careful not to run over an opponent in his reckless determination to secure the ball.

Brock saw it. Without Cole, Luke's angry intensity was gone, and he was avoiding foul trouble.

The team missed Cole's high-percentage shooting, but was now less reliant on a single player. Justin stepped up to fill the void, knocking down mid-range jump shots and driving to the hoop, where he'd feather in a finger roll for a score. "This is the best he's played all season," McHue said.

Brock was pleased with what was happening on the floor. As an assistant, it wasn't his job to develop strategy or set the tempo of the game. And he wasn't a basketball technician. But he was a team builder, and, without Cole, it seemed the boys had found a new togetherness. If, when he returned, he could get him to play unselfishly like the team was doing here, the Grizzlies would be hard to stop. There wasn't much time left in the season, but there was still a chance.

As the game wore on, Brock again let his eyes stray across the floor to watch another man cozy up to Ronnie Jepson. He had no claim on her. He was still a married man. But he was disturbed by this man's sudden appearance and his obvious interest in Ronnie. Roland Donigan wasn't a sculptor. And he didn't live in New York City. But the situation seemed to replicate what had happened only months before when he'd watched his wife, Celia, stray from him for a more sophisticated man. His marriage had been destroyed and he agonized over the loss. For months, he'd wake in the night drenched in sweat from wrestling with his failure.

For the next hour, the boys ran up and down the court with renewed energy and the Grizzlies put a victory in the win column. Despite the team's jubilation, Brock's heart was in a slow burn. As the players walked off the court with their heads high, he followed them toward the locker room. Halfway there, he turned to look at Ronnie and Roland. They stood laughing and smiling. Roland bent down and hugged her. Brock didn't see Ronnie's response as he stepped into the locker room and steadied himself for the talk Buster would give the team. It wouldn't be inspirational. But he'd keep quiet.

Brock knew he didn't know enough about basketball to be a varsity coach, but somehow, he wished he could lead this team … to fix what had been missing. And right now, he wanted to fix his life. He didn't like competing for love, but if he had to, he'd fight for it. In basketball or romance, he didn't want to lose again.

Donigan left Glory Grove after the game and settled in for the long drive home. He wanted to spend more time with Ronnie and the few hours at the game had his male desires ramped up to a high level again. But he'd learned his lesson from the mistakes he'd made on their evening in the hotel. He couldn't rush things but was still determined to win her over for the bank and himself. And after he'd seen Justin play basketball, he was convinced the boy was the kind of athlete who'd give his own son's team a chance at winning a league championship in football.

This wasn't football, but the skills Justin exhibited on the basketball court would translate over to the football field. He was quick on his feet and had soft hands when handling the ball. It was also clear the team looked to him for his leadership. He wondered why Justin hadn't scored more in earlier games, but he guessed it was because of the little sophomore guard he'd read about, who was now oddly absent from the team.

Donigan pondered his strategy as he sped through the occasional flurry of snowflakes that drifted down onto the freeway. As he traveled north, he set the cruise control on his Jaguar to a steady seventy mph. He wouldn't hurry. It would give him time to think. He kept the satellite radio off to concentrate on the challenge he faced. How could he pressure Ronnie without scaring her away, to convince her to agree to his proposal? A hard sell wouldn't work. He'd made the mistake of coming on too strong with Ronnie at the hotel. He'd let his desires overwhelm his good judgment. He regretted it. But he wasn't going to give up.

*Perhaps it would be better to communicate directly with Justin himself. Then Justin might convince his mom.* He laughed as he felt his head nodding slowly in the affirmative. He loved it when he solved a simple problem. *Damn, I'm good*, he thought.

As he sped through the evening shadows, he schemed. Glory Grove would play a few basketball games close to his home. He would make sure to be in attendance at a few of those games. If he could get in Justin's ear, he might persuade him to consider the opportunities that would come from attending a larger high school and playing football for a team at a higher level.

Donigan tripped off the cruise control as traffic slowed on the outskirts of Spokane. He finished his thoughts. His strategy seemed especially plausible after watching the basketball team play. Justin's talents were going to waste playing with the boys from Glory Grove. *All I have to do is convince Justin … and Ronnie will come with him.*

# CHAPTER 20

# BUMPKINS

A FRIDAY NIGHT GAME was scheduled with the Coolidge Cadets, a private inner-city institution. It served as an alternative for students in trouble with the law and heading to juvenile detention. If a student behaved for a specific period of time, they were allowed to return to their communities and their record was wiped clean. The boys from the Grove knew about the school and realized this wasn't a normal athletic contest. The game was held in an old armory ... no bleachers, no fans, and no cheerleaders or band. The building was like the lives of the students ... cold and depressing.

The parents who were allowed in were seated in steel folding chairs circling the gym floor with their backs against a brick wall. The game was a form of street ball, similar to an intramural contest, except the results mattered in the rankings kept by the high school establishment officials.

As the boys began their warm-ups, Jimmy Ivory looked over at their players, a mix of ethnicities, some Black like him. *That could have been me if Coach Brock had left me in Seattle.* He knew of boys from his old Hill district in Seattle who had been sent to similar facilities. Some returned to lead a normal life, but others graduated to adult penal institutions when they couldn't adhere to strict rules.

When the teams gathered around the center circle for the opening tip, Jimmy stood next to one of the Black athletes from Coolidge. "Bruh, you look like a raisin in a rice bowl," the player smirked as he stretched his legs, his body swinging from side to side. "How'd ya' end up with them bumpkins?" He gestured over at Jimmy's teammates.

"Didn't want to end up here, like you," Jimmy said.

"Damn, that's nasty." The boy bristled.

"No disrespect, cuz," Jimmy said. "It's a long story. But it's sic. These are good dudes."

"Whatever. We'll see if they can ball. Wanna bet?"

"Nope. Saving my Benjamins. Gonna buy a cow so I can fit in at the Grove." He laughed at his own joke and watched the Coolidge player mumble to himself as he walked away. But somewhere in his consciousness, he wondered if he meant it. He'd been watching the cows every night and had developed a fondness for the animals that surrounded him as he and Sassy made their rounds.

Jimmy was glad when the referee blew his whistle. He relaxed. The sound echoed off the empty gym walls and ended the tension he was feeling. He wasn't sure how friendly the conversation had been or if it was leading somewhere he didn't want to go. But he soon forgot what had been said. Except for the idea of buying a cow. That thought lingered.

Play on the court was fast and the boys from Coolidge were relentless. Coach McHue's slow-down offense couldn't keep pace with the run-and-gun action of the streetball players from the academy. Even the constant encouragement from Brock Gallagher didn't seem to right the ship. Having Cole on the floor might have made the score closer, but even that wasn't a sure thing. When the game ended, the Grizzlies quickly retreated to their cramped locker room and changed clothes. They were a quiet, subdued busload of teenagers as they moved away from the city. The whole experience had a depressing effect … strangely unreal.

"I'm glad that's over," Luke said, as he crammed his body into the hardbacked bus seat next to Jimmy. "I don't know whether to feel sorry for those guys or just happy I'm not one of them."

"You'd be right either way," Jimmy said. The bus lurched forward out of the parking lot. "Let's breathe easy. We're heading back to the Grove."

When Jimmy and Brock arrived back at the farm, they noticed lights on in the barn. As the car came to a stop, Richard came around the corner of the loft, carrying a spotlight. He walked straight to them. When Brock rolled down his window, cold air came rushing in. "Problems?" Brock asked.

"Yeah, I've got a very uncooperative cow in the corral. She needs help and I can't get her into the barn. Glad you two showed up in time."

"Okay, let us throw on some work clothes."

Once they were dressed, they hurried to the corral, dodging frozen puddles. With their flashlights, they found Richard standing over the cow in the far corner of the enclosure. He waved them over. "Let's get her up and into the barn where we'll have more light to work with. We're going to have to pull this calf. She's had feet and a nose out and has been laboring for over an hour."

Jimmy followed the men into the pen and the three of them rocked the cow into an upright position. They forced her to her feet and as she wobbled forward, they guided her through the entrance of the building. "Let me get a rope around her head," Richard said, "so we can get her into a stanchion."

Richard's toss found the mark, but the old cow was agitated, her heavy breathing funneling cold vapor into the air … dragon-like. She wanted no part of being in the enclosed space. She spun around, shot forward, and headed back towards the barn door. Brock and Jimmy blocked her path. She barreled through them, like they weren't there, knocking Jimmy to the ground, her hoof crushing his thigh as she stomped out the door.

Jimmy let out a groan. "Holy crap," he moaned. "Damn, that hurt."

"Is anything broken?" Brock asked, rushing over to check on him.

"I don't think so," Jimmy said through clenched teeth. "Help me up."

He stood gingerly and hopped on his good leg, wishing the pain away. Finally, he put some weight on the leg and breathed. "I'm okay." But his voice hinted otherwise.

While they stood recovering from the collision, Richard retrieved the end of the rope and began snugging the angry bovine to a corral post. With Brock's help and Jimmy's assistance holding the spotlight, the two men got chains on the calf's feet and made quick work of finishing the delivery. The little heifer calf gulped for air as soon as it hit the frozen ground. Brock bent down to pick it up. He cradled it in his arms and headed into the house to warm it.

"Jimmy, I'm going to turn this crazy mother loose, so you'd better hobble on out of here before she stomps on your other leg," Richard said.

Jimmy spun around. He didn't need to be told twice. He limped along after Brock, testing his leg as he went, hoping it wasn't a serious injury. The team had a game scheduled with the Ralston Raiders on the road the next day. It was important for the team. How effective could he be with a cow-stomped leg? And the thought he'd carried for the last few hours about buying a cow hadn't left him. This incident hadn't discouraged him. He would just make sure that when he bought his cow, she was a bit more docile.

# CHAPTER 21

# QUESTIONS

**FRIGID TEMPERATURES SETTLED** on the valley along Cold Creek. When Brock's alarm clock radio pulled him from his bed Saturday morning, the weather report wasn't good. An arctic outbreak with high winds was predicted to seep into their part of the state. Sub-freezing temperatures on winter wheat with no snow cover could damage the crop. It was a simple formula; fewer bushels equal less income. Brock recognized the irony. Money generated from these high winds could reduce those worries.

Brock had been so busy with teaching and working with the basketball team, he hadn't taken time for himself … to sit and think. So before the team headed west to take on Ralston, he drove out to Piney Ridge and parked where he could look out over the rangeland they owned. The landscape spread out before him. With the clear morning skies, he could see for miles. In the distance, smoke rose from the chimneys of neighboring farmhouses.

Brock bristled at the idea of wind towers ruining the view. Why did this area have to live in the shadow of a wind farm built to provide heat to thousands of city dwellers living miles from Glory Grove? He tried to put it out of his mind. He just wanted to relax and remember why he'd found himself here. He'd only been back in Glory Grove for eight months, but the changes in his life had been significant. As he sat with the engine idling and his windows cracked open to breathe in the scented air from the surrounding fir trees, he enjoyed the warmth of the old pickup's heater blowing at his feet.

The peace he sought … to find happiness on the farm with the people of the Grove, away from the trappings and hubris of his former life as a celebrity coach … seemed simple enough: live on the farm without the distractions and drama. Yet it was getting harder to realize. The wind company had created disharmony among neighbors. His new job as a teacher and coach had him dealing with teenage life-and-death dramas. And even Ronnie was weighing the opportunities she'd been offered and might leave.

He sat still, taking in the scenery, but his mind wasn't at peace. The moment of solitude was interrupted by the memory of his wife Celia. He studied his wedding band, rotating it on his finger. Only a month had passed since his aborted trip to Seattle. It was her letter asking for independence that convinced him, at a critical juncture in his life, to turn around and return to the farm. It left him with nagging feelings of failure.

It was the one thing he couldn't ignore. He needed to talk to Celia. He reached for his phone. From this vantage point on the ridge, he had good reception. He dialed his wife's number. It rang once.

"Hello, Brock."

It was good to hear her familiar voice. She'd been part of his life for seventeen years and seldom had they had a harsh word … until her adventure into drug use.

"It's nice you called," she said.

Her tone was sober and sweet at the same time. He always loved that about her. The memory filled him with sadness and starting a conversation was awkward. "How are you?" was the best he could do. Three words that masked what it would take to express how he was feeling.

"I'm okay."

"Do you have time to talk?"

"Sure, I'm at the gallery, but it's quiet this morning. I can talk as long as you want." Brock could hear her shuffling papers as if she was settling in at her desk. "Is life good back in the Grove?"

"I'm staying busy. I'm working at the school now. And there's always a lot to do on the farm."

"Good for you, and how's your mom?"

"She's hanging in there and has good days and bad. She gets pretty weak and tired but still has a positive attitude."

"Bless her. Tell her hello from me. I miss her." She paused and lowered her voice. "And I'm sorry things fell apart like they did. She was always very kind to me."

"I reassured her our problems had nothing to do with her … or me coming back to the farm," Brock said. "She would have done anything to keep our marriage from falling apart."

"But I think you and I always knew it might end up like this," Celia said. "We just didn't have enough in common and needed to go our separate ways. You belong over there. That's where you're happy. And I belong here. Sometimes things happen for a reason, don't you think?" There was a short silence. "You are happy over there, aren't you?"

"I am," Brock said. He was, and he was happy to admit it but was reluctant to list the reasons why life was more difficult than he'd hoped. So, he pivoted. "Are you? I have to ask about the drug problem. Are you able to handle it alone?"

"I'm fine. I know you think I should have stayed in rehab longer, but I learned a valuable lesson in the short time I was there … that you must take one day at a time. That's what I'm doing. I work on it every day and I haven't had any setbacks. I just stay really busy working, and I don't hang around anyone or anything that might tempt me."

"Good for you. I'm proud of you." He was relieved at her answer and relaxed, knowing they could have a cordial discussion after their breakup. But now he hesitated to ask the question he was struggling with. A question he'd never thought he'd ask. But things needed to be resolved. Their bank accounts were still together, and their house in the city was in both of their names. If they weren't together, why were they married?

He closed his eyes and no longer saw the countryside in front of him, just the vision of his beautiful wife as she looked when they were happy newlyweds. He forced his voice to ask the question that needed to be answered. In a measured tone, he said, "Celia, you asked to be alone, and I respect that, but we need to settle some things. I guess what I'm asking is where do we go from here? … Should we make it official and get a divorce? I think it's time."

Brock returned to the farm after his conversation with Celia. It had been a morning to reflect and resolve issues. But the day didn't allow for long periods of solitude. The basketball team was heading west to Ralston to take on a league foe, the Raiders. The Grizzlies had defeated their old rival in football a few months earlier and derailed the Raider's usual trip to the playoffs. Brock and McHue warned their boys to be ready for a team seeking revenge.

The game was scheduled as a doubleheader with the girls' varsity playing at 6:00 p.m., followed by the boys' varsity at 7:30. To save money, the two teams traveled together, so the boys were prepared to sit for nearly two hours waiting for their game to begin. Several parents followed the team, expecting fireworks between the two rivals.

Roland Donigan circled this game on his calendar and made the short drive from his home in Spokane. He wanted to visit with Justin alone to start filling his head with the notion of playing football for his son's team.

Back in Glory Grove, Ronnie had been asked to stay late at the bank. It was an unusual thing for her boss to ask, and she didn't quite understand why he'd made the request. But she agreed, although she was disappointed to miss the game. She loved watching her son play and enjoyed time with Brock when he wasn't on the bench with the team.

When the Grizzlies' bus pulled into the school parking lot and the players unloaded, a few of the car-crazy teenagers noticed a cranberry-colored Jaguar, with its engine running, sitting away from the other cars in the parking lot. It stood out as if a spotlight was shining on it, glistening in the overhead streetlights. When the boys stepped outside the bus, they could hear its motor. It made a soft purring sound. A man in a leather jacket sat behind the wheel, reading his phone.

"Wow. Someday I'm gonna have a ride like that," Luke said to the handful of boys who were studying the vehicle.

"Sure, and I'm gonna walk on Mars," Jimmy said. "Unless you're going to rob a bank, I'd lower my expectations." He limped along beside his friend, still sore from his collision with the cow.

"Geez, Ivory, cut me some slack. But you're right. I'd make a piss poor bank robber. They'd pick me out of a lineup for sure."

Luke followed his teammates, who had turned and were slowly strolling to the gym entrance. They were a few yards behind the girls, who hurried into the locker room to dress for the game. When they entered the facility, the boys checked out their surroundings. The gym was even smaller than the one in the Grove. Jimmy scratched his head, "I don't get it. Their football field is like a college field but look at this rinky-dinky basketball court."

"Must have spent all their money on football," Luke said. "They do get jacked about football. Let's hope their basketball team isn't any better than this old gym."

Justin chuckled at his friends. They were new to the school's basketball facilities so had mistakenly jumped to conclusions. He interrupted. "Sorry to spoil your fantasies, guys, but this is their practice gym. The game court is over there."

He led them through the double doors and as they stepped inside, they took a deep breath. A college-sized court was sandwiched between school-colored bleachers on either side. Championship banners hung from the end walls. Luke and Jimmy began counting the number of football league championships the team had won. Of course, plainly absent was one from the previous year when the Grizzlies pulled an upset and defeated the Raiders on Ralston's home field.

"I'm getting why they took it so hard," Jimmy muttered. His mind filled with the importance of the Grizzlies' gridiron victory in November. "They probably don't like us very much, do they?" He threw back his head and grinned up at the banners. "Let's add to their misery."

"You'd better strap on your superpowers then," Luke said, laughing. "They'll remember you for sure."

The man in the leather jacket had watched the high school kids get out of the bus and drift into the Ralston High School gym. He had his eyes on their leader, Justin Jepson. Even amongst his peers, Justin stood out as an athlete. It was still early in the evening, and he planned to wait a few minutes until some of the crowd arrived so he wouldn't be too obvious. While he waited, he scribbled notes … bullet points he'd casually use in his conversation with Justin. It was in his nature as a banker to have the details all planned out in advance. But first, he would need to find a way to get Justin away from his teammates so they could visit quietly.

Donigan also noticed the boys' coaches as they got out of the bus. He didn't know the head coach, but he remembered Brock Gallagher from the short introduction they'd had when Ronnie first visited the bank. *Big fellow*, Donigan thought. *Football coach type, probably more brawn than brains. Shouldn't be a problem.*

When the time came, Donigan slipped on his leather gloves and slid out of the auto into the chilly late January evening. He raised the collar on his leather jacket and followed some of the early arriving fans making their way into the gym to watch the girls' contest. He had a momentary twinge of guilt, knowing he was missing his own daughter's game while on this mission. But this was more important to his other child, his boy who needed a better quarterback on his football team. He'd make it up to his daughter later.

Inside the building, he spotted the Grizzly boys grouped together on the far side of the gym, their legs stretched out, relaxing like they were at a summer picnic. A few were lying prone on the bleachers, their eyes closed. He made his way to them and climbed up to where Justin was sitting. Some of the players recognized him as the man in the Jaguar.

Donigan stepped in front of Justin and extended his hand. "Justin, my name is Roland Donigan," he said. "I'm a friend of your mother's. Wondered if I could have a few words with you?"

All the boys turned their heads and stared, wondering what was happening. The fellow looked like a very important person. Maybe a college recruiter … they knew it might happen.

"Sure," Justin said. "Is there a problem?"

"No, not at all. I just wanted to get to know you. Your mom has told me a lot about you. And I wanted to meet you in person. Do you think we could talk privately?"

Justin was impressed by the man's well-kept appearance and polite demeanor. "Sure, we can move away from these jocks if you want. We have time before we start dressing for our game."

They moved to the other end of the bleachers, sitting beside each other. Donigan handed Justin his business card—stiff cardboard edged in gold trim and with raised gold letters—the special cursive lettering indicated he was president of Ronnie's bank.

Donigan got right to the point. "I know your mother from her work at the bank in Glory Grove. We have been discussing an advancement in her career. And I thought I'd see what you thought about the idea. I know you lost your father in an accident last fall. I'm terribly sorry for your loss. But I think the bank can make your mom's life, and yours, a great deal better." He paused, not wanting to overwhelm the young man with too much information too quickly.

Justin sat in stunned silence. He didn't know any of this. Donigan explained the offer he'd made to Ronnie … a salary increase and a chance to manage her own branch of the bank. "This is the opportunity of a lifetime," Donigan said, looking right into Justin's eyes. "But I know it affects you as well."

The banker turned on his charm. Now, it was about Justin. He explained. "If you and your mom make the move, I could get you into St. Peter's High School. You'd be playing sports at the highest level in the state. And you would have the chance to show your athletic skills by leading a team full of first-class athletes. A lot of those kids will end up playing at the next level. I know you have friends in Glory Grove, but you can do so much more at a higher level of competition. There will be college scouts watching games." Donigan dropped his voice to express his sincerity. "My own son would be on your team, and he'd love to play with someone of your talent."

Justin was caught off guard. He wasn't aware of the offer his mother had received from the bank. He knew she had gone to the bank head-quarters a couple of times, but assumed it was just some sort of training. The news hit him like a slap to the face. He'd adjusted to life without his father. He missed him, but didn't miss the chaos that came with Cort's angry outbursts, especially when he'd been drinking. The times before his auto accident had been the worst, when his dad had physically abused Ronnie, acting out his resentment towards Brock Gallagher.

Recently, Justin's life had returned to a more normal pace with just him and his mom living alone. This sudden revelation from Roland Donigan made his mind spin. He stood and shook his hand and thanked him politely for the information. "I should get back with my team," Justin said. "We need to get ready for the game." He made his way down the bleachers and didn't look back. He wasn't going to listen any more without first talking with his mother.

When the game began, Brock and Coach McHue noticed how distant Justin seemed when he was on the floor. He played with angry determination and scored enough points to impress even a casual observer, but his spirit and enthusiasm were strangely missing. Brock had spotted Donigan in the crowd and had seen him talking with Justin. Did his presence bring about the change in Justin's attitude? His suspicion of the man was heightened. *This guy's up to no good,* Brock thought.

When Justin returned home from the game with Ralston, Ronnie was anxious to hear all about it. She'd waited up but had fallen asleep in the recliner. It was almost midnight when Justin came in the door. "So, how'd it go?" Ronnie said, clearing her head from sleep as she threw the blanket off her lap.

"It was okay, Mom," Justin said. "We won." There was none of the spirit Justin usually exhibited after a victory.

"That's it? I need more details." She rotated forward in the chair.

"Well, we won by eight. Jimmy was kind of hobbled by his sore leg, but I scored twenty-two points. The coaches were happy."

"You don't seem too excited about it. Something wrong?"

"I guess not. But I met a man." He handed her a business card. "He talked to me."

Ronnie's eyes scanned the thick paper with fancy print. She blanched. *Damn you, Roland Donigan.* She'd kept the bank's offer to herself until she could sort out all the "what-ifs" and "now whats?" "I'm sorry," she said. "I didn't want you worrying about something until I knew what I thought myself."

Justin tossed his gym bag on the sofa and flopped down next to it. He laid his head on the backrest and exhaled. He was tired from the game and the bus ride, and agitated from the encounter with the banker. "He kind of caught me off guard. Took my mind off the game a little."

"What did he say?"

"Oh, just that the bank had made you an offer and how it would be good for you to take it and good for me to play ball with a different team from a bigger school."

"I should have told you right away, but he shouldn't have talked to you. It's a decision we will make together."

"He said I shouldn't hold you back."

Ronnie tightened her jaw. "That was out of line, Justin."

"Doesn't matter. If it's true, I don't want to stop you from something bigger, if that's what you want."

Ronnie's eyes were wide open now. The last thing she wanted was for Justin to feel any pressure. He was her number one priority. He'd lost his father in an accident, and he'd shouldered the burden of caring for her during the aftermath. She realized the sudden news and pressure applied by Roland Donigan had soured his usual rosy mood. Justin was most happy when he was playing ball. Hearing him say the team had won and he'd been the high scorer, yet seeing that he didn't seem happy, hurt.

*I should have been there to shield Justin from Donigan*, she thought. She'd experienced his forcefulness at the hotel and was becoming aware of his desire to manipulate every situation. She'd rebuffed him in a kind yet forceful manner. But this was about their future … Justin's future. She could sacrifice if it gave her son a better life. Now Justin would be in on the conversation.

"I should have been at the game," Ronnie said. She looked over apologetically at her big, sensitive son. "I don't know why, but John, at the bank, asked me to stay late. It really wasn't that important. And John seemed nervous about asking me …" She caught herself in mid-sentence, as a suspicion crept into her mind. "Anyway, I'm sorry I wasn't there. I would have asked Mr. Donigan to leave you alone on a game night. And told him that I will be the one to talk to you about any offer he makes. He shouldn't get between us."

"Sure, Mom. It's no big deal." He rocked forward on the couch. "We should get to bed if we're going to church tomorrow, or we'll be sleeping through the sermon."

"Good plan." Ronnie pulled herself out of the chair. "Then we'll pray for a good outcome to this messy business. Let's shut all this out of our minds until later." She took her son's hand and helped him off the couch.

As she settled into her bed, the incident kept swirling in her mind. She'd told Justin to forget about what had happened. But she couldn't. For the next six hours, she tossed and turned. She was mad at Roland Donigan. And she was mad at herself for letting it come to this. Sooner than later, she'd have to make a decision.

# CHAPTER 22

# ATTITUDE

**BROCK WAS FREE SUNDAY** afternoon, so he agreed to meet Tim in town.

"Let's have lunch at The Steak House," Tim said.

Brock changed into some casual clothes after church, headed back into town, and found a spot in a corner booth at the restaurant. At the agreed time, Tim ambled in, nodding to a few of the patrons and giving a hearty greeting to his closer friends. He headed for the booth where Brock sat.

"Take a load off," Brock said, as he folded up the newspaper he'd been reading. He gestured to the cushioned seat across from him.

"You sure you want the company?"

"Only because it's you. I can ignore anything you're going to say." He looked up at his childhood friend. "Why aren't you working?"

"Cause it's Sunday and I work for the government. We get days off, just like you lazy schoolteachers."

"Fair enough. Can I buy you lunch?"

"Can you spare the expense?"

"Just this time. Teachers don't get paid much."

"Didn't take you long to catch onto that party line, did it?" Tim flopped down in the booth as if he'd set the right mood for a deeper conversation.

"Okay, you got me. What did you want to see me about?" Brock asked.

Tim shrugged. "Nothin' really. Just your attitude." His smile turned serious.

"So, I drove all the way back to town just for you to pick a fight?" Brock shook his head. "Things never change, do they? Just like old times. You were always trying to fix my mood."

"Yup. I've always been there to pick you up when you're down." Tim's eyes squinted. "I guess no different than on the football field in high school. I'd rush over to help you up after you'd been blown up by some monster linebacker and your eyeballs were spinning in your head."

"I'll give you that. So, what's wrong with my attitude?"

"Nothing a good talkin' to can't fix. You just seem out of sorts lately. You got constipation, or something more serious?"

"Sure, something like that." Brock sipped his iced tea, looking intently at his friend, appreciating his concern. "I don't know, just kind of stuck in a bad place." Brock massaged his forehead with his fingers. "Can't get over what happened to my marriage."

"Oh, hell, is that all? That wasn't your fault. Celia had something to do with how it ended … running off like that." Tim didn't look up, just picked at a callous on the palm of his hand. "I might be out of line here, but I'll bet you just can't stand the thought of losing."

"So?"

"You know you've always gone sour for a bit after losing. Never got used to it. You know why?" Tim looked across the table. "Cause you almost always win. Hell, when we lost the state championship game our senior year in football, you didn't smile for a month. Mad at Cort Jepson. Mad at the coach. But mostly mad at yourself."

"I think you're exaggerating."

"Nope. And of course, it probably didn't help that the next day we started basketball practice. Didn't have time to grieve over the loss. And I know how much you didn't like hoops."

"And now I'm pretending to be a basketball coach."

"I know. That's kind of iconic isn't it?"

"I think you mean ironic."

"Well, whatever. But you didn't like basketball 'cause you were a piss-poor player. Granted, you always looked good … made the girls swoon, but couldn't make a shot unless you closed your eyes first."

Brock's hands tightened around his glass of tea. "I wasn't that bad. And at least I looked good. That's more than I can say for your sorry ass."

"No, what I think your problem is, is you're too damned determined to win at everything you do." He halted his talking while the thirty-something waitress, a perpetual smile fixed on her face, poured his coffee.

"You gentlemen ready to order?"

"Thanks, Jill." Tim winked up at her. "Just give us a minute."

"Anything for you, honey," she patted his shoulder as she turned away.

"As I was saying, Brock, you always try to win at damned near everything."

"There's nothing wrong with trying to win."

"Sure, but it's not going to happen all the time. Sometimes you win and sometimes you lose. But you, sometimes you just can't let it go. Face it, Brock, you're on the winning side of most things in your life … way more than most people. Maybe you need to work more on dealing with loss."

Brock's gaze lifted to look Tim in the eyes. His chest tightened. "I dealt with the loss of my dad. I handled it didn't I?"

"You sure? I'm not sure you ever did. You just kept on living. Being the man of the house for your mom. Maybe you're still trying to prove yourself to him. Even though he's not here anymore."

Brock looked past Tim through the windows of the café at the eighteen-wheeler, loaded with logs, passing through the little town. He could almost picture his father, strong and determined, at the wheel of their grain truck.

"This is different. My dad didn't leave by choice. Celia did."

"So … your wife sent you a letter saying she wants to separate. You lose … and now you're pissed. But Brock, and don't take offense here, Celia was a prize."

"What?"

"Yeah, I think she was a consolation prize 'cause someone stole Ronnie from you."

"Now you're getting personal."

"Yep. It's called being best friends. And you're going to listen to me. Celia's gone and Ronnie is here. What the hell you thinkin'? Feeling sorry for yourself again."

Brock leaned back, his head against the back of the booth. "You're not helping."

"Brock, I'll bet when the Rams cut you from pro football, you went into a slide, didn't you? You wouldn't answer my calls for a month."

"Maybe I just didn't want to talk about it."

"Yeah, but when the Rams sent you packing, you didn't have many options. Unless you wanted to play in some little rinky-dink arena league. But here you get a second chance … with Ronnie. She's right there waiting for you."

"You think you're pretty smart for an old bull rider with a bad knee. Maybe you should get a couch and get paid for all this psychoanalysis." Brock pushed his iced tea aside.

"Maybe, but I couldn't pronounce that word you just said."

"Okay, that's true. Next option, you could be a bartender, listening to everyone's problems."

"Oh, no. One customer like you is plenty. And me behind a bar in a tavern would be nothin' but trouble."

"True again." Brock crossed his arms and leaned back in the booth. "Okay, this therapy session is over."

Tim pulled the cap off his head and dropped it on the seat next to him. "Your time is up. What are you buying me for lunch?"

# CHAPTER 23

# NEIGHBORS

**ON MONDAY MORNING,** Irene answered the phone while Richard was out feeding cows. Jimmy and Brock had already left for school. The call was from one of the neighbors, Delbert Leachman, asking if he and a few of the other local ranchers might come talk to the family about the proposed wind project. Leachman farmed nearby. He had taken over the farm from his father, moved him to town, and bought out his sister. Local gossip claimed he'd talked her into selling cheap, way below market price.

Irene was surprised he'd called. The man wasn't normally friendly with the Gallagher family. There had been a few disputes with him over recent years, mainly about his cattle appearing on Gallagher's pasture ground. Mostly they were just small things … leaving gates open and ignoring noxious weeds. They never rose to a point of open conflict. Instead, the families developed a silent understanding to stay away from each other and out of each other's business.

"Of course, Del, I'll pass the word along to Brock and Richard," Irene said. "I'm sure they won't object to a meeting. I know this situation has been on our minds lately. We're not exactly sure what we want to do."

"Well, you need to understand that our group has decided we want to sign on to the project and think we need all the neighbors to agree so Wind Driven doesn't back away." Leachman's voice was rough like sandpaper. "We don't want to take any chances on losing this opportunity."

"I see," Irene said. "We'd certainly listen to your point of view, but can't say for sure we're going to agree with you. We're trying to stay open-minded but it's still our decision to make."

"Well, that's what we need to talk about, Irene. There is a lot on the line here so let's get together and talk about it. Maybe some evening we could come over. What would be a good time?"

Irene said they'd be in touch and hung up the phone as she heard Richard coming in the back door for his morning cup of coffee. "Morning, Irene," he said as he settled into his favorite kitchen chair. He noticed the troubled look on her face. "You get a nuisance call from a telemarketer already this morning?"

She poured the steaming black coffee into Richard's "Knock Knock" mug. "No," she said, "it was Del Leachman. Wants to come over and talk about windmills."

"Oh, great. Delbert Leachman." He took off his glasses and wiped the lenses with his handkerchief. "The trouble with Del is he's only friendly when he wants something." He blew hard on the coffee. "What's he got in mind?"

"Didn't really say, other than he wants us all to sign our leases with Wind Driven. Not sure what difference it makes if we don't sign."

"I swear, if that man would just focus on his own business, we'd all be a lot better off. I think I spend more time herding his cows off our property than I do taking care of our own livestock." He paused to sip from his cup. "I think maybe he's gotten himself into some trouble with the bank. If he doesn't have the fanciest pickup in the county, he starts twitching. Living a bit above his means is what I think. And then there are his frequent trips to the casino." Richard laughed. "Speaking from experience, I'm pretty sure that empties your pockets pretty fast."

Irene nodded. "Too bad his wife Cindy left him. She was a nice girl. If she was still around, he'd be a little better off. She just couldn't rein him in."

"Well, I figure this meeting he wants has everything to do with the money Wind Driven is offering. It's got a lot of people talking. Can't say as I blame them. It would help us too, you know."

"I know," Irene said. "But I also know we've never been so desperate for money that we'd sell our soul to the devil. And sometimes I think there is a bit of a devil in what that company is promising. It all sounds too good to be true. That fellow, Tony Marcellus, is a bit too slick for my liking. He seems a bit like an insurance salesman or a used car salesman … no offense to those professions. But he lists all the good things about wind towers without talking about the negatives. And from what I've read, there are negatives to the whole deal."

She began ticking off the list. Dead birds. Roads cutting through pastures and fields. Giant concrete anchors buried deep into the ground. Blades that can't be recycled. Red flashing lights. And the noise. "We'd better think this through before we sign onto something like that."

When Brock arrived home after basketball practice, Irene filled him in about the phone call. "I really don't know that fellow at all," he said to Irene. "Except for what Uncle Richard says. He's none too fond of him. But a meeting with the neighbors isn't a bad idea. Let's see where that takes us."

Two nights later, pickup trucks started arriving in the Gallagher driveway, bringing Leachman and three other ranchers who bordered Piney Ridge. Irene had brewed fresh coffee and had two plates full of cinnamon rolls ready for the guests. She invited the men into their little dining room, and they all gathered around the table. The ranchers removed their hats and offered to remove their boots, as a courtesy to Irene, but she wouldn't think of asking such a thing.

"Well, what's on your mind?" Brock asked after the men had settled in. "I know you want to talk about Wind Driven, but is there something special we should know?"

"I guess I can speak for the group," Leachman said. "Me and the fellows here think this is a golden opportunity that doesn't come along very often. Ranches along this ridge have never been blessed with a lot of income. Now, because of the wind that usually pushes us around, we've got the chance to cash in on something. Kind of like Texans sitting on a pool of oil, but we're sitting in a spot where the wind doesn't stop blowing. Why not take advantage of it?"

The other men in the room nodded their heads.

"I can sure understand your thinking," Brock said. "And none of us would blame you for signing up with Wind Driven. But it's kind of up to each rancher, isn't it?"

"Well, that's the rub." Leachman leaned forward with his elbows on the table. "Your farm is right in the middle of the project the company wants to build. Mr. Marcellus says that unless you sign, the company may decide to look for another location. It seems like, in the eyes of the company, it's an all-or-nothing kind of a deal."

Brock looked around the table at the other ranchers. They were solemn-faced, as if they were participating in an intervention for a relative and they really didn't want to be there. "What about you men?" Brock said. "Is that what you've been hearing?"

Walter Smith spoke first. He was the oldest of the group and had been ranching his whole life. His weathered face was evidence of his decades raising cattle. "I think that's true, Brock, from what we've been told. We're not here to put any pressure on you and your mom and uncle, but it seems like a lot rides on what you decide." He looked over at Irene. "You and I aren't spring chickens anymore, Irene. A little annual income from something as simple as a wind tower could make our retirement a lot more pleasant. I wish it wasn't such a drastic thing, but we're not going to be around that much longer anyway. This would make it easier on these young folks."

Irene leaned back in her chair, studying the faces of her neighbors. She was feeling pressured by the men and didn't like it. *What would my husband do if he were alive?* He would know exactly what to say. But he'd been gone for a long time. Still, she didn't think he'd be persuaded by the arguments the men were making. Max had been an independent thinker and wasn't afraid to go against the crowd if he didn't think it was the right thing to do.

Brock scooted closer to the table and cleared his throat. "What makes you think Wind Driven isn't just getting you to do their dirty work, having you come here to put the pressure on us? Seems a little sketchy to me. If they want our signature, they should come and make the case themselves."

"Even so," Leachman said, "do you want to take a chance on ruining this for the rest of your neighbors?"

"Well, all the neighbors aren't on board, you know that, Del. You heard Harold Olson at the meeting the other night. He, for one, is dead set against it. And I'm sure there are others," Brock said.

"Well, there might be ways to bring him around," Leachman said. "He rents some DNR ground from the state. The government might not like it if they found out he was running more stock on it than allowed. It would only take a complaint or two to start an investigation."

Brock's voice rose with his anger. "You know that isn't true. Are you going to start lying to the authorities to get what you want? Is that the game you're playing, Del?" Brock would have spit in the dirt if he were outside. "That doesn't seem too neighborly to me."

"Sorry you feel that way, Brock. But sometimes you have to get down to business to get what you want," Del said. His fingers drummed on the table, emphasizing his point.

"You got something in mind for us if we don't sign?" Brock asked.

"Can't say. Don't want it to come to that. Just hope you see the wisdom in putting your name down on the lease and we can all get along."

Walter Smith cleared his throat. Everyone turned to him. "You all need to settle down," he said. "We've always all got along, and I think we still can. We'll work something out and still be friends in the long run."

"Let's hope so," Irene said, her voice soft and reassuring. "We've been friends and neighbors too long to be angry at one another."

Her summation seemed to set a marker. The meeting had ended. The men rose from their table and everyone but Del Leachman thanked Irene for the coffee and rolls. They admired her and didn't enjoy the harshness that had bubbled up among them. As they stepped out the door and fixed their hats against the breeze that was blowing, no one looked back. They'd said their piece and didn't plan to bother the Gallaghers again. Everyone except Del Leachman.

# CHAPTER 24

# PAPERS

**CELIA CALLED BROCK.** She reached him just as he was headed for bed on Monday night. "I'd like to drive over … to say goodbye," she said. Her return had another purpose. She was bringing papers for Brock to sign … to end their marriage. Brock agreed to meet with her the following Friday. There would be time before the team left for their game with Cabin Creek.

Brock hadn't seen Celia since he checked her into a rehab facility in November. It was shortly after she left treatment that she wrote to him asking for a separation, hoping for a fresh start. "I could never be happy in Glory Grove," she admitted. Their lives had taken separate paths. She wanted to deal with her situation alone.

When Celia's car pulled into the driveway, Brock steadied himself. This wasn't going to be a pleasant reunion. As he watched her walk up the sidewalk, he remembered what his initial attraction to her had been. She was still beautiful. The disturbing downfall she had taken with her drug use, and the toll it had taken on her body, had clearly been reversed. The color was back in her face. Her blond hair, cropped and blackened during her days of social experimentation, was back to its normal color. Her casual dress showcased a spirit of freedom and happiness. For a moment, he was once again captivated by her appearance.

He took a deep breath as he opened the door. "Hello, Celia," he said. "Come in, please. It's nice to see you. You're looking well."

She acknowledged him with a bob of her head. "Thanks. Good to see you too, but gawd that's a long drive. I'm a little weary. I could use some coffee."

*Still straight to the point*, Brock thought. She always despised the drive from Seattle. He led her into the kitchen, the one room where Celia had been most comfortable on her rare visits to the farm. She settled into a chair and laid a formal-looking envelope in front of Brock.

"This must be what you're here for," Brock said. He looked down at the document before walking over to plug in the coffee maker.

When he returned to the table, she patted his cheek as she had always done each evening when he got home from work at Brighton High School. But now there was little affection in her touch. "There is no hurry. Let's just talk for a while. I see the farm hasn't changed much. Still has the smell of cows and pigs." She cringed. Then, triggered by a more pleasant aroma, she turned toward the oven. "It smells like your mom's been baking."

"That's Mom, trying to make us happy with food. Just for you, she made snickerdoodles."

"Bless her heart, but I'm trying to keep my weight down." Celia's lips puckered in a sad frown. "Is she here?"

"She'll be back soon. She and Jimmy went for a drive."

"Oh, that's sweet. So, is Jimmy adapting to life in farm country?"

Brock answered without pause. "He's part of our family now. He's great to have around and good for my mom."

"How's she doing with her cancer?"

"She takes it a day at a time. She still likes to go on drives, and being with Jimmy lifts her spirits."

"Good for her. And how about you, Brock? Are your spirits good? Everything okay with you?"

"I'm staying busy teaching and helping coach basketball. Basketball … it wasn't a job I really wanted but I like working with kids. And here on the farm, we're almost done with calving season so maybe I'll be getting a little more sleep when winter is over."

"It sounds like a happy life. But I bet you miss the city, don't you?"

"Not really. Too much confusion for a farm boy. But there are problems here in Glory Grove too."

"Yeah, what's this about wind towers? I saw signs when I passed through downtown … like protest signs. Why would anybody be opposed to green energy?"

"It's complicated."

"It brings some money to these little places, doesn't it? I've read some about it. But I suppose you're too stubborn to take the easy money."

"Well, Mom's not too excited about it." Brock stood up to get coffee for the two of them.

"She won't live forever, you know."

Those words weren't what Brock wanted to hear. "She'll be around for a while longer, I hope."

Celia ignored his comment and swerved onto a different train of thought … a memory from their early years. "You know, when I married you, you were heading to the NFL. Those were exciting times, weren't they? I had visions of living in one of those big California mansions. Somehow that didn't work out like I thought."

*Was she kidding or revealing a long-held truth?* He thought back to his rookie year in the pros, and the fancy apartment they lived in. Was his failure to make it big in professional football a secret resentment she'd held during their seventeen years of marriage? Those thoughts raced around in his head. "Sorry it didn't work out. I know Glory Grove isn't like Los Angeles."

Celia forced a smile. "Those days were a lot of fun, even though it didn't last. You tried hard and took a beating. I admire you for it. But now, living out here on this farm, I just think you could do better." She blew on her coffee Brock had poured. "I don't know anything about those windmills, but if it makes your life better, why not take advantage?"

"Our life here is good enough. We get by. I'm not sure living in the middle of a wind farm would make it any better."

"Sure, peaceful and easy in farm country, like you wanted. And you have a family now with your mom and Jimmy and all those Grizzly boys. I know this whole town is like family to you. That's something I was never able to give you, was it?"

Brock stroked his chin. He thought of their failed attempts to start a family. "It's okay, Celia. I'm not blaming you. And you have to know life here is not that easy. There are a lot of challenges that come with living here."

She laughed. "And you were always most happy when you had a challenge. Remember how you struggled at Brighton the first few years? Don't tell me you didn't enjoy that."

Brock thought of their first years in Seattle after he'd been dropped by the NFL. They pinched pennies on his beginning teacher salary, and he worked hard to turn a losing high school football program into a winner. "It wasn't so bad, was it?"

Celia's forehead wrinkled. "It was all right. But can you do it again? Be happy with the challenges in this little town?"

"I'm going to try. But right now, I've got a half dozen things weighing me down."

"So, six times the joy when you get them all solved, right?" She sighed and stared at him over her coffee.

Brock noticed she was still wearing his wedding ring. It put a lump in his throat as he remembered the times in their early marriage when she'd urged him forward and cheered him on when things improved. He loved her for that. "I've missed you, Celia," he said matter-of-factly.

"But you have something better here, don't you?"

Brock could sense her envy. Perhaps because she was still searching for happiness in her own life.

Celia pulled back her hair and wrapped it with a band. "And I'll be happier chasing my dreams too." She wiggled in her chair as she'd always done when excited. "I'm working with some other galleries now. I'll be traveling back to New York soon."

Brock leaned back in his chair. "So, we are just two people heading in opposite directions. But we can still be kind to one another, can't we?"

Celia slid over next to him, grasped his hands, and pulled them up to her face. "I need to leave," she said, humming softly. "Keep me in your prayers. I'm stronger now but I need any help I can get." As she finished her sentence, they heard the rumble of the farm pickup coming up the driveway. She released his hands and leaned back in her chair. She tapped on the envelope with the divorce papers. "This will make it official … formal and all. I'll leave them with you so you can sign them." Her fingers toyed with the document. "And Brock, if you get a pot of wind money, feel free to share." She smiled the "come on" smile that had drawn him in when he first spotted her at a college dance.

"I wouldn't count on that," Brock said.

"Sure, sure." Celia waved her finger. "But I don't want us to fight over anything. It's good we don't have children to worry about. But this is sad, isn't it?"

Brock shook his head to clear any sadness from his mind and leaned forward to lift her chin. "We won't fight. I can promise that." He steadied himself, imagining he was in the final scene of a sad movie. "One kiss for old times' sake?"

He pressed his lips against hers. It had been an evening ritual in their home for years. He expected to have memories come flooding back. They didn't. Instead, there was an empty void. Despite the coffee she'd been drinking, her lips were cold, with the faintest hint of wine and lipstick.

As Celia pulled back, staring into his eyes, she smiled a tiny smile. "So can I count on you if I need help?"

"You know where I'll be."

"I do. In Glory Grove, of course."

The door opened and Irene and Jimmy walked into the kitchen, laughing … happy to see Celia again.


After meeting with Celia, there was little time for Brock to reflect on the enormity of what had just taken place or the implications it had for his future. The Grizzly basketball team was heading into the mountains to play the Cabin Creek Cubs that evening. They needed a win to move their league record to 6–3. A loss would severely hamper their chances of making the district playoffs. Only four of the twelve teams in the league would qualify.

Cabin Creek was a small town that had sprung up at the turn of the century around a lumber mill. The mill shut down when the environmental movement put restrictions on the number of logs taken from the forest. What was left was a remnant of what had been. Not a ghost town, but a place with better memories of their past than hope for their future.

Still, families clung to their roots and found other ways to make a living … guiding hunts or aiding snowmobilers and cross-country skiers. The town was situated in a narrow valley with access to the Blue Mountains. It had always been a place where boys learned to hunt and fish before they ever picked up a basketball.

Their Cubs' typical season in basketball reflected the community's priorities. They had never sent a team to the state tournament and seldom had a winning season. When the Grizzlies drove into town, the Cubs' year was no different. They were sporting a losing record, and the turnout of fans was minuscule. The ones who were there were mostly dressed in camouflage clothing as if they were planning on a winter outing in the woods … which in fact was true, as many were heading out that evening to get an early start to their winter cabins in the forest.

As predicted, it was an easy win for the Grizzlies and a chance to rest the starters. The two- and three-games-a-week schedule had left many drained of energy or suffering from nagging injuries. Jimmy was still limping from the thigh bruise from the cow. But even with tired and injured players, the Grizzly offense worked well. It centered around Luke's inside game. He muscled up shots in close for easy scores. If he missed, he rebounded his own missed shots for second attempts.

The Cubs had no one who could match his strength. "That big boy would make a good logger," one of the Creek fans muttered as they watched him move through the Cub players as if he were a bulldozer working through a forest.

Even Derek Baker, the fifth starter who seldom scored and specialized on defense, knocked down a few shots, as did Les Colquit, who'd been moved up from the junior varsity to fill the spot created by Cole's absence.

The victory sent the Grove fans home happy. Buster McHue was buoyant when he climbed onto the team bus for the return trip. The players grinned at his animated speech, his arms waving in circles as he spoke. It wasn't his usual demeanor. It hinted at what he thought this team might accomplish in their stretch run.

"Okay, men, get to bed early, we have a big game tomorrow. We're on a roll, let's keep it going."

Brock agreed. The team still had a chance to succeed. He was happy for the boys. But as he sat across the aisle from Coach McHue, he couldn't help but think of Celia and of his own failings. He reclined as far as his long legs would let him, leaned his head back on the winter coat he'd wadded up into the shape of a pillow, and closed his eyes. *There will be another game tomorrow*, he thought.

# CHAPTER 25

# FIGURES

**THE DEADLINE FOR THE GALLAGHER FARM** to submit their budget to the bank was February 1. Since the death of her husband, Irene had done the books and had become proficient in balancing their annual budget and monitoring their cash flow. Since her illness had progressed, the preparation of the budget was nowhere near complete. And with the setback in her prognosis, she was scheduled for an early visit to the hospital for a checkup. The budget deadline was only days away and Brock knew without their annual lending limit approved by the bank, the farm would be in trouble. With the increasing cost of all farm inputs—fertilizer, herbicides, and fuel—plus the cost of maintaining the machinery, loans from the bank were necessary.

Brock was a successful coach and a good teacher. But working with numbers was far down on his list of talents. He reached out to Ronnie. "We might be in a little bit of trouble here," he confided to her during one of their frequent phone calls.

"What's the matter?"

"Mom didn't get our budget done and it's due soon."

"Are you asking for help?" She laughed softly. "You realize I'm your banker, right?"

"Yes, and you're a tough one. But do you have any ideas for getting us out of this jam?"

"If I help, your budget will be pushed up to John at the bank, but he's fair. So sure, I can help."

Ronnie agreed to visit the farm on Saturday. She and Brock were both weary from their trip to Cabin Creek, but if they worked quickly, they could finish the paperwork in plenty of time to get to that evening's home game with Liberty. Richard had taken Irene for her doctor's appointment. They planned to stay overnight so Irene wouldn't be exhausted from the travel. Brock would tend to the livestock.

When Ronnie arrived at the farmhouse, the sun was shining and the ground was bare. It was a beautiful late winter day with only a slight breeze. The weather channel had forecasted a cold front with snow moving in … a positive development, since snow would protect the vulnerable young wheat plants. And since the storm wouldn't arrive until Sunday, the school went ahead with their scheduled basketball game.

"Let's take a look at your books," Ronnie said when she stepped into the kitchen.

"Wow, not even a 'Hi, Brock, how're you doing?'" He noticed the tiredness around her eyes. "It's fun being a basketball mom, isn't it? Gotta love those away games."

"Especially on mountain roads in the winter," she said. "But it was a good game. And we all made it home safely. The boys are playing well. Good coaching, I guess." She stepped around the table and gave him a hug. "If we're going to get this paperwork done before the game, we can't get distracted." She playfully put her hand on his chest and pushed him away.

"Okay, Miss Banker, where do we start?"

Ronnie opened the farm ledger and scanned the figures. Irene hadn't learned to use a computer spreadsheet. But on quick examination, Ronnie found she had all the numbers entered perfectly in easily read handwriting.

"This won't be too hard," she said. "We just have to move last year's expenses into a realistic forecast of next year's income and expenses. You can help with that, can't you?"

"I can try, but I'll be doing a lot of guessing."

"And that's all it is, really. It's just a best-guess scenario. A farm business is the hardest to predict, with changing weather and volatile prices, let alone trying to guess how much your machinery repair bill will be."

They pored over the accounts and Brock did the best he could to be of some help to Ronnie. At noon, he stirred in his chair. "My head hurts from all this. Can I fix us some lunch?"

"It's about time you offered." She set her pen down, leaned back in her chair, and pulled the hair back from her eyes.

Brock stepped behind her, put his hands on her shoulders, and massaged her neck. "Thanks for helping. I'm not sure what we're going to do if Mom leaves us. And she will leave us some time, I know."

"You'll figure something out." She rotated her head back and forth, her shoulders arching upwards. She inhaled. "This feels good. No one at the bank does this for me." She shook her head. "But we can't take too long a break, or we'll never get this done." She popped up out of her chair, cleared the papers off the table, and began setting it for lunch.

In the afternoon, the wind picked up. Brock could see the tree limbs outside the kitchen window moving back and forth. "Looks like the weather's changing," he mumbled.

Ronnie didn't respond. She focused on trying to find enough income in the new budget year to match the expenses they'd predicted, and still have enough margin to allow the bank to secure the loan.

"It looks a little tight," she said under her breath. "This is going to take more work than I figured. Let's go over these expenses one more time and see if we can ratchet these down a bit."

Brock stood and walked over to the coffee maker to freshen his coffee. "Now you're making me nervous," he said. "What's happening here?"

"I hate to say it, but losing that truck in harvest last year and the lost crop from the fire set you back a bit. And some extra expenses have come in from Irene's cancer treatment. Insurance covers most of it, but it's never enough."

"What'll we do?"

"This is the hard part of budgeting. We've got to look at every projected expense and see if we can cut out something." She pursed her lips, closed her eyes as if she were looking for an answer, and inhaled deeply. "We'll make it work."

As they labored, looking at every detail, darkness crept over the farm. They were so wrapped up in their exercise they weren't aware the wind had shifted, now coming out of the north. It was only five o'clock, so he and Ronnie still had time to get to the game. But the weatherman had missed the mark. Snow was coming earlier than predicted. Without the sun, they failed to notice it piling up outside their window. First, inches, then half a foot. The gentle breeze that had been blowing all day had shifted into a stronger wind.

The pair were nearly done making changes to the budget and had become drained by the struggle. They were startled when the kitchen phone rang. Ronnie jumped as if it had been an electric shock. She'd been deep in thought, putting the final numbers to paper, making subtle changes to the budget so the farm had enough margin to get the loan approved. It was tight but manageable.

Brock rose from his chair and grabbed the receiver. "Hello."

"Coach, it's Jimmy. They've canceled our game. The other team isn't going to drive down with all the snow and drifting. It's like a blizzard here in town."

Brock glanced out the window and stared at the bare tree limbs whipping against one another like an awkward science fiction sword fight. "Hold on, Jimmy," Brock said. He dropped the phone, walked over, and peered out. "I didn't see this coming," he said, glancing over at Ronnie. He retrieved the phone.

"Jimmy, I think you'd better stay in town tonight. I'm sure Tim's got an extra bed. Looks like nobody is traveling anywhere for a while."

"Got it, Coach. Can you take my turn checking the cows?"

"Of course. No cows look close to calving right away. I've got it covered." He hung the phone back in its cradle.

Brock turned to Ronnie. "You'd better call Justin and tell him you won't be home tonight."

"What?"

"You're spending the night here. You're not driving along that canyon in this kind of storm."

"Are you sure? You didn't plan this did you?" She walked over to the window, laughing softly to herself. "This is like some cheesy plot in a daytime soap opera."

"Hey, sometimes things happen that are out of my control. I could never arrange things this well. You and me all alone together in a farm-house, by the fire in a snowstorm."

"Okay, you're right. You're not that creative … but if you want to follow that script then you'd better stoke the fire. And shouldn't you go check your cows? Now that I've arranged for your budget to balance, I know you can't afford to lose any livestock in a blizzard."

"Well, that kind of throws cold water on the mood, doesn't it? Now you're sounding like the banker everyone complains about."

"You know how we accountant types are. Just the black-and-white facts, sir. But I'm going with you to check the cows. I need to clear my head."

"Okay, better bundle up, it's going to be a bit nippy out there."

They put on their heavy coats and stocking caps, pulled on over-shoes, and wrapped scarves around their necks. They each grabbed a flashlight. When they stepped outside the back door, they were blasted by a swirling wind against their faces. Heavy snow spiraled sideways and danced in front of the light beams.

Ronnie held onto Brock's arm as they stomped through snowdrifts in the pasture. As they trudged along, dark black forms came into view, and eyeballs reflected from the light. After the warning from Ronnie about the loss of any livestock, Brock wanted to make sure they were all okay until morning. He could count the twenty cows left to calve they'd put in the pasture closest to the barn. Their backs were against the wind and snow covered their coats. But they didn't seem panicked by the storm.

"What are we looking for?" Ronnie raised her voice against the wind.

Brock stepped a little closer to Ronnie, so he didn't have to shout. "Just for any signs that one of these old girls wants to deliver a baby tonight. Sometimes when a cow gets stressed by a sudden change in weather, it will force them into early labor. But they all look like they'll be all right for now. Let's get back to the house before we end up stuck in a snowdrift."

He grabbed her by the arm and leaned into the wind. They used the footprints from their travel to make it easier to walk through the deepening snow. When they reached the back porch, they shook the snow from their coats and hung them on hooks to dry.

"Glad you stoked the fire," Ronnie said as she tiptoed to the living room fireplace and sat on the sofa. Her cheeks were pink, and her eyelashes were tipped with ice. "That was rather exhilarating." She rubbed her hands up and down her arms. "Hope those cows stay safe. When will you check them again?"

"I'll go out again at two o'clock in the morning. That's my usual routine." He sat down beside her and put his hands up to the flames to warm them. "Maybe we should talk about tonight. Like who's going to fix dinner, and where you're going to sleep."

Ronnie put her cold hands on his stubbled face. "I'll help fix dinner and I'll sleep right down here by the warm fire. You are still, after all, a married man."

"Right."

They found enough ingredients in the kitchen to put a meal on the table. With the wind still blowing hard, they hurried, fearing the storm might create a power outage. They dined on pork chops, fried potatoes, and corn. She'd also put cheese-covered bread in the oven. As the wind howled and the snow swirled outside, they laughed and chatted as they ate.

"I'd offer wine, but you won't find it in this house. Mom's not too keen on the consumption of alcohol."

*Good thing for me*, Ronnie thought, *it always seems to lead to trouble.* She tipped her water glass as if offering a toast. "Here's to Irene," she said. "Now you won't be getting inebriated when you have cows to look after. You have to go back out there in a few hours. I don't want you staggering through the cowherd in the dark." She glanced toward the door. "You might get lost, and I want you to come back. Someone needs to stoke the fire."

"Funny," he said. He crumpled up his napkin and threw it at her.

After they finished dinner and cleaned the dishes, they moved back into the living room. Ronnie asked about the family photos on the wall. She'd been to the home when she was a teenager but hadn't been observant at that age … more worried about making a good impression on Brock. Now she wanted to know more about the family.

Brock talked about his forebearer's immigration to the area. How they had staked a claim to the land they were on and the struggles they'd gone through to keep it in the family. His father was the fourth generation, now he was the fifth. The financial gymnastics they'd spent the day working on was just the most recent attempt to keep the farm going.

Brock loved talking about his family. But he suddenly got serious. He was grateful for Ronnie's help. "Thank you for coming out today. I'm not sure how I could have got this budget done without you."

She turned away from the fire and looked into his eyes. "Glad to offer my talents. It's what I do every day at the bank. It's just more personal in your case." She patted his hand, smiled, and then admitted to her sudden exhaustion. She'd had a busy couple of days. "I really need some sleep. So do you if you get up again at two o'clock. But I need to get out of these cold clothes. Does your mom have a nightgown I can borrow?

Brock laughed at the image. "Uh, I'm not sure you'd fit in one of Mom's nightshirts. But let me find you something."

He returned after a few minutes of searching with a silly smile on his face. "How would this work?" he asked and held up a practice jersey from his days on the university football team. "Might be a bit roomy but I think it'll look good on you."

She laughed and blushed. "Does this mean I made the team?"

"Well, after all the work you did today, I think at least you've got the coach's attention."

Ronnie grabbed the jersey and tiptoed into Irene's bedroom to change, while Brock warmed himself by the fire. When she returned, she did a slow spin in front of him. He had to catch his breath before he could utter his approval. "Umm, I think you've moved up on the player roster," he said. "I'll have this vision in my head for a long time."

He found some blankets and made her a bed on the couch, near enough to the fireplace to keep her warm, even if the power went out. He took her hand and held her close for a time. Together alone, they seemed to be free from life's worries. There was no one needing their attention. No one pulling them away from each other. No one saying, "This isn't right."

Brock released her from the embrace. "Good night, Veronica O'Malley."

She backed over to the couch, lay down, and snuggled into the blankets. She closed her eyes and let out a long happy sigh. "Good night, Coach Gallagher."

He climbed the stairs to his bedroom and undressed, but kept his clothes nearby so he could get up and out quickly to check the cows. He wished she were with him but understood their situation. Life was unsettled and moving awkwardly. There was little heat upstairs and the night was bitter cold, so he added extra blankets, pulled them up close and tight, set his alarm, and fell asleep.

At two o'clock, the shrill, pulsating sound of the alarm lifted him from his slumber, and he dutifully rose from the bed, shivered in the cold while he slipped into his clothes, made his way to the back porch, and bundled up for his trip to the pasture.

The wind had settled some, but snowflakes still danced in front of his flashlight and lashed at his face. The footprints from their earlier walk were already covered, but he knew the route. As he trudged, with his hat pulled down over his ears and the hood on his coat tight around his neck, he found the cows, still huddled where they had been earlier. He paced through them, counting them off to make sure he had checked all twenty.

"Good girls, no emergencies yet," he muttered to the herd, then turned and headed back to the house.

With the wind at his back, it was a quick hike. Once inside, he shed his coat, then tiptoed into the living room and placed a few more logs on the fire, trying not to wake Ronnie. With the heat from the fire, she'd thrown off most of the covers. The light from the fire cast an orange glow on her body and he stood motionless, watching her and listening to her measured breathing. Even as she slept, her beauty made him pause. "Sleep tight, my sweet banker," he whispered, then turned and made his way to the stairway. In the darkness, he headed up to his room.

Near the top step, he suddenly felt her presence moving behind him. He didn't look back, and he didn't say a word, but kept climbing. Silently in the darkened bedroom, he slowly stripped off his heavy clothes and crawled into bed. She followed, lay down beside him, pulled herself near, and held him close.

# CHAPTER 26

# ADJUSTMENT

**COLE KNIGHTON RETURNED** to school after his two-week absence. He'd spent a few nights in the hospital after the Brookside game and his aborted suicide attempt. He'd also attended daily sessions with a counselor. Back in the Grove, his mother Goldie devoted her time to making sure her son got the care he needed, driving Cole to appointments, and sitting in when the counselor requested her presence.

It was during those sessions that she realized much of Cole's problem began with her. She'd been a dominant force in his life, while isolating herself and her son from others. She rationalized that her focus on Cole made her a good mother, when in reality, it had led him to be either shy and dismissive of others, or combative and arrogant like her.

*I have to change my ways,* she told herself. It was a hard, bitter pill to swallow, but it was necessary if her son was going to recover fully from his emotional breakdown. She wasn't quite sure what to do or how to do it. But she knew it needed to start with her behavior at basketball games.

Back in school, Cole could hear the whispers as he passed other students in the hallway. His absence had been noticed, and rumors of his actions filtered through the teenagers, although no one knew exactly what had occurred. He'd been told by the counselor to expect the attention but to ignore it and know it would pass with time. "Walk with your head up and with a smile," the woman had told him. "They are teenagers. Their curiosity will soon fade."

He wasn't as concerned with the regular students as he was with the members of the basketball team. There was no one on the team who he could consider a friend. And in reflecting on his actions, it was clear why he'd been disliked by those closest to him on the starting five. He'd blamed the football players, but in discussions with the counselor, she'd made him realize he needed to look to himself to remedy the situation.

Brock called the therapist at the hospital to ask if she thought Cole was ready to return to a normal life and join the basketball team. The woman hesitated, until she remembered it was Brock who'd first brought Cole into the hospital.

"Every case is different," she said in a soft but authoritative voice. "But I think Cole has benefited a lot from our visits. And his mother now seems determined to give him the support he needs."

Brock pressed the phone closer to his ear. "So, is it safe to put him out in front of people again? These high school basketball games come with some intense pressure on a young person."

The therapist didn't hesitate. "Frankly, though one never knows for sure, it might be the best thing for him right now. He needs to get back into a social setting with his friends and teammates. If it was me, I'd put him out there and keep an eye on him. But I think he'll be fine. I know he wants to be back playing basketball again."

Brock thanked the woman. At least now he had something to tell Coach McHue. The coach was anxious to put his best players on the floor. It was the most talented team he'd ever coached, and he didn't want to come up empty again. He could already imagine the naysayers blaming him for messing up a team with so much potential. Going into the playoffs without their best shooter would put the Grizzlies at a disadvantage.

When the two coaches met before practice, they agreed to wait a few days before letting Cole scrimmage with the starters again. They had a week before their final two league games, so they'd know whether Cole was in shape to go full speed.

Coach McHue met with Cole and Goldie the day before Cole returned to school and said they'd let Cole back on the team but thought it best to work the teenager into the rotation slowly. Feelings needed to heal.

Goldie didn't put up the fuss McHue had expected; instead, she nodded politely and said she agreed with the proposal. "We want whatever is best for Cole," she said, purposely adding, "and also what is best for the team."

The coach held back a relieved smile. He was happy with her response and could see things might be headed in the right direction. "Thanks, Goldie," he said. "Brock and I have been worried how this might turn out, but it looks like we're all in agreement. You know how important Cole is to our team." He rubbed his head. "But the health of our players is more important than anything else. Let's go slow and see where it takes us."

Cole didn't dress down when he attended his first practice after the incident. When McHue called the team together, he motioned for Cole to join the circle. The coach kept his remarks brief and to the point. "Fellows, as you can see, Cole has rejoined the team, but he won't be playing for a day or two. He's been working through some issues, so he'll be with us but won't be at full strength."

The team stood motionless, silent, as they avoided eye contact with their former star teammate. Their sneakered feet seemed stuck to the hardwood, as their teenage minds swirled with images of suicide and how Cole's return would affect the team. But their curiosity about Cole's suicide attempt quickly evaporated, as McHue began talking team strategy for the upcoming game with the Dillon Dragons. The boys all knew they would have a better chance to win if Cole could play.

When McHue finished the short announcement and said, "Okay, run some laps to get warm," the boys left the circle with an energized sprint, glad to be away from any serious implications they couldn't really understand.

Yet, there was one player who couldn't let the words escape his mind. *The only issue Cole has*, Luke Palmer thought, *is between his ears*. He wasn't pleased to have the sophomore back on the team. They'd done well enough without him, and he'd been relieved to be rid of his theatrics and selfishness. Now Cole was back.

# CHAPTER 27

# BEAR

**THE GRIZZLY BEAR WAS PEELING.** Brock noticed it again on his snowy commute to school. Flakes of brown paint had fallen onto the snow surrounding the concrete silo on which the bear had been painted. It left the animal looking like he suffered from a deadly rash. Even portions of his face, with the ferocious stare, were missing. *Much less terrifying with only one eye,* Brock thought.

The silo, used for storing grain, rose nearly 150 feet, capped by an American flag perched on top of the headhouse. The bear, painted on its east wall, was the first thing passing motorists saw as they entered the city limits of Glory Grove. Like so many other things in the small farm town, it had faded over time. Since he'd first noticed the bear's deterioration, Brock found his eyes drawn to it each time he drove to town from the farm.

One evening, Brock invited Tim to come out for a meal on the farm. He promised a steak dinner. As Tim was chasing the last few bites of meat around his plate, Brock brought up the subject of the fading bear. "Tim, I think we need to paint the bear."

"Oh, great," Tim muttered, as he threw the last bits of steak into his mouth. "You went and bought a bear, and now you want to paint it?"

"You know what I mean. That elevator bear is looking rather pathetic, don't you think?"

"Yup, and now I know why you invited me to dinner." He kept chewing. "But I gotta agree, that old grizzly has been shedding fur for a lot of years. But you and I aren't painters, are we? And it'll take a barrel of paint to fix him." Tim took a long sip of his coffee…a long slurping sound only he could manage. "But I bet you have a plan, don't you? And it probably involves me repelling off the top of that old grain elevator."

Brock leaned back in his chair. "Tim, I spent my teenage years hanging out with you … and you and I lived to talk about it. Why should you be worried?" Brock glanced over at his mother, who was listening in on the conversation, a knowing smile on her lips. She'd always worried when Brock headed out with his rambunctious friend.

Brock continued. "This isn't about you … but the kids on the basketball team. The one thing those boys are missing is a bonding experience. They aren't playing like a team. And the business with Cole Knighton has them all shook up. We need something to bring them together. I think that old Grizzly bear might be the answer."

Tim twirled his fork like a baton. "Boy, you row with a big oar, don't you? Why not something small like raking leaves for old ladies?"

"Hear me out," Brock leaned back in his chair. "I think this group needs something big. Most of them played in the football champion-ship. They've been on a big stage, so it'll have to be something big to capture their imagination."

Tim set his coffee down and dropped his head as if he were resigning himself to the idea. "Lordy, Brock. Why do you make everything so complicated? Don't you have enough things on your plate?" He shook his head and let out an "I can't believe I'm agreeing to this" laugh. "Okay, I'm in, as long as I don't have to climb on any ladders or swing from a rope. I've always wondered about the view from up there … must be damned spectacular. It might be the one time in my life I'll be able to look down on all the good citizens of this little burg."

Brock was pleased he had at least one person who would agree to the plan. He immediately started listing the steps he'd have to take in order to make it happen. "I'd better talk with Buster. Sometimes he doesn't understand the meaning or the value of team bonding. It'll take some convincing, but it'll be worth the time if we can get this team back on track. And if nothing else, it might make the bear look like he has a little life left in him. It'll send a message to the people in this town—the Grizzlies won't fade away."

They agreed if they could get a green light from Coach McHue, Tim would try to convince the county road department to donate the use of their bucket truck to get up next to the elevator. And finally, they'd ask the boys to knock on a few doors to see if they could get some funding for the paint and supplies.

"How old is that bear painting anyway?" Tim asked. "It was there when we were in high school, I know."

Brock glanced over at his mother, who'd been enjoying listening to the two men as they hatched their plan. She tilted her head back and looked up at the ceiling as if she might find the answer to their question by staring long enough at the painted tiles. Finally, she dropped her shoulders, indicating she knew the answer.

"I know exactly when it was painted and by whom. The painter was a fellow named Peter Martin Green. People here just called him Paint Man Green. Nice man … very creative sort. Handsome too, in his own way, with his painter's hat cocked off to the side and a cigarette in his mouth. He finally ran out of things to paint here in the Grove so moved on to Portland, Oregon … became pretty famous for his artwork. I think that bear was maybe the last thing he painted here in town." She closed her eyes and sighed. "He's gotta be pretty old by now, if he's still alive."

Brock noticed the hint of sadness in his mom's demeanor. He wondered if it was some special memory she'd recalled, or if she was sad because of her own age. "Maybe we should see if he's still around and have him come back to help with the project … give us a guiding hand."

Irene chuckled and her lips turned up in a sweet melancholy smile. "That would add some intrigue to the project," she said. "Most people here wouldn't know who he is, but he'd make an impression, for sure."

Coach McHue, to Brock's amazement, loved the idea. "Whatever it takes to get this group headed in the right direction," he said. "I promise I'll be there to watch, but my feet won't leave the ground."

Tim was successful in getting the equipment needed from the county road department. "Looks like a worthwhile project to me," the head man said. "I'm guessing the top of that bear is almost one hundred feet above the ground. Our truck shouldn't have a problem getting up there. I've been thinking for years we need to get that old bear spruced up a little."

More excited than all the grown-ups were the members of the basketball team. Brock brought it up at practice a few days after he'd cleared the idea with Buster McHue. A few of the players had dreamed of climbing to the top of the elevator and painting their girlfriend's name with a rattle can. But fear of heights coupled with fear of getting caught by the local police had kept it as only a dream.

The group was divided down the middle, between those who couldn't wait to get up in a bucket with a paintbrush and those whose legs turned to rubber just thinking about being so high in the air. There weren't many chances in the town of Glory Grove to rise above the standard one or two-story buildings. Nothing in the town came close to matching the height of the towering grain elevator.

Brock questioned the boys about their wishes to participate and let them know they'd need to get a waiver signed by their parents if they wanted to be among those willing to go airborne to reach the Grizzly. "Okay," he said, scanning the group, "who thinks they want to be among the climbers? And don't be embarrassed if you don't want to go. We're going to need ready hands to do the job supporting the painters."

A few hands shot up immediately. Justin and Luke were the first. Then Les Colquit, the skinny freshman who'd played a major role on the football team. "I'll go, Coach," he said. "But have fun telling my dad." He laughed. It had been a struggle just to get his dad's permission to turn out for football.

"We'll work on it," Brock said, a smile on his lips. "Anyone else? The rest of you will be mixing paint and cleaning up afterwards. This is going to be a total team project."

When given that option, several others raised their hands to become painters. Derek Baker joined in, and so did Jimmy Ivory, along with several of the other varsity players. Every one of the starting five was on board except for Cole Knighton, who had turned thoughtful and reserved after his suicide attempt. Brock was reluctant to put him on the spot after the depression he'd gone through but felt he needed to include him. "What about you, Cole? You want to be part of this?"

"I'm not sure, Coach. I'm not scared of heights, but I don't want to get in the way."

"Don't worry about that. We'll find a way of making sure we all work together."

The boys were excited about the project and word spread throughout the school. Soon principal Colquit called Brock into his office. "Brock, I've heard about your plan and think you should put a stop to it," he said. He leaned forward in his chair and put his hands down on his desk. "Not that I think it's a bad idea, but the school can't expose ourselves to that amount of risk. We'd be liable if anyone got hurt. I'm sorry, but the school can't be involved in anything like that."

Brock anticipated Colquit's stand. "Yessir, I thought you'd say that. So, I'd like this project to be done independently of the school. I'll take full responsibility."

"Are you sure you want to do that … take a bunch of teenage boys up in a bucket truck to the side of an elevator? That's pretty risky."

"We'll make sure they're all supervised, and we'll follow all safety protocol," Brock said. He was used to Colquit's timidity and was ready to reassure him. "We won't take any unnecessary chances. But the boys need something to bring them together. Let us give it a shot."

"Okay," Colquit nodded. "I might be there to watch … unofficially, of course. And very happy to watch from the ground." His lips curled up in a satisfied smile. "And make sure the bear looks good when you're done."

The final step Brock faced was finding the painter who'd done the original work on the bear portrait. Thanks to Irene, he had a name: P.M. Green. She'd said he had moved to Portland, Oregon. Brock offered, as special credit to a bright student in his government class, the challenge of finding Mr. Green.

A few days later, the boy had the printout of an article from a Portland newspaper describing the retirement of their local artist. Soon they had a phone number, and Brock punched in the numbers on his phone. Two rings later, there was an answer.

"Hello, Green here …" The voice on the line was strong but friendly, with the rasp and resonance of a man who'd smoked his whole life. Brock was drawn to it and relaxed with the sound of it.

"Mr. Green, my name is Brock Gallagher and I'm calling from Glory Grove. Do you have time for a chat?"

Green chuckled. "My God … a voice from a splendid little town I can never forget. I have nothing but good memories of that place … and the people. Sometimes I wish I'd never left." He paused. "And your name is Gallagher? Any relation to Max Gallagher, the farmer?"

"Yessir, my father. He died a long time ago in a farm accident, but my mother still runs the farm."

"Irene." There was the sound of Green's breathing in, then a long pause. His voice dropped to a sincere tone. "How is she?"

"She has some health issues, but right now is taking one day at a time and still feisty as ever."

"You might know she and I were pretty close before I left town."

Brock remembered his mother's subtle emotional reaction when talking about Green. He wasn't quite sure how to respond to the painter's revelation, so he pivoted back to the reason for his call. He reminded Green of the bear painting on the elevator and the need for a fresh coat of paint on the old Grizzly.

The painter laughed. "I remember that old bear well. One of the bigger projects I've ever done. Took a lot of brown paint. I was as brown as the bear by the time I was done. It was the last thing I painted in the Grove. That was a long time ago."

Brock got to the point of his call. "I know this is asking a lot, but is there any chance we could convince you to come back to the Grove to guide our little group when we try to freshen up the bear? None of us are professionals and we want to do a good job."

"Man, oh man," Green said, his voice rising with each word.

Brock knew he was asking a lot and was afraid he might have struck out. But Green continued.

"To be honest, I'm retired now and have been looking for something to keep me busy. You bet. I would love to get back and visit the old town. When do you need me?"

So, he and Brock laid out a plan. It was coming together faster than Brock had even imagined. Seemed now the whole community was on board, talking about the project. With the help of the original painter, it would only be days before the first splash of paint was splattered on the Grizzly's massive belly.


When "Paint Man" Green arrived in Glory Grove, Brock was there to meet him. From their first handshake, Brock felt an affinity for the elderly painter. They'd agreed to meet in front of The Steak House during Brock's lunch break on an early afternoon in February. The latest snow was rapidly melting, and a warm blue sky gave evidence the frigid winter was giving up her grip on the valley. Sidewalks in the town were drying and steam rose from the concrete.

When Green's car pulled into a spot behind Brock's car, there was no question in Brock's mind that this was the man he'd been waiting for. He was in a nondescript cargo van, white with a bit of rust on the lower rear panels. On the side, a decal strategically placed below the driver's window simply read, "Paint Man."

Green took no time in shutting down the engine and hopping out of the driver's seat. *Pretty spry for a senior citizen*, Brock thought, as he watched him bounce up to the sidewalk. He stepped toward Green and extended his hand. "Welcome back to the Grove," he said as he grasped the man's calloused hand. "I'm Brock, thanks so much for coming."

Green tipped back his white painter's hat and broke into an infectious grin. "You didn't have to tell me who you were, you look enough like your father to be his twin. And you've got your mother's blue eyes." He breathed in as if inhaling the atmosphere of the location. "It's great to be back in this little town. It hasn't changed much in forty years; The Steak House is still in the same spot." His eyes sparkled with amusement. "And still probably serving up hot beef sandwiches with the best of them."

"That's a fact," Brock said. "Are you hungry? Can I treat you to lunch? You can order one up and see if it still tastes as good as when you left."

"Absolutely. Best idea I've heard all day."

"And we've got room in our house. You're welcome to stay with us."

Green looked pleased but shook his head. "No, I don't want to put you out. I can stay at the motel here in town if they still have one. I've noticed a lot of the stores are out of business here."

"Like all these little towns, I guess," Brock said. "But we do still have a motel. They keep it open and still cater to travelers. I think they are clean and have modernized enough to stay in business."

"Okay. I'll check in there, but I would like to see your mother. She was a good friend to me when I lived here."

"Why don't you come out to the ranch sometime? Do you remember how to get there?"

"Sure, twelve miles out on Sullivan Road and turn in at the silver mailbox." His head bobbed as he recited the directions.

"That's it," Brock said. "So, let's get a bite to eat, and we can talk over the project." They made their way into the old restaurant. A few heads turned, as folks do in a small-town eating establishment. They recognized Brock and nodded to say, "Hello," but there were only curious looks directed at the painter.

The men ordered food and began to talk. "So, tell me about your mom," Green said. "You mentioned she has some health problems."

Brock was willing to share, sensing Green had a genuine concern for his mom. "Mom has a rare form of cancer, which doctors say will take her life soon. But right now, she's feeling good and stays busy on the farm. If you remember my mom, she won't go down without a fight. We're doing all we can to keep her happy while she's going through this."

"Cancer … that's heartbreaking." Green's lips tightened. "That's the one diagnosis no one wants to hear. But I'm not surprised she'll fight it as long as she can. I would expect as much from Irene. She was always full of life. And it seems like she has passed her attitude along to her son." Green glanced up from his sandwich to look at Brock. "But I think you got your looks from your father. How long has he been gone?"

"About twenty years. I was in high school. He died in a farm accident. Mom's been running the farm ever since. She and my Uncle Richard."

"I'm not surprised she could handle it. She was an amazing woman."

Brock noticed when Green talked about his mother, he had a distant look in his eyes. There was something there; he just didn't know what.

# CHAPTER 28

# MISSING

THERE WERE TWO LEAGUE GAMES SCHEDULED to wrap up the regular season. The Grizzlies needed at least one win if they were to make the playoffs. First, they would travel to Dillon for a game with one of the surprise powerhouses of the league. A Cinderella favorite of the media, the Dragons had surprised everyone with their success and were gaining a following from the newspaper writers of the area. The young redheaded center for the Dragons, Brett Talbott, was one of the league's leading scorers. It didn't bode well. In games featuring big post players, Luke was often stymied with foul trouble. Without his presence, the Grizzlies found it hard to keep up with their opponent.

But the team had buried the memory of earlier difficulties and the mood on the Grizzly team bus, as they traveled to Dillon, was jovial. A 12–3 overall season record was the best the team had produced in years. The previous Saturday night game, which had been cancelled due to the sudden blizzard, gave the boys an extra day of rest, so everyone now seemed reenergized.

With a win against either of their final two league foes, the boys from Glory Grove would earn a spot in the district playoffs. Many of the team's fans would make the Friday evening trip to Dillon, so there wouldn't be an emotional letdown from the players. There had been spirited practices leading up to the game. Even Brock, who warned Buster McHue about the strength of the Dragons, was feeling optimistic.

The preceding week, Brock took Cole under his wing. Brock was a football coach and didn't pretend to be a basketball expert, but he recognized the value of team play. As the team scrimmaged, he would subtly point out to Cole how an extra pass would give the team an advantage. "Movement off the ball can create openings," Brock said. "When you're moving, either Jimmy can get the ball to you for a quick shot, or your movement will distract the defense and open things up for Justin or Derrick." Cole kept his eyes on the action and nodded as if he was seeing the game from a different perspective.

Brock didn't stop there. "That doesn't mean you can't score twenty points, but they may come in a different way. Or it might let some of the others add to the score." He glanced over at the boy, knowing when Cole took the floor again in a game, he'd still be looking for a way to score points. That was his role and his focus, and it wasn't a bad thing.

The Dillon gym was the perfect venue for Brett Talbott. It had survived years of use and many years of failed bond attempts to build a new facility. Rickety wooden bleachers rose up from the dark stained hardwood to meet red brick walls. The ceiling seemed especially low and incandescent lighting left visitors feeling a bit dizzy and depressed, as if they were being sequestered in a penal institution. The odor from the aging facility mixed with the sweat of teenage boys added to the sensation.

This was Brock's first visit to the school since he'd played there nearly two decades before as a member of the Grizzly team. But he could remember it well. *I like this old gym*, he thought. *I never tired out here.* The length of the floor from baseline to baseline was the shortest of all the gyms among league schools. It took little effort to travel from one end of the gym to the other, even at a full sprint. It was a big relief to the big men. And it was a decided advantage to the tall, scarecrow-like center for the Dragons. He never had to leave the game to catch his breath.

When the game started, Brock sat next to Cole Knighton. The coaches made the hard decision not to play Cole. It was too soon. But they would keep him involved in the game as they brought him back to full activity. By sitting next to Cole, Brock could continue to help the boy see how certain actions on the floor could lead to better results.

Les Colquit, the skinny freshman, was nervous being a member of the starting five, as he had been used primarily on the junior varsity. But he'd been an important key to the football team's success so was already bonded with the other starters … all football players.

Lester Colquit, the principal, was happy with his namesake's promotion to the varsity. He slipped into a seat close to the bench and listened in on the conversations during the routine time-outs. He could also hear fragments of the conversations between Brock and Cole, discussing game strategy. *Good decision we made to put Brock on the bench with Buster*, he thought. If anyone could turn that kid around it was Brock. Even if it meant putting his own son back on the bench, he wanted the best for the young sophomore who had flirted with suicide.

As the game unfolded, the Grizzly coaches' main concern was keeping Luke out of foul trouble. If he was relegated to the bench again, the Grizzlies' chance of a win would be almost nonexistent. Both teams moved the ball methodically, eschewing any attempt to run a risky fast-break offense. "We can't risk it on this short court," McHue warned. The teams traded baskets throughout the first quarter. The Dragons routinely worked the ball into their big man and Luke's reluctance to collect fouls resulted in easy buckets by the slender giant.

The Grizzlies countered with their outside shooting. With Cole on the bench, it was Jimmy and Justin who found the range and kept the game close. With the success of the Grizzly outside shooters, the Dragons could not risk dropping into a zone defense. So the week of practice was put to good use. Repeatedly, the team ran a ball screen, pick and roll offense. Justin would come up out of the post position and screen Jimmy's man. Jimmy either found a clear lane to the basket or, if the defense followed him, Justin would roll to the basket for a quick pass and easy bucket.

"Good work!" McHue hollered. He was pleased with his game plan. The action on the floor was not frenetic, but methodical and fierce. The fans who had squeezed into the little gym were rubbing against one another like passengers in an overcrowded subway, waiting for the doors to open at the next stop. They were on the edge of their seats, as neither team could pull ahead. The lead seesawed back and forth several times, but as the halftime buzzer sounded, the score was knotted, 24–24.

The crowd let out a collective sigh as the teams headed to the locker room. It was a respite from the noise of the bands and cheerleaders' screaming during the game. The Grizzly coaches followed their players through the dark entrance, with Cole by their side. "What do you think, Brock?" McHue asked. "We've made it to halftime and Luke only has two fouls. That puts us in a pretty good situation."

"We finally tamed him down a little," Brock said, leaning over so

Buster could hear over the noise of the crowd. "Do we turn him loose now or play this out and hope for a close win at the end?"

"I think we keep the reins tight until the fourth quarter and then let him try to put the brakes on Talbott. We'll stay close if the boys keep shooting like they have been, and they don't shut down our pick and roll. Then we can break it open at the end."

Brock turned toward Cole. He studied his face. "Do you have any thoughts? Do you see anything we're missing?"

Cole was caught off guard for a second, then rebounded. "I think they'll try to stop that screen by Justin and start switching on defense. If they do start switching men, that leaves Justin one-on-one with a lot smaller guy. I think he could own that little guy."

Brock grinned. "Nice call. Anything else?"

"Well, maybe it's too much to ask of a freshman, but I've watched Colquit shoot in practice. He's money most of the time. If the defense sags off on him to try and stop Jimmy or Justin, I think he could be a weapon."

Brock looked over at McHue who was listening to the conversation. Their eyes met. *The kid might be right,* they both agreed without saying. Whether they won or lost this game … progress had been made.

As the second half played out, an old habit emerged again. Early in the third quarter, Luke bit on a Talbott pump fake and hammered the tall boy. It was his third foul, and he followed a few minutes later with a reach-in foul, his fourth, trying to poke the ball out of Talbott's hands as he started his post move. Luke's head hung as he trotted slowly to the bench, not even waiting for the coach to make the move.

"Now we're in trouble," McHue said out loud to no one in particular.

And as if he were prophesizing, the team, without Luke, could not keep up with Dillon's inside game. Despite desperate attempts by the remaining members of the team, the Dragons quickly established a lead and would not relinquish it. Forced to take outside shots, none of the remaining Grizzly players could find the target often enough to counteract the points Talbott was flushing through the twine.

"We needed Cole," McHue mumbled, as the clock wound down. "He'd better be ready for our next game." Now the team's fate rested on the results of the final regular season game, and the return of Cole Knighton. It was only a week away.

# CHAPTER 29

# TRUCE

**GOLDIE KNIGHTON WAS DETERMINED** to change her life … to do everything possible to ease the stress on her son. She couldn't take the place of Cole's missing father. But the confrontation in the stands with Peggy Palmer was partly to blame for her son's behavior, despite the bravado he'd shown at the game. Goldie was going to heed the advice of the therapist. *I need to face the situation head-on,* she thought. She'd visit Peggy Palmer. She knew where the Palmers lived and drove to their home one evening while the boys were at practice.

As she climbed out of her car and paced up the crumbling sidewalk in front of the home, her heart pounded like a hammer. She took a deep breath, working up her courage. She no longer felt strong and dominant, ready to be a physical bully. Cole's crisis had taken that out of her. She knocked gently half a dozen times on the weathered wooden door and waited.

When the door flung open, Peggy filled the space, her tousled hair falling on her shoulders, a television remote in her hand. When she saw who had knocked, she stepped back, the color fading from her cheeks as if she expected a punch to the face. "It's you," she stammered. The two words, nearly inaudible, were all she could utter. She grasped the remote as if she were holding a weapon.

"Yes, it's me," Goldie said softly. "Can we talk? I have something I need to say."

Peggy waited for the harangue that was to come. She backed away cautiously.

Goldie tipped her head down slightly and sighed. "You know I've never been very polite to people, but I want to apologize for acting the way I've been at the games." She looked over at Peggy. Goldie's hands were trembling. "And I shouldn't have yelled at your son, Luke. He's a good player."

Peggy stared at the usually brash woman ... confused. *Was this an act?* She relaxed her posture and flipped the remote onto a chair behind her, slightly less worried about a physical confrontation. "And so is Cole," she said softly. "Why isn't he playing? The team needs a scorer." Then she partly answered her own question. "Luke says he has some kind of injury. I hope it's nothing serious."

"That's why I wanted to talk. I need to share with someone." She lowered her voice and glanced around the room, to make sure no one else was there. "I don't have any friends I can talk to. May I come in?"

Peggy had never heard Goldie speak with any voice other than the one at the highest decibel level, berating the referees or coaches ... and sometimes her son. Goldie's voice was now actually soft and pleasant. Calming in fact. But she still wasn't convinced this wasn't a way to get back at her for the confrontation she'd created during the basketball game. She remained wary.

Goldie continued. "I'll tell you about Cole's injury if you promise not to spread it around."

Peggy nodded. "Of course, I don't have a lot of friends in this town either … at least who I can share secrets with. Come in if you don't mind the mess. You know my men, they aren't real tidy."

Goldie stepped through the doorway, moving slowly, and pulled the door closed behind her. She turned back toward Peggy and began to tell her story. "Thanks for listening. First, I want to say right out, Cole will be fine. You might have heard; he thought his father, Clarence, was coming to watch him play against Brookside. He was over the moon thinking his dad might come to watch, even though he can barely remember the man." She gritted her teeth, thinking of her former husband. "I couldn't convince him not to get his hopes up. Then when Clarence didn't show, Cole went into a tailspin."

"There are a lot of rumors," Peggy said.

"I'm sure they are floating around our good town." Goldie closed her eyes for a second, thinking of the dangerous thing Cole had done, flirting with suicide, then continued. "His injury isn't physical. There is nothing wrong with his body." She bit her lip and stared at the floor before saying, "It's emotional. He's fighting through some depression. But the coaches are kind enough to treat it like an injury. They're taking it slow and want to be sure he's okay before they'll put him back on the court."

Peggy saw the tears in Goldie's eyes and recognized the situation for what it was. Goldie didn't have to give a full explanation. It was clear; Cole had fallen into a dark place … similar to a place Peggy herself knew very well. It mirrored her own difficulties, dealing with an emotional crisis. She thought of the recent night in the park with Luke and how close she'd come to heading back down a dark path, one that she knew would eventually kill her. A slower process than what Cole was considering, but still with the same sad ending.

Without thinking, she reached out to the woman who only a few weeks earlier had slapped her in front of the entire crowd of Grizzly fans. She extended her hand. Goldie grasped it and held it tight as she was led into the Palmer's living room.

The final game of the season was a home contest with the Thomasville Titans. Folks in the Grove community were cautiously holding their breath, hoping for the best but anticipating the worst. Basketball in the Grove had never experienced any success to speak of, so Grizzly fans weren't getting their hopes up. At the Cozy Corner, the men found ways to hold back any hopes that the team might finally earn a spot in the district tournament. They could list the excuses and reasons aplenty for failure, preparing for the inevitable collapse of the team.

"Old Buster will find a way to choke this away," Homer Johnson said, holding his coffee, stirring the creamer he'd dumped into the brew. "He's never been to the playoffs so we shouldn't expect it to happen this year."

"Yup, and he's been sitting Knighton on the bench for almost a month, nursing some kind of injury. If that kid doesn't play, there's no way we can beat the Titans. Our boys will start missing shots and throwing the ball away. They'll shrivel up into little blobs of goo, looking to the bench for courage and only finding McHue, sitting there scratching his head."

"I heard Knighton may play again," Homer said, delighted to share some inside information he'd gleaned from his secret sources. "That might give us a fighting chance."

"Sure, until that redhead rattles the rest of the boys with her screaming."

"You're right," Homer said. "Might as well close the door on this season." He dropped his spoon on the table as if surrendering his sword to the enemy's victorious army. "Better break out the bats. Maybe those kids can do better with baseball."

It was unanimous … the Grizzlies' season would be over after one more game. Still, there was a sense of accomplishment that hovered over the table full of pessimists. The boys had put together a winning season. That was reason enough to celebrate with a second cup of coffee.

As the Grizzlies went through their warm-ups for the game against Thomasville, the fans began to arrive. Tim and Peggy Palmer, as was their custom, found their spot in the front row. They settled in and watched as other die-hard basketball devotees made their way past the ticket booth. The crowd seemed even more excited and animated than usual, anticipating what could be the final game of the season for the Grizzlies or, with a win, a ticket to the district playoffs. If they achieved that feat, it would be their first appearance in the tournament in decades.

Goldie Knighton had not been to a Grizzly game since the night of Cole's attempted suicide. Grove fans hadn't missed her verbal theatrics, so when they saw her in line at the ticket booth, there were more than a few groans of displeasure and rolling of eyes.

"Look who's here," Tim said elbowing Peggy as he spoke.

Peggy hadn't recounted to Tim the news of Goldie's visit to their home, wanting to keep it to herself, especially because of the vow of secrecy about Cole's reason for being absent from the team.

"Here we go again," Tim muttered, as he tapped the program on his knee. "Can't say I've missed her."

He slumped back into his cushioned seat but quickly sat up erect when he realized Goldie was walking directly toward them in front of the seats along the side of the court. "Hold onto your hat, Peg. Looks like Goldie's coming to give you another whack." He bristled.

But when Goldie slowed to a stop in front of them, Peggy rose from her chair and extended her hand.

"Hi, Goldie," Peggy said.

"What the hell?" Tim shook his head.

"Sit with us, Goldie, please," Peggy said. "We'll cheer together tonight."

Goldie's lips pulled tight into a reserved smile. "I would love that," she whispered, "if that's all right with Tim."

Tim looked at Goldie and then at Peggy, then shrugged his shoulders. "I have no idea what the hell is going on here," he said. "But if you two promise not to start another catfight, I'll stay here with you."

Not all the fans from the Grove had arrived yet, but the ones who were there could barely believe what they were seeing. "I'll be damned," Homer Johnson said. "Miracles do happen, I guess. If those two women can get along, I suppose anything can happen."

"Like a win by the Grizzlies over the Titans?" his friend asked.

"I dunno, maybe. I guess that's what I mean, but don't get your hopes up. The game hasn't even started yet, and those two women might still get their tempers up again. At least that would be worth the price of admission."

If theatrics were what the capacity crowd was hoping for, they were sorely disappointed. Homer and his friends were quietly eased into complacency watching quality play from their Grove team. Cole Knighton played only sparingly … coming off the bench for a few minutes in each quarter to rest one of the starters. His usual frenetic play was strangely subdued, similar to his mother's cheering. Her voice was nearly absent from the crowd's vocal eruptions when a great play happened or when a controversial call by a referee was made.

"Let's go, Grizzlies!" she'd yell, but cheering by the crowd easily drowned her out, since no one could hear her as she sat in the front row with Peggy and Tim and purposely kept her voice to a minimal volume.

When Cole entered the game, she and Peggy applauded politely, under the watchful eye of Tim and the others, who still couldn't believe what they were seeing. Helping cool any emotions was the fact that the Grizzlies jumped out to an early lead and held fast to it throughout the game.

Cole's absence from the team during his therapy had helped the other starters gain confidence in their abilities. When Cole trotted onto the hardwood as a substitute, they didn't hesitate to run the offense as if he were just one more tool in the complete toolbox.

When the final buzzer sounded, the clock showed a twenty-point victory for the Grizzlies. It was a complete anticlimactic end to the regular season, but Grizzly fans were ecstatic over the result. "Well, I'll be," Homer Johnson said, as he rose from his seat. "The Grizzlies are going to districts. What'll old Buster do now? He's usually thinking about his golf game at this point in the season. I guess sometimes miracles do happen."

Parents and fans rushed to the floor to surround the players and congratulate them on their victory. Tim and Peggy stood by their seats, soaking in the scene, watching the jubilant fans fawn over the players, including their son. Luke received a hug from Ashley as she stood on her tiptoes to fling one arm around his neck, her clarinet clasped awkwardly under the other.

The couple spied Luke's parents and wandered over to them. Ashley was nervous about being with Peggy. But Peggy walked straight toward her with a smile on her face and put her hand on her arm.

"Ashley, we meet again," she said with her hair swinging from side to side. "I think I owe you a thank you for calling my son a few weeks ago. You're my guardian angel, I guess." She rubbed her hands together. "Funny how it sometimes takes a teenager or two to keep me on the straight and narrow." She glanced over at Luke and winked as if to say, *I like your girlfriend.*

Ashley blushed. She wanted to say "I'm not worthy," … but just stammered, "I don't know …"

Peggy laughed at the girl's shyness. "Give me a hug then." She stepped closer and put her arms around the sophomore, like a mama bear embracing a cub. "We're all friends here," she said, looking over at Goldie. "Because we're all going to the playoffs." She clapped her hands together and did a little dance. "I can't wait."

Goldie watched her new friend exhibit an act of pure unbridled joy. She wished she could be so carefree. But her son Cole was standing across the floor talking with the coaches. When he saw his mother with the Palmers, he was confused. *What is she doing?* He didn't move toward them but stood still … watching. He wasn't ready to join in the celebration. Not yet. Not with Luke Palmer.

# CHAPTER 30

# UP

**BROCK HAD TAKEN A GAMBLE.** If the Grizzlies had not won against Thomasville, a team-bonding experience would have been a hollow exercise. He'd taken that gamble and now, with the victory, it seemed even more important than ever that the team was fully united for their playoff run.

When the sun rose on a Saturday morning, it was clear with a warm breeze filtering down the valley ... a notice to everyone that winter was losing its grip. The basketball team had worked through their league schedule with just enough wins to earn a spot in the district tournament. With a couple of victories in that competition, the Grizzlies would move on to the state tournament ... something the citizens of the Grove couldn't yet believe.

Still, the team had not been able to win against superior competition. Cole's absence had cost them a couple of wins and the coffee shop fans were keenly aware of the team's early weakness ... their inability to work together. "Those wins didn't come from team play, but from the fact we have better players," Homer Johnson noted over coffee. It wasn't a formula for making any kind of run in the playoffs.

Brock hoped his plan for team bonding would help bring the team together, and maybe patch up the animosity between players. With a week break before districts, it gave him enough time to gather the boys together to work on the elevator bear. As the day approached, he thought more about the risk he was taking, shouldering full responsibility for any mishaps that might occur. He put it out of his mind. If he didn't, he might panic and call the whole thing off.

Peter M. Green was as excited as the boys he was working with. He showed little evidence of his sixty-plus years of life and his nasty smoking habit. There was a smile on his lips and color in his angular cheeks. "Looks like the temperature is cooperating," he said. "The boys won't freeze, and the paint will stick. This will do just fine."

Brock followed Green's instructions and assembled the necessary scrapers, paint, and brushes. Tim, meanwhile, rallied the county crew and positioned the bucket truck at the base of the elevator. Before the boys arrived, Brock and Green rode up the side of the silo for a test run in the double buckets which were lifted hydraulically by Tim, on the ground. "This is a darn sight easier than what I had to do forty years ago," Green said, as they started up the side of the building. "Back then it was scaffolding and ropes and white knuckles."

Brock nodded silently and stared at the scene below … the little town stretching to the west, following the curve of Cold Creek, which drained the runoff from the nearby mountains. It was home to a few thousand people who, almost to a person, claimed to be die-hard Grizzly fans. Many would soon gather to watch the progress. Looking down, Brock realized his legs felt weak and were shaking ever so slightly.

As a college and pro football player, Brock experienced dozens of cross-country air flights at 30,000 feet. The height didn't bother him then, but this was different. A light wind moved the waist-high buckets, gently but perceptively. And as they rose, the human sounds from below gradually faded away. The concrete structure was within arm's reach, and the closeness added another dimension to the sensation of height. As the sun rose in the east, it cast their shadows on the wall. Brock never had a desire to be a rock climber, those daredevil souls you see in movies and videos. He wondered if this might be a similar sensation.

They moved higher and higher, reaching the clawed feet of the Grizzly, and then, working their way up the length of the torso, they eventually reached the bear's angry face and stared into the remaining eye that hadn't peeled away from the concrete. Brock chuckled to himself. This experience was something the boys who ventured up to this height would never forget.

"Well, Brock, this should be quite the adventure for your young athletes," Green said as he pushed the bill of his painter cap back on his head and flicked ashes from his cigarette. He watched them flutter down. "We can get started soon but we should have an adult ride up and down with each one of them until they feel comfortable. Then we can let them go to work."

Once they were back on the ground, Brock checked the list of pairings he'd made. He planned to share it with the boys when they arrived. Since the first day would be used only for scraping off the old paint, the boys would each take a short shift before being lowered to the ground for the next pair to ascend.

At the appointed hour the varsity players arrived. They were bleary-eyed, but still giddy from their victory the night before. Brock tried to calm them down by going over some basic safety rules: no bouncing in the bucket, no dropping anything from any height, and always keeping a safety harness on. Goggles would be provided when scraping and painting. The boys were nervous, pacing around him as he spoke … except Luke, who carried on with his tough guy exterior.

Justin nudged his big friend. "You aren't nervous, are you?"

"Me? Hell, no, why would I be nervous? As long as no one tries to throw me out of the bucket, I'll be fine."

Justin nodded. "This will be something to remember when we're old and gray. If we live that long. When we get the bear looking good, it'll still be around when our own kids graduate high school." He rubbed his hands together, anticipating the moment when his turn would come.

As Jimmy and Brock climbed into the buckets for the first demonstration ride, the other boys, clearly nervous, laughed and chatted, anxious for their turn to come. They shuffled their feet as they craned their necks skyward. Their focus was broken by P.M. Green. "Okay, fellas," he said, grasping a steel brush in one hand and sandpaper in another. "Each one of you will get these. When you get up there," he pointed to the bear, "you're going to look for any loose paint and scrape away. We have to get the old loose paint off so we can give that old Grizzly a new look." He flicked cigarette ashes onto the ground. "If we work hard, we can have this done in no time."

The adults took turns riding up with each player to familiarize each one with the experience. The boys would come down laughing and smiling … almost everyone. As they climbed out of the bucket, Brock noticed Luke's complexion was a pasty gray, like the sandpaper they'd use on the peeling bear. "Everything okay?" Brock asked.

"Sure, Coach. Just need a second to get my legs under me." He stumbled away from the other boys and his coaches.

Brock followed him. "It's okay if you don't want to go again. That's why we're giving everyone a short ride first."

"No, I'll be fine, just not quite used to the height," Luke said, pulling in a big breath.

After everyone had their orientation ride with an adult, the boys were paired up for their twenty-minute shifts. When he composed the list, Brock made sure the most nervous of the boys had a stronger individual by their side. He'd first send Justin with Jimmy, knowing each of them would bolster the other's confidence, and how anxious both were to try out the lift. The boys on the ground could see how safe the operation was and use it to calm their nerves. After that, each assigned pair would spend twenty minutes scraping off old paint as per Green's instructions.

Brock's biggest concern was sending Cole Knighton up with another youngster, considering his recent trauma. He didn't want to single him out from the rest. Instead, he thought he should send him with the strongest man on the team; Luke could intercede if Cole made any kind of desperate move.

Luke grumbled when Brock asked him to go with Cole, but he wasn't given a choice. The boys agreed and climbed in, fastened their belts, and headed skyward. Brock paced nervously as he watched them reach the Grizzly, where they could begin to scrape. He couldn't hear their conversation, but hoped they might reach some sort of reconciliation and settle the differences they'd expressed during practice and games.

In the bucket, the boys were silent, not looking at one another until they came to a stop. "I guess we start scraping now," Cole muttered. He began to slip on his goggles.

"Guess so," Luke said, but as he reached out with his steel brush, he looked down and when he did, he felt his legs turn to rubber. The blood drained from his face.

Cole stared over at the big boy. "You all right?"

Luke slowly sank to the bottom of the bucket and stared down at his feet. "I can't do this."

"What do you mean, we're supposed to scrape for twenty minutes. Are you sick?"

"Shut up, Cole."

"You scared?"

"I just want down."

Cole looked down at his teammate … the one who had given him the most problems. "Should I holler at the coach and ask them to lower the bucket?"

"Gawd, no. I don't want to look like a wimp." Luke sat, legs spread wide, and his head lowered to his chest. His eyes were squeezed shut.

"Okay. I'll scrape and you can sit. They'll take us down soon enough."

"And then you can tell everyone what a wuss I am. Bet you can't wait."

Cole thought for a second and rocked back and forth. "I'm not one to talk, after what I did when my dad didn't show up for the game. I'm sure everyone in school is talking about what a dumb shit Cole Knighton is. You can't be as embarrassed as I am."

Luke opened his eyes but still stared straight ahead. "Jeezus, Knighton … why would you do that anyway? Nothing's worth pulling that stunt. So what if your dad didn't show up? Hey, I didn't even know my dad until last fall. You can live without a dad … I'm proof of that."

"But look at you now. Big stud. Good friends. Local hero. Cute girlfriend. You've got it all." Cole began nervously scraping as he talked.

"Sure, but I can't shoot a basketball worth crap. If I'm not within five feet, it ain't going in. But you've got all this talent, and you were going to throw it all away for nothin'."

"I was pretty sure the team wouldn't miss me."

"Oh, boo hoo. Well, we wouldn't miss you being a ball hog and your flapping gums … that's for sure."

Cole turned, ready to be angry, his hand cocked to throw his steel brush into Luke's face. But his anger suddenly disappeared when he saw Luke cowering at the bottom of the bucket. Luke was laughing. Well, not really laughing … but a crazy combination of terror at being so high and relief at hiding his fear with the words he had spoken.

Cole studied his teammate. Was he laughing or crying? Whatever it was, it made him begin to laugh himself, slowly at first, but soon his eyes were watering. He was trying hard to hold it back, but he couldn't help but find humor in the ridiculousness of the situation. He was stuck in a bucket seventy-five feet in the air, a Grizzly bear staring at him with one eye, and this huge bully of a boy—his arch nemesis—cowering at his feet. "Look, man. I won't tell anyone you're afraid of heights if you'll get the guys to shut up about what I did."

"And why should I?" Luke lifted his head and squinted at Cole.

Cole's laughter faded and his eyes drooped. "Because I still want to be part of the team, and I want to win ball games. What I tried to do, it really scared me. But I learned something while I was in the hospital." He hesitated to get his words right … to repeat what he'd learned. "I can go through life without a father, but I can't go through life all alone. Even my pushy mother isn't enough. But mostly I learned I don't want to die. Guess that means I'm going to have to try to get along with you and the football players."

Luke slowly reached out his big hand. "Deal," he said. "Now help me up."

Cole grasped Luke's hand and pulled. The big junior cautiously rose to his feet, knees bent, keeping his eyes straight ahead, breathing hard. He wouldn't look down again. Not until the bucket hit the ground. "You know, I learned the same thing when I burned my leg in a wheat fire out on the Gallagher farm. I thought I might die. Really scared the shit out of me. Then, I couldn't play football and gawd I missed it. But I found out who my friends were and why I liked them."

Luke leaned into the slender sophomore. "Listen, Knighton, the football guys don't hate you. But until you lighten up and show us some respect, we won't give a crap about you, either. Try playing ball with us … share the ball a little. Justin and Jimmy are good players. We played well without you. We'll be even better with you. Give us a chance."

As he talked, Luke cautiously began to scrape the brown paint off the bear. His eyes were turned away from Cole. "We need you, Knighton. It's time we all tried a little harder to get along, or …" Luke suddenly went erect and reached over to grab Cole's hoodie, acting as if he was going to yank him out of the bucket.

Cole dropped his brush and went rigid. "Oh, shit."

But it was a playful gesture. Luke released his hold. "Made you wanna pee your pants, didn't it, hotshot? Okay, that wasn't nice, but I couldn't resist. Anyway, let's skin this bear. I'm not going to look down. But, if I do, and if I pass out again, just let me lie there until we hit the ground and then tell the team the bear killed me."

The two boys stood together … scraping and brushing until the old Grizzly lost some more hair and the bucket began its descent. They talked throughout the rest of their time slot … everything from girls to jump shots to dealing with Coach McHue. When they finally stepped from the lift, Brock noticed something new in their body language. Something had happened. He didn't care what, he just knew somehow it was good.

# CHAPTER 31

# CLOSURE

**EVERYONE IN TOWN WAS EXCITED** about the basketball team. Except for John Eberhardt, the veteran bank manager at Glory Grove. He had other things on his mind. As the head of the local bank, John had been Ronnie's mentor since she started working for the bank as a teller right out of high school. Her unintended pregnancy and hurry-up marriage to Cort Jepson curbed any dreams she had of going to college, perhaps even to join her high school boyfriend, Brock Gallagher. With the baby's arrival six months after her graduation, she faced reality and took a job with the bank.

John, a middle-aged expert in finance, welcomed her without judgment. He pushed aside rumors concerning her sudden marriage to Cort Jepson, though he did think Jepson wasn't a good fit for such a nice girl. Veronica O'Malley had been a good student in school and an upright citizen growing up. Her one mistake, if the rumors were true, shouldn't condemn her to a long-term reputation as a misguided individual.

*Mistakes happen to even the best of people*, John told himself. He knew she'd moved to town as a child and was raised by a single mother. From her first day on the job at the bank, John could see her potential. She was bright and personable, well-groomed and polite. She related well to the other employees and to the customers. He took her under his wing and soon became almost like a father to her. As time went on, she took on more and more of the responsibilities of running the little branch bank.

Given her close relationship with John, Ronnie was mystified by his sudden nervousness around her. He seemed distracted by small things and snapped at one of the young employees over a small mistake. *I've never seen John act in this way,* she thought.

For several days, she tried to ignore the sudden change in his behavior. Then one evening as the employees were exiting the bank, she caught sight of him sitting alone in his office with his head in his hands. He'd taken his glasses off and loosened his tie. The color had drained from his usual rosy cheeks. He thought she had gone with the rest of the workers so was surprised when she slipped into the office and asked, "John, are you all right?"

Her words made him sit up and open his eyes. "Oh, Ronnie, I thought you'd left. I'm just tired," he said. "It's been a long week."

Ronnie smiled. "It's only Tuesday, John." She slid into the chair opposite his desk. "Is there something going on at the bank that I'm not aware of? You've been acting different the last couple of weeks."

John put on his black-rimmed glasses and smoothed his thinning hair. He leaned back in his chair. "I don't know how to tell you this. We have a situation. And it concerns you." He tapped nervously on the desk. "And it shouldn't. And let me be clear, it's not your fault in any way."

"Am I being fired?"

"Goodness, no. Just the opposite. Mr. Donigan wants you to manage one of the branches in Spokane."

"I know. I already told you he'd made me a wonderful offer. But I'm not sure it's what I want to do."

"Well, it's looking more and more like he's trying to force you to say yes."

"What do you mean? He can't make me take a job I don't want."

"Ronnie, he's playing hardball now."

"How? There is nothing he can do to me to force me into a job I don't want."

"He can close the branch in Glory Grove." John said it so suddenly and matter-of-factly, it took an instant for Ronnie to comprehend what he was saying. But seconds later, she folded her hands over her chest as if she were having a heart attack. She sucked air into her lungs and leaned toward John. "He can't do that. Why would he do that?" Her voice was trembling.

"Well, the first thing he says is we're overstaffed, and we need to cut expenses. He suggested either we drop your salary down to minimum wage to save on labor costs, or we'll have to close the branch. But my intuition says it's because he wants you with him, and he wants your quarterback son to come with you. I've always thought of him as a shrewd businessperson, and now I can see how he gets things done. He's a bit of a bastard, is what I think now."

Ronnie was shocked. She'd never in her career heard John Eberhardt use a swear word. It showed just how serious he was. "So, he's threatening to close the bank in Glory Grove if I don't take the job up there? And leave the people here without a bank and the girls here without jobs?" Ronnie stared at her hands … thinking … confused by this sudden revelation. The branch bank had always been profitable. The lease on the bank building was small and other than the few bank tellers they employed, their costs of doing business was minimal.

John looked over the desk and fixed his eyes on Ronnie. He cleared his throat. "I think this is all about you."

"Why? What's this have to do with me?"

"Ronnie, I think he may be interested in you for more than a professional relationship."

Ronnie's face flushed, remembering the night in the hotel. "That's just wrong," she stammered, her voice rising in anger.

John continued. "I think he's using this threat as a way to get you to agree to his offer. That seems to be what he's hinting at. It's not on paper like that, but it doesn't have to be. He wields a lot of power with the board, and they won't question a decision to close a little bank like ours."

"But how can he justify closing us down?"

"Well, we aren't a big player in their overall picture. We've always kept our heads down and do just enough business with the farmers here to justify our existence. Now, with the potential for windfarm money that would circulate around if the Wind Driven project goes through, I'd hoped it would put us on a more solid footing. But if the farmers don't sign leases and the project doesn't get green-lighted, he may use it as another reason to shut us down."

"I can't believe he'd do that." Her eyes were now nearly closed as if without vision she might see some logic to the situation.

John stroked his chin, looking like a professor explaining some complicated problem to the brightest student in a calculus class. "Roland Donigan is a man who gets his way. He usually doesn't have anyone say no to him. I think he's frustrated and may do whatever it takes to achieve his goal."

"And now I'm even less interested in the job or the man." Her teeth were clenched. "I've been pushed around way too much in life to let something like this happen. I'll let him know I won't play his game."

John sat without moving a muscle, trying to think of the correct advice to give to someone he cared deeply about. He lowered his voice. "Just be careful. He could always shut us down out of spite. I'm not sure what else he might do. And we don't even know if what I'm guessing is true."

Ronnie rose from her chair, reached across the desk, and gripped John's hands. She realized just how important the man had been in her life and how much she cared for him. "I'm sorry. I'll do what I can. It's my fault. I'll try to fix it somehow."

Ronnie was confounded. If what John Eberhardt said was true, Roland Donigan was being a bully, threatening to close the only bank in Glory Grove. Worse yet, he was using the threat to get to her. And it seemed, as a sidenote, it would put more pressure on farmers to give up their land to the wind company. That would impact the Gallagher family and others on Piney Ridge.

She admitted, at first, that the idea of leaving the little town for the city and all it had to offer for herself and her son Justin had a strong appeal. Also being wined and dined by a handsome man, with his looks and sophistication, was flattering, although his unwanted advances at the hotel still made her cringe.

She had struggled for weeks trying to sort things out. She was a newly single mother, on shaky financial ground and responsible for a teenage son with a seemingly bright future. The lure of a more lucrative life with a boss who'd let it be known he had a romantic interest in her was flattering.

Now, it seemed there was an ugly side to Mr. Roland Donigan. Even when she'd been forced to push back on his sexual advances, she'd excused his behavior due to the wine he'd consumed and the signals she had unintentionally sent during their dinner and dancing. She partially blamed herself for his approach. But her rejection seemed to make him more determined to make her his prize, through any means he had at his fingertips—including threatening to close the bank.

Ronnie left the meeting with John seeking some sort of resolution. It was not in her character, but she was determined to be as wise and cunning as the man himself. An abrupt refusal would anger him. He backed away before, but maybe not a second time. He might seek revenge and have her fired or close the bank. If she strung the decision out too long, he might grow impatient and start pestering her son to influence his mother. Justin didn't need that in his life.

Once she was home, she brewed a cup of tea, kicked off her shoes, and sat down at her tiny desk, alone with Franny. The cat curled up on her lap. Franny couldn't offer advice, but her warmth and slow motor-boat purring calmed Ronnie. She picked up her pen and began to put words on paper.

"*Mr. Donigan*," she wrote, then laid down the pen, leaned back in the chair, and closed her eyes. "What can I say, Franny?" she murmured softly as she reached down and rubbed the cat's neck. Franny didn't answer, so she picked up the pen again and started to write.

> *"Roland, I am flattered, both personally and professionally, by your employment offer. It is thrilling to know you would consider me for such a promotion in the bank. Working for the bank has been a blessing for me for nearly two decades. John Eberhardt has been a guiding hand and a terrific mentor. He has trained me well, or such*

*an offer of promotion wouldn't be possible. However, in a recent conversation, he indicated there might be some discussion, at the upper levels of the bank, about cutting back on the number of small branch banks in the organization. It would be a heartbreak for me if Glory Grove's branch was being considered for closure. It has always been (and still is) my dream to someday become manager at this location when John chooses to retire.*

Ronnie rolled the pen around in her hand and stirred in her chair. Franny stayed firmly stuck to her lap. "Okay, Franny," she said. "Here comes the tough part." She needed to pen her conclusion, careful to use delicate language.

*"I sincerely thank you for considering me for an advancement, and for the time we've spent together. But I feel as of now, it is best for me to remain in Glory Grove, and for Justin to stay with his teammates. And I hope to maintain my position as assistant manager. On a personal level, I would like to reserve the right to say that someday I might wish to move up in the organization and take on a larger role and perhaps to see more of you. You have gone out of your way to make your proposal hard to resist and I do appreciate that very much. It is just not the right time for my son or me to make such a move. I'm sure you can understand.*

*Sincerely,*

*Ronnie Jepson*

Three days later, Roland Donigan was at his desk combing through the bank's receipts and expenditures for the month of February when his secretary brought in the day's mail.

"Thanks, Norma," he said. "Anything of interest today?"

"Just the usual, Mr. Donigan, although there is a letter from the woman you interviewed last month. You know, from Glory Grove. I didn't open it. Looked kind of personal." She smiled as she turned to leave the room.

Donigan inhaled but tried not to show his eagerness to pull the letter from the stack. "All right, I'll take a look at it later," he said. But as soon as the secretary left the room, he pulled a letter opener from his desk drawer and slipped the blade under the flap. He slid it the length of the envelope and carefully lifted out the contents.

The words were in cursive … *an artistic style to them*, he thought. He skimmed the full text, then let his eyes move back to the top of the page where he began to read every word carefully. When he finished, he dropped the pages onto the desk and leaned back in his chair. He closed his eyes and dropped his head.

"Dammit," he said, under his breath. "I can't believe she'd say no. What more do I have to do?" But as soon as the words left his lips, he paused and sat up straight. *But she didn't really say no, did she? All she really said was "later."* It wasn't over. He picked the letter up in his hand and slid it back into its envelope. He opened the top drawer in his desk and carefully laid it on top of his personal papers.

He clucked his tongue as if he were chastising a misbehaving child. She said "later." He would just have to find a way to make it sooner. He recognized his obsession, but so what? He'd pull enough levers to entice Ronnie Jepson to come to him. He rarely lost in his dealings, especially when it came to manipulating people … especially women. His looks and wealth always led to conquest. Even his divorce was on his terms, despite his own infidelity as the cause for the separation. His lawyers made sure the settlement was entirely in his favor.

This effort to win Ronnie was an intriguing challenge. She should have jumped at the incentives he was offering. And his move to threaten the bank in Glory Grove with closure should have pushed Ronnie into a corner. Yet, her letter left him frustrated and looking for angles to convince her to move. He'd tried persuasion and subterfuge. His next move might have to be even more heavy-handed.

The linchpin might be Ronnie's love for her son. If Ronnie was influenced by Justin's desire to stay in Glory Grove so he could play sports with his friends, there might be a way to sabotage that program. He'd watched Jimmy Ivory and Luke Palmer at the basketball games he'd attended. They were the key to the success of the team. And from talking with the people in the Grove, who were friendly and open in sharing their town's news, he'd discovered the boys both transferred in, just before the fall season.

Why had they come to this little farm town? If he could find a way to undermine their eligibility for sports, he might have found a way to convince Justin it would be better for him to move to a larger high school. If Justin was willing to transfer, Ronnie might see the light and accept the bank's offer.

Donigan had connections. One of his college friends was on the state's governing body for all interscholastic activities. He could make a phone call and have his friend check the eligibility rules for transfer students. It was particularly interesting that Jimmy had conveniently moved to Glory Grove with his coach, Brock Gallagher, just prior to the football season. His participation on the football team had been key to the team's appearance in the state championship game.

If he could take Jimmy's eligibility away, perhaps the program would collapse.

*It will take time*, Donigan thought. But he could be patient when the prize was so important to him. He'd only spent one night with Ronnie Jepson in his arms. But that was enough to make him determined to win her over … no matter how long it took or whatever the price. He'd start making inquiries and consult with his legal department. His career with the bank, crunching numbers and studying budgets and performance objectives, although being quite lucrative, had dulled his senses. This pursuit of Ronnie and Justin awakened something inside him. The chase alone was exhilarating. And the victory in the end could be even more fulfilling.

He wasn't defeated, just stalled. He would find a way.

# CHAPTER 32

# NERVES

**IT WAS VALENTINE'S DAY,** and the men of Glory Grove dutifully dropped by the Glory Be Flower Shop and bought flowers for their wives. Brock felt a bit awkward when he stepped into the store.

"Something for your mother?" the elderly attendant asked.

Brock hesitated. "Sure, that's right. She deserves some flowers."

"Well, it's probably none of my business, but an elderly gentleman was already in this morning wanting to buy a special arrangement for Irene. I think this will be a good day for her."

*There are no secrets in this town*, Brock thought, and wondered if it was Peter Green who'd ordered the flowers for his mom. He obliged the sales lady and picked out a small arrangement for his mother. Then he did what he'd really come for and requested to have a half dozen roses delivered to the bank for Ronnie.

"Oh, that is so nice of you," the woman said. "The bank must serve your family well for Ronnie to deserve this." She winked.

"She does," Brock said. "Keeps us going, for sure."

The lady calculated the total and Brock paid in cash. He left the store wondering how long it would take for the gossip to spread. But a rumor of this flower order would not make the gossip headlines for people in the Grove. They were now too much in a state of restless anticipation. The basketball tournament was only days away. To stir their emotions even more, thanks to Peter Green and a small group of teenagers, a fresh-looking Grizzly bear was staring down at them from the town's towering grain elevator. It was back to its shiny, stoic, ferocious, intimidating self, complete with the angry gaze that had been missing for decades. Both eyes now looked out as if daring any intruder to step out of line.

The citizenry, without expressing it in so many words, was filled with pride over the fresh image. Even the men gathering for coffee at the Cozy Corner Drive-In were impressed. "The old bear is looking good," one man said, initiating the morning chat a few days before the district playoffs were to begin.

"Can't argue with that," Homer Johnson said. "But even with a fresh coat of paint on the bear, and everybody excited about getting to the district tournament, I still think old Buster will find a way to fritter away any chance we have of going to state." Johnson stared down at the creamer he'd dumped into the brew. "Even after all these years of coaching, he's still new to the playoffs, so we shouldn't expect much."

The group lingered over their coffee and returned to the discussion about the newly painted bear. One of the chattier men proposed a new topic. "With that bear looking so good it'd be nice if our basketball team could look a bit more intimidating."

"I don't know," Homer Johnson said, "that Palmer kid with that tattoo looks pretty scary to me."

"True," the first man said. "Maybe next he should get a big old bear tattoo on his other arm."

"There's room for one on that massive bicep of his," Johnson said. "Maybe we should all chip in and help him pay for one."

"Naw, I've got a better idea. If we're going to spend money to change the image of the Grizzlies to match the slicked-up bear on the elevator, we need to start at the top. Let's get old Coach McHue a new red tie or sweater or something … make him look the part of a champion-caliber coach for what will most likely be his last game this year."

The men around the table all nodded and a few grumbled as Homer took off his seed cap, dropped a five-dollar bill into it, and handed it to the farmer sitting next to him, who was already reaching for his billfold.

Buster wasn't aware of the gift coming his way. He was at home feeling the pressure of high expectations for the basketball team and embarrassed for forgetting to get his wife the chocolates she always loved to get on Valentine's Day. The upcoming tournament had him forgetting everything but basketball.

Four teams earned a spot in the district tournament. It was a loser-out affair. Two wins would send a team to the state tourney for a shot at bringing home a trophy. The Glory Grove Grizzlies had never been to the state tournament while Buster McHue was their coach and had only been there twice before, once in the 1940s when many of the area's schools' best athletes, who had reached their eighteenth birthday, chose to enlist in the WWII effort. Ironically, most of the boys from Glory Grove were exempted to stay home to work on their daddy's farms. Those Grizzlies had an advantage against other decimated teams. That trip to state came with an asterisk.

The team's other appearance was in the 1920s when the Grizzlies had a bunch of athletes muscled up from manual labor hauling sacked grain. They'd won close games against even bigger schools with weaker players. Scores then typically were in the twenties and the one and only victory Glory Grove had at the state level was a nail-biting 20–19 victory over a team from a fishing village from a west coast seaport.

The deflated game ball from that victory rested in the corner of the school's trophy case … a lonely tribute to a long-ago victory.

In the upcoming tournament, the three other teams who made the playoffs were the squads who had notched victories over the Grizzlies in games played earlier in the season. Pine City with their big man, Wallitas from the Indian reservation, and Coolidge, the alternative school with the street-smart boys who loved to run and gun. Brock and Buster worked on a game plan for each of the potential opponents. First up were the Cadets from Coolidge.

"We don't match up with those freewheeling playground ballers," Buster said. "They're too fast, and live and die on fast breaks and shooting threes. Our only chance will be to slow them down and face-guard their shooters … no help side defense or hoping for a missed shot. Just maybe, if we can challenge them early, they'll get frustrated and try too hard to break open the game with quick long shots. Hopefully, Luke can plug up the inside game, but we have to shut down their outside shooting or we won't have a chance."

Brock admired Coach McHue. But he couldn't understand the man's tendency to accept losing. He knew basketball as well as anyone he'd met. But the old coach's weakness came from failing to know the boys and what was in their heads. It was the one thing Brock could offer the team.

That evening at home, McHue fell back in his recliner, thinking about the upcoming game with Coolidge. His wife handed him his nightly shot of Jack Daniels on ice. She'd forgiven him for having forgotten her chocolates on Valentine's Day. "Is the team ready?" she asked. "Or should we not talk about it? You've kept to yourself most of the season and it's worked out so far."

Buster took the glass and raised it to his forehead, cooling his brow. "Not much to say, honey, we're in the hunt and I'm a nervous wreck. I don't even know how to act."

"Just act proud. You deserve this."

"Do I? I've been handed two great athletes, Jimmy and Luke, who came from out of town. And now Brock Gallagher is doing this team bonding stuff to get the kids to work together. I wouldn't even know where to start with things like that. So, if I win, do I deserve any credit for this team?"

Eunice sat down in a chair beside him. "Listen, you old grump bucket, if anyone deserves a break here, it's you. You've shepherded the kids from the Grove around for years, with a bunch of mediocre athletes and without a thank you. Now that you've got some good boys, you're getting cold feet. This team of yours, and I mean yours, has more wins than any team in years. And you're the coach. Don't complain about that."

Buster put the glass to his lips and sipped while Eunice continued. "And if things go well and you get to the state tournament, there will be enough credit to go around for everyone. And it will be your name on the ball in the trophy case. Buster, take what you've been given and be happy for it."

Buster laid his head back and closed his eyes. "I'm just not used to this and don't want to miss my shot at doing something special."

"And because of your worrying, you've missed all the happiness you could have enjoyed along the way."

"I know. But we've reached our first goal. And the whole dream may come crashing down in a couple of days. And if it does …" He couldn't finish his thought because Eunice had walked over and cupped his face with her hands.

"And if it does," she said, "your wife will still love you very much. Now, finish your drink. Dinner's almost ready. Happy Valentine's Day."

"Yes, dear." Buster swatted her behind as she walked away.

# CHAPTER 33

# DISTRICTS

**THE GRIZZLY TEAM AND HALF** the town traveled for the first game of the district tournament. It was held in the nearest big city with a community college, a venue with a modern basketball arena situated in the middle of the campus. The Grizzlies would face the Coolidge Cadets, the league team that had given them one of their largest defeats a month before.

The team arrived early to get their bearings before taking the floor. The coaches wanted them to be relaxed and ready to go when the time came. It also gave Buster and Brock time to get their own minds prepared for the contest. But minutes before the teams headed to the locker room to dress down, Brock saw a familiar face coming down the corridor leading to the gymnasium: Roland Donigan.

The man approached him with a smirk on his face and confidence in his stride. *The arrogant money man*, Brock thought to himself. He'd become all too familiar with the man's appearance at Grizzly basketball games. And Ronnie had told him of his threats to close the bank.

Donigan swerved in front of Brock, altering his path. "Coach Gallagher," he said, acting like an old friend. "Nice little team you have. Are they ready for battle tonight?"

Brock nodded. "Ready as they'll ever be." He was used to casual chit-chat from parents before a big game. It was a way for them to calm their own nervousness about what was to come and their desire for their sons to perform well in the spotlight of high school sports. But Brock wasn't ready for what Donigan said next.

"I know one thing," the banker said. "If you keep that little showoff guard on the sidelines, it will give Justin Jepson the opportunity he deserves to show his talents, don't you think?"

Brock bristled. "Well, if you're referring to Cole Knighton, he will play tonight. And Justin will be glad to have him on the floor. We're a better team with everyone healthy."

"Sure, but as you and I both know, Justin is your best player. He needs to be leading this team … or go somewhere that will showcase his talent."

Brock was silent for a moment, then raised his head and looked Donigan in the eyes. "I don't know you, sir. And I can only guess at your motives, but I know enough to tell you that you're sticking your nose where it doesn't belong. You've put a bug in Justin's ear about moving away. He doesn't need that kind of interference at this time in his life. You need to stop bothering him, and for that matter lay off the pressure you're putting on Ronnie to take a new job. She'll make up her mind when she's ready."

Donigan's smile faded. "I'm not sure this is any of your concern. I'm giving Ronnie a chance to improve her life, get out of your dying little town, and set herself up so she never has to worry about money again. And to give her son the chance to be a football star on the biggest stage."

"And what if they don't want what you're offering?"

"They'd be foolish to pass up a chance like this. They need to take a hard look at where this town is going and get out while they can."

"So, you're trying to convince her by threatening to close the bank in our town or by harassing her son?" Brock's voice was now rising with each word.

Donigan didn't back down. "And who made you her guardian? She didn't seem to care about you when I took her dancing in Spokane … far from it. She was probably glad to be away from hayseeds like you." Donigan's sarcastic smile grew wider … flashing his perfect white teeth.

"I'm her friend," Brock said. Color was rising in his cheeks. "I've known her for a long time, and I know she doesn't rattle easily. But she's still dealing with her husband's death, and you are creating turmoil in her life. Whatever she decides is up to her, but I think she'd be better off here than working for a man like you. And as far as Justin is concerned, he'll be a star no matter who he plays for. So, Mr. Donigan, you know how I feel … I want you to back off. Got it?"

Donigan's lips parted again, this time like a dog baring its teeth at a stranger. "Spoken like a has-been football jock who can't look the truth in the face. Gallagher, I won't be backing off. I won't lose this. She'll be working for me. Count on it. And your prized quarterback will be playing in the city leagues next year. You can bank on that, too. Now if you'll excuse me." He turned and brushed past Brock, while simultaneously tipping his head to an attractive young lady passing by. She smiled self-consciously but couldn't help but be impressed by the banker's good looks.

Brock resisted the temptation to follow Donigan and smack him alongside the head. "Keep cool," he said to himself. He was aware of the manipulative power Donigan used for his self-interest. A physical confrontation played right into his hands. The banker was smart, clever, and driven. Brock knew men like that while playing in the NFL. Those types often got their way at the expense of others. Brock would do what he could to fight it here. The price he'd pay if he failed would be especially painful.

When the ball was tossed into the air for the opening tip-off, almost all the seats in the modern gym were filled. Ashley Summers was there with the pep band. She and Luke settled on a pregame ritual ... a kiss on the cheek before the team dressed, then a two-finger salute to one another before the first whistle.

Coach McHue, sporting a new red tie, watched the display but couldn't quite figure out why Luke was saluting. Brock, fully aware of the youthful romance between the two teenagers, smiled knowingly, hoping Luke's temporary diversion might calm him down a notch or two before his aggressive instincts got him into more foul trouble.

Just as Coach McHue had predicted, the Cadets sprinted from one end of the court to the other, seldom venturing into the key to contest Luke Palmer's strength, unless it was on a fast break, trying to beat the Grizzlies down the court. If their breaks didn't work, they reversed course and hoisted shots from beyond the three-point line. The Grizzly players, meanwhile, took McHue's coaching to heart and stuck close to their opponent in a tight man-to-man defense. They tried to cut off any penetration to the basket. Cole Knighton was especially determined to challenge the Cadet's best shooter. The coaches, pleased to have him back on the court at full speed, encouraged him from the sideline.

If there was a weakness on offense in the Grizzly game, it came from Cole's reluctance to let fly with his usual aerial bombardment. Instead of his standard determination to shoot at every opportunity, he chose instead to pass up shots to find Luke inside, or a streaking Jimmy Ivory as he broke towards the bucket.

McHue turned to Brock, a puzzled look on his face. "Coach, did you tell him not to shoot?"

Brock shook his head. "He's trying to be a team player."

McHue stared at Brock with a look of bewilderment and frustration. "But we need the points."

Brock waved his palm slowly up and down to settle the older man. "It'll be okay. Let him work this out."

"He'd better not wait too long."

Brock nodded. "Let me talk to him at halftime."


As the team retreated to the locker room at the half, red-faced with sweat dripping from their foreheads, they trailed by a half dozen points. Doubt was creeping into the minds of the players. They had given one hundred percent of their effort and still couldn't match the success of the boys from the reform school.

As they sat, scattered in front of their lockers, still breathing hard from the last flurry of activity on the court, the coaches walked in with equal concern on their faces. They had a solid game plan to defend against the run-and-gun style of the opponent and hold the foe to minimal points, yet they trailed. Their offense seemed anemic. Luke was frustrated by the athleticism of the Cadets, and Jimmy's speed was matched by the street ballers. Justin was solid but his points weren't enough.

While the coaches conferred, Luke turned and leaned into Cole. "Knighton, you're giving the game away. You gotta start shootin'."

Cole dropped his shoulders. "I'm trying to fit in. Remember what you said about me hoggin' the ball?"

"Fitting in is one thing, but losing a game isn't how to make friends," Luke said. "We see what you're doing, but geez, man, we need points. That's what you're here for ..."

The coaches moved into the room and McHue stood still, waiting for the team to hush. The boys noticed how flushed his face was and saw a slight tremor in his fingers as he spoke. Was he sick or stricken by fear that his chance of moving on to state was slipping away? When he spoke, his voice was more pleading than coaxing, like a spurned lover begging for another chance.

"Good effort, fellas," he said. "You've held them to a season-low, but we're still behind. We gotta get our offense rolling. Move the ball, find the open man, and make your shots. Let's challenge these guys. That crowd out there is there for one reason. They think you have a chance to move on to state and they don't want to miss it if you can make history." He started to turn to Cole, but in the boy's fragile state he couldn't risk calling him out.

Luke saw the opening. "Coach, can we be alone here for a minute?"

McHue's face crinkled up in wonder. "I don't ..." he started to protest but Brock gently pulled on his arm.

"I think we should step out for a few minutes, Coach," Brock said. Buster nodded and followed Brock out the door.

Luke waited until they were gone and out of earshot and asked all the others to sit down, then pulled Cole up in front of the bench and put his arm around him. Cole looked away from the others and stared at Luke, wondering what he was going to do.

Luke silenced the boys. "Everybody, listen up. This is going to be our last game if we don't get it together. I don't know about you, but I sure as hell don't want it to end." He stared at his teammates and raised his index finger and thumb an inch apart. "We're this close to making it to state," he said as he laid a hand on Cole's shoulder. "But if my little friend here doesn't find the basket in the second half, this season is done." He stared down at Cole. "Now, Knighton, we all respect what you're doing, letting us have a piece of the action. But right now, we couldn't give a friggin' flip about our stats. We need a win. Right now, right here, we are going to bury any hatchet we might have had for you before tonight. We all know what you can do. It's time for you to do it."

He turned to his teammates. "So, we're all going to get behind Cole and he is going to lead us to a win in the district playoffs. Forget everything that's been going on. Right now, we need to show those cocky Cadets and the people out there that we know how to play ball. If Cole is open, he's going to make 'em pay."

Jimmy and Justin and the others clapped their approval. Whatever had happened to shift Luke's feelings for the sophomore wasn't important now. They needed Cole's offense—and now it seemed just as important that Cole needed them.

Justin, claiming his spot as team captain, jumped to his feet. The other members of the team followed his lead. "Take us out," he said, pointing at the two boys standing by the door. "Cole, you first … we're right behind you."

Cole's head was swimming. He'd come so close to abandoning this team … and his life. Now he was being lifted up by those he'd resented most. As he jogged through the doorway with Luke's hand on his shoulder, he was floating. He felt that, even if he never scored another point, he'd won a bigger victory. He gasped for air from the lump in his throat. He wouldn't let them down. He fought back tears as he passed in front of Goldie and Peggy. Goldie clapped her hands but didn't say a word.

During their halftime break, the Coolidge coaches conferred and concluded Cole wasn't their main threat. He had only attempted a half dozen shots and was forcing passes to his teammates. "Knighton isn't going to shoot, so we're going to a zone defense," the head coach told his players. "We'll focus on plugging up the middle and stopping that big man of theirs."

The change in strategy by the coach, which seemed logical at the time, would ultimately yield a death blow to the Cadets. As the defense sagged off on Cole, he took to heart the admonitions of his teammates and began lofting a long-distance barrage on the Coolidge team. The six-point deficit quickly turned into a lead and by the end of the third quarter, the Grizzlies were leading by double digits. Moving the ball quickly from side to side against the zone allowed Knighton enough open space to find the range and hit his target.

The Cadets reversed course in the fourth quarter, switching back to a man defense, but it was too late. The Grizzlies, buoyed by their raucous crowd of fans, were not going to let the probation boys rally. They matched them stride for stride as they raced up and down the floor. As the seconds ticked down, Jimmy dribbled the ball in the back court. The Cadets, knowing a loss was imminent, backed off and waited for the final buzzer.

A month earlier, Jimmy's Black Coolidge counterpart had ridiculed the Grizzly team. Now, as the teams parted ways, he sidled up to Jimmy.

The trash talk disappeared. In a serious but deflated compliment, he nodded toward the celebrating group of Grizzly players. "So, bruh, I guess the bumpkins can play," he said quietly as he extended his hand.

"I think so," Jimmy said. He saw the sadness in the young man's face. He pulled him into a respectable hug. "Good game."

# CHAPTER 34

# COZY

**DON BAKER SET HIS ALARM EARLY** to make sure he could get to the Drive-In and have the coffee brewed before any of the regulars arrived Friday morning. He anticipated the discussions that would erupt around the table as the men put in their two cents about the Grizzlies' victory over the Cadets the night before. He chuckled to himself as he guessed which man would start the conversation and which one would insist the win could be the Grizzlies' last. And, of course, someone would theorize how Buster McHue would find a way to lose the next game.

It wasn't long before he had his answer. The door flew open, and Homer Johnson stomped his feet on the welcome mat as he slammed the door behind him. He let out a holler. "Hey, Don, is the coffee hot?" Without taking a breath, he continued, "Can you believe how that lucky old coach pulled out a win last night?"

Don snatched Homer's cup down off the rack and splashed the fresh brew to the brim. "Gosh, Homer, I don't know what you're talking about." He grinned as he reached over, careful not to spill the contents. The old red mug with the Grizzly logo had been Homer's special cup for a generation.

"Come on, Don, you were there. Those street kids had us on the ropes until Knighton got going. Was he hot in the second half or what?"

Don had traveled to the game with Richard Gallagher. On their way home, as Richard's pickup wound down the lonely highway, with the moon on the horizon, they tried to make sense of what had happened. They couldn't quite put their finger on it. So Don didn't have any answers for Homer. "Something sure turned around at halftime," he said, glancing over at the old gentleman. "Maybe Buster is a better coach than you give him credit for."

"I wouldn't go that far," Homer said as he steadied his cup. "Could be the long layoff helped Cole get his act together. He sure found his shooting touch." Homer shuffled over to his usual spot at the round wooden table with room for ten grown men. "Funny thing, though. Did you notice Goldie hardly made a squawk? Maybe she's got laryngitis or something."

As he finished his thought, the other men started to drift in and fill their cups. They knew they only had a day to think about the upcoming district championship game between the hometown boys and Pine City. The men tried to act nonchalant as they gathered, concealing their excitement over the team's rare appearance at districts. Usually, in late February they would be sharing their opinions on the weather, or the price of grain, or whose prostate was acting up.

However, this morning they had only one thing on their minds. Was there any chance the Grizzlies could pull off a win and lock in a spot in the state tournament?

Soon the table was surrounded, and conversation and laughter bubbled up. Every man put in his two cents. There was no conclusion reached for how the boys had notched the victory or whether they could win the next contest. That is until Slim Mathers, a man who usually just sat and listened, staring into his cup, raised his hand as if he were interrupting a classroom of gifted orators.

"I think ..." he started, in his usual slow-paced drawl.

"Uh oh, Slim is thinking again," Homer said, cutting Slim off halfway through his sentence. Laughter filled the room. "But don't let me stop you. This has to be good."

Every head turned and even the chatterers stopped talking. Slim hesitated, cleared his throat, and continued. "I think," he said again, "we won because of the red tie we bought him. You know, I picked it out. Made him look good, don't ya' think? But if he loses now, we'll take it back."

Nine heads all swiveled back and forth slowly in an "I can't believe he said that" sort of motion. The comment finished the topic, and the men began to talk about the weather.


After the convincing victory over Coolidge, the Grizzly boys discovered a newfound confidence. Luke and Cole were in harmony. Their mothers had surprisingly developed a friendship and were visiting on an almost daily basis. With the help of that relationship, Peggy steadied herself and was back on solid ground, avoiding using alcohol to calm her nerves.

Luke and Ashley were together whenever time and schedule allowed ... in the halls at school or at the convenience store during Ashley's breaks. It was Ashley who could calm the big boy down and take his mind off the battle he would face against Pine City's big post.

On the Gallagher farm, there was a lull in the calving schedule and Brock and Jimmy were catching up on their sleep. Brock was relieved when Ronnie told him about the letter she'd sent Donigan. After witnessing Donigan's persistence, Brock wasn't convinced it was over, but it put his mind at ease for now.

To brighten everyone's attitude, the weather warmed, with no late winter storms predicted for the week. The day between games for the district championship gave Brock and Coach McHue time to plan for the pivotal contest. The only obstacle keeping the Grizzly basketball team from reaching the state tournament was the Pine City Mustangs and Milo, their big center. In their first game, Luke Palmer spent most of the contest sitting on the bench in foul trouble. If the Grizzlies were to advance, keeping Luke on the court was the key.

Coach McHue met with Brock the day after the Coolidge win. "How do we handle the big guy, Milo Ruttinger?" Buster asked as he scanned the roster of the Pine City players.

If Brock had been asked about defenses on the football field, he'd have had a ready answer. A four-two front with a nickel back. Or a three-four with a spy shadowing the star player. But with basketball, he was out of his element. He had learned a lot working with the veteran round ball coach, but he couldn't begin to scheme a defense for basketball.

Brock said the obvious. "Keep Luke out of foul trouble. But I don't know how."

Buster rubbed his head, his mind wandering off into a world of $x$'s and $o$'s. "Maybe a triangle and two. Part man. Part zone. We surround the big guy with three players in a zone and man up their two guards. With Justin and Derek Baker helping Luke defend the big guy, maybe we can stretch the game and share the load of defending their star."

Brock looked at Buster, who was lost in his thoughts, still staring at the roster. *The guy is smart*, Brock thought, *like a chess player.*

Buster continued as if he was talking to himself. "We'll milk seconds off the shot clock. Slow the game down into fewer possessions. Try not to turn the ball over. Then there'll be less chance for Luke to stumble into unnecessary fouls."

As Buster was speaking, Brock loaded the game film from the team's first meeting, and while rain pounded the pavement outside the school, the men watched the screen, searching for weaknesses in the Mustang defense.

Hours later, as the coaches exited the school and stopped to lock the outside door, they noticed two youngsters across the street. They were playing one-on-one in a neighbor's driveway. A hoop without a net hung from the garage. A slight drizzle still fell from the sky. The boys, not yet teenagers, were laughing and jabbering as rain soaked their clothes and the ball bounced through puddles. "I'm Cole Knighton," the smaller one yelled, lofting a long jumper toward the rim.

"And I'm Luke Palmer," the second boy answered as he drove his shoulder into his small friend.

The two men smiled at one another. The hoop game was alive in the Grove.

# REMINISCE

**WHILE BROCK AND JIMMY** were heading back to the District Basketball Tournament, Peter Green told Brock he'd visit the farm to keep Irene company. She'd decided before the season started not to attend basketball games unless the Grizzlies qualified for the state tournament. As much as she wanted to watch Jimmy and the team play, she knew her health wouldn't allow frequent evenings sitting inside a drafty old gymnasium. An almost predictable seasonal cold or flu might end her life sooner than she wished.

However, Irene promised herself that if the Grizzlies qualified for the state tourney, she would risk it to watch Jimmy lead the team in search of a trophy. And, of course, Brock would be there on the bench with old Buster McHue. She knew Brock felt out of place helping coach basketball, but it gave her another reason to want to go.

Green arrived on the farm just after lunch and bounced up the sidewalk, cradling the bouquet he'd ordered for Valentine's Day. He was anxious to see his old friend. *Try to stay calm*, he told himself. He'd only been in the Grove for a short time but had been anticipating this moment since he arrived. It would be the first time in over forty years they would be together. The last time he'd been with her, he left feeling as if his heart had been ripped out of his chest. He'd been in love with Irene Caruthers ... before she became Max Gallagher's wife.

They'd spent time together in their early twenties and had become close friends. He wanted their relationship to be much more. She was high-spirited and adventurous, unafraid of risks. He loved being with her. When they were together, he felt whole, like he could tackle the world head-on. He had talent and energy. She had spirit, always smiling and laughing, her blue eyes sparkling.

But then along came a handsome young farmer named Max Gallagher, a serious, determined man who everyone in the community respected. Where Green could offer adventure and playfulness, Gallagher offered a home, and the challenge to make a useful life in an idyllic setting with acres and animals and space. Irene fell in love with the idea.

When Green paid his last visit to Irene, she showed him the diamond on her hand. "I'm in love, Peter," she'd said. Her face glowed with the anticipation of becoming a wife and a respectable member of the little community. The life Gallagher offered had a stronger pull than being partners with a fun-loving fellow with a paintbrush.

Green still remembered the crushing heartache he felt when she kissed him on the cheek to say goodbye. He didn't blame Irene. She made a good choice, but still, he wondered if she might have been just as happy with him. He let those thoughts bounce through his mind as he knocked on her door.

"Peter," Irene laughed as the door swung open. For a few awkward seconds, they stood looking at one another, searching for the person they once knew. "Please come in," she finally said. "Flowers for me? Where have you been for the last forty years?" Her familiar sarcastic humor toyed with Peter's memories.

"Just waiting for you to call," he smiled, and tipped his painter's cap as he handed her the flowers. "So, thank heavens that old Grizzly bear needed a paint job, or I would never have seen you again."

She smiled. "The bear has faded and so have we." She took his hands in hers. "Come in. Let's catch up. We have a lot to talk about."

As they settled onto the sofa, Green looked at Irene, his eyes studying her face.

"Oh, Peter, stop staring, I know I'm a wrinkled old thing," Irene laughed.

Green reached over and patted her hand. "Irene, you're just as beautiful as ever."

"And you're full of it, just like always."

"So, you still won't marry me?" He shifted on the cushion as he laughed.

"Don't you think I'm a little old for that?" she said. She waved him off with her hand.

"Never too old, I say. I figured maybe this time you'd change your mind."

Irene became serious. "Peter, you know I cared for you back when we were dating. It was awfully exciting for me being courted by two handsome men at the same time."

"But you showed me the door and married the big strong handsome guy ... the most eligible bachelor in the county." He reached into his pocket and grabbed for a cigarette but stopped himself. "Can't say as I blame you. A good-looking farmer versus a skinny little painter with no money. It really wasn't much of a contest, was it?"

"Oh yes, it was. I loved being with you; you always made me laugh. But I had to make a choice. And I fell in love with Max and with this farm. I was swept away by it all."

"So, if I'd had a farm, you would have been mine?" He grinned playfully, knowing what her answer would be.

"I can't see you as a farmer."

"Nor can I, my sweet lady. I wouldn't last a month unless I could paint murals on the walls of every farm building on the place. But I hope you know you kind of broke my heart when you gave me the heave-ho. I couldn't paint a straight line for a couple of months, you know … thinking about you."

"I'm sorry."

"But it got better when I moved to Portland and found Gladys. But I did miss this little town. And I missed you."

Irene began pulling herself up out of the chair. "Peter M. Green, we've talked enough about our romantic past. Let's leave it behind. And let me fix something for us to eat."

Green stood and gently helped her up from the chair. "Let me help with a meal. I'm a good cook too, you know." He extended his arm, and they made their way into the kitchen.

The afternoon passed quickly, as they shared stories about their life's journey. Irene told how she and Max had married and set about to start a family. But after several years without children, they'd sadly adjusted to the fact that it might never happen. Then, one spring morning, after missing her monthly period once again, and afraid to tell Max if it was a false alarm, she felt a movement in her stomach. She was pregnant.

It was a joyful moment and months later, a beautiful baby boy was born. They named him Brock Matthew Gallagher. Her life was complete. And despite the ups and downs of farm life, she went about her chores as perhaps the happiest woman in the world. They had a wonderful twenty-three years of life together before an accident took Max's life.

"I'm sorry," Peter said.

Irene continued. "It was like a bad dream. One day you're so happy you think nothing can change the way you feel, and then the next thing you know the bottom falls out from under you. But I still had Brock. He was my rock. I couldn't spend a lot of time grieving because of him. And the farm kept us busy." She gazed over at her old friend. "And now tell me about your adventurous life. I know you well enough to know you've had lots of excitement."

Peter cleared his throat. He needed a cigarette but resisted. "Well, if you have to know, once I got over the heartache of being rejected by a beautiful young lady in Glory Grove," his eyes crinkled up, "I packed my things and headed west. Found a nice community of artists, settled in, and made a good life for myself. You won't believe this, but that old Grizzly I painted was key to getting some good jobs. I showed photos of what I'd done here, and before I knew it, I was being paid handsomely for painting murals in Portland. Never got rich but loved every minute of it. You know, even in a big city there are small communities that reach out to help. Not like the Grove but with some of the same compassion for one another."

"And I see you have a wedding ring. Tell me about your wife."

His eyes fluttered with the question. "A wonderful woman. Full of energy like you. She was part of the art community. I'm a painter. She was an artist. It was a good mix. I painted with a broad brush. She used delicate strokes. Oh, how we loved arguing over who had the most talent. Of course, I knew she did … just didn't want to let her know it. She died ten years ago. She was working on a beautiful piece of art in her studio, a painting of the Oregon Coast … children playing on the beach, when she leaned back in her chair and stopped breathing."

His lower lip trembled for a second, then he regained his composure.

"Life was never quite the same after that. We raised two daughters, grown women now, one's a lawyer and the other is an accountant. They help take care of me, checking in from time to time. Neither one is artistic … wouldn't you know. But some of the grandkids like to draw so there is hope." He relaxed in his chair. "It's been a good life, Irene. And even better now because I get to see you again."

The next day, Painter Green headed out once again to the Gallagher farm. He'd asked Irene if she'd like to go for a drive. "I would love that," she said. "I don't get away from the farm very often unless it is for doctor visits."

It wasn't like she didn't enjoy her life. Despite her illness and some bad days, Jimmy routinely filled her in on the activities at school and the drama taking place on the basketball team. They shared a common interest in the cows, as the bulk of the herd was nearing the end of the calving cycle. Irene watched the herd from her kitchen window and Jimmy still took his turns walking the pasture.

And it wasn't only Jimmy who kept her company. Richard always came for coffee in the morning after Brock and Jimmy left for school. Their daily visits centered on farm work and planning. There was now also open and honest talk of the pressure they were feeling from some of the local ranchers to sign with the wind farm.

Brock kept a close eye on his mom and her medical needs, scheduling appointments and filling prescriptions. Recently he'd become aware of Irene's uptick in spirit when she heard Peter Green was back in town. She was adding touches of makeup to her face and was more selective in choosing clothes to wear, as if she was preparing for an important upcoming event.

It made Brock happy to know that even if his mother's days were numbered, they could be filled with happiness instead of dwelling on her present situation. The only drag on her mood was the decision the family was going to have to make concerning the wind lease.

When Green called Irene offering a drive through the country, she didn't hesitate. "Well, Peter, if you can get me up in that old van of yours, I'd love to go for a ride." There was a little giggle in her voice.

"Yes, dear friend. If I have to, I'll just pick you up and throw you in."

That afternoon, when Green arrived and pulled up in front of the yard gate, he snuffed out his cigarette. He'd been driving with the windows down to discharge some of the smoke for Irene's sake. She met him at the door. She had her coat on and a scarf around her neck. Her eyes sparkled with anticipation. Green noticed how that hadn't changed in all the years they'd been apart. As they made their way to the van, Sassy followed along, rubbing her head on Green's hand.

"Okay, pup, I see you," Green said. "I suppose you want to ride, too." Sassy's tail wagged her answer, beating against his leg like a metronome setting the beat for a ragtime jazz piano solo. "What do you think, Irene, can the dog ride along?"

"She'd love that. The last ride she took was to Seattle for the football championship game. She enjoyed riding and now she tries to climb into any van that pulls up at our house. I'm kind of surprised she hasn't left with the UPS driver."

Green helped Irene up into the bucket seat and then lifted Sassy through the cargo door. The pup quickly worked her way between the front seats and sat proudly with her head leaned up against Irene's leg. Off they went. Green drove slowly, making Irene as comfortable as possible. They wound through the country roads, each one bringing a memory to Green's mind. He and Irene had gone on drives like this when they were dating. When he pulled over at a turnout, neither of them spoke of the place. It was where they'd spent a few special evenings watching the sunset.

Green surveyed the horizon. "Still as beautiful as it was when we were young," he said. "There are some great vistas in this country. Too bad my wife couldn't have seen them. She would have loved putting these images on canvas."

"I wish I could have met her," Irene said. "She sounds like a lovely person. And the paintings would be nice to have since it might not be long until all this beautiful country looks like an industrial site."

Green looked over. "What's going on that I don't know?"

Irene looked out to the distant hills as she stroked Sassy's head. Her face turned sad. "They want to build a wind farm out here on the ridge. Maybe as many as two hundred towers."

Green's shoulders curled in. "And ruin this beautiful countryside?"

"I'm afraid so. Some folks see the dollar signs and can't resist. And I really can't blame them … it would pull a few people out of their money troubles."

"You included?" Green pushed the cap back on his head, a curious look on his face.

"I guess. We're in the center of the proposed project. Richard says the money would almost guarantee we'd never have to sell the farm."

"Sure. But it would be like watching the scenery being murdered.

Having lived in the city for so long, I wish they could leave the country-side alone. Folks need to understand it's worth saving a few undeveloped areas without all the trappings of civilization. People need to get out of the cities and breathe. And besides, the electricity those wind farms produce isn't for you folks here. It's all for the city people."

Irene was struggling with the topic. Was she being selfish, wanting to deny the installation of wind towers on the Gallagher property? Afterall, the city folks need electricity too. And she knew it wasn't possible to build wind towers in a city. Today's citizens would never go back to living without lights and heat, or air conditioning. The power had to come from somewhere. But why did it have to come from the land she loved so dearly?

Green was working himself into a crescendo with his diatribe. He reached for a cigarette but remembered how sick his friend was. "Those people won't have to look at all the towers. They won't see the red lights and listen to the noise. They only know it'll light up their houses. That's exactly why those towers end up in places like Glory Grove. Because there aren't enough people here to protest. They can walk all over you, and nobody cares."

Irene was impressed with the passion her old friend had for the situation. "Well, we do care, Peter. But it's not an easy decision and we're feeling a lot of pressure. One of our neighbors even threatened to cut off our water if we didn't sign."

"Oh, those big wigs have you right where they want you … I've heard it before. They are throwing out their nets like they are trawling for fish. Some people want to take the money and run. While others just want to be left alone. That's the way communities like Glory Grove get divided over this kind of so-called progress. I wish I had a vote. I know what I'd say. I'd say, 'Take your towers and build them somewhere else … not in this beautiful countryside.' But I guess I don't live here so I don't have a say."

Irene looked over at the man. She studied his face and sighed. "I've missed you, Peter Green. You haven't changed a bit … still wanting to fight the good fight." She turned her body toward him. "I'm happy you're back in the Grove. Life is better with you here; I want you to know that. And not just because the bear got a new coat of paint."

She reached over Sassy and patted Peter's arm. "If I was still in my twenties, I'd slide over there and curl up beside you, like I used to do." Sassy followed Irene's gesture with her eyes and calmly laid her head on Green's lap.

Irene laughed like a very mature schoolgirl. "But now I guess you'll have to settle for a border collie."

Green smiled. "That will be enough."


The shortness of a February day sent the couple hurrying back to the farmhouse. The pleasantness of warming spring temperatures rapidly turned chilly as the sun began to set. Peter pulled up to the sidewalk in front of the house and scurried around the vehicle to help Irene onto the ground. He took her arm as she lowered herself.

"I wish I could hop out like I did in the old days," she said as she found her footing.

"Oh, but we're so much wiser now," he said. "Look at me, I haven't had a cigarette all afternoon. I must be getting smarter with age."

Irene's lips parted in a grin as she looked over at the man holding her arm. "You didn't smoke because you don't want me to die any sooner than I already will. And I appreciate your consideration. If you'd give that habit up, you might live a little longer yourself."

He bowed his head, trying to think of something witty to answer. All he found was a quick, "Yes, ma'am." Then he added. "I'll abstain as long as you'll hold my hand when my cravings begin."

Irene didn't miss a beat. "Stay with me as long as you want, Peter. Even if you have to sneak out once in a while to fill your lungs with smoke. I can ignore your vices. I just enjoy having you around."

"You're making me giddy with that kind of talk, young lady," Peter said. He paused for effect. "What do you have going on this evening? Can I take you to dinner? I know where there is a well-stocked kitchen." He nodded toward the house.

"Yes, and then after we eat, we're going to turn on the radio and listen to the ball game. The Grizzlies are playing Pine City in the district championship tonight and I want to hear how Jimmy and Luke are doing. They're like family now. Good boys. They've added a lot to my life. And now you're here. My life is pretty full, don't you think? Surrounded by men. I always liked it that way." She batted her eyes in movie star fashion. "And I still do."

Green laid his cap down on a chair as they stepped into the warmth of the home. He watched as Irene ambled toward the kitchen. He followed behind her. He didn't reach for a cigarette.

# CHAPTER 36

# REMATCH

**THE BLEACHERS WERE FILLED** as the Pine City Mustangs and Glory Grove Grizzly players burst from their respective locker rooms. The crowd rose from their seats while the bands played the school fight songs, each in turn. They were amateur musicians making music they'd memorized since their first introduction to high school band.

Ashley Summers, while playing her clarinet, kept her eyes on Luke as he sprinted down the sideline in front of her, a smile on his face. He followed Justin toward their basket. Jimmy Ivory trailed right behind. These boys had become her best friends since the beginning of the school year and all the drama that took place with the football team.

While the players warmed up, the opposing cheerleaders met in the corner of the gym, making nice to each other before the verbal battle began with their rehearsed cheering from opposite sides of the court.

Ashley hoped to one day be a cheerleader. She twice tried to make the Grizzly squad (once in the fall and again for winter sports) and failed both times. *Perhaps next year*, she thought. Despite her desire to be on the cheer squad, she liked being in the band, sharing the fun with the other band members, and watching her fun-loving teacher.

The arena was buzzing in anticipation of the big game for the league championship. Ashley watched Milo Ruttinger, the giant center for the Mustangs. He didn't seem like a dastardly villain. He seemed more like an oversized, soft giant who might still sleep with a stuffed animal at night. She laughed to herself at the thought. Still, tonight he was the enemy … the one person who could end the Grizzlies' quest for a rare trip to the state tournament.

Before the team left to dress for the game, she and Luke sat together, holding hands. She could tell Luke was on pins and needles thinking about the night's contest. He was also reliving the embarrassment he felt in the two teams' first meeting. He'd spent most of the game sitting on the bench in foul trouble.

She tried to calm him. Yet, when he stood to leave and she kissed his cheek, she felt him shiver … not from the kiss, but from his anxiety. He was game-ready. *Hopefully not for football*, Ashley thought.

After the teams were announced, Brock took his place next to Buster. "I think we're ready," Brock said. Buster could only nod, too nervous to speak. The boys had spent two full practices polishing the new defense, determined not to let Milo Ruttinger beat them. From the first moments of the game, every fan could see the strategy unfolding. Ruttinger was surrounded by three boys denying him his usual post moves.

Still, some of the Grizzly fans were concerned. "Come on, Luke," Peggy Palmer whispered, "Don't foul … please don't foul." On every play, Tim leaned his body in whichever direction Luke was moving, silently duplicating his every move. Peggy tried moving with him, releasing his force, until she finally grew tired of the shadow dance and shifted closer to Goldie to avoid further body blows.

Goldie's eyes focused on the battle her son Cole was facing, keeping the Mustang guards in check. Cole was determined to hold up his end of the bargain. Since his teammates had bottled up the big man, the Mustang guards were free to assert themselves, trying to keep stride with the Grizzlies outside shooting. Cole was being tested … no longer solely an offensive force. He now prided himself on his defensive play. "Good job, Cole, you make us proud," Goldie whispered.

Across the floor, the Pine City fans were worried and frustrated, knowing their chance for a state berth rested on the shoulders of Milo Ruttinger. He'd led them to a spot in the district championship and now their hopes were fading. Their hearts were hurting as they watched him get stymied by the three-pronged attack of the Grizzlies.

Milo had always been a soft lovable boy. The families in Pine City had virtually ignored him until, by the end of his grade school years, he had outgrown his parents and most of the high school students. He eventually towered over every person in Pine City. However, his demeanor kept him from becoming a bully. Often it was the opposite, as smaller boys realized he would not retaliate to their bullying. He was too bashful and withdrawn to play football. But in this basketball season, he'd finally found his moments of glory. He was the league's leading scorer, and his team was highly ranked in the state polls. Now, as they cheered their team on, the Pine City faithful suffered personal angst watching Milo, seemingly caught in a trap with no way out.

Despite his cautious play, Luke was tagged with two fouls before halftime. "Dammit. This isn't good," Tim groaned. The coaches encouraged him to keep his cool. Their strategy was working perfectly. If Luke could keep his inclinations to physically dominate under control, the Grizzlies could claim the district crown.

The boys from the Grove led by nine points at halftime, and the third quarter was mired in a back-and-forth affair. Every time the Mustangs made a run, their spurt would be answered by a Cole three-point score or a drive to the basket by Jimmy. Milo Ruttinger was no longer a weapon. The Grizzly fans rose to their feet as the fourth quarter began and most, especially the students, stayed on their feet for the remainder of the game. Luke eventually got tagged with two more fouls—one on a silly reach-in—however, it came with less than a minute to play. He smiled at the referee. This one wouldn't matter.

As the clock wound down and the seconds ticked off, the entire Glory Grove fandom were united in their cheer. *We're on our way to state … We're on our way to state …* they repeated in sing-song fashion until the buzzer sounded.

Milo Ruttinger lowered his head, the color gone from his cheeks. His lower lip pushed out like a child who'd been scolded for spilling Kool-Aid on a carpet. His heart was breaking. If the Grove fans had noticed, they might have been sympathetic, but that emotion was trumped by the relief and joy they were feeling for their own team. They'd waited too many years for this moment, and they were going to enjoy it.

Brock turned to Buster McHue and patted his shoulder. "Congratulations, Coach, you've done it."

"No, Brock, we've done it. You and me and those kids. You helped bring us all together." He reached for Brock's hand and shook it hard. "Couldn't have done this without you." He had barely finished speaking when his arm was purposefully pulled back by his tearful wife, Eunice. She leaned into his protruding middle and kissed his cheek. He was at the same time receiving pats on the back from numerous ecstatic Grove fans.

But Buster continued to look Brock in the eye. He calmly mouthed two words. "Thank you." Then, with one arm around Eunice, he turned toward the fans and raised his index finger high into the air.

# CHAPTER 37

# DOGS

**BROCK ROSE BEFORE THE SUN WAS UP** on the morning following the game. He saddled Dolly and climbed on for a quick ride through the pasture before church. It felt good to be in the saddle. He'd spent hours riding when he was a boy. His spirit was soaring after the team's victory, yet he still needed to free his mind from some of the other things troubling him. He returned to Glory Grove seeking the warmth and serenity of the place of his youth. Yet, as he took stock of his present situation, he was struck by how many complications had come to pass. Whichever way he turned, it seemed, he was buffeted by a strong headwind.

He was comforted by the fact his mother was still with him. Although she was slowly failing, she was well in spirit and had a strong desire to face each day with a positive attitude. She was—as she had always been—his role model. And now she seemed energized by the return of Peter Green to the Grove.

On the other side of the coin, his move home had magnified the weakness in his marriage to Celia. Divorce papers had been delivered. It was going to happen, and he'd come to terms with it. Now, a former love had returned to his life. It eased the pain he felt from the pending divorce, but even that relationship wasn't on solid ground if Ronnie changed her mind and left the Grove for a better life.

The one thing that should have been solid, the anchor to which his new life was tied—the farm itself—was threatened by the intrusion of the wind company wanting to change the world around them.

Those were the big things in everyday life, but just as pressing to Brock was the thing of immediate concern to the people in the Grove—a sports team that was making its citizens proud. He had grown to care for these boys, particularly one fragile soul who'd nearly ended his own life. Could they take a giant step forward … bring home hardware from the state tournament and make school history?

Like a juggler with spinning plates overhead, Brock worried about his new reality, finding it hard to keep any or all of the platters from crashing to the ground. Those thoughts disappeared as Dolly crested the hill. His ride had taken him to the water gap his family shared with Del Leachman. As he approached, he noticed tracks. *From a four-wheeler*, he thought. They led to the wooden gate posts his father had placed in the ground two decades earlier. The gate was the entrance to the lane leading to the spring where the ranchers shared water. The old cedar posts lay strewn about on the ground.

Now, three-inch iron posts had replaced the wooden ones and two sixteen-foot steel gates were hinged to the posts. A padlock dangled from one end of the open gate. To Brock, the message from Del Leachman was clear. Sign the wind company lease or lose the water.

Brock eased himself down from Dolly's saddle and tied her to the metal post. He stepped lightly through the moist soil to the trough. Water in the tank rippled in the breeze. It bubbled up from the inlet pipe at the bottom of the tank. He reached down and rinsed his hands, letting the water slip through his fingers. He cupped his fingers together, splashed some on his face then lifted some to his lips. He swallowed. It was cold and pure.

"Mother Nature's finest," he said out loud. Dolly's ears twitched forward at the sound of his voice. "But maybe not for us for long." He walked back, untied the reins, and climbed back into the saddle. He guided the mare to the trough and let her drink. *While you still can.*

Brock hurried back to the house and told his mother what he had found and that he was going to visit Del Leachman. "Just take it slow," Irene said. "Maybe he's just bluffing. If we rile him up, we might really lose access to that spring."

"It looks like he's already made up his mind," Brock said. "But he needs to know we can't be pushed around like that. This is as close to extortion as you can get in farm country."

Three large dogs came running out to greet him when Brock pulled into the driveway of the Leachman house. They weren't friendly. *Guard dogs*, Brock thought, *Rottweilers.* As he cracked the pickup door open, the barking intensified, and the lead dog lurched through the opening, nipping at Brock's hand. The black dog's white teeth showed through a rust-colored muzzle. Brown spots extended up from dark eyes like miniature horns. *A devil dog*, Brock thought. He tugged the door shut to keep the animal's one-hundred-and-twenty-pound body from forcing its way through the opening.

He was trying to figure out his next move when the dogs heard

Del Leachman's voice. "Down, boys … get back." Leachman stood on the front porch of his house, hatless with an unbuttoned shirt. His eyes were squinting into the sun, clearly waking from sleep.

"Morning, neighbor," Leachman said, his voice croaking through his first words. "You're out and about early today."

Brock unconsciously looked down at his watch as he opened the door. He didn't comment on the fact it was already eight o'clock and most farmers had been up for hours. He eyed the dogs to make sure they were still retreating. "Just thought I'd swing by and visit about the gates you put up at the water gap. I rode out that way this morning and saw what you'd done. Are you trying to send us a message?"

Leachman nodded and cleared his throat. "Just trying to get ahead of things," he said.

Brock was heeding his mother's advice. He didn't want to start an argument but needed to express his disappointment at Leachman's actions. "Del, your father and mine were good friends. Your dad was generous enough to give us access to your spring. In turn, we would share any excess hay we'd raised when your stocks ran short. That cooperation has lasted for a long time."

Leachman buttoned his shirt as Brock spoke, acting as if he wasn't listening.

Brock continued to talk. "I hope we can disagree about the wind farm without this turning into some kind of feud. Our cows need water, and you need a good neighbor."

Leachman yawned and finished tucking in his shirt. "Well, good neighbors try to help each other out in a lot of ways. We can be great friends, and both have more money in our pockets. All we have to do is sign those leases. That seems pretty simple to me. Unless you'd like to continue to scratch and claw to make a living up on this rocky ridge.

That's up to you." He stared over at Brock. "It's going to be a lot harder if your cows can't get water."

Leachman was ending the conversation. He turned and headed back to his house but threw a few final words over his shoulder. "Sorry if the dogs scared you," he laughed. "I guess the Rotts can't tell a friendly neighbor from a stubborn one. So let me know which you are, so I can let these fellas know the next time you come by to visit." He walked back into the house, leaving Brock staring at the closed door.

While Brock was having words with Leachman, the phone rang in the Gallagher kitchen. Irene picked it up. She always tried to have breakfast ready for Brock and Jimmy ahead of church. Jimmy was worn out from the two days of basketball he'd experienced in the week and was still in bed.

"Hello," Irene chirped. She was in a good mood, knowing the basketball team had notched a ticket to the state tournament and she would be going. She assumed it was someone wanting to talk about the game. The community would be buzzing with excitement. But the call wasn't about basketball. It was about wind.

Sally Smith was on the line. "Sally, how are you? It's good to hear your voice. We haven't talked since you left town." Sally was Del Leachman's sister. She'd married a man she met in college and lived in Colorado.

"It has been a while, for sure. What's it been, fifteen years? Anyway, I hope I didn't wake you," Sally said. "I can never figure out the time difference. I want to ask you about a letter I received from some wind company. Something about leasing some of our farm ground."

Irene was confused. Why would Sally have gotten a letter from Wind Driven when everyone knew she'd sold her share of the

Leachman farm to her brother? As she held the receiver to her ear, Irene remembered what a talker Sally always was. She seldom stopped to take a breath.

"After we sold our share of the farm, we found out Del hadn't been real fair with us. I trusted him to pay us a fair price, but I think he took advantage of my ignorance about property values. As you might expect, I'm not very happy with my baby brother."

"Sure," Irene said. "I can understand how you feel. But why would you be getting a letter from the wind people?"

"Well, the one thing I didn't sign over to Del were the mineral rights to the farm. You know, my husband is a geologist; that's why we're in Colorado. He just thought maybe someday there might be oil deep down in that mountain range. I talked to an attorney, and he thinks since I'm still half-owner of the mineral rights … that might include the wind. That's why I received the letter."

Irene took it all in, realizing how it complicated Del Leachman's desire to enroll his farm with Wind Driven.

"I need your advice, Irene. I trust your opinion. I only wish I had talked to you before I sold the land."

Irene pulled a chair over to the phone and settled in. "Sally, feel free to call anytime. It's nice to stay in touch and I appreciate your confidence in me. However, this is a complicated situation. How much time do you have? This could be a long conversation." Being as polite and diplomatic as she could, Irene let Sally know what was happening regarding the wind project and tactfully described the unpleasant pressure her brother was applying to the neighbors to get them to sign.

Sally listened without interrupting until Irene was finished. "So, what if I don't sign, what happens?" Sally asked.

"I'm not sure." Irene paused. "But I'd think since you are part owner of the mineral rights, Del can't enter your farm into a lease without your signature. Still, I'm not sure wind is the same as mining or drilling. That's up to the attorney. And I must be honest; if you don't sign, you might be giving up a pretty big pot of money."

There was a long pause on the phone. Silence. That was unusual for Sally. Irene said, "Sally, are you still there?"

"I'm here, Irene … just thinking. The money really isn't a problem for us. But maybe it is for Del. What if I tell my brother to stop threatening you folks about cutting off your water, or I won't sign the lease? That isn't civil of him to suggest that."

"That's nice of you. It might help."

Sally slowed her speech. "I may not sign anyway. I'd hate to see the ridge dotted with those wind towers. I loved that country growing up and wish I could live there now. But my husband's work will keep us here for now. I always thought someday we might come back to the Grove to retire, but we won't if we're surrounded by wind turbines. I have some serious thinking to do. Thanks, Irene, for your time."

When Sally hung up, Irene stayed seated in her chair, replaying the conversation in her head. She didn't like to interfere in other people's business. But this was different.

# CHAPTER 38

# HAROLD

HAROLD OLSON, THE MAN MOST OPPOSED to the wind turbines, was in church the same Sunday morning Irene received the call from Sally Smith. Brock made a habit of taking his mom and Jimmy to the eleven o'clock worship service. Despite his short visit with Del Leachman, he had just enough time to get there before the service began. They had become so regular with their attendance that the other churchgoers didn't give them any special notice. Brock was happy with that, although Jimmy liked being noticed. The attention he received from the basketball fans and, of course, the church ladies made him feel good.

"They are treating me special," he said to Irene, one Sunday as they rode home.

"Don't let it go to your head," she said. "Just remember why we go to church. It's not for you to start a fan club."

"Okay, Irene, I'll pray for forgiveness for acting big," Jimmy teased. He glanced over at Brock, who was grinning, remembering how his mom had said the same to him when his high school sports career took off.

As people moved past the greeter and into the sanctuary, there was a sudden ripple among the attendees. It happened when Harold stepped in the door at the back of the room wearing a dark suit and tie. He wasn't a regular but did faithfully attend on Easter and Christmas. "Why do you suppose Harold is here today?" one older parishioner asked as she leaned out from her pew. She wore old-fashioned hearing aids and spoke loudly to compensate for the plugs in her ears. Everyone heard.

"Must be something big," her friend whispered. "He hardly ever gets off his tractor." They didn't know that Harold was there not on a religious quest, but to see Brock, hoping to catch him on a Sunday. He was furious at their neighbor, Del Leachman, and wanted to share his angst with someone.

Harold was overdressed for a routine Sunday service and, with his serious demeanor, resembled a pallbearer at a funeral. With the pressure on folks to sign leases, perhaps he thought it was appropriate dress for the battle he was anticipating. Erecting wind turbines on Piney Ridge might be a death knell for the farm life he was living. He sat down in the vacant row behind the Gallaghers and said hello to Irene, but didn't say another word, waiting for the hour-long service to conclude before speaking.

As the young minister finished her message, she nodded to those assembled, staring casually at Harold. "See you next Sunday," she said, smiling. Harold paid no mind. He rose, his big frame towering over Jimmy and Irene. He waited for Brock to turn then asked, "Brock, can I have a word?"

Brock could see Olson was even more serious than usual. "Sure, Harold, let's step outside so we won't bother the others." He turned to his mother. "Mom, why don't you and Jimmy head down to coffee hour and let me visit with Harold."

When the men were outside, away from the others, Harold let Brock know what was on his mind. Del Leachman was making noise, threatening to make accusations against him for overgrazing ground he leased from the Department of Natural Resources. The DNR ground was a large part of Olsen's pasture acreage. If he lost the lease, he'd have to cut his cow numbers in half.

"But Harold, you don't overgraze."

"I know that, but what if they believe Del? I don't want to take a chance. Maybe the state will force me to allow towers on their pasture land, but I'll be damned if I'll let any wind turbines on my farm ground."

"Sounds like we both have a problem with Del. I had a not-too-friendly visit with him this morning. We don't like being threatened any more than you. But Del's only thinking of the money. That's his motivation. There should be some way to counter that without it getting ugly. Let me think on it. We have some time before Wind Driven imposes their deadline."

As they stood talking, Brock's mind was already thinking through their options. If Olson threatened to sue Leachman for making false accusations against him, he might back off when he realized he'd have to hire an expensive attorney. He couldn't afford that.

The water the Gallagher family used on Leachman's pasture was an established custom … a historic easement. That might win in a court with the right judge. Brock was thinking like a coach, running through the options, searching for the right play … establishing a game plan. If he chose the right way to defend against Leachman's attack, they might avoid ending up on the losing side.

Brock stood with one foot on the church steps. He wished he could help this big man … a man who simply wanted to be left alone to do what he did best … farm the land. "Harold, I don't think you'll lose your lease. He's bluffing. And you don't have to sign anything—no matter how much pressure you'll get from the others. This is still a free country. You have rights. Don't forget that."

Harold nodded. "I'm going home to get some salt out on the ridge before we turn our cows out. I hope we can do something about Del. He's getting awful pushy about this, and I don't like being pushed around." He turned and strode out, his shoulders broad against the sun. As he left, he reached up and removed his tie.

Brock studied the man. *This rift between old neighbors could be more harmful than the damage the wind farm does to our land,* Brock thought. These were hurt feelings that could last a generation. But in this case, if Del Leachman wanted a confrontation, he shouldn't want it to be a physical one. Not with Harold Olson. That wouldn't last long … unless Del brought his pack of dogs.

CHAPTER 39

# ATTACK

**DEL LEACHMAN'S SILVER PICKUP** came flying up the driveway early the following Saturday morning. It headed straight toward the Gallagher house. Brock and Jimmy were inside, easing into the kitchen chairs as Irene prepared breakfast. Jimmy's favorite day of the week was Saturday, when the family's activities slowed down and they all sat down for breakfast before heading out.

Jimmy delighted in how his new family gathered around the kitchen table and chatted about the week's activities, sharing the highs and lows, and what lay ahead. He'd not had that living alone with his mother in Seattle. But here, despite their fragmented schedules with cows, basketball, and doctors' appointments, the entire family made it a priority to eat together on Saturday morning.

Irene let Jimmy sleep in, knowing how an active high school teenager could be overwhelmed by a busy schedule. But Jimmy was awakened by the sizzling of frying bacon and the smell of bread soaked in egg, cinnamon, and butter browning on the frying pan. He came bounding down the stairs, sleepy-eyed, with a smile on his face. This was the standard routine, so it seemed unusual for anyone to visit on Saturday morning.

"Maybe one of our cows got out on the highway," Irene said, as she cautiously flipped strips of bacon over in the frying pan.

Brock stood up and peered out the window. "Maybe," he said, as he balanced the coffee cup in his hand, "but whatever is on Del's mind, it looks like he can't wait to share it."

Irene rocked back and forth in her slippers as she studied the French toast on the grill. "With the attitude he's been carrying around lately, this probably won't be a courtesy call. He may have heard what I told his sister on the phone the other day." She patted the toast with the spatula as if hoping the gesture would settle down whatever would happen next.

"I'll go see what he wants," Brock said. He set his coffee cup on the table, slipped on his boots, and headed out the back door. He was only a half dozen steps into the yard when Leachman spotted him.

"I've got a bone to pick with you," Leachman shouted. At the sound of his voice, the single Rottweiler inside the one-ton Ford pickup began to bark. It was the same *devil dog* Brock faced at Leachman's house. He pressed up against the windows, seeming to share his master's anger.

"Calm down, Del," Brock said, trying hard not to raise his voice. "What brings you here on a Saturday morning?"

"Your damned family, that's what," Leachman said. His words were slurred. His cowboy hat was pulled down on his head, but his eyes squinted into the sun as it began to break over the roof of the house. "Your mother has been talking to my sister and filling her full of lies. Now she's talking like she might not sign the lease with Wind Driven."

"I'm sure my mom wasn't trying to do wrong by you," Brock said. "You know my mother. She never sticks her nose in other people's business." He paused for a moment. "Unless it's to protect her farm or her family." Brock's hand pulled into a fist.

Irene heard the voices through the kitchen window. She could hear enough of what Leachman was saying to know some of his anger was directed at her. She slid the frying pan off the burner and moved as fast as she could onto the back porch, stopping to slip on a warm coat with Jimmy's help. As she stepped out the door, he followed close behind.

Leachman turned when he saw them coming. He staggered, wobbly, until he steadied himself with one hand on the hood of the Ford. "Well, look who's here," he stammered. "The whole clan, ready to gang up on me. Well, I don't give a damn whatever you have to say. You and that lumbering oaf, Harold Olson, are gonna ruin this thing for all of us. I've got bills to pay—a lot of us do—and I won't let you stand in the way of us making some easy money. I've tried to persuade you folks in a respectable manner. But if me and the neighbors can't reason with you, nice and friendly-like, we might have to try another approach."

Brock bristled. "That's enough, Del. You've been making some pretty serious threats against us. Just know, if you shut off our water, we can find another way to take care of our cows. Whether we sign the lease or not is our decision to make … not yours. We won't be threatened by you. You can decide what you want to do. Leave us out of it." As his voice was climbing in volume, Brock inched closer to his mom and Jimmy.

Leachman spat at his feet. "I've half a notion to turn my dog loose to see if he can make you see the light," Leachman said. He stumbled to the door of his pickup and reached for the handle. The dog inside was circling inside the vehicle, teeth bared and saliva dripping from his gums. "I don't see much worth saving here anyway. An old nosey woman and some Black kid from who knows where. My dog would love to tear into him."

Irene prayed Leachman was bluffing. But clearly, he was boozed up and wasn't in control of his emotions. It was the threats to Jimmy that made her tremble. She stepped in front of the boy. "That's enough of that kind of talk," she said. "You need to go home and sober up. Come back when you can act like a good neighbor."

"I ain't done," Leachman said. He pointed his finger at Irene. "Let's see if my dog here can make you see it my way." He reached for the door handle.

Richard Gallagher was in the barn tending to a new calf, anxious to head into breakfast with the family when he'd heard Leachman drive in. He recognized the sound, a deep rumble from the muffler, and knew it was his least favorite neighbor. The silver truck impressed anyone who saw it coming down the road, with its chrome wheels, roll bar, and grill guard.

At night, the running lights looked like a circus show coming to town. *All for show*, Richard always thought to himself when he'd meet the truck on the road. *He's put enough money into that pickup to make a down payment on a combine.* He wasn't sure where the money came from to afford such a vehicle, but reminded himself it was none of his business.

The shouting coming from the driveway got Richard's attention and he stuck his head out of the barn door to see what was happening. He could see the argument taking shape—a conflict unfolding. He was reluctant to join the group, happy to stand away, but ready to help if they needed it. When he heard what Leachman said about Jimmy, his heart sank in his chest. *No, Del, this is not happening*, he thought.

He spun around and trotted a dozen steps down the side of the manger to where his rifle hung on the wall. He pulled it off the hooks that held it high above the feed sacks and hurried back toward the door. As he walked, he inserted the clip and chambered a shell. "I'll use it if I have to," he said under his breath. No one was going to hurt Jimmy Ivory if he could help it. For years he had tortured himself for being too late to save his brother, Max, as he lay dying. That guilt hung over him every single day of his life since. He wouldn't let himself fail again, especially for the young man he'd taken under his wing.

When he reached the door and peered out, Leachman was screaming. "Dammit, Gallagher, say you'll sign that lease, or I swear I'll turn this dog loose on your boy here. No one in town will believe it wasn't an accident. Hell, he's not one of us anyway."

"Del, you're talking crazy. Just cool down and we can talk this over." Brock was demanding. He was no longer trying to reason.

"I'm done talking. Brock, say you'll sign that paper. And Irene, you're going to call my sister back and let her know you've changed your mind. She'll listen to you."

Richard had heard enough. He flipped the scope down from the barrel of his gun. This was too close a shot to use a scope. He could line up the iron sights on his target and finish the business. He leaned against the doorframe to steady himself and slid his finger onto the trigger. He brought the rifle up to his shoulder, took a deep breath, and let it out slowly. He focused on his target. His heart pounded in his ears.

Perhaps a drunken Del Leachman didn't intend to open the pickup door. Perhaps it was supposed to be a veiled threat to convince the Gallagher family to bow to his wishes. Whatever the move was, when Leachman grasped the door handle and lifted his fingers, the strength of the Rottweiler made his intent or lack of it a moot point. The door flew open, and the dog exploded out of the space.

Brock instinctively pulled his mother aside and screamed at Leachman, "Del … call him off!"

Leachman stumbled, knocked backward by the force of the dog. He sprawled on his back like he'd fallen from a ladder. "Stop. Stop. I didn't mean to," he babbled, as he struggled to regain his feet.

The dog paid no attention to Leachman. In seconds it lunged at the three adults huddled together. Brock kicked violently at the aggressive attack, but the dog pounced and locked his jaws on Jimmy's leg. Jimmy screamed in pain, the dog ripping at the jeans covering his leg. As he struggled to break free, the dog only grew more vicious, snarling and biting with a fury never seen before on the Gallagher farm.

Jimmy staggered as his legs tangled around the dog and he toppled to the ground. Brock kicked repeatedly at the dog and the Rottweiler released its grip, only to scramble upward toward the boy's neck. Jimmy's screams intensified as a whirlwind of dust rose from the driveway, broken only when a black streak came flying from the porch of the house.

Sassy, the little border collie, sprinted full speed toward the attacking dog. She lunged, her little teeth snapping at the flank of the Rottweiler. Instantly, the larger animal spun away from the humans and changed its stance to fend off the little pup. He charged, ready to sink his teeth into Sassy's throat and finish the pup, but before he could reach her, a deafening explosion came from the barn. Then there was silence.

The dog lay dead. Richard's shot found its mark. Blood oozed from the gaping hole in its chest. It was eerily quiet as if the reverberation had sucked any noise from the air. Jimmy's screams ceased and Irene stopped praying. Even the sparrows in the barn were silent, stunned by the blast.

Jimmy crouched in the gravel driveway, clutching the wounds on his lower leg as he rocked back and forth in pain. Del Leachman stood, his shoulders slumped, eyes staring blankly at the body of his dog, trying, in his intoxicated, confused state, to make sense of what had just happened.

Brock surveyed the scene. He tried to calm the adrenaline coursing through his body, but it didn't ease. He moved with the speed he'd known as an athlete and quickly checked on his mother and Jimmy. Blood pumped through his veins as he turned toward Leachman. With his muscles trembling and with the strength of two men, Brock grabbed the big man by the collar and threw him back onto the ground. Adrenaline trumped good sense as he swung his boot into Leachman's ribs. The rancher groaned and lay still, his hands covering his face.

Brock studied him for a moment to make sure he wasn't going to respond, then turned and hurried to the barn. He covered the fifty yards in seconds and peered into the darkened building. His uncle was slumped against the hay manger, head down on his chest. The rifle was positioned between his legs. His cheek rested against the barrel of the gun.

Without looking up, Richard knew it was his nephew. "I didn't want to," Richard whispered.

Brock laid his hand on Richard's shoulder. "I know. I know. It's okay. You didn't have a choice."

Richard's shoulders curled in and his hands shook. "I couldn't let our pup die. Jimmy's seen too much death already. He loves that little dog."

"Uncle, you did right. You had to, now come help pick up the pieces."

"Is Jimmy okay?" Richard looked up at Brock, worry on his face.

"Scared … and has dog bites. You need to take him to the emergency room … find out how serious it is. And I need to get Mom back into the house. She didn't need this. And we have to call the police. Del has to answer for this." Richard dabbed his eyes with his sleeve as he stood up and exhaled. He walked out with Brock.

Leachman was back on his feet but he wasn't combative. His drunken anger was gone, like a child whose tantrum had subsided. He walked over and stared down at the dead Rottweiler. "Why'd you go and do that?" he mumbled. He kneeled down and awkwardly picked up the animal and folded it into his arms. He carried him to his pickup and tossed the lifeless body into the cargo box.

Leachman wiped blood from his hands on his pants as he turned toward the family. He stared at them with dull black eyes and uttered a single sentence as he climbed into his pickup. "Why can't you people understand?"

# CHAPTER 40

# PANIC

**BUSTER WAS RESTING IN HIS EASY CHAIR** Sunday afternoon before the state tournament was to begin. He hadn't yet learned of the commotion on the Gallagher farm. As he watched an NBA game on television, his heart began to race. He could feel the rapid pounding in his chest. As he tried to pull himself out of the recliner, his muscles trembled and sweat dripped from his forehead. He struggled to catch his breath.

"Eunice," he called out.

"What?" Her voice came from the kitchen.

"I think I'm having a heart attack."

"I doubt it," she said, laughing. But when she walked into the living room and saw him, she gasped. She put her hand on his forehead. "You're hot," she said. "Tell me what's happening."

"My chest hurts," he put a hand on his heart. "And the room is spinning around."

She grabbed his wrist and took his pulse. Rapid beats. Her face tightened. "I'm calling an ambulance," she said.

Buster laid back down and closed his eyes. *Is this the end?* he thought. *Why now, so close to my dream?* But by the time the ambulance pulled up in front of the McHue house, Buster's pain had subsided. He tried to wave off the ride to the hospital, but Eunice insisted. "We have insurance," she said. "You're going, and we're going to make sure you're okay."

Buster grumbled. "I need to get ready for tomorrow. Brock and I were supposed to meet tonight to go over our plans."

"Let's make sure there is a tomorrow, my darling," she said.

The EMTs loaded Buster into the ambulance on a gurney, keeping him steady. "We'll have you there in no time, Coach. And we can monitor your heart as we go, just to be safe."

Buster was embarrassed by the attention, but he was shaken by the crushing feeling he had momentarily experienced. It was as if the world was closing in on him and he couldn't fight his way out of it. He lay on the gurney, closed his eyes, and surrendered to the situation.

Hours later, after the doctors had checked out all his vital signs and monitored his condition, an elderly physician stepped into the exam room with Buster and Eunice. "Good news, Mr. McHue. Your heart is fine. I know how scary something like this is, but we're convinced this is a classic case of a panic attack. It isn't something that can kill you, but anyone who experiences one says it's terribly frightening. Still, in most cases, just as what happened to you, it only lasts a short period of time and doesn't do any permanent damage to your body."

"Why now?" Buster said. "I've never had anything like that happen to me before."

Eunice looked over at him. "Buster, you know why, don't you? It's the basketball game."

Eunice noticed the doctor's puzzled expression. "Buster is coaching a high school team in the state tournament next week. It's something he's dreamed of for a long time. It's bringing on a lot of stress."

"Of course," said the doctor. "That would do it for sure. You might have to sit this one out or it could happen again."

Buster looked over at the man. "Not a chance, Doc. I'm going to the game and I'm going to coach. I'll just stay calm."

Eunice laughed. "And how are you going to do that?"

"Don't know, Eunice … but I won't miss this one chance. Brock can help. And the kids know what to do. They've finally started working together. I'll just sit and enjoy the ride."

"We can prescribe a mild sedative to help if you'd like. I can see this is important to you," the doctor said. "Just remember, a panic attack won't kill you … you might just think you're dying until it passes. And maybe you'll never have another. But if you do, you'll know not to be terrified. It will pass. And you'll be fine."

The man patted Buster on his knee and nodded to Eunice. "You can go home now. Get your husband some rest. It sounds like he has a big week in front of him. Everything will be okay."

# CHAPTER 41

# RICHARD

**ON MONDAY MORNING,** Richard Gallagher dragged himself out of bed before the sun was up and tried to shake the dreams from his mind. Once there was enough light to see, he'd head out to feed the cows. He added logs to the fire and sat with a cup of coffee in his hand. He hadn't slept well, thinking of the part he'd played in the confrontation with Del Leachman. Knowing he'd killed a dog nearly made him sick to his stomach.

The doctor said the dog bites on Jimmy's leg weren't deep and would heal quickly. But it was a worry. What effect would it have on the basketball team? Even more frightening … would Del Leachman come looking for him? A police report had been filed, but no arrest made. These crisis moments brought his own life into focus.

His mind wandered away from his daily routine. He began to think about the offer the family had received from Wind Driven. It was the wind company's insertion into the lives of Grove citizens that led to

Del Leachman's bizarre behavior. Richard was also now thinking about his own future. That was unusual. He didn't often look ahead, going through his daily activities … feeding cows and pigs, doing fieldwork to raise the crops, and repairing machinery. His only entertainment was watching local sports or games on television. But over the last few months, his life had changed.

Jimmy had become a favorite part of his routine. He delighted in their frequent conversations and friendly verbal jousting. Through the recent calving season, they spent hours together delivering calves and patrolling the pastures. He'd watched Jimmy deal with the joy and heartbreak of calving, as well as being injured by a runaway cow and a vicious dog. He admired how the sixteen-year-old managed to keep a positive attitude through each situation. It was his feelings for Jimmy that made him reach for the rifle two days before.

These changes in his routine were a blessing to him. Since the death of his brother, he had borne the guilt for his hand in Max's death. It was an avoidable farm accident. He'd been partially to blame for his brother's fatality, arriving late at his workplace while Max worked alone. He couldn't shake that fact, even though Irene and Brock had long ago buried any ill will towards him. Since then, he'd moved through life, hiding his hurt by being the jolly fellow, full of jokes and beer and surrounding himself with others looking for a good time.

But then in June, Brock returned home to be with Irene and a light seemed to shine on his life. Every day now seemed brighter, with Brock sharing responsibilities on the farm and Jimmy by his side, always asking questions and laughing at his jokes.

Now, the wind company offered something more. They wanted to shower the families on Piney Ridge with money for doing little more than putting names on a piece of paper. Richard thought of the possibilities. Perhaps there could be a new pickup truck for him to drive. His house could get a new roof and siding. He might travel. He always dreamed of going to the famous rodeos and stock shows in Fort Worth and Denver. Maybe he could attend some Seattle Seahawk football games, or he could take a cruise to Mexico and, if luck would have it … find a wife. It was all just a dream. But why not dream a little?

Some folks said wind towers were a blight on the landscape. He wouldn't argue with those who thought that. But couldn't a person turn a blind eye to the scenic alteration for some personal gratification? He was deep into those thoughts when he heard a car pull into his driveway. He peered out the kitchen window and watched Brock amble to the back door. Richard swung it open before Brock had a chance to knock.

"Good morning, Uncle," Brock said, as he stepped into the mud room. "Hope I didn't wake you."

"That's a funny one," Richard said. "You knew I wouldn't be sleeping much after Saturday's blowup. Besides, farmers and ranchers always beat teachers out of bed, you know. What brings you by so early?" He motioned for Brock to join him in the kitchen. "If I'd known you were coming, I'd have scrambled some eggs or something. But the coffee is hot."

"I don't need any breakfast," Brock said. "I know how well you cook." He pretended to shudder. "But I was heading to school and thought I'd drop by to ask a favor."

"Haven't I done enough already?" Richard said, shaking his head. "I hope it's nothing too hard. If it is, the answer is a big fat no."

Brock hesitated, rocking back and forth on his feet. "It's not hard, but maybe a bit uncomfortable for you."

"Good gawd, what now? Another one of your team-building adventures? I'm not going to climb up the side of some grain silo for you."

"Nothing like that. I just need you to give someone a ride to the game next week."

Richard exhaled. "Sure. No problem. I could use the company."

Brock relaxed his shoulders. "Great. I'll let her know."

"Wait, what? Who's this *her*?"

Brock cleared his throat before rapidly spitting out the answer, as if by saying it quickly, Richard wouldn't hear the name. "Goldie Knighton. Her car is in the shop, and she doesn't have a way to get to the game to watch Cole play."

Richard plopped down in a kitchen chair and put his head in his hands. "You have got to be kidding. Goldie Knighton? I won't even sit near her at a basketball game. Now you want me to put her in my pickup and drive her for two hours to a game and then bring her back? I think I'd rather repel off the side of the elevator."

"So, I'll take that as a yes, then," Brock smiled. "I'm pretty sure no one else will take her, so the honor falls to you. Don't worry, she won't bite. She's calmed down a lot since Cole had his problem."

"You're going to owe me big time for this favor. I may take a week's vacation during harvest next year, just to make it close to even."

"Sure, sure, whatever you say, Uncle. I'll let Goldie know you'll be calling." Brock turned and headed towards the door. "Gotta run ... my students will be waiting."

"Yeah, run, you good-for-nothin' teacher," Richard said. As the door closed, the aging bachelor sat in the kitchen, his head tipped back looking at the ceiling, thinking how he'd rather wrestle a mad cow than spend time with Goldie Knighton.

Two days later, Richard pulled up in front of the Knighton home and stepped out into a misty gray Wednesday morning. A slight breeze rattled the still-empty tree limbs that reached out into the street. He looked forward to the basketball game scheduled at noon but wasn't nearly as anxious to spend time coming and going with Goldie. He didn't know much about her, but had seen and heard enough of her at basketball games to think there wasn't much to like. If Brock hadn't asked this as a family favor, he would never be here walking up the steps to her front door.

When his finger pushed the doorbell, the door flew open. Goldie greeted him, a happy smile on her face. "Sir Richard," she said. "I heard your monster pickup pull up. I hope this isn't too much trouble for you." The light was bright enough for Richard to see Goldie's face. Her eyes, big and round, stared at him with delight. "I know you probably didn't volunteer for this." Her eyes instantly morphed into crinkled little happy slits, as she spoke. "I'll get my coat, and we can be off, unless you want to come in for a bit. And please say no, 'cause you don't want to see how messy my house is."

"No, that's fine," Richard said. "We should probably be on our way. I'm sure you don't want to be late for this game."

"That's for sure. I wouldn't miss it for the world. You are a lifesaver. I'm forever in your debt. I was afraid I'd have to stay home, sad and pathetic, listening on my cheap little radio." She turned and left Richard standing at the door. He could see in just enough to notice the starkness of the furnishings. The living room was clean and tidy, but the furniture was the kind made popular decades earlier. *Kind of looks like my place,* he thought.

Goldie returned with a woolen jacket zipped tight around her fully formed body. The collar was pulled up around her neck like she might be headed to a ski slope. Richard's wit bubbled up without thinking. "Hey, Goldie, the heater works in my pickup," he said. After the words came out of his mouth, he regretted his glibness. He wasn't sure if she could be teased without taking offense.

"Well, you never can be sure," she said. "Old farmers like you sometimes drive around with their windows down." She laughed.

"Okay, I see where this is going," he glanced over at her as they stepped down off the porch and headed for the pickup. "Better be careful with your sarcasm. I'm known around the area as the town's master of witticisms."

"Wait, are you sure you want to know what people around town think you're the master of?" She stared over at him, grinning.

"Boy, we haven't even left town, and we're already off and running." He chuckled. "Can't wait to see where this conversation will take us."

"Gird your loins, Big Boy," Goldie said. "Let's make this a fun trip."

When they reached the pickup, without thinking, Richard opened the passenger side door for Goldie.

"And now, you're trying to get on my good side by being a gentleman," Goldie said, as she grabbed the strap on the door frame and hoisted herself into the pickup. Her black clad legs slid easily onto the seat. "But if you were a sneaky devil, you'd have given my tush a little boost to make this climb a bit easier."

That comment made Richard smile. She could match his rat-a-tat humor without missing a beat. He hadn't been with a woman since his college days. And the few times he did socialize with single women it always ended badly … humorless girls, dull and uninteresting. Those dates were more painful than entertaining. But this … but this wasn't a date … was it? He cleared his head as he circled around the Ford to reach the driver's side door. Why was he feeling a little dumbstruck?

After all, this was Goldie Knighton. What he was suddenly feeling made no sense at all.

Two hours later as the couple entered the city, they took a breath. The time they'd spent on the road was nonstop chatter, a back-and-forth of puns, jokes, and anecdotes. If either of them paused for a moment, the other jumped in with a comeback to top the last silly contribution.

As he slowed the Ford, Richard realized he hadn't laughed so hard since he'd dared to smoke giggle weed in college along with some of his friends. Unlike that, this laughter didn't come from some artificial high. It was just fun being with someone who could match his irreverence. He couldn't believe the woman who seemed so abrasive at ball games was so much fun to be with. He slowed the pickup down, knowing they would arrive at the arena in a few minutes and their two hours of fun would end.

"This trip wasn't as bad as I thought it was going to be," Richard said, feigning seriousness.

"Oh yeah, wait until you drive me home," Goldie said. "Especially if we lose. I can be real nasty."

"Well, then, let's pray the Grizzlies can win this game."

"Hey, Richard," Goldie said, "what do you think people will say when they see us walk in together? I can only imagine." She paused. "Or do you want to go in by yourself and I can come in five minutes later?"

"Not a chance," Richard said. "Let's give the locals something to gossip about." He thought for a moment. "In fact, if you really want to mess with people's minds, let's go in holding hands. That will blow the tops right off their heads."

Goldie squirmed in her seat. "Holy crap, Richard ... I think I'm in love with you."

The bachelor, Richard Gallagher, didn't even look at Goldie. He just smiled. He knew she was joking. But ...

# CHAPTER 42

# STATE

**TO THE SURPRISE OF MANY** in Glory Grove, especially the men at the Cozy Corner, the Grizzly basketball team was headed to state. It was a sixteen-team tournament. Eight teams would leave with a trophy. Two losses would send a team home empty-handed.

Since they had fought their way to be league champions, albeit with four losses on their season record, the Grizzlies were seeded as the number eight team in the tournament. Their first game was scheduled for noon on the opening day of the four-day event and matched them with the number nine seed. Their opponent, the Madison Mounties, was from the northwest part of the state—dairy country. The team was filled with tall, athletic farm boys with Dutch pedigrees, who were perennial participants at state.

"We might as well dip our toe into the pool right off," Principal Colquit said to Brock as he stepped into Brock's classroom on the Monday morning before the tournament began on Wednesday. "A noon game should get our boys cranked up early. They won't have time to get any butterflies."

"The butterflies might still be asleep at that hour," Brock said, looking up from the papers he was grading. "We appreciate the school for paying for the hotel Tuesday night. If we had to drive over Wednesday morning, the boys would be rolling out of bed early and then taking a long bus ride. There aren't many teenagers who are ready to win a basketball game with that schedule."

Colquit nodded, a satisfied look on his face. "I know my son wouldn't be excited about getting up that early. But Brock, I want you to know all the success you're having with these sports teams is putting a strain on our school budget." He shook his head to conceal his smile. "We may have to ask the voters to pass a levy this spring." He fidgeted with the papers in his hand. "No pressure, but I think it'll help if your boys can bring a trophy home. Maybe then the good citizens here will be more inclined to vote in favor."

As Colquit spoke, he stared at the basketball team photo Brock had pinned on the bulletin board next to pictures of U.S. presidents. "Good looking bunch," Colquit said as he stepped out of the door. "I'd better let you get ready for class."

Brock appreciated how far the principal had come since they first met in June. Back then, Colquit tried everything he could to run him off and kill the football program. However, once his own son, Lester Jr., became an important piece of the football team, the man was eventually one of Brock's biggest supporters.

Young Les Colquit was on the roster of the boys who would suit up for the state tourney. He wasn't on the starting five but was one of the first players sent in off the bench, especially now with Jimmy's injury. He had earned the privilege, but Brock knew his presence on the team made the principal a much bigger supporter of athletics than he would have been otherwise.

Brock wondered how the team would react when they stepped onto the arena floor, under the bright lights and in front of television cameras. It helped that they'd been in the spotlight before, playing in the state football championship. *But this is basketball, and this is the biggest stage of the year*, he thought. He shared the same concerns as the hundreds of Grove fans who would attend. Most of them weren't even alive the last time the Grizzlies were a participant in the tournament. Just being there was a success for the little town.

The next step would be more difficult. To bring home a trophy, the team had to find a way to win at least two of their first three contests. If they lost the first two games, they would go home with only the experience to remember. For a team to claim a trophy, they had to play through Friday without two losses.

As Brock checked off the details, he pondered the difference in logistics between arranging for a football team's one-game event in a state championship and basketball's lengthy state tournament. Of course, taking a team of twenty-five players and all the gear needed for a football team was a bigger challenge than a dozen kids with gym shoes and a duffel bag. But the four-day tournament had its challenges.

On Wednesday, as Richard and Goldie stepped through the arena doors, hands clasped together, heads turned. The fans from Glory Grove were interspersed with others from competing schools, as they meandered through the concourse preparing to watch their boys compete. Only those from Glory Grove took a second look at what they saw ... one of the town's favorite characters, Richard, with a woman many people in the Grove steered away from.

It added to the odd feelings they were experiencing. Their mood bordered on disbelief because their young men were set to play in the big state tourney. It seemed like a fantasy. So, seeing Richard and Goldie holding hands simply added to the feeling they were living in a dream world.

While the fans were in a surreal reverie, Buster McHue was floating a few inches off the ground. His doctors had prescribed a mild sedative to counter the nervousness that led to his recent panic attack. As he and Brock walked together into the arena, leading the members of the team through the tunnel toward the locker room, Buster felt like he was in a different world. He had anticipated that feeling, thinking he'd be pinching himself when they got to the state tournament. It was something he'd always wanted. But he didn't expect the blurred thinking that clouded his mind. Try as he might, he couldn't focus. How could he lead his team if he couldn't think straight?

"Brock, are you ready to help me today?" McHue asked quietly as they walked.

"Sure, Buster, like always." Brock assumed McHue was simply looking for moral support. The old coach turned to Brock as they reached the locker room door and laid a hand on his shoulder. "I think I need more help than usual," he said. "The drugs I took to calm me down have my brain all messed up. I can't seem to concentrate."

Brock stepped aside as the boys filed through the door. When they'd all gone into the room and were out of earshot, he turned to Buster. "Get off your feet for a while, Coach, and let me get you some water. The excitement here is probably making things worse. I'm sure your mind will clear in a few minutes."

"I hope so," Buster said. "But if it doesn't, you may have to lead this team."

Brock had to catch his breath. He'd been on the sidelines of critical football games and knew how hard it was to focus all one's attention on the action. But if Buster was now asking him to make decisions in a basketball game at the state tournament with hundreds of fans staring over his shoulder, that was a different thing altogether. He'd feel like an embarrassed sixth grader being asked to explain his answer in front of a classroom of his peers. Sure, he wanted to lead. He loved the feel of battle. And he yearned for a sense of victory. But did he have the right tools in his belt to pull it off?

Of the sixteen teams qualified to play at the tournament, many were perennial participants. The team from Glory Grove was the exception. They were the team with the longest absence from the annual event. Still, their recent appearance in the small school state football championship had people curious to see if these same athletes could succeed at another sport.

Despite the tournament starting on a Wednesday and their game scheduled at noon, every Grizzly fan who could skip work and make the trip was there. Brock's mother lived up to the promise she made to Jimmy and was in attendance, ready to cheer on the boys. Although he worried about her health, Jimmy was thrilled she would be there for him.

The most optimistic Grove fans booked hotel reservations for five nights. Others would make the two-and-a-half-hour trip from the Grove each day. Brock would stay with the team, but he reserved rooms for his mom, Peter Green, and Ronnie. Richard would have to make a daily commute to check on the cows.

Irene made the trip with Peter Green, who doted over her as if they'd been together as a couple for years. He spent the day before the game preparing his van—checking all fluids and tire pressure and vacuuming the interior. He emptied the ashtray and threw away his cigarettes and even bought a blanket to keep Irene warm. When he got to the farm, he carried her suitcase to the van and helped her climb in. "Buckle up, honey, off we go," he said.

"Fire up this old rocket," Irene said. She grinned like she was on her first date.

The boys in the locker room went about their business. Except for Cole, they had all gathered in a similar locker room at a football stadium three months earlier, facing the same trepidation of appearing on a big stage. Now, they were nervous but self-assured in their ability. The two-game district tournament seemed to have built their confidence to a new level. It was a good time to believe in themselves.

When the team was ready to run onto the floor for warm-ups, Coach McHue leaned against the wall and asked the players to quiet down. He had prepared a motivational speech. He steadied himself for a moment, looked around, and spoke. Inside his head he was struggling with his emotions. But despite his mental deficiencies, he wanted the boys to see him as assured and ready for the task.

There was the usual redness in his cheeks and sweat visible on his forehead, but the boys noticed his voice being uncharacteristically shaky. They wondered if it was just the pressure of this being his first appearance at state, or if there was something else going on. They listened intently just the same.

McHue began slowly. "Men, if this is a dream for you, I want you to know this is also a dream for me … and for all the Glory Grove fans that will be cheering you on out there. It's been a long wait for Grizzly fans. But I know you're ready. You deserve to be here." He paused and took a deep breath.

"We all know the difficulties we've been through this season. It hasn't been easy, but right now this team couldn't be in a better place. You are all healthy and prepared." McHue wasn't going to draw attention to Jimmy's leg injuries. Although there were some serious flesh wounds, most were superficial. Despite the pain, he was determined to play.

The coach continued. "You have the town behind you and with Brock's help here, we are going to put you in the best position possible to win out there today."

McHue paused and then became quiet as if he were reaching for the words to say next. There was a long awkward silence in the room as the players looked around at each other, wondering why the coach had stopped talking.

Brock stood next to the coach. He recognized immediately McHue had lost his train of thought and instinctively reached over and put his hand on the older coach's shoulder. He turned to the boys. "And this fine man deserves your best effort out there on the floor. Give him every bit of energy you have to make it happen." He looked over at McHue. "Coach, shall we take the floor?"

McHue nodded and the boys jumped to their feet, clapping their hands as they filed through the door. It was time.

# CHAPTER 43

# ACTION

**WHEN THE BUZZER SOUNDED,** marking the start of the game between the Grizzlies and the Madison Mounties, it was the third game of the day in the four-day marathon of small-town high school hoops. Thousands of fans had come to watch the teams, bands, and cheerleaders represent their hometowns.

For Grizzly fans, it was a joyous occasion. They were now rubbing shoulders with the elites, including those teams who consistently placed a gold ball or plaque in their school's trophy case. The usual Grizzly faithful had assembled, huddled together in the plastic bleacher seats, nibbling on popcorn or pretzels to replace the lunch they might be missing.

Brock and Buster McHue stood watching the boys in their pregame warm-ups. Buster was calmed by the antidepressant, but still lightheaded because of it. "You doing okay, Buster?"

"I think I'll be all right," McHue answered. "Just wish my brain was working better. If we can keep up with the Mounties and get a lead, maybe the kids won't need a lot of coaching from me."

"Perfect plan, boss. From the game film I've watched, I think we match up pretty well from the looks of them. They don't have anyone as intimidating as Luke. We can use that to our advantage."

When the boys finished their warm-ups, they gathered around the coaches. McHue turned to Brock and asked him to give last minute advice. Brock stumbled to find words but did his best impression of a savvy basketball coach. He repeated the plan he and McHue had fashioned earlier.

"We'll start with a man-to-man defense until we see how they play it. On offense, if they're playing man-to-man against us, we'll push the ball inside until they start sagging off our guards, then Cole can light 'em up. Now go out there and expend some energy. Those boys are as sleepy as you are, so get revved up. But remember ... stay composed, crash the boards when you rebound, and be patient with your shots. You can do this."

Brock surprised himself with his own verbiage. He'd listened to McHue for a full season, and it had seeped into his consciousness. Still, he knew he was a poser. He didn't have the basketball knowledge Buster possessed. *Please get out of the fog, Buster. These boys are going to need you.*

Both teams were content to stick with a man-to-man defense. That was disappointing in one regard, since Cole's long-range shots were more available if the opposing guards were constantly shifting and expending energy. However, by playing "man", the Mounties were giving up the inside to Luke, who quickly found the lane open to his post moves. He was single-handedly making the Mounties pay a price.

Brock leaned over to McHue so he could hear above the din from the crowd. "Boys are doing well, Coach. If Madison doesn't change up, Luke will win this thing all by himself."

"Too early to get excited," McHue said. In the stands, Tim and Peggy were sitting with Goldie and Richard. If there hadn't been so much excitement on the floor, the crowd of Grove fans would be gossiping about them. But when the boys scored, the fans cheered wildly, and the cheerleaders waved their pom poms. Ashley sat in the band keeping track of Luke's points in her head … sixteen as the first half wound down.

When the teams headed to the locker rooms, the Grizzlies had put up thirty-two points to only twenty from the Mounties. McHue waited until the boys were seated. He seemed calm and attentive. "Good half, men. But that team isn't used to losing. They'll put up a fight. I expect they'll either double up on Luke or go to a zone. If they do, we have them right where we want them. Cole and Justin will get their shots."

Buster noticed Jimmy limping. "How's the leg holding up?" It was heavily bandaged.

"I'm okay, Coach. I'll make it." He grimaced as he patted his calf.

"Good man," McHue said. "But let's give it a rest in the third quarter. We have a good lead, so Les can spell you off. We have more games to play, so we won't push it too far."

During the intermission, the crowd from the Grove was as nervous as a father waiting on the delivery of his first child. Could this really be happening? Could their boys pull out an opening-day win?

When the game resumed, the Madison coach had made adjustments as McHue predicted he would. They fell back into a two/three zone defense to ward off Luke's easy trips to the basket. It worked, but only for the first few minutes of the third quarter.

The Grizzlies responded by rapidly rotating the ball from side to side. The guards from Madison began to tire and couldn't close quickly enough on Cole. His threes began to fall and the lead at the end of the quarter remained at a dozen.

When the final quarter began, Jimmy was back in the line-up. Despite the extra strength he provided on defense, the Mounties began to surge. They were frantic, clawing their way back into the game. Their coach had a plan. And it was working. They allowed Luke to get the ball close to the basket, but as soon as he started to shoot, they'd collapse on him and purposely foul. It put him at the charity stripe.

For his part, Luke recognized his own weaknesses. First was his tendency to anger. But more critical at this stage was that any shot from the free throw line was like a game of chance. He looked over to his coaches for some kind of advice. McHue didn't offer any. Luke's frustration didn't help his shooting either. Over half of his free throws careened off the rim.

The Mounties' comeback had begun. With four minutes left in the game, they'd pulled within six points. The Grizzlies' dream of a first-round win was very much in jeopardy. Brock noticed McHue staring off into space. "Coach, should we call a time-out?"

McHue snapped to attention. "Yes, yes … call it."

When the team gathered around, McHue was silent. Brock looked at the players. There was trepidation on their faces. "What's going on here?" Brock asked.

Luke's voice was panicked. "Coach, I'm getting hammered in there and I can't make a free throw. I'm going to lose this for us." His eyes darted between Brock and McHue.

"You might, Luke if you don't calm down," Brock said. "Relax, trust your teammates. They're going to help you win this." He didn't have any other advice to help the big teenager. But Cole had an odd smile on his face as he raised his hand. The boys all turned to him. "What is it, Cole?" Brock asked.

Cole changed expressions. He crunched his face into a make-believe angry mask, acting as if he were playing the role of a coach. "Doggone it, Luke, you dumb Grizzly … it's easy." The boys stood spellbound, waiting for what he'd say next. "Listen. When you take a free throw, don't think. Just relax. Then say to yourself, 'I'm Cole Knighton, and I can't miss.' Then, you'll be perfect."

Those words a few weeks earlier might have got him punched in the face, but now the absurdity of it elicited a laugh from every boy in the huddle.

Luke snorted. "Great advice, hotshot. You're a frickin' genius." The players, including Luke and their coaches, laughed. Brock saw the fear was gone from their faces.

Brock turned to Buster. "Can I suggest something else, Coach?"

McHue nodded.

"Jimmy, go ahead and feed the ball to Luke, but Luke, the instant you touch the ball, get it back out as quickly as you can to Cole or Justin. Their players will be out of position. It'll open things up for our shooters and take the strain off you."

Jimmy gave a thumbs up, ignoring the throbbing pain in his leg. He liked the plan—play inside/out and relieve Luke—let the others win the game. In the end, Cole nailed a three-point shot to ensure the victory as the Glory Grove fans—their voices hoarse from cheering—counted down the final seconds. The team celebrated as they ran back to their bench.

Tim and Peggy Palmer slumped down in their seats, exhausted from the anxiety they'd been feeling. Goldie jumped up and did a little dance and Richard, impressed by her lack of self-consciousness, tried his own awkward imitation of it. He hoped no one was watching. Ashley let out a giant sigh and waved her clarinet in the air. And Irene leaned over to Peter Green and whispered in his ear, "Now aren't you glad you came home for this?" He smiled a contented smile.

As the players headed into the locker room to make way for the next set of teams to take the court, Brock walked along beside Buster. "Great job, Coach," Brock said.

The old coach didn't hesitate. "I'll be better tomorrow, I promise."

Brock silently prayed he would be.

# CHAPTER 44

# ELIGIBLE

MCHUE WAS BETTER THURSDAY. With the midday victory on Wednesday, the Grizzlies were now playing in the winner's bracket. The game was scheduled for four o'clock in the afternoon. The extra time gave the players and the coaches time to rest. Buster's fog was lifting.

As he and Brock sat in the hotel's coffee shop making plans for their next game, Principal Colquit came striding toward them, nearly colliding with the young waitress.

"Morning, Sir," Buster said. "You look troubled. Did one of our players get out of line?"

"No, maybe worse than that." His words came in rapid fire. "I got a call from our regional rep on the state activities board. Seems they are investigating the eligibility of our two transfer players … Jimmy and Luke."

"That's crazy," Buster said, looking nonplussed. "These boys have been playing sports all school year. Why now?"

Colquit was just as perplexed as McHue. "I told him that, but he said someone on the state council raised concern about those boys and how they suddenly showed up in Glory Grove and made such an impact on our team."

Brock set down his coffee and pushed his plate to one side. "That's nonsense, coming right now. Anyway, can we find out who's stirring this pot?"

Colquit shrugged. "I don't know any of the people on the council. But I can try to find out."

Brock held his hand up. "Let me make some calls, Lester. I know enough people in this business to maybe get to the source. I'll get on it. But what does this mean for today? We have a game to play."

Colquit strummed his fingers on the notebook he was carrying. "The rep said since we've been alerted and we know about the eligibility question, if the boys play and they're declared ineligible, we'd have to forfeit the game results."

Brock slapped the table. "Doggone it, Lester, this isn't right. Now is not the time to be punishing kids when they've done nothing wrong."

Buster waived him off. "We're not benching anybody. Those two are a big part of the reason we've made it this far. We're not shutting down now."

As the clock ticked down to game time, Buster focused on details, but Brock's mind couldn't get past the eligibility question. He knew there shouldn't be a problem. What had triggered the sudden investigation from the state board? The question shook him, but he forced himself to put it aside. The team had a chance to elevate their opportunities for a trophy—even a chance at a state championship—if they could get past the number one ranked team, the Vancouver Christian Riptide.

Brock and McHue studied the Vancouver roster and game results from their season and realized this would be a monumental task. The starting five for the Tide had the stature of a college team. Three of their players stood over six feet, four inches. They hadn't lost a contest all year and most of the games they'd played were decided by over twenty points.

"This will take a miracle," Buster said, glancing up at Brock. "I'm not sure even the heavenly host can save us in this one."

"Maybe they'll all come down with food poisoning before the game," Brock said, as he rocked back in his chair. "Not that I'd wish them any harm, but just to even things out a bit. Have you got a genius plan up your sleeve?"

"Nope. Maybe we should consider benching Luke and Jimmy until we get this game behind us. I hate to surrender so easily, but if I were a betting man, I wouldn't put a lot of money on our chances. We probably don't have a shot in this one so we could just rest them for tomorrow."

"I'd hate to see that," Brock said, "they deserve to play, and our fans have come to watch them. Besides, there is no reason they should be declared ineligible."

"Then we're on the same page. We'll do our best to make this a competitive game, but I can almost predict what will happen. With that much length on their team, Luke can't handle them all, so he'll get in foul trouble. Without him, it will get out of hand quickly. But we won't wave a white flag. Maybe the referees will swallow their whistles and Luke can stay in there for a while. On offense, we'll try to get Jimmy pushing the ball on fast breaks and hopefully, Cole will keep the hot shooting streak going. If we play good sound defense maybe we can make it competitive long enough to pull off that miracle in the end."

Brock chuckled. "I knew you'd figure something out. Don't count us out until the buzzer sounds." Brock straightened his posture. "But as soon as this game is done, I'm getting on the phone to figure out what the heck is going on with the state board."

The Riptide were as advertised. Their starting group was all seniors who'd played together since grade school. They'd taken home the second-place trophy the year before and were determined to capture the championship banner. To them, the Grizzlies would be just a bump in the road. In warm-ups, they were confident and nonchalant as if they were using this as a practice game before the real competition began.

The one and only weakness of the Vancouver team was their tendency to slack off on outside shooters, knowing they owned the inside game. To the dismay of the Tide fans, the rag-tag bunch from Glory Grove came to play. From the opening tipoff, Jimmy pushed the ball down the court quickly and found Luke inside, who wisely passed back out to an open Cole Knighton. His shooting touch was on target. On their first four possessions, Cole nailed his shots and the Grizzlies jumped out to an early 12–4 lead.

Grizzly fans were ecstatic, on their feet cheering wildly for their boys. Was there an upset in the making? Across the arena floor, the Vancouver coach went into histrionics, jumped to his feet, and signaled to the ref for a time-out. He waved violently for his boys to huddle. He could be seen shaking his fist at the bunch, exhorting them to wake up.

They did. They tightened their defense on Jimmy and Cole and began to methodically pound the ball inside where Luke, despite his best effort, couldn't corral all their big men. It was clear, the best team on the floor was the one from the state's west side. McHue and Brock kept the boys playing hard, but Luke was soon in foul trouble and Cole was stifled by their defensive pressure. The Grizzlies fought back several times to pull within a single-digit score, but their efforts were turned back by the Tide.

When the game ended, the Grizzly boys were drained of energy. They were disappointed, but still upbeat, knowing they'd given everything they had against superior opposition. As they exited the floor, they smiled up at their fans. The Grizzly audience applauded them. They all shared in the pride they felt for the boys, unaware of the drama unfolding about the eligibility question. Residing in the back of their mind was the fact that a win by the team the next day would guarantee they would leave town with a trophy. It was something the Grizzlies had never done before.

Even the men from the Cozy Corner were on their feet, politely clapping for the boys and their coaches. "Pretty good," Homer Johnson said. "Pretty good."

"Yup." Slim Mathers agreed. "Buster can keep his tie."

It didn't take much time before Brock was on the phone, working through his contacts to get to the bottom of the eligibility problem. His former athletic director knew one of the state board members of the athletic association. That man in turn gave Brock the name of the individual raising the charge. Brock made the call.

Brock was polite but probing. "Sir, I've heard you have made an inquiry into the eligibility of two of our players," Brock said, after explaining who he was and how he'd coached the boys through the state championship game in football.

"That's right, Coach," the man said. "I really don't have any information to give you other than there was an inquiry from a friend of mine who seemed to know a lot about the Glory Grove program. He thinks there might be something going on there that isn't on the up and up."

"Can you tell me who this person is? I'd like to know if there is some reason he is making a claim like that."

"I won't give you the name but he's a prominent citizen and a leader in the banking industry over there. I don't think he'd steer me wrong on this."

Brock's anger exploded. He knew. It was Roland Donigan. He didn't need any more details. "Your friend, Roland Donigan, if I may be frank, is using you." Brock took a measured breath. "I don't know what your friendship rests on, but I can tell you, what he's doing is for personal reasons. And it's a lie. He's messing with the lives of our boys, and it needs to stop. Those two boys have met every eligibility requirement. Now, in the middle of the state tournament, you are raising this question. If I were you, I'd call the board chair and ask him to back off, or this won't look good for you or the board."

"But I ..."

"But nothing," Brock said. "Call Donigan. Tell him to get his nose out of our team's business. Tell him I said so. Otherwise, I'll be making a call to his superiors at the bank and let them know how this man operates. I want your board to withdraw the inquiry by the end of the day. If you need the dirty details of why your friend is acting this way, I can spell it out for you. But I think if you'll call Donigan, he'll back off. Got it?"

"It sounds like you're threatening me, Coach."

"I am. You're doing someone else's dirty work for him, and it needs to stop. Do I need to call your chairman?"

"No, sir. I think your message has been received. Thank you for your call."

Brock set down his phone when the conversation ended. He tried to catch his breath and calm his racing heart. But he wasn't finished. The banker was playing games. Brock's whole life was filled with strategizing to win games. It wasn't an idle challenge. He'd now need to move on to additional pressure. Soon, he'd call John Eberhardt, the bank manager in Glory Grove, to see how far he could push. Donigan had threatened Eberhardt and the branch. Brock needed to gauge John's willingness to help.

With a plan in place, Brock settled back. He remembered his promise to have dinner with Ronnie. They would join Tim and Peggy at a restaurant close to the hotel. *I'll share what I know with Ronnie and my closest friends before acting,* he thought. But his anger was still boiling, and it was directed at the slick banker who was messing with his life. He wasn't about to give up on Ronnie or his team without a fight.

# CHAPTER 45

# BLOOD

AS BROCK PULLED HIMSELF OUT OF BED Friday morning, he was still mulling over the situation with Donigan. He hadn't seen him in the crowd for the Grizzlies' first two games. But he knew he'd eventually show, even if only to see if his meddling had achieved his desired results. Since the Grizzlies were now in the loser's bracket, Friday's game was a two o'clock affair versus another foe battling for a pass to the Saturday trophy games. With a win, the boys from Glory Grove would be guaranteed the hardware that had always been missing from the school's trophy case.

As the coaches prepared, they could see there was a good opportunity for success. The Blue Lake Buccaneers matched them in size and, like them, lost four regular season games. They'd taken their game to overtime on Thursday and were beaten on a last-second shot by their opponent. Buster McHue recognized it as an advantage.

"Those kids will be tired from all the energy they gave." He nodded knowingly. "And the disappointment from that tough loss could play in their minds a bit. We can take advantage," he said.

As the crowds gathered for the game, Grove fans continued to fill the section of the arena assigned to them. Tim and Peggy always arrived early and found seats near to the court, as if by being close they could infuse some of their nervous energy into their son. It seemed to work. Throughout the tournament, the big boy seemed to grow stronger and more determined. He also routinely received an emotional lift from Ashley. As a band member, she made daily trips from the school to the arena to share the experience with her bandmates. Their band instructor wouldn't let them lag and had them playing at any break in the action.

After the team's loss on Thursday, Ashley had hurried down from the stands to console her boyfriend but found him in good spirits. "That was a helluva battle," he said, sweat dripping from his forehead. "But I was outnumbered." He assured her the Friday game would be different. "No way we're losing with a chance to play in the trophy round," he said.

Ashley admired his optimism and recognized the fire in his eyes. She suspected he'd either win or go down fighting.

Richard and Goldie, after two trips and five hours together on the road each time, had become less of an oddity to the Grove fans and more of a welcome addition. They had always loved Richard's fun-loving attitude and were relieved to see the dramatic shift in Goldie's behavior when the two were together.

The table was set. When the teams took the floor, the Grizzly fans stood and cheered. There was no chance for a championship. Those dreams were gone and there was disappointment. But with a win on Friday, the team would get to compete on Saturday in the trophy round. It was more than any Grizzly fan had dreamed of when the season started.

Roland Donigan sat away from the Grove crowd as they began to fill the seats for the game. He was waiting, hoping to catch Ronnie Jepson. She would be here to watch the Grizzlies play, either to win a spot in the trophy round on Saturday or, he hoped, to leave the tournament empty-handed.

Donigan knew that without Luke and Jimmy, the Grizzlies didn't have any chance of winning. He wasn't surprised, with his influence, how easy it was to call in a few favors and manipulate the situation. This challenge to win over Ronnie and her son Justin had become an obsession. He savored the challenge. So much of the privilege in his life had come with little effort. This situation offered the stimulation he needed.

As he sat watching the basketball fans stream into the arena and fill the bleachers, he studied each face, waiting for the one he couldn't put out of his mind. When she appeared, his heart raced, like a schoolboy laying his eyes on his prom date, dressed like a model and waiting for his arm. *Silly,* he thought. She was just a small-town widow without wealth or sophistication. But it was her natural beauty and innocence that made her more attractive to him.

She walked slowly down the concrete steps, watching the boys down below. She was wearing a red Grizzly t-shirt and form-fitting blue jeans. A black jacket was wrapped around her neck. Her auburn hair hung to her shoulders.

Donigan was ready to pounce. He stood and made his way toward her. He reached out to tap her on the arm when he froze in his tracks. Brock Gallagher was hurrying up the steps to greet her. At the same time, Brock spied him and slowed his approach. Ronnie was positioned between the two men, unaware of Donigan standing behind her. Her face was frozen in a curious gaze, wondering why Brock's expression had changed so quickly from a warm smile to an angry stare. She swung around and knew. Her shoulders pulled inward, and she stepped back to let the two men converge.

Brock reached out and put his hand on her arm. "Ronnie, this man and I need to talk," he said, as he made his way past her to reach the banker.

"Donigan," Brock said, staring up at the man. "You shouldn't be here."

Donigan bristled. "Don't tell me what I can or can't do. I'm here to cheer for Justin." He said it loud enough for Ronnie to hear.

Brock moved closer, stepping up so he could stand on Donigan's level. "You're here to see how well your pathetic play worked." He glared at Donigan. "Well, it didn't. The boys are playing. They aren't going to be disqualified. But you should be."

"Go to hell," Donigan snarled.

Brock stuck his finger in the banker's chest. "Butt out. Leave our kids alone." He glanced down at Ronnie. "And I think I can speak for her too. Get out of our lives."

Ronnie backed away while nodding yes. She was embarrassed by the scene and glad there weren't more people in the stands. However, she was pleased with how Brock was standing up to this man. It might cost her the job at the bank. It might cost the town a business that the people depended on. But Brock was making a stand that needed to be made.

Donigan wasn't cowed. He was a strong athletic man. No one touched him like that. He instinctively grabbed Brock's hand when it touched his chest. *I'll show this meddling ex-football player*, he thought. He lowered his shoulder and drove it into Brock's body. The two men pivoted on the narrow slick steps and tumbled into the seats. Donigan's face caught the arm of a chair. Blood gushed from his split lip. The basketball fans nearest to them turned to stare at the commotion.

This was a show neither man wanted. They pulled themselves to their feet and, like schoolboys on the playground, backed away.

"That's enough," Ronnie said, as she pulled Brock away from Donigan. "Let's go, this is too much. People are watching."

The banker jumped up, his hand to his mouth. "We'll see you in court, Gallagher," he said, as he wiped blood from his lip.

As Buster predicted, the Blue Lake Buccaneers were sluggish and uninspired when the game began. They hadn't shaken off the disappointment from Thursday's overtime loss. The Grizzlies took an early lead, but the Bucs fought back. They weren't a physically imposing team size-wise, but they were a tough bunch. Brock knew about them since, like the Grizzlies, they'd made a run in the football playoffs in the fall. They weren't talent-laden but were muscular and fast, not winning with size or technique, but with physicality and determination. Once the hangover from their Thursday loss was out of their system, they began to turn it on.

"They're a feisty bunch," McHue said, looking over at Brock. "Gotta admire their energy. Our boys better step up."

"We might have to get them back in football pads," Brock said. He studied the action on the floor. "This might be a foul fest."

Predictably, since it was the third day of the tournament, the referees were weary and in no mood to call incidental fouls. The three men were seasoned veterans and had officiated many state tournament games. But they weren't young, and they'd been running up and down the court since early Wednesday morning. They were tired and reluctant to extend the length of the game.

"They are letting 'em play," Tim said to Peggy as they sat near the floor in the stands. "Luke is going to like this. No blood … no foul."

Tim rocked back and forth in his seat thinking of the action that lay ahead. "It might be Luke's time to shine."

The Buccaneer defense was tenacious, hands constantly harassing Cole and Jimmy, the Grizzly guards. If there was a loose ball on the floor, players from both teams dived on it, wrestling for possession.

The style of play suited both teams. They had all played football and weren't afraid of physical contact. Luke especially enjoyed the relaxed officiating. He could bang around under the basket without the constraint he'd shown all year, dictated by the referee's whistle.

Coach McHue, on the other hand, was unsettled by the combative nature of the game. "That's a foul," he'd yell at the referee closest to him if Jimmy or Cole were the recipients of a hard push or slap to an arm.

Brock tried to calm the old coach, afraid the rise in his emotions might trigger another health crisis for the man. "The boys are okay. They can handle this," Brock assured Buster.

"It's got our kids playing rat ball," McHue shot back. "This isn't basketball, it's roller derby."

Brock wasn't as concerned as Buster. The tactics by the Buccaneers weren't what the boys had faced all year, but they knew how to react. They could keep pace, and no one was in foul trouble. It was a game where the stronger-willed team would survive. He trusted the boys would somehow stay composed despite the nature of the battle.

At halftime, the teams headed to the locker room with the Bucs holding a small, 32–30, lead. Goldie Knighton watched the boys jog off the floor. She was trying to restrain herself. Since Cole's breakdown, she'd stayed composed through the last few games. However, watching Cole getting battered by the Buc guards had her slipping back into her old angry attitude.

"Come on, ref," she yelled at one point. "This isn't a boxing match, for gawd's sake."

Richard leaned over and gently pulled on her elbow. "Tell him how you feel, Goldie," he said. He was mocking her, making light of the situation to calm her down. "You know that old man with the striped shirt can't hear you," he said. "I saw him taking out his hearing aids just before the game started."

"Oh, shut up, you old farmer," she said back to him, shaking her head. She threw a couple pieces of popcorn into his face and laughed. "You'd probably know all about growing old, wouldn't you." She leaned into him. "I'm just trying to protect my boy." She was serious.

Richard looked into her eyes. "Your son seems to be handling himself just fine. This is how boys begin to grow up."

Goldie exhaled and put her hand on Richard's thigh. "You're right. I'll keep quiet. I have to now because I need a ride home."

"True. And I'd miss your company if I had to drive home alone." He laid his hand on top of hers.

When the third quarter began, the action on the floor stayed the same. Once when Cole raised up for a long jump shot, his legs were taken out from under him. No whistle blew. He sprang to his feet and raised his right hand with three fingers extended. He didn't complain to the ref … satisfied with the points. Still, despite Cole's occasional scoring burst, the Bucs continued to torment the Grizzlies with their aggressive play and began to slowly pull away.

Richard held Goldie in check, but Brock wasn't doing as well with Coach McHue. He became more and more agitated watching the boys being manhandled and with the game slowly slipping away. Early in the fourth quarter, as Luke battled for a loose ball under the basket, the Buc's muscular post player snatched the ball out of Luke's hands and swung his elbows violently from side to side, head high.

The elbow caught Luke in the eye socket and sent him to the floor.

Blood oozed from his cheek. Instantly McHue jumped to his feet, his face bright red with anger. He rushed to Luke, screaming at the referee as he approached.

"Are you blind?" he hollered. "What's it take to get a foul called?"

The referee closest to the action puffed his chest out. "Off the court, Coach, and I mean now."

McHue stood staring, his heart pounding in his veins. "Not unless you call a foul, you worthless zebra."

"Here's one," the bespeckled man said. He raised his hands to form a perfect "T."

"Not good enough!" Buster screamed. He stood holding a towel to Luke's face.

"Okay, here's another." The man pursed his lips, making his mustache extend out from his face, like a porcupine threatening to swing his quills. "That's two … now get off the floor and out of the gym."

Brock stood watching. Spellbound. *I don't believe what I'm seeing,* he thought to himself. Buster had never acted like that before. Brock's second thought was, *How am I going to coach the team through the rest of the game?*

Buster, who spent his whole twenty-year career dreaming of coaching a Grizzly team in the state tournament, turned and, without looking, waved his hand in disgust at the referee. He walked slowly towards Brock. The natural color was returning to his cheeks. "I think I got my point across," Buster said. A sly smile appeared on his lips. "I think we'll be okay now, Brock. Just bring it home." He turned and headed for the exit.

Brock didn't know whether to be angry at the old coach or humbled by the man's confidence in him. But no matter, Buster's tactic seemed to work. Once Luke's face was mended, he returned to the floor with a renewed passion. The other four starters also rallied and made the most of the remaining time in the game. Jimmy found his way to the basket on a couple of occasions by leaving the Buc's player grasping for air as he spun through the defense. Cole did his part, forcing successful shots through the hands of Buccaneer players planted in front of his face.

With only seconds left on the clock, the game was tied. Players from both sides were drenched with sweat, mouths open, sucking in as much air as possible, and hands on thighs at every break. The Buccaneers were frantic. They'd lost an overtime game the day before and were desperate not to fail a second time.

There was a sudden break in the action when a Buccaneer player batted the ball out of bounds. The crowd hushed, waiting for the action to resume. Eight seconds showed on the clock. The Grizzlies had the ball under the Bucs basket. Fans from both schools waited nervously in anticipation of a dramatic finish to the game. Having used all his time-outs, Brock could only stand in front of the bench and try to communicate from a distance.

Justin stood next to the referee, trying to catch his breath. "You can run the baseline," the man in stripes offered. "No penalty for that." Justin nodded and while the referees checked with one another to make sure they were ready, Justin contemplated the gravity of the moment. An errant pass or a five-second clock violation would give the Buccaneers the ball back under their own basket with a chance to claim the victory.

As he stood waiting for the ball, Justin looked over at Brock standing mid-court in front of the Grizzly bench. Brock clapped his hands to get the team's attention and yelled something. Justin was momentarily confused, but the command seemed clear enough. He'd heard it before, just not in these circumstances. "Bright Fire! Bright Fire!" Brock yelled twice at the top of his lungs. It took Justin a second to absorb the meaning of what Brock had just ordered. But the implications were clear.

*Bright Fire* was a Grizzly football play, designed for a quarterback and his top receiver. As the team's quarterback, Justin had practiced it with Jimmy many times throughout the fall football season … it was a pick play to free Jimmy from the defensive back and send him streaking down the football field, deep into the opponent's territory.

Justin's arm would rocket the ball to his sprinting friend. If the play was successful, it could break open a close grid contest … an explosive move that would demoralize the opponent. However, if it came up short, it would seem reckless and foolhardy to critics in the stands. The play had nearly won a game for the Grizzlies when they played for the state championship just a few months before. Only a missed call by the official denied the team its championship trophy.

Justin turned his eyes to Jimmy, who also heard the command. They both understood. They'd been under Brock's tutelage long enough to know he was turning his experience as a football coach into a make-or-break effort for the basketball team. Risky. If the long-range toss by Justin went awry—too long or was fumbled by Jimmy—the Buccaneers would be handed the ball under their own basket with a good chance of making a last-second shot to win the game.

A safer play would be to get the ball into a nearby Grizzly player, run out the clock, and try to win the contest in overtime. Coach Brock had weighed the odds in his head and was going for broke. It was a huge gamble, but both boys were thrilled by the call and the confidence their coach had in them.

The referee reached for his whistle, put it to his lips, and signaled for the play to begin. He flipped the ball to the Grizzly captain. Justin had five seconds to make the pass. The sixteen-year-old knew he had to wait long enough for Jimmy to break free. He faked a pass to Luke standing at the free-throw line. At the same time, Derek Baker hustled over to set a screen to free Jimmy, who darted forward as if he were to take the inbounds pass but wheeled around Luke and sprinted hell-bent on getting to the opposite end of the court.

The referee was counting, marking each number with the wave of his hand. *One … two … three … four.* His hand was ready to drop for five when Justin jumped sideways, stood on his toes, and cocked his arm. Unlike the football that he'd mastered, there were no laces to guide the ball, no point to push through the air. But, still, it was a ball. He could make it happen. His big hand grasped it firmly, then let it fly. The ball flew like it was shot from a cannon.

Despite the throbbing pain in his injured leg, Jimmy broke free, well in front of the trailing defender. He looked back and caught sight of the spinning sphere. For an instant, his mind snapped back to the pass he'd caught in the early December state football championship game that should have been the game-winner for the Grizzlies. He couldn't repeat that mistake. He'd finished too close to the end line and the referee claimed his toes were out of bounds. This time he leaped, collected himself, and extended his arms. The ball dropped into his hands. He secured it, making sure not to let it slip as he dropped to the floor. He glanced down at his feet. His toes were well within the black line that marked the boundary of the playing surface.

Justin put enough sizzle on his throw to get the ball past the defender. But it left no room for Jimmy to maneuver. If it had been a few feet shorter, Jimmy could have easily laid the ball into the basket with seconds to spare. But now he was too far under the rim, and the defender was racing to cut him off from the basket.

Jimmy didn't hesitate. With only seconds left, this wasn't his time to be a hero. Trailing the defender was Derek Baker, the solid, trustworthy member of the team who had not once during the season been the leading scorer or made an important shot. He was the uncelebrated fifth cog in a wheel … never considered one of the stars. As fate would have it, he now had his chance.

Jimmy spun around the defender and deliberately dropped a well-placed bounce pass to Baker who slowed his pace enough to get both hands on the ball. He fumbled it awkwardly for a second before finally corralling it. He rose up in perfect form, as if it was just another warm-up drill, and lifted the ball towards the basket as the clock reached double zero. Fans from both teams were screaming so loudly that as the ball arced toward the target, the old men from the coffee shop couldn't hear the horn sound to end the game. Homer Johnson, standing on his toes, turned to Slim Mathers. "Does it count? Does it count?" He elbowed his lanky friend.

"I think maybe it does," Slim said, eyes bright with excitement. He enunciated his words and shouted them close to his friend's ear so Homer could hear. "The referee raised two fingers," Mathers said. "That means it's good. By golly, Homer, I think we just won the game."

Grizzly teammates mobbed Derek Baker. Jimmy was the first to reach him. He leaped into Baker's arms—their smiles worth the price of admission. On the sideline, Brock sank to the bench, leaned back, and breathed a sigh of relief as he watched the boys celebrate.


Roland Donigan had retreated to sit high in the upper reaches of the arena. He seethed as he watched the Grizzlies celebrate their victory. A text had just come through on his phone. It consisted of only a few words. "Investigation of eligibility showed Grizzly players meet all standards." He'd always assumed the investigation would yield those results, but hoped the disruption in the short term would derail the team's success in the tournament and make Justin realize he'd be better off leaving his friends behind. But his strategy failed. And he'd stepped out of line. His lip throbbed. From a distance he could see Ronnie as she stood cheering for her son's team. And he watched Brock as he joined the Grizzlies in their celebration … winners, ready to take on the next foe.

# CHAPTER 46

# FINAL

SATURDAY'S GAMES WERE A REWARD to those teams that had survived the season's three-month marathon of games and the first three days of the tourney. It was also a reward to parents and fans for their patience and fortitude in attending every game and supporting their teenage athletes.

Only the two teams vying for the "gold ball" given to the victor had any amount of pressure on their shoulders on Saturday. The other six teams would each leave with a trophy, although with minor differences in the lettering on the plaque.

For the Grizzlies, a win or loss would make them either the fourth- or sixth-place team in the tourney. To Coach McHue, his two decades of frustration would come to an end. He'd already achieved his goal.

On Friday night, the Grizzly players sat in a small hotel banquet room and ate dinner together for the last time as a team. The coaches knew this might be a time to let them know how proud they were of the efforts they showed throughout the important final games of the season. Coach McHue was giving a typical dry unemotional speech when, without warning, his voice cracked, and he was overcome by emotion. He struggled to continue but he couldn't get his words out.

"We love you, Coach," Luke hollered out. The other boys clapped. Buster pulled himself together.

"And I love this team," he said, a catch in his throat. "I couldn't have asked for anything better. Tomorrow, win or lose, it's been a great ride."

After dinner, the boys dispersed and headed to their hotel rooms, to rest and watch some Friday night basketball on a sports channel. Cole Knighton was thumbing through a souvenir program, a thick glossy publication with photos of each tournament team. Towards the back of the document, several pages were filled with scoring records for teams and individuals. Cole's finger slid down the page, his eyes scanning the names on the list of the top twenty scorers and their point totals over the last fifty years. He was intrigued by the possibilities. His conclusion? His name could someday be on that list. He didn't make it a goal, but the seed was planted.

The game was scheduled for three o'clock, the second contest of the four-game finale. It gave everyone from Glory Grove time to check out of their hotel before heading to the arena. Brock decided he had time to go see his mom and offer to help pack up her things. He'd visited her each day and found her full of energy. Her vibrant spirit was surprising, considering the stress of being at the games and dealing with her health. Sometimes he'd watched her in the crowd, laughing and smiling with her hand on Peter Green's back. *It was a good move, bringing the Paint Man back to town,* he thought.

When he knocked on the hotel door to Irene's room, to Brock's surprise, Green answered. Brock laughed. "This is scandalous. Alone with my mother in her hotel room."

Green played along. "Only if you think an old man helping his friend with her luggage is a sin."

Brock stood at the door, lowered his voice, and looked into the older man's eyes. "Thanks for being here … for Mom. You're a good man, Mr. Green."

The coaches and team arrived at the arena a few hours early. After four days, it was now a familiar place. The boys were relaxed and looking forward to the final game. Brock saw his uncle coming through the door, making his way through the security check. Goldie was behind him but had been detained by security to check her purse. "She's not carrying explosives, is she?" Brock teased.

"Not that I know of," Richard said. "But with Goldie, you can never know for sure."

"Hope this hasn't been too much of a problem for you," Brock said. "I know it must have been a hassle to get all the cows fed and pick up Goldie to get here."

Richard grinned, a twinkle in his eye. "Well, Goldie has been helping me feed. Says it's the least she can do to help repay me."

Brock wasn't sure how to respond to the news. He was speechless, saved only by Goldie as she sauntered over toward them.

"Hi, Brock, they didn't arrest me," she said, looking back at the security guard. "But I've come ready to abuse the referees."

"Not if you're going to sit with me," Richard said, nudging her with his elbow.

"Oh, you old farmer, I just want to have a little fun."

"Lord, woman, can't you ever stop?" They stared at each other as if Brock wasn't there.

Richard looked at his nephew. "We'd better go before this gets out of hand." He winked at Brock. "Good luck today. Bring home some hardware." He and Goldie turned and walked away. As they did, Goldie leaned towards Richard and gently reached for his hand.

The crowds in the arena had slimmed down since half the teams had already left town empty-handed. The championship game would bring a crowd and media but those who played during the day had only their hometown fans to cheer them on. The Grizzly coaches were trying to get the boys to stay focused. As they gathered in the locker room, it was Brock's turn to speak.

"Listen up, guys!" Brock hollered out to get their attention. "I've got a couple of things I want to say before we head out. As you know, I know a lot more about football than basketball. But being on the bench with Coach McHue, I now know what it takes to win basketball games. Secondly, I want to thank you boys for letting me ride along with you on this journey. Without you, the old bear on the elevator would still be shedding his fur, looking like he was ready to be put out of his misery."

The boys laughed, remembering their time in the bucket, high above the town.

"And finally, I want to compliment you on coming together like a family. It took a while, but I think you've found out how important that is in life and in sports."

Luke and Cole exchanged looks and knew Brock had put them in a better place.

Brock wasn't done. "Oh, and there is one last thing I want you to do for me and Coach McHue. Does anyone know what that is?"

The boys looked around for someone to answer. Finally, Les Colquit spoke up. "Win this game?"

"You got it. Now let's finish this season on a high note. Let's leave this place the right way … with a victory."


After their hard-fought win on Friday, the Grizzly boys were ready for a struggle. Luke had stitches on his cheek … *a babe magnet* … he'd told Ashley. Jimmy had a fresh dressing on his leg, which was healing nicely. The referees were again letting them play, only calling obvious violations. Each team had their scoring runs and throughout the first quarter the score seesawed back and forth. The advantage Glory Grove had was the pinpoint shooting of Cole Knighton. Whenever Silverton took the lead, it was answered by a three-point score by the sophomore shooting guard.

When the Silverton coach called a time-out, Brock and Buster chatted among themselves while the boys took a breather.

"Cole is in a zone," Brock said to Buster. "If he keeps it up, we should be able to weather anything the Miners can throw at us."

McHue agreed. "And Luke's doing a great job underneath. If we can slow down their fast break points, we should be able to pull this out.'

When the action continued, Justin, Jimmy, and Derek Baker stepped up their game, scurrying back to slow down the fast break the Miners had been running. When the horn sounded to end the half, the Grizzlies had a comfortable eight-point lead.

In the locker room, McHue scanned the stat sheet. He called Brock over. "Look at this Brock. Cole already has eighteen points. At this rate, he's going to have pretty big numbers."

Cole knew his point total. Although he'd become more of a team player after the understanding he'd reached with Luke, out of habit he still kept the tally in his head. He didn't intend on challenging the record book, but remembered that any score over thirty-four points in the game would add his name to the top twenty scorers in the tourney's history. He wouldn't chase it, but if it came …

The second half went much like the first. The Miners' smallish guards were too short to defend against shots by Cole. For the coaches on both teams, it seemed the Grizzlies were destined to go home with the fourth-place trophy. "Let's let some of the bench players in, so they can experience this," Buster said as the fourth quarter started.

"Agreed," Brock said. "Although, I think Cole may be closing in on his season's high. Let's leave him in there and see where it goes. He needs to be rewarded for the way he's turned his life around."

Even with the Grizzly backups on the floor with him, Cole still found a way to score. With less than a minute left, and with Cole's thirty-three points in the books, McHue put the other four starters back in so they could enjoy the final minutes of their season together.

As the clock ticked down toward zero, the Grizzlies led by eight. Still, the Miners continued to pressure the boys from the Grove. They were playing hard to the final horn. As Jimmy brought the ball up the court with only a few seconds left, he began his drive. The Miners' guards chased after him, leaving Cole open. Jimmy dished off. Cole was ready. One more score would put him in the record books.

Cole knew it. It was his chance to do what he'd practiced for all during the hot summer and football season. It was automatic. He rose up and, despite his weary legs, he was energized by the moment. The words in his head were the same. *I never miss*, he thought. *Make your mama proud.*

The ball left Cole's hand as it had over a dozen times during the game, with precision and purpose. Everyone in the Grizzly section of the arena waited for it to find the net … ready to rise and cheer for the fragile sophomore guard and for the team's victory. Happy tears were streaming from Goldie's eyes. She and Richard were on their feet, along with Tim and Peggy. "Bring it home, Cole," Tim hollered.

However, when the ball left Cole's hands, it didn't track toward the rim. Instead, the spinning orb arced downward toward the outstretched fingers of a bewildered Luke Palmer.

"What the heck?" Brock whispered

Luke's eyes widened as the ball came toward him. He instinctively reeled it in and hesitated for one moment, before he spun to the basket. A smile appeared on his bandaged face. *Nice touch, you little showoff,* he thought as he laid the ball gently off the backboard and into the basket. As the horn sounded, he turned and pointed at Cole, then raised his arms in a gesture of jubilation.

*Perfect finish* … Cole thought, as he ran over to embrace his friend.

# CHAPTER 47

# ACCEPTANCE

IN THE DAYS FOLLOWING THE TOURNAMENT, Coach Buster McHue wasn't feted by the Glory Grove community. There was no resounding praise for bringing home a fourth-place trophy, and no glowing editorials in the local newspaper. Perhaps if the team had won a state championship there might have been a parade. But there had been a break in the wintry weather, a signal spring had arrived.

Farmers in the community weren't thinking about basketball, they were warming up their tractors. Fields needed to be prepared for spring seeding. Cattle would soon be turned out to pasture, but first, the calves needed to be worked. Cowboys and cowgirls of all ages would converge on local ranches, moving young calves—both bulls and heifers—through runways and chutes to doctor each of the animals. Bull calves were castrated, and all calves were branded for identification. They would receive vaccines and supplements to improve their health. Any calf with horns would have them removed. The gatherings of like-minded neighbors often became a social event, with laughter and good times, as they were an hours-long mixture of hard labor and dusty, dangerous work. Occasionally a beer or two would be passed out at the end of the day.

When the Gallaghers pulled their calves into the corral to begin working them, Richard turned to Jimmy. "Pick out a heifer you like, Jimmy."

"What for? You want me to bulldog it?"

"Yeah, like you'd win that battle. No, hotshot. Pick out a heifer we can keep in the herd for a cow. With all the work you've done, it'll be your payment."

"You mean I can own her?" He looked over, wide-eyed, to see if Richard was serious.

"Yes, and knowing you, you'll pick some silly gosh awful stupid name to stick on her." Richard rolled his eyes.

"I can do that," Jimmy said. He thought for a moment and then with mock seriousness, pointed to his forehead. "I've got it." He paused for effect. "How about I name her … Goldie?" He broke out in laughter as he turned to run.

Richard growled. "Smart ass." He swatted with his hat as he stumbled after Jimmy as if he were giving chase.


Life's cycles were repeating themselves.

Still, even without much of an outward celebration for the basketball team's success, there was an upbeat mood on the streets of Glory Grove. The high school students were basking in a newfound pride in their athletic achievements. A small ceremony was held by the student body to place the plaque won by the basketball team in the school's trophy case.

As captain of the team, Justin Jepson did the honors, with a beaming Principal Colquit and Buster McHue by his side. Sophomore Ashley Summers, frustrated by the rejection of her attempts to become a cheerleader, volunteered instead to be the school reporter. She captured the scene at the trophy case with a camera borrowed from the journalism class. She would submit the photo to the *Glory Grove Gazette*. It would be the first photo credited to her, in what she dreamed might become a career. Luke was her biggest fan and became her favorite subject.

Buster didn't expect any special attention for the team's achievement. It was the self-fulfillment he had sought. Reaching that goal gave him all the satisfaction he needed. But there was a special kind of honor that came his way. It didn't happen in a ceremony but came a few days after the tournament when he happened to meet Homer Johnson on the sidewalk in front of The Steak House. "Hey, Buster, nice job with the team this year." Homer extended his hand. "Say, why don't you join us for coffee sometime? The boys love to talk about sports."

Buster was dumbfounded. He'd coached for nearly two decades and had never been asked to coffee before.

"Sure, I'd like that." He tried to hide his enthusiasm. "Your group is at the Cozy Corner, right?" Buster asked, but knew all about the groups. Everyone in town knew which men met in which location.

"That's right. Every morning but Sunday. Doors open at 5:30. We'd be glad to have you."

So, Buster got what he wanted most of all … respect from the locals. From that day on, it became part of his usual before-school routine. He fit right in, drinking coffee, telling stories, and listening to the men second guess every other coach in the town.

The day after returning home from the tournament, Brock met with John Eberhardt at the local bank. He scheduled the visit to see if, as manager of the Glory Grove branch, he would consider pushing a complaint up the ladder to the bank's governing board. Brock wanted to propose a formal complaint be made by Eberhardt about Donigan's threats and his borderline harassment of Ronnie.

Eberhardt listened and waved a pencil in the air cutting off Brock's sentence. "I'm ahead of you on this, Brock. I already made some moves of my own. I know some of the older members on the big board. I also know they're not fond of Donigan's arrogance. And they have become concerned with his recent lack of attention to bank business. They listened to what I had to say but said unless I had proof of harassment or blackmail, there wasn't much they could do."

Brock slumped back in his chair "I see. I guess we have to put up with him then."

Eberhardt shook his head. "I haven't finished," he said. "There's more. After the game Friday, a cell phone video appeared of Donigan pushing you down in the stands at the arena. That video was shared with all the board members. They've seen enough. They're calling him in to ask for his resignation. If he'll resign, he'll get a severance payout, but either way, he's done with the bank."

Brock sat up straight. "My gosh, that happened fast. What's that mean for our bank here in the Grove? And what about Ronnie?"

"From what I can see, our branch is safe ... even if the wind farm money never comes through. And he has no excuse to keep pestering Ronnie. If he does, she can seek a restraining order. I think she'd do it." Eberhardt hesitated, then looked Brock directly in the eye. "Brock, you know she's in love with you." He let his words hang there for a moment. "She didn't take that job because of you.

She's like a daughter to me, so I'm asking you to be good to her. She deserves that."

Brock rose from his chair. "I will, John," he said, as he reached out to shake Eberhardt's hand. "I will."

# CHAPTER 48

# MARCELLUS

**A MEETING WAS SCHEDULED** with Anthony Marcellus the week following the state tournament. Brock arranged for a substitute to cover his classes for the morning, so he and Richard were both there to listen to the man's final proposal. Irene was prepared … coffee brewed and pastries on a plate in the center of the kitchen table.

When Marcellus stepped from his rented SUV, Sassy was there, tail wagging, to greet him. She had no memory of how the man shooed her months earlier. She also had no notion of the ruckus the man and his company had stirred in the community of Glory Grove.

A soft morning drizzle had Marcellus even more reluctant to have a dog near him. "Stay back," he mumbled. "I don't need the smell of wet dog to follow me around the rest of the day." His glare made the little pup retreat a step or two, giving him a clear path through the gate leading into the yard. He stepped to the front door and consciously pulled his lips back to force a smile. He knocked.

Inside, Richard watched through the window. "You can tell he's a stranger here … coming to the front door. Neighbors know better."

"Be nice," Irene said. She looked in the mirror over the kitchen counter and brushed back her hair. "He's just showing his manners."

"Just playing nice to get our names on a dotted line," Richard said, glancing over at Brock who was nibbling on the apple turnover he'd lifted off the plate.

"Brock, you could have waited until we all sat down," Irene scolded.

"Sorry, Mom, couldn't resist." He threw the last bit of the turnover into his mouth and swallowed, licking his lips. "Preparing for the lecture, I guess," he said.

There was a solid knock on the door. Irene made her way into the living room to greet Marcellus. "Good morning, Anthony," she said as she opened the door to let him in. "Nice to see you again."

"And good to see you again as well. Please call me Tony." He reached out and shook her hand. "I hope we can do business today."

Irene's smile faded. "We'll see about that."

"Well, Irene, I think we should talk some more before you decide one way or the other."

Irene nodded. "Please come into the kitchen; the men are waiting."

Marcellus felt his optimism fade. He'd hoped to use his charm with this elderly woman to convince her to sign the lease he had in his folder. This might be a harder sell with men involved.

Brock hadn't met the man but wasn't surprised by his dress or demeanor. Casual, friendly, and just a bit too polished for a farm visit. "Hi, I'm Brock. Irene is my mother," he said as he stepped over to shake the man's hand … a firm grip but with a businessman's soft hands.

"Brock, nice to meet you, and Richard, it's good to see you again."

Irene motioned for everyone to sit. She poured coffee and offered the pastries. Richard took both. Marcellus waved off the sweets. "Too early for sugar, I think. But," he said, "I'll take some coffee."

The next two hours were a repetition of the proposal Wind Driven had made earlier to Irene. Marcellus directed most of the discussion toward Brock, assuming he had the power of persuasion over his mother. Brock probed him with questions. "How many towers did the company think might be on Gallagher land? How tall? How many roads would it take and how much concrete would be poured? What was the revenue generated from each turbine? What benefit was there for the people in Glory Grove?"

Marcellus was patient and answered each question. The one he didn't answer straight out was a specific question Brock dropped into the conversation. "Did you suggest to my neighbors that the project might be scrapped if our family didn't sign?"

The cool demeanor of the salesman suddenly changed. He blinked and pushed back in his chair. "I'm not sure what you're asking."

Brock leaned onto the table. "We had a neighbor threaten to cut off our cattle's water source. Then he turned his attack dog loose on our family. All because he thought you, sir, had threatened to pull the plug on this project unless our family signed."

Marcellus recovered his poise. "I'm not sure where he may have gotten that impression; we certainly didn't stipulate that in our communication to your neighbor."

"Okay, then is there any truth in that fact? Does it affect our neighbors if we don't sign?"

"I really can't say. That decision is made at a higher level. I'm just the salesperson. I don't design or oversee the project."

Richard jumped into the conversation. He hadn't said a word throughout the discussion, but his frustration had been boiling up. "I think you've been telling some tall tales."

"Excuse me?"

Brock interrupted. "Well, sir, our neighbor was so convinced of it, he was threatening our cattle and our lives. If you weren't making it obvious to him, then he jumped to some pretty interesting conclusions."

Marcellus squirmed. "Obviously there was a serious breakdown in our discussion. And if that's the case, I apologize." He pulled the cup of coffee to his lips and sipped. "I hope no harm was done?"

"Only dog bites to a good young man and the wits scared out of Irene," Richard said. He didn't mention his own trauma from having to kill a dog.

Irene was looking straight at Marcellus, not with anger or forgiveness, but with serious questioning of his truth-telling.

Marcellus looked past the three, avoiding direct eye contact. "I'm terribly sorry if I was responsible for any of that. I hope a misunderstanding like that won't influence your decision on signing the lease. I think it's clear from our discussion it would be a benefit to all of you and the future of this farm."

Brock was done talking. He leaned back and stared at Marcellus. "If we do, it won't be because of you."

Irene cleared her throat. "Anthony, I think we have all the information we need. We'll let you know what we have decided within a few days. Don't take our anger about the incident we just went through as an indication we won't consider your offer. It won't be an easy decision."

"Of course." Marcellus pulled together all the papers and brochures he'd scattered across the table and tucked them neatly into his file folder. He left the unsigned document on the table for the family to study, hoping they would attach their signatures to it. He thanked Irene and the men for their time and stepped out of the kitchen, through the living room, and out the front door.

Outside, Marcellus again shielded himself from Sassy with his folder and crawled into the car. He threw the papers onto the passenger seat and turned the key in the ignition. He let out his breath with the sound of the engine. As he put the car into reverse, he stared over at the farmhouse and shook his head. "Damned stupid farmers," he said.

# CHAPTER 49

# FLIGHT

**BROCK WAS ALONE WITH HIS THOUGHTS.** He sat on a crumpled rockpile—a precipice jutting out from the bluff overlooking the canyon. He could see the tiny stream, Cold Creek, as it meandered around rocks and fallen logs. The ripples of fresh mountain water glistened as it tumbled down sections of the narrow passage between boulders. With the April sun, the last of the winter snowpack was rapidly melting, increasing the stream's flow.

He and Ronnie had come here to be alone, away from the school and the farm and the town. When they reached this spot, she kept walking up the trail, knowing Brock needed some time to himself … time to make a decision. She also needed time alone.

As he warmed himself in the morning sunshine, Brock thought back to the morning in January when Tim challenged his attitude. Now, in the stillness of the morning, Tim's words came back to him. They'd parked themselves in his brain, spilling out from time to time. "*You can't handle losing 'cause you're too damned determined to win everything you do. And when you don't win, you just can't let go."*

Brock wrestled with the charge. He had failed at his marriage and accepted it, hadn't he? He and Celia had parted ways. Her absence no longer weighed on him. Did he ever love her? Yes, but on the flip side, looking back on their time together, did she ever truly love him? Once his short stint in the NFL was over, she had drifted and then ultimately strayed.

So, he'd lost. Yes. Or perhaps, it was really a win … for both of them.

If he was keeping score, the winning over the last few months had been life changing. With Cole Knighton, he'd almost failed. He was late to the moment, but in the end, he may have saved the young boy's life and given meaning to Cole's mother. And without even trying, through Goldie, he had enriched his Uncle Richard's life. He relaxed and breathed in the fragrance of the Douglas Fir and White Pine that towered up behind him. He took off his cap and let the wind blow through his hair. With his eyes closed, he listened as the wind whistled through the tree branches, and he could hear the distant sound of chipmunks and blackbirds announcing to the world they were happy to be alive.

The scorecard hadn't been completely finalized. His mind was searching for more wins. Helping Buster McHue bring home a trophy with the basketball team was clearly a big one. It would certainly be considered so, even though they'd fallen short of claiming Brock's dream of a state championship. *Someday … somehow,* he thought; football was only months away. But Buster reached the elusive goal he so desired. Brock could see it in Buster's demeanor when they passed in the hallway at school.

With his own family, it had been years since Brock had seen his mother quite as happy as she was with Peter M. Green by her side. They seemed to breathe new life into one another … and Green no longer had a cigarette dangling from his lips. Even if the relationship only lasted a brief while, it was a win.

A final reckoning was far from complete. Roland Donigan still hovered over their lives. Ronnie was embarrassed by how her actions had led to the banker's obsessive behavior. And to Brock, he'd said, "I'll see you in court," as they parted at the basketball arena. Was that going to happen?

Worse yet, after the dog attack on the farm, Brock had assaulted Del Leachman. He regretted it. And since the district attorney was continuing to investigate the case, there might be repercussions.

Brock put those worries aside. Today was the day he'd make the final decision on the wind farm. His mom had let her feelings be known, with the caveat that since she most likely wouldn't even live long enough to see the first tower, she'd leave the decision up to the men. Richard seemed so enthralled with his new relationship with Goldie, he'd stopped even thinking about wind turbines.

Either way, Brock decided, he wasn't sure if the result could be considered a win or a loss. The verdict lay far out in the future. But he was here to decide … here, where his mind was uncluttered and free to think.

He reached down and picked up a pinecone and studied the intricate pattern, perfect in its symmetry. As he turned it over in his hand, the motion seemed to calm him, counting the rows and numbers of seeds in each row. The breeze blew harder now, moving the bunchgrass on the surrounding hills. He searched the valley for signs of life. Across the way, a group of whitetail deer meandered up a steep ridge, not in any formation but moving to and fro, searching for the best of the fresh grass. They were not being pursued, simply moving slowly … marking time.

The corporation, Wind Driven, had disrupted the steady deliberate hands of nature's timepiece that had always been with the citizens of Glory Grove. Now, the people were divided … some pushing the hands of the clock forward … progress, they claimed … with a pot of gold waiting for them. Others were grasping the clock hands, dragging their feet against the machine that was pulling them to a place they didn't wish to go.

Brock yearned for a time when only nature's cycles moved the people. Slow, steady progress. He'd lived in a city … the height of civilization. Now, he chafed under the threat of bulldozers and concrete trucks rumbling through the countryside and blading their way across this beautiful ridge.

Brock's thoughts returned to the time he and Ronnie lay on the ground among giant windmills dotting the countryside in someone else's world. Now those same giants could one day be stacked from one end of this magnificence to the other, in a show of man's strength to control and shape. It might be inevitable. Glory Grove needed a revival. Was this it? Would life be better off if he inked his name to a piece of paper, giving up control of the Gallagher farm?

A black padded folder lay at his feet. Inside were the lease papers from Wind Driven. He took off his gloves and reached down to lift it onto his lap. The sun had warmed the padded surface of the file, and it felt good in his hands. He opened the folder and pulled out the contract from Wind Driven. A simple signature was all that was needed to bring wealth to the families owning land along the ridge. Their lives would be changed dramatically. The community would also change. The camaraderie and warmth of farm and ranch neighbors, sharing emotions based on good weather and hard work to earn a living, would be challenged. Now there would be haves and have-nots. Despite friendships formed over a century of living as a single community, jealousies would surely arise. Promises to share the wealth would be tested. Promises by the corporations would also be tested.

Would birds die? Would blinking red lights and the whirring of spinning blades spoil the draw for nature seekers who visited here for the beauty of pristine views?

Brock opened the folder and stared down at the document. His eyes scanned down the page to the bottom … to the line needing his signature. Weeks before, he'd signed another important document that would change his life—the divorce papers for Celia. He recognized it was the right thing for him to do. This document, though less personal, also had emotional ramifications. He stared at it, then lifted the page. It fluttered in the wind. He reached into his shirt pocket for a pen and clicked the button on the end, over and over, as he stared into the canyon.

He turned his gaze to the sheet of paper in his hand requiring his signature. He stared at it again, then carefully laid the pen down on a nearby rock. On impulse, he folded the paper lengthwise from top to bottom. He fingered the corners of the page and folded them over. Once, twice, three times. As a boy, he'd learned the procedure from his father over a quarter century ago. He could feel the presence of Max Gallagher as he finished the folds and imagined his father's smiling face looking down.

Brock lifted the delicate paper creation above his head, admiring the finished product, a sleek miniature aircraft. Would it fly? He rose from the rock on which he'd been sitting, breathed in, and slowly let the air out of his lungs. With a gentle snap of his wrist, the tiny aircraft, carrying the dreams of some and the fears of others, took flight, caught the mountain breeze, and lifted toward the heavens.

He hadn't heard Ronnie as she approached him from behind but was happy she'd returned. "A perfect flight?" she asked. Her voice was soft and understanding. She put her arms around him and laid her head on his back. They watched as the tiny aircraft drifted lazily in a circle above Cold Creek as if surveying the terrain, looking for a safe spot to land. It seemed to be in no hurry to reach its destination below.

"Ronnie, I hope I'm doing the right thing." He waited for her response—some kind of assurance, but there was no answer, only the wind covering the silence. He turned, needing her reaction, only to find tears streaming down her cheeks. He lifted her chin and looked into her eyes.

"What? Ronnie?"

She looked away for a moment, then cautiously returned his gaze. She stroked the front of her jacket and left her hand resting in the center of it. She took a breath and stared down at her trembling fingers. In a voice barely over a whisper she said, "Just do what is best for our family."

Brock stood motionless for a moment, studying her face to make sure he'd interpreted her words correctly. He saw the answer in her eyes. And he knew. A freak February blizzard had changed their lives. He reached for her hands, pulled her in, and pressed his lips to hers. They turned, holding one another, watching the little airplane below. And had no regrets.

# ACKNOWLEDGMENTS

**A SINCERE THANK YOU** to those who offered valuable suggestions to help polish this story.

Among them…

Maureen Scoggin, Stephanie Daud, Tom Fitzsimmons, Terry Brandon, Doug Janachek, Lillian Heytvelt, Ernie Kimble, Tai Bye, and my wife Kayleen, a lovingly honest critic.

Thanks also to Bobby Haas, a remarkable editor, and Kiki Ringer, a knowledgeable resource in dealing with the publishing world.

A tip of my farmer cap goes to our son Torance for his patience as he keeps the family operation running in real time while I'm off dreaming up a fictional world.

# ABOUT THE AUTHOR

GARY BYE lives with his wife in rural eastern Washington among the rolling hills of the
Palouse. When not writing, he spends time
helping his son manage the family's grain and
cattle ranch. His debut novel, *Glory Grove*,
earned the Silver Award Medal from the
Independent Book Publishers' Ben Franklin
Awards for Best First Book – Fiction, as well as being named winner
in the sports fiction category by the 2024 American Fiction Awards.
Gary developed his writing and photography skills working as the
associate editor of a magazine for the nation's largest youth organization and has contributed articles to several leading agricultural magazines. Research for stories has taken him to nearly every state and
many foreign countries. Drawing inspiration from his experience as a
community leader, teacher, coach, farmer, and family man, Gary often
finds his creativity sparked while driving a tractor or working with the
cattle herd. Although he has enjoyed living in big cities, he recognizes
the endearing qualities of small towns…the opportunities they present,
and the challenges they face. To arrange a book club talk or presentation,
visit: www.GaryBye.com.